UNNECESSARY ENEMIES

FINDING A PLACE FOR MAYSON

A Novel

DAWNN B SOMMERVILLE

Copyright © 2020 by Dawnn B Sommerville

ISBN: 978-1-7353537-1-5 (Print)
ISBN: 978-1-7353537-0-8 (ebook)

Foreword

Gays, lesbians and Christianity: they are often assumed to be completely incompatible. Can a person who is gay or lesbian also be a Christian? This is the question this book attempts to examine through its characters' stories, experiences, and beliefs. Assumptions each group holds about the other ignites the anger and embitterment between some churches and gay communities. This anger spills over into society and perpetuates division among people who may have other commonalities that can bridge the gap. Thus, this book makes an effort to balance this conflict through the experiences of Mayson, whose life is ingrained in both communities despite their opposition.

Based in the 1980s, in the fictitious town of Benton, the experiences of Mayson speaks to the heart of a divided segment of people with well-meaning intentions. The words "gay," "lesbian," and "homosexual" are used periodically throughout the book based on the character's background or content of the subject matter. For example, "gay" is a word that is more commonly used for same-sex male attractions now, but in many Benton churches, during this time period, the word "homosexual" was still in use.

In referring to gays and lesbians in this book, the word *Human* is often used as a replacement. This is done for the sake of perspective, but the reader should be aware that the characters are using the common labels (gay, lesbian, or homosexual) as in their real world. The descriptive word *Human* was used by the character, Phyllis, Mayson's mother, to avoid other common terms in describing her son's sexuality. Primarily, the use of the word *Human* *i*s substituted throughout this book for the following reasons:

It provides a commonality that brings all the characters to the same level of being or basic existence.

It shows the redundancy in labels when an effort is made to differentiate from others.

Out of the variety of names and labels used to differentiate from one another, we yet have the commonality of being human as designed by our Creator.

In order to distinguish differences, but emphasize a point of commonality, which also includes a need for consideration and respect for their beliefs and values, the *Human* description could be used for those in the church as well. However, in determining the use of the word *Human* for which group, it was decided that the gay and lesbian community's overall description as a gender minority and their past struggles and efforts to be heard was taken into account. Thus, the substituted word *Human* for the gay and lesbian community was deemed more suitable.

It is an honor to share this story of Mayson with you and his journey to self-discovery. For all who open themselves to the almighty God, this book hopes for a resolution that God will ultimately bring people together through his union and communion with humanity.

CHAPTER 1

The Search for Mayson

"Not knowing can leave a lot of room for the imagination."

Those who were home that evening in the Hendricks' neighborhood were glued to their television sets; including the family matriarch, Phyllis Hendricks. Usually on a Wednesday evening, Phyllis would be in the den, watching her favorite television program of the 1984 season, Highway to Heaven. A show that she included with a large bowl of popcorn with its viewing. But tonight, she and her family were not relaxing with their favorite shows. The news of the dead body of an unidentified man had been televised yesterday and it was rumored that the body could be that of Phyllis Hendricks' second child, 22-year-old Mayson.

Phyllis was friendly with her neighbors, and there was not much that went on that people in her neighborhood didn't know about each other. Mayson's recent situation was not something that Phyllis discussed with her neighbors, but it was obvious in the neighborhood that for the past year, Mayson had not been seen. People had been by to comfort Phyllis. Some tried to assure her that the body could not be Mayson's. Others, uncertain of what to say to the family, would give a quick wave as they passed the family, adding, *We have you in our prayers.*

It had been over a year since Mayson moved out of his family's home. He missed his family and found it difficult not seeing them on a regular basis. He started to come by their home for weekly visits or meet his mother at a restaurant for lunch. His younger siblings, 14-year-old Lamont and 15-year-old, Idelle, called Idee, were glad to see him when he came by. However, since Mayson had left their home and church, they were at a loss for words when it came to engaging in their usual past conversations. Funny stories about who did what at church or in the choir were no longer the same.

Mayson had not spoken with his best friend Reanna in a while. So

Idee made sure she provided Mayson with any little bits of information she heard about his colorful friend. Idee knew that Reanna was a safe bet for engaging Mayson's interest. But even sharing the humorous gossip about his friend Reanna, whose calls he had stopped returning, became of less concern to Mayson. He had often sensed that she always knew he was not the Mayson that the church wanted him to be. He knew that Reanna would not treat him any differently now that everyone knew his secret, yet he could not see himself including her in his new life.

Now that his family and church members knew that Mayson was homosexual, his interaction with them was now awkward and uncertain. People who had known him since he was a boy became strangers to him. With each encounter on the street, Mayson had to think quickly about how he should address them. Pretend he didn't see them and go the opposite direction, or talk as though the matter of his sexuality was unknown? Neither was an ideal option. In the past, running into someone from the church led to hugs, laughter, and good conversation. But now, Mayson felt fear each time he saw someone he knew from his church, Greenlawn Community Church--GCC, or anyone who knew him. They had heard the rumors about Mayson's sexuality, but it was not the same now that the reality of it was set before them.

Whenever their pastor spoke about the sins of homosexuality, Mayson would notice his mother fidgeting with her purse or some other distracting gesture. "Homosexuality" was a word that Phyllis would make much effort not to say. Instead, she would say "Humans." Mayson found it interesting that his mother substituted the word "Human" for homosexual, but he never asked her why. Mayson felt that talking about it meant that it was proof that it was so. That he was homosexual. He would not even tell her when his classmates called him effeminate names. As he got older, he developed his own understanding of why his mother referred to homosexuals as Humans. Knowing her heart, he concluded that it was her way of saying that we all have one created identity when it comes to God.

As for his siblings during this difficult time, the reality of Mayson's being Human left Lamont and Idee uncertain of how to interact with him. When Mayson first left their home, Phyllis had her hands full making sure he was okay and helping her other children adjust to a household that no longer included their beloved brother. Lamont had not given much thought to his sexuality, but he began to wonder about himself. He wondered if he should be as sexually aroused or advanced as the other boys in his class. He thought about the girls who had made advances towards him whom he had brushed off. After seeing all that Mayson was experiencing, he had hoped that he was not a Human like Mayson. After Mayson left one day after his weekly family visit, Lamont overheard his mother crying in her bedroom. He tried to assure himself that he was not Human like Mayson, and he would never make his mother cry. In his room, he allowed himself to focus on two girls in his class he thought were cute. He also thought of the time when he talked his older brother J.R. into letting him go with him to an R-rated movie. He recalled his feeling of arousal from a love scene. However, doubt reared again as he wondered, could the arousal have come from the male actor rather than the actress? Lamont was not one for opening up to others, but he was scared at the thought of being like Mayson. It was one of the few times that he wanted to talk to someone. He dared not choose his mother as it would make her more upset. Mayson was too deep in his own problems to discuss this with him. He could not take Idee seriously enough to think she could help. Talking with his father was never an option. He loved J.R. and looked up to him, but he knew that J.R. was too "manly" for him to discuss his sexual curiosity. J.R. was better for talking to about his feelings for girls, but not his possible interest in boys.

When Mayson visited his family's home he did so when he knew that his father, Ed, would not be home. He'd sometimes call ahead and check with Lamont to be sure his chosen day was not one where his father would be there. His relationship, or lack thereof, with his father was a problem that existed years before Mayson moved in with his partner, Tony.

Mayson and Phyllis had their weekly lunches as usual, but after a few months, Mayson began to cancel his family dates and simply stopped coming to the house. Several months after leaving home, Mayson began to have little to no contact with his family. Phyllis called him each week, whether he answered or not. She didn't have it within herself to go to the condo where he and Tony lived, so her phone calls were her only way of keeping in contact with her son. Often when she called, Mayson was home and answered. He always sounded glad to hear from her. He'd sometimes tell her that he was just about to call her. He'd routinely tell her how busy he was with his job. Phyllis would give him updates on what was going on with the family, church or the neighborhood. She'd try so hard not to talk about Tony, but when their conversations would hit a lull, she would ask, "So how's your friend?" Without much detail, Mayson would often respond, "Fine, but he works too much." He knew to end any comments about Tony with that. He was aware that his mother really did not want to know any more about Tony. Before they hung up, Mayson would assure her that he would keep in regular contact. From their talks she would assume that they were back on course with their daily contacts and weekly family visits, only to find weeks had passed and she had not heard from her son. Phyllis worried about Mayson, but she felt she had no one to talk to about him.

CHAPTER 2

Family Time—Earlier Days

"Mayson, it's 12:30AM. Where have you been?" asked Phyllis.

"Some of us went to My Place Buffet after the service. I thought you knew that," replied Mayson.

"How was I supposed to know that?" asked Phyllis.

"Remember when Pastor Upshaw was about to dismiss service? He mentioned that our choir was ranked #1 last week as the most inspirational choir in the state. He said they were going out to My Place Buffet to celebrate. He said that all were welcome to join in on the celebration."

"I didn't hear all that," said Phyllis sternly.

"I think Idee was whispering in your ear about something at that time," said Mayson, grinning at the thought of his chatterbox sister.

Everyone in the neighborhood knew that if you wanted to find the Hendricks family on a Sunday, you'd better start looking for them at church. During the week, it was also not uncommon to see church members, including their beloved pastor, Earl Upshaw, pastor of Greenlawn Community Church (GCC), frequenting the Hendricks' home with various church activities. Pastor Upshaw, a 68-year-old family man, married for 37 years and father of one adult son and two adult daughters, he pastored one of the most prosperous and well-known churches in Benton, Ohio. His church was well known for his powerful sermons and talented choir. Many had declared that the songs and ministries that came from GCC would bring you to your feet in praise. And if you came in burdened, you would not leave that way. Pastor Upshaw's sound doctrine and compelling voice were all over the airwaves. His sermons would precede and end with a selection from the choir.

Mayson and his family had been attending GCC since Mayson was 5 years old. Phyllis was over the Youth Empowerment program, which included the teens from the church, community and in-house church projects. Last year Phyllis had the young people to put together a drive for donating items for opening a GCC thrift store. They gathered enough items to open the thrift store 30 days ahead of schedule. The teens at GCC really liked Phyllis. When Pastor Upshaw decided to start the Youth Empowerment program, Phyllis was his only choice for the position. He knew how much the young people liked and respected her. Phyllis was grateful to the pastor for allowing her to work with the youth. As the oldest of 9 siblings, her mother often left her in charge during her absence. So, working as the leader in the youth department, was not a difficult role to fit.

In passing conversations, Pastor Upshaw often asked Phyllis about her family. During the days when Mayson was living in her home, she would give a general response that her family was doing well. After changes that led to Mayson's departure from her home, she noticed that her pastor seldom mentioned her family. On one particular Sunday evening after a special service, post Mayson's departure, Phyllis caught her pastor's eye as she was leaving among a throng of mingling church members. Phyllis was preoccupied in thought and her eyes appeared as though she had been crying.

"You okay, Sister Phyllis?" asked Pastor.

Phyllis imagined herself bursting into tears and falling into her pastor's arms. Instead, she felt resentment for him at that moment. In her mind, she blamed him for her son's estrangement from his family and the church. The image of her breaking down before him soon dissipated. Phyllis sniffled a little and responded.

"I'm okay," Pastor, she said.

She gave him a quick smile and turned toward the exit, inching her way through the crowd.

Phyllis Hendricks was the 40-year-old matriarch of the Hendricks' household. Her firstborn, from her first marriage, was Clifton Harmon, Jr. whom everyone called J.R. He could have been called Junior, but Phyllis didn't want him to go through life feeling secondary to his father. J.R. was in his last year at a local college outside of Benton. His skills at baseball, basketball and football had earned him a partial athletic scholarship.

Phyllis became pregnant with J.R. when she was 18 years old. She and J.R.'s father were high school sweethearts who married as a result of Phyllis' pregnancy. The marriage lasted for only a few years. J.R. was

Cliff's only son, and Cliff wanted to make sure that J.R. had the foundation of his presence throughout his life, unlike his own father, who had never been around. J.R. inherited his father's love for sports and played a variety of sports from the time he was 8. He had a special interest in football. His father would make it a part of their visit to include throwing the football back and forth during their visits. He wanted to influence and strengthen this athletic part of J.R. that was also one of his favorite sports.

When J.R. turned 15, he told Phyllis that weekly visits with his father were not enough. He asked Phyllis to let him live with his father and his stepmother Irene. Phyllis, not wanting J.R. to leave her at such a young age, had to think fast.

"Your father wouldn't want the responsibility of caring for you on a full-time basis. You know his job as a firefighter keeps him busy," she said.

She knew that Cliff adored J.R., but she had hoped this explanation would work.

"I talked to Daddy and he was fine with it," he said.

"What about Irene?" asked Phyllis.

"Oh, she said she had no problems with it either," he said, with a look that showed he knew she would ask that question.

Phyllis had problems with this request at the beginning, but Cliff had always been a good father, and Irene, who couldn't have children of her own, seemed to enjoy J.R.'s company. After several weeks, Phyllis agreed to let J.R. move in with his father.

Phyllis' second husband, Ed, the father of Mayson, Idee, and Lamont, was a handsome man. He was tall, with chiseled features that reminded you of a black Cary Grant. His job at Benton's local assembly plant brought in enough income to support the whole household. Ed had been working there since he was 20 years old. He had been offered promotions but turned them down, as he didn't want the extra responsibilities of actually managing others. Still, his managers, eager to retain such a dependable and knowledgeably employee, gave him regular and generous raises. Ed would constantly talk about being at work for overtime, but his paychecks didn't always reflect all those alleged hours. Phyllis knew that her pretty-boy husband was involved with other women. But she never had to concern herself with his money going to other women. Quite the opposite: the women seemed to financially take care of Ed in order to retain him in their presence. On payday, he'd come home to give Phyllis his paycheck, minus a couple of hundreds from what he called "pocket change."

Phyllis' focus was on the well-being of her children. Ed knew Phyllis' heart was with their children more than him. They had an unspoken agreement to keep the status quo of their marriage. Ed could keep his "overtime" going as long as he took care of his responsibilities at home, was Phyllis' stance. As a result, Phyllis never had problems with Ed handing his paycheck over to her as he walked out the door with a few dollars in his own pocket between "overtimes."

Idee was the only girl and family diva. Her sense of style for just the right wardrobe started as young as 3 years old. She would cry and whine if Phyllis dared to dress her in pants or any kind of denim. In addition, whenever she wore new clothes, she made sure that everyone would be aware of her adorable outfit at church, as she'd walk up to fellow members and point at her colorful ensembles. At 15, with the exception of including pants in her wardrobe and not being as directly showy, not much had changed for Idee's external displays. At school, Idee was known as "Miss Hollywood." Her school outfits were always the latest in teen fashion, and she never failed to accessorize, right down to the occasional toe ring. Phyllis tolerated her clothes-horse daughter's habits, as shopping together was a special mother-daughter bonding time for them. It was one of the few times that Phyllis felt she could "hang out" with her only daughter.

Phyllis had conflicting thoughts about Idee's obsession in her appearance. For a while, she wondered if Idee's taste had something to do with her own past. When she was dating Cliff, who was a popular athlete at their school, she wore clothes specifically to get his attention. She thought that maybe God was punishing her through her daughter for seducing Cliff. After Phyllis gave birth to J.R., her clothing changed to a more conservative style. The change had had much to do with Cliff's mother description of her as looking "loose." It concerned her that Idee put forth so much effort to get people to notice her. When Idee was younger and demanded so much attention through her colorful clothing and untamed verbiage, Phyllis had hoped it would be a passing phase. However, when Idee came into her teens and her wardrobe changed from colorful to excessive, Phyllis became concerned about the source of Idee's need for such attention. She thought maybe if Ed would spend more time with Idee perhaps she would not need so much attention from others. So, she asked Ed to spend a Saturday with Idee because she thought that she needed that time with him. He hesitantly agreed. On the Saturday they spent together, Idee came back home bouncing up and down hugging Phyllis as though she had not seen her in years.

"Look at what Daddy bought me," she said, as she leaned her right ear toward Phyllis."I've wanted these earrings for months," she squealed.

She then went to her room to call one of her many friends to tell them about the earrings. When she left the room, Phyllis could see the exhausted look on Ed's face.

"Is she always like this?" he asked.

"Oh yes!" said Phyllis, laughing at Ed's dumbfounded expression. "What happened to the movies and lunch?"

"We had lunch, but the movie changed to shopping time," he said.

He then took out his wallet, pulled out his credit card and flipped it over to Phyllis.

"I applied for that last month," he said. She caught the card with little effort.

"You know how much I despise shopping," said Ed.

"I know," said Phyllis with a giggle.

After that day, Ed and Idee never again spent any specially planned time together.

Phyllis was grateful that her daughter's need for attention did not include sexual activity. In their mother-daughter moments, Idee often shared how she feared the thought of having a baby. She told Phyllis that she could not stand the prospect of all the pain that went with it. Idee had a few boyfriends, but they were short-lived. Idee told Phyllis that once they didn't get what they wanted from her, she would not hear from them again. Phyllis would encourage her that when the right guy came along and stayed with her, she would know he was the one she should marry someday. And then it wouldn't be difficult for both of them to express that side of themselves to each other.

Lamont, Phyllis' 14-year-old youngest child, had his father's features. He was tall but lacked his brother Mayson's lankiness. He was the shyest of all the children. Phyllis also found him to be the most affectionate. He would often give Phyllis the biggest hug for no apparent reason. Lamont was a loner and never had as many friends as Idee or Mayson. When at home, he could either be found in his room listening to his Walkman or watching television. He liked watching the big television in the den, but on days when his mother wanted to watch her programs, Lamont would retreat to his room without complaint to watch one of his many action shows.

Lamont was a brilliant student with little admiration for school. His teachers would often share with Phyllis their frustration in getting him to follow through with his high academic capabilities. He'd usually start out the semester with excellent grades. Close to the end of the semester his grades would drop to C and low B averages. It was as though he feared getting high grades, one of his teachers told Phyllis. Phyllis had also done well in school. If she had not gotten pregnant at such an early age, her goal was to go to college and become a teacher.

Phyllis tried all she could to get Lamont to share with her why his grades faltered close to the end of each semester. He'd only reply that he didn't know, or he'd try to do better next time—which he would not. Unlike Mayson, Lamont was not one to open himself to long and in-depth communication. He didn't have the drive that Mayson had when it came to challenges, instead, he lived off mediocracy.

Lamont's handsome features didn't go unnoticed by the girls in his class. But Lamont would never allow himself to engage in their bids for his attention. Initially, he was not aware that the girls were attracted to him. When some of the girls were tired of trying to be subtle, they would simply make vulgar sexual offers. Lamont ignore them as though he didn't hear them, or occasionally lie that he had a girlfriend. These sexual come-ons were something that he'd tell Mayson about, but wavered about sharing them with his mother. He knew of the teachings at his church about lust and fornication. He also knew that there were a few occasions when the thought of engaging in some of the acts the girls propositioned made his body react in ways that he definitely didn't want to share with his mother.

The one time that Lamont told Mayson about all the attention he was getting from girls, Mayson expressed amusement. He'd awkwardly responded as though Lamont was lucky for such attention. Lamont could tell that Mayson was trying to sound like the other boys he heard at school or in their neighborhood. He asked Mayson whether he had ever had sex with a girl. Lamont recalled Mayson responded that he had a devotion to

God and wanted to wait until he got married. They never brought up the conversation again.

Lamont liked hanging out with Mayson. Mayson never discouraged Lamont's tagging along with hm and his best friend Reanna. Lamont was never much trouble and Mayson liked the fact that he was among the very few that Lamont felt comfortable with. Lamont also got along well with Idee. Despite Idee's self-absorbed personality, she too would try and find some time for Lamont. It baffled her how someone could be as quiet and isolated as him. She'd try and make up for it by watching television with Lamont or bring things back for him whenever she went out with her friends. As for his oldest brother, J.R., there were a few times when J.R. invited Lamont to hang out with him at ball games. After a day out with J.R., Lamont would usually return home looking for Mayson as though he had to make sure that Mayson was okay with his hanging out with J.R. Phyllis liked the time that J.R. spent with Lamont but could not help but feel bad for Mayson. J.R. never spent any time with him. She wanted to believe that it was due to their personality differences.

Mayson and his mother had discussed Lamont's need to venture out. They both agreed that Lamont's time with Mayson was a start for him to meet other people. Mayson didn't swear, drink alcohol, or express any signs of being sexually active, so he knew Lamont was in good company with him. However, his friend Reanna had a different side to her. On days when Lamont was with them, Mayson expressed to Reanna his concern when she would tell Mayson details about her relationships with her boyfriends. Mayson would ask her to tone it down when Lamont was around.

Mayson, Phyllis' 20-year-old second child was the gentlest of her four children. He was tall and thin like Ed, but lanky. His facial features, including his very light complexion, were those similar to Christopher Reid, of Kid and Play. His mother Phyllis, had what he described as a pecan brown complexion, and his father was about one shade darker than her. His mother, Lamont, and Idee were all of similar complexion. Idee looked like her mother and Lamont like his father. Mayson was tall like his father, but his lankiness and facial features sometimes made him feel as though he stood out. Mayson didn't look much like either of his parents, although a few people would say his eyes were like his mother's. Phyllis had a picture of his paternal grandfather, whom Mayson had never met, in the family album, and he could see that he looked more like him than either of his parents. Mayson was self-conscious about his light skin. When he was in high school some of his classmates would call him "white boy," which he disliked intensely. Mayson was not comfortable with most of his physical features, but the one thing he prided himself on was his hair. It grew fast, sometimes too fast for Phyllis to get him a decent haircut. Now Mayson wore his bushy afro to his shoulders, similar to the Jackson 5 during the 70s. His hair often got him compliments. Some girls at his high school offered to braid it for him.

Mayson was usually mild-mannered. It took a lot to anger him, but when it happened, he'd burst like a broken dam. Phyllis admired Mayson's tendency to think optimistically of others, but she also worried it would make him vulnerable. Unlike Lamont, whose mediocre grades were because he only did enough to get by, Mayson struggled in school even when he did his best. During his junior year in high school, his teacher informed Phyllis that if Mayson could get a score of at least 79 on his next test, it would be enough for him to make a passing grade. When Phyllis relayed this, Mayson began to study evenings and weekends. He had his siblings quiz him until he was able to answer almost every question. Mayson passed the test with an 85. Phyllis baked him his favorite German chocolate cake as a reward. He was able to graduate from school with a C average. He worked at a discount store part-time in high school, and his boss had assured him that if he stayed after he graduated, he would bring Mayson on full-time with the possibility of working toward becoming the assistant manager. Mayson did stay after graduation, but the store closed down six months later. For the past two years, Mayson had worked odd jobs, including part-time work at a janitorial cleaning company. He kept that job longer than any of the other jobs. He told Phyllis that it was just a stopgap until he decided what he wanted to do.

Mayson had managed to come to terms with his father's lack of regard for him. He resigned himself to the view that it was not just him that his father didn't like, but Lamont as well. He knew that his father loved Idee, because he would find time to laugh and talk with her. But Mayson saw himself and Lamont as two boys for his father to bark at about mowing the lawn or taking out the trash. Mayson didn't mind if the barking was actually his father's concern for keeping the house up, but he could tell that it was more about his father's attempt at "acting" like a father when he made his appearances. Phyllis helped Mayson to believe that his father's low regard for him and Lamont was more about who his father was as a man and not about their self-worth. This sounded reasonable to Mayson, yet he longed for a normal family that included an attentive father. He liked J.R. and admired his relationship with Cliff, Sr. Mayson envied those times when Cliff would come to the house to pick up J.R. for their weekends together. Cliff was always nice to Mayson when he came to the house.

One weekend, before Cliff was to pick up J.R. for a morning fishing trip, Phyllis called Cliff and asked him to invite Mayson to go along. Cliff assured Phyllis that he would like to ask Mayson to come, but the last time when his wife Irene suggested the same thing, J.R. responded that he would not go on the trip if Mayson was going. Phyllis contemplated asking Cliff why he thought J.R. didn't want Mayson to go, but she was afraid of what the response might be. Instead, she asked:

"Well, did you talk to J.R. about his attitude towards his own brother?"

There was a brief silence over the phone.

"I did but he only closed up and didn't have much to say. They are different boys, he added. And us trying to force them together is never going to work."

"It scares me when I see a little of your mother's shunning attitude in him," said Phyllis.

If anyone else made this comment about my mother, I would be highly offended, thought Cliff, but he knew Phyllis was right. He often saw his mother in J.R. but never wanted to admit it.

CHAPTER 3
Young Phyllis and Clifton, Sr

Unrestrained young love can lead to grown-up decisions

(I)

Seventeen-year-old Cliff and eighteen-year-old Phyllis were high school sweethearts. Being older than your boyfriend was not the norm for relationships in Phyllis' mind, so she would often tell people that Cliff was one year older than he actually was. They had been a couple for two years before she became pregnant with J.R. in their senior year of high school. Cliff was special and the longest relationship she ever had. She had gotten pregnant three weeks before her eighteenth birthday. Phyllis never thought she would be sexually active and pregnant in high school. She had wanted to wait until she was married to have sex, but they often found themselves in isolated places with opportunities and aroused emotions.

Cliff was stunned at the news of Phyllis' pregnancy. His father was not around for him to confide in and he dare not tell his mother, as she never liked Phyllis anyway. He would not consider going to his other relatives for help for fear his mother would find out from one of them.

Cliff was the only child of his mother. His father left them when Cliff was eight years old. His parents, Florence and Willie Harmon, had been separated for nine years, but they never divorced. Willie had since been living with another woman and fathered four other children with her. Florence told her family that she didn't have the money to file for divorce from her husband. When she secured a well-paying job as the head cook at a popular restaurant in their hometown of Lanear, Ohio, she then said she needed the additional income for Cliff's college education. Years later, due to her shrewd savings and investments, she became the owner of the restaurant; after that, she didn't give any explanation as to why she and her estranged husband had not officially divorced.

Phyllis was the oldest of her siblings. Her mother, Ida Mae Potter, relied heavily upon Phyllis to help her take care of the home and Phyllis 8 other siblings. The family received a small income after the car-accident death of Ida Mae's husband, but it was not enough to adequately care for a family of 10. After Phyllis' father died, her mother developed the reputation of *"another woman"* in Lanear.

Despite (or maybe because of) her questionable reputation, Ida Mae brought in enough income to keep her family off the streets. Ida Mae didn't have a regular job . But somehow the bills were paid. Phyllis never asked her mother where her additional money came from. As an adult, Phyllis had an idea where it had come from, but never had her mother to confirm it. She recalled her mother leaving the home on a few occasions to *"take care of something,"* as her mother phrased it.

On a warm Sunday afternoon, while sitting on a bench near their high school track, Phyllis and Cliff sat as they looked into the sky. Both knowing they had a lot to talk about but were unsure where to start.

"I don't think my mother would be the best person to tell about us at this time. There are 9 mouths in my house that my mother has to feed. Can you imagine what she would do if I tell her that now there's a 10th child on the way?" said Phyllis.

"Come on, Phyll. We have to talk to someone. Might as well be your mother..." Cliff paused..."rather than mine," he said.

Phyllis could see the fear in Cliff's eyes. Reluctantly, she agreed to tell her mother.

At school the next day, Cliff and Phyllis were both nervous. They met at lunch to talk more. Phyllis had second thoughts and decided to tell Cliff that she changed her mind about telling her mother. Phyllis only had an orange and milk on her tray. Her stomach was too upset to eat anything else. Cliff had everything that he was allowed to eat on his. They sat in the corner of the cafeteria near the fire exit door, far away from the other students. Phyllis pushed her tray to the side and leaned in to talk quietly to Cliff. Cliff began to eat immediately.

"I can't tell my mother about the baby. I need for us to wait a while until we can come up with a different plan," whispered Phyllis.

"A plan?" Cliff asked as he dropped his fork to his plate, splashing a little spaghetti sauce on his shirt. "I thought we had agreed that we would tell your mother this afternoon. We can't wait too long," he said.

"I know, but I'm scared," she said.

"Scared of what?" asked Cliff.

"Scared of what my mother might do to me," responded Phyllis.

"What could she possibly do to you, Phyll? I think your imagination is getting the better of you," said Cliff, as he stopped eating. "We definitely can't tell my mother right now. She'll accuse you of getting pregnant on purpose. She told me a few months after she met you that you would find some way to trap me."

"And? I hope you're not thinking the same," said Phyllis, alarmed.

Phyllis was aware from the first day that she met Mrs. Harmon that the woman didn't like her. She knew that keeping this secret from her was not going to make her embrace her. She had met Mrs. Harmon at one of Cliff's baseball games one summer. From the frown on her face in seeing Phyllis in her high, almost over-the-thigh shorts, to her avoidance of eye contact with her, she made it known to Phyllis to keep away from her and Cliff. After the game, Cliff and his mother had a terrible argument about Phyllis. She told Cliff that Phyllis was the type to trap a boy. He was not sure what she meant by trapping him but had an idea. His friend Jason had gotten his girlfriend pregnant and he was now having money taken from his paycheck at the auto-parts store where he worked. After this argument, Cliff seldom spoke about Phyllis to his mother.

In an effort to see if he was still seeing Phyllis, Mrs. Harmon would bring Phyllis' name up from time to time, referring to her as "Miss Loose." Cliff would either ignore her or give a quick *she's fine*. He had resolved to leave these two women separated in his life.

"Of course not!" responded Cliff to Phyllis' question of his thought about his being trapped by her.

"Okay Cliff, we'll tell my mother, but this better turn out right," said Phyllis.

Cliff smiled at Phyllis and breathed a sigh of relief as he started back eating.

(II)

As Phyllis and Cliff approached Phyllis' house, they agreed that Phyllis would go in first to get things going with her mother, and Cliff would stay out on the porch until she called him in.

Ida Mae was home washing clothes when Phyllis came into the house. She didn't look up as Phyllis walked through the door. She was watching the old wringer washing machine carefully to prevent it from jamming. Phyllis stood near the door for a while as she looked at her mother's old, loose-fitting housedress and short wig that was slightly askew on her head. The fact that she had her wig on while washing meant that she had been out at some point during the day. Her mother's faced looked dry and worn, as she seldom slept a full night. She had suffered from insomnia since Phyllis' father died. Phyllis sometimes felt as though she had two mothers. Some days her mother looked rough and disheveled and on others she looked like a glamorous movie star. When her mother dressed up, her make-up made her skin and eyes vibrant. She'd wear a beautiful long brown wig and short dresses in solid colors that accented her voluptuous shape. She dressed like that on those days when she would come home with enough money to pay for their bills. At that moment, Phyllis wished her mother was adorned in her better wig and make-up. She despised the harsh appearance of her mother that was mostly seen by people her mother didn't feel the need to impress. She thought if her mother was dressed up, it would make it easier for her to talk to. It would be like talking to someone else.

"Mama, I need to talk to you," said Phyllis.

"You see I'm busy girl," said Ida Mae.

"Mama, this is really important," said Phyllis.

She was about to put a wet shirt into the wringer but held it in her hand and looked Phyllis in the face. Phyllis could see the dread and anticipation mingled in her face. Almost as if she knew what Phyllis was about to say.

"Well, what do you have to say to me?" asked Ida Mae.

Phyllis felt her knees shake as her voice trembled.

"Wait, I have to get Cliff. He's on the porch," she said.

As Phyllis left to get Cliff, Ida Mae put the wet shirt in the washer. She pulled out one of the chairs from her kitchen table and fell into the seat, her body limp with anticipation of the news. One of the chair legs was short and made the whole chair wobble. She moved back and forth as she thought about the need for a new kitchen set.

Cliff came through the door, his eyes shifting from Ida Mae to the floor.

"Hi Mrs. Potter," said Cliff.

Ida Mae glanced at Cliff without greeting him and immediately looked back at Phyllis.

"Phyllis, I don't have time for games. What do you have to tell me?" she asked.

Cliff heard the tension in Ida Mae's voice and began to wonder if she was the right choice to break this news to after all.

Cliff moved closer to Phyllis as he saw her shaking.

"Mama," she began to cry. "Mama," she tried again. "I'm pregnant."

Phyllis lost sight of her mother's stretched eyes as tears began to flood her vision.

Cliff moved away from Phyllis as he felt his body tremble with fear. It all seemed so unreal. He could not open his mouth to speak.

Ida Mae was always a mystery to Cliff. Whenever he came by to walk with Phyllis to school, Ida Mae would open the door, look at him and yell to Phyllis that he was at the door. She did this every time. He could never tell whether she liked or disliked him because she never had anything to say to him. Cliff had planned all the words he would say to Ida Mae that afternoon, but nothing came from his mouth as Phyllis continued to cry.

Ida Mae turned her whole body around to the kitchen table, covering her face with her hands as she rested her elbows on the table. She rubbed her face as she could hear Phyllis crying and repeatedly saying, "I'm sorry Mama, I'm sorry."

Ida Mae took her hands down from her face and with a heavy sigh and drained countenance, she looked at Phyllis as though Cliff was not in the room.

"What are the boy's parents going to do about this baby?" she asked.

Cliff was startled by this response but managed to speak.

"Mrs. Potter, I have not told my mother about the baby. We thought you could help us," he said.

"Help you!" Ida Mae shouted. "Did I tell you to get my daughter pregnant? How am I supposed to help you? I got children of my own I have to help. Clark, you are asking the wrong mother for help," said Ida Mae.

"It's Cliff, ma'am," Cliff interjected quietly.

"I don't care what it is," she screamed as she pounded her fist on the kitchen table. "You need to tell me what you are going to do with your baby."

Ida Mae turned her attention back to Phyllis and asked her how far along she was. Phyllis could barely talk as she tried to catch her breath to answer her mother's questions. She finally managed to say that it had been 8 weeks since she had had a period.

"You know I don't have enough money to take care of this mess," said Ida Mae.

Phyllis began to cry even harder. Cliff moved closer to Phyllis to support her, but did not put his arms around her in front of Ida Mae. He stood next to her with his arms alongside him but slightly touching Phyllis' shoulder from behind. He wanted her to feel his presence. He straightened his back as though he was going to stand up to Ida Mae.

"I will get a job to care for the baby," Mrs. Potter.

Ida Mae looked at Cliff condescendingly.

Ok, Cliff! she said, emphasizing his name sarcastically. "But who's going to pay her medical bills in the meantime while you look for a job?"

Cliff looked startled and no words came from his mouth again. There was a long silence in the room. No one opened their mouth as Ida Mae stared up at Cliff from her seated position. Phyllis cried harder. After about 10 seconds of silence, Ida Mae then turned her seat back around to face Cliff and Phyllis more directly.

"You really want me to help you?" Ida Mae asked.

"Yes, ma'am," said Cliff.

"How old are you, boy?" Ida Mae asked.

"I'll be eighteen next month," said Cliff.

Ida Mae leaned back in her chair with her hands folded across her chest.

"Do you and Ida Mae plan to marry before this baby comes?" she asked.

Having never considering marriage and scared of saying the wrong thing, Cliff responded what he thought would be a safe answer.

"I would like to marry someday," he said carefully.

"The military has a solid future with good benefits," said Ida Mae.

"Now, since you did ask me, I suggest you go and enlist. Phyllis will be graduating from school in a few months. She can join you after she's had the baby. I will only help you if you will be responsible enough to join the military for your family," she said.

Cliff looked at Ida Mae with curiosity and shock. At this point marriage was not his only concern. He didn't anticipate the talk with her going in this direction, or that a solution would be proposed so fast.

He walked toward the table and took a seat on the opposite side of where Ida Mae was sitting.

"The military?" repeated Cliff.

"That's what I said," responded Ida Mae quickly, as though she was squaring a deal at a flea market.

As the tone between Cliff and Ida Mae took on more of a conversational interaction, Phyllis slowly stopped crying. She wiped the tears with the backs of her hands as she took the seat next to Cliff.

"I don't know," said Cliff as he looked down at the floor shaking his head. "I'm not sure how my mother is going to take my joining up," he said.

"How old did you say you are?" asked Ida Mae flatly.

"Soon to be eighteen, but…"

Ida Mae cut him off.

"And who did you come to for help?" she asked.

"You," said Cliff, feeling as though he were in a courtroom.

"So, what does your mother have to do with this?" asked Ida Mae.

Cliff looked across the table at Ida Mae with defeat on his face.

"How do I get information about the military?" asked Cliff.

"I have a friend who knows a recruiter for the Marines. I'll talk with him today and let Phyllis know where he wants to meet you," said Ida Mae. Phyllis felt embarrassed. She suspected that this *friend* was the source of her mother's questionable income.

"Okay," said Cliff in a soft voice.

CHAPTER 4

Reanna

Friendship starts from the head and moves to the heart.

(I)

Reanna Harrison was Mayson's best friend. She was five years old when she and her family joined GCC. Her mother Evelyn and stepfather Morris Brewer had been married for several years. Her younger brother Chuckie was their biological son. Reanna and her older sister Elaine had the same biological father. He was a police officer who died in a motorcycle accident. Elaine was four and Reanna was eight months old when their father died. Elaine had a few vague recollections of their father, but Reanna had no firsthand memories of him at all.

Morris was a nice man who never had a harsh or unkind word towards the girls. He provided whatever they needed. However, Reanna saw his kindness as more of a duty to help her mother, rather than any specific affection for her and Elaine.

When Reanna was a child, Morris' older brother lived in the basement of their home. He babysat Reanna when she got home from school until her parents came home from work. Chuckie was the only one they could afford to send to an afterschool program and Elaine stayed with her best friend after school. Morris' brother molested Reanna from when she was six until after she turned seven.

Against Morris' wishes, Evelyn filed charges against her brother-in-law. Upon his release from prison, they never heard from him again. During that time, Reanna went through a period of nightmares and sexually acting out with her toys and other objects. The Department of Child Protective Services recommended counseling for Reanna. Evelyn took Reanna for counseling for two months, but stopped because she felt she could help Reanna herself with love and by making sure that she never put her in that situation again. The strain on Evelyn and Morris' marriage during that time led to a temporary separation. They reconciled after receiving counseling from a pastor in the community. Prior to the counseling, neither Evelyn nor Morris attended church on a regular basis, only on Easter for the children. They also joined the pastor's church but stopped attending when he moved the church to a different part of town. By then, they had developed a love for church, so rather than stop going, they join GCC. Eventually, the trio of Mayson, Reanna, and Lamont formed.

As a young teen, Reanna would sincerely commit to a life with God on Sundays, but before the week was out, she would be back into her old ways of living. She was in and out of being *saved,* to the point that no one bothered to ask anymore. She told Mayson that she was so tired of repenting that she decided to be in the church than out until she could get it right. Mayson reminded her that the church taught that once you sin, you must always repent to God and the church.

"I know I'm a sinner and not what God wants. One day, I'll get this right and let everyone know later about the *out* days," she would say." Besides, they need as many people in the choir as possible," she'd add wryly.

In their early teens, Reanna and Mayson often shared their dreams of having a beautiful home and nice cars. This future did not include education or career type. Unlike Mayson, Reanna worked various odd jobs from fast food to manufacturing companies. She lived off and on with her mother and stepfather. When her finances were good, she'd get her own apartment. But when her funds were limited or non-existent, she moved back in with her parents. Her mother allowed her back home with no questions asked. She blamed herself for Reanna's molestation, therefore, allowed the back and forth living arrangement.

Reanna had beautiful light brown eyes and long, thick eyelashes that most people assumed to be false. She had dimples in her cheeks that Mayson would describe as *"too adorable."* He liked seeing her laugh because the dimples would become deeper and it sometimes made her look like a little girl, he'd often tell her. Despite her natural beauty, she wore an excessive amount of make-up. She had an obsessive thought that without foundation, people would stare at the small area of acne on her cheek. Mayson often tried to discourage her from wearing make-up, but she would tell him that she felt naked without it.

24

Despite the fact that they both sat under the same teaching at GCC of abstaining from sexual immorality, Reanna would often confide in Mayson about her different boyfriends and her "activities" with them. With an effort not to show it, Mayson looked forward to hearing about her activities with her boyfriends. Occasionally he'd eye Lamont when he thought she was going too far. There was only so much that he wanted Lamont to hear, so he'd caution her to change the subject. When Lamont was not around, Mayson would hang on every word. But after hearing her stories, Mayson would caution Reanna with common-sense realities about her behavior, laced with the occasional verse of Scripture. But he did it with a smile on his face. Once, Mayson tried to psychoanalyze Reanna by telling her that she must have such a sexual appetite for so many boys because she didn't know her father and had a distant relationship with her stepfather. Reanna never shared with Mayson about her molestation. She couldn't bring herself to talk about it with anyone, not even her mother.

Reanna knew that Mayson was mesmerized by the stories of her sexual escapades. She gathered that her friend Mayson was a virgin but she also knew that his hormones were raging as much as hers. She knew much more about his romantic desires than he suspected. Branson was the most attractive boyfriend that Reanna had been with. He was on the wrestling team and it was obvious that he worked out daily. Mayson had come across Reanna and Branson one day when they were sitting in a booth at a fast-food restaurant. Reanna introduced them to each other, and she recalled how intensely Mayson stared at him while extending his hand out to shake his. After the meeting, Mayson constantly asked Reanna about Branson. "You just want my man for yourself," Reanna said to Mayson one day with a laugh. Mayson blushed a little and she laughed more. Reanna would occasionally make insinuating remarks about Mayson's sexuality in hopes that he would open up to her, but despite their closeness, this was one thing that Mayson would not confide in Reanna. As much as he loved his friend, he knew that she could not keep secrets. Telling Reanna something as personal as his sexuality was the equivalent of announcing it to the entire GCC congregation.

(II)

"GCC is invited to Shiloh Church for an appreciation service for Pastor Martin next Sunday," said Reanna, talking on the phone with Mayson.

"Are you going?" asked Mayson.

"Yeah, I think I'll go. My family's not going, so I think it'll be good for me," said Reanna in a devious laugh.

"Here we go again in our seeking a man at church venture," said Mayson. "I thought you were seeing someone?"

"I am, but it doesn't hurt to look. Remember that bearded guy who works at SaveTime grocery store?" she asked.

"Yes," Mayson said.

"Okay, his name is Mitchell Carter and he goes to Shiloh. I want to see what he's like in a church setting," she said.

"Well, I'm going. My mother, Lamont and Idee will be there. Unlike you, I have nothing to hide from my family," said Mayson.

"Mayson, you have a lot to hide," laughed Reanna.

"I'll see you tomorrow girl," said Mayson, ignoring her comment and hanging up.

Shiloh Church was at its 500-seat capacity. Mayson was dressed in his best blue button-down shirt with gray slacks. The church would get warm during services, so he decided to not wear the matching jacket. His hair was fully picked out and had a bounce that he could feel as he walked.

He sat in the second row of the church near the front. Mayson liked being as close to the front as possible. He wanted to feel the presence of all that happened during services. He also liked seeing the musicians play their instruments and hearing the choir at close range. Mayson loved music and singing, but he was not highly skilled in either. He would lead a song whenever given the chance. He could sing on key, but his voice often sounded strained whenever he tried going out of his range. Whatever the level, he led congregational songs whenever possible.

Mayson was known in the church for his inspiring testimonies and congregational lead singings, during Praise and Testimony service. One time, Mayson was holding one of the choir member's eight-month-old baby in his arms while he led an especially inspiring congregational song. Mayson was so enthralled by the song that he broke out in a praise dance while holding the baby. One of the ushers came and got the baby from his arms while Mayson continued to dance in praise, hair bobbing up and down.

While sitting in the pew at Shiloh Church, Mayson looked around the church for Reanna, who was chronically late. He was trying to save a seat for her, which was becoming more and more difficult as people poured into the church. The usher had warned Mayson that at some point they would need to put someone in that seat as the church continue to fill.

Each time Mayson would see the church door open from the side of the building, he would crane his neck to see if it was Reanna. Finally, in walked Reanna dressed in a tight pink top, a short skirt that curved around her bottom to show off its shape, black pantyhose, and pointy high-heeled shoes. She wore her hair in a finger-wave style that neatly framed her oval face and also made her look older. Compared to what she wore at the clubs, this outfit was tame. She was allowed to get away with her eye-opening attire at GCC because when she sang in the choir, she wore her choir robe, which completely covered her. On days when she did not have her choir robe on, a few of the church mothers spoke to her about dressing more appropriately for church, but Reanna would either pretend not to hear them or simply walk away.

Mayson stood up halfway as he waved Reanna over to come and sit with him. She squeezed between the pew as she passed the knees of others and Mayson's long legs to sit next to him. Lamont scooted over so she could sit. He knew that Mayson and Reanna liked to talk during the service, so he made sure not to be between them.

"What did I miss?" asked Reanna as she adjusted her skirt and put her purse between her and Lamont.

"Nothing much. They just finished the opening prayer," said Mayson.

The side door opened again and in walked two young ladies, Deandra Rowe and Veronica Lambert. Mayson had seen the college girls around at various churches and from events at the university, Benton-Hawk University.

Those that lived in the town referred to the university by its full name. Students referred to the school as Ben-Hawk or, as printed on their t-shirts and sweatshirts, BHU. BHU was not a well-known university, but it demanded high standards from its employees and students.

Expulsion from the university was not uncommon, especially when it involved initiation pranks.

Deandra and Veronica were roommates in their junior year at Ben-Hawk. Deandra, petite, beautiful glowing caramel skin tone, long cornrow braids and an inspiring minister, which she does not admit to, is one of the leaders of their campus bible meeting groups.

She also did a church seminar on leadership at her own church. Mayson liked Deandra and always looked forward to hearing her lead prayer or share so eloquently during Praise and Testimony service. He vaguely remembered Veronica's name because Deandra would sometimes refer to her to lead the opening prayer.

Mayson knew that Deandra attended Faith on A Mission Church. He remembered that he and Deandra had sung in their district choir together once. She sat next to him in the choir and they had a brief conversation about Ben-Hawk University. Mayson liked the way Deandra appeared so sincere about her spiritual life.

Mayson first saw Veronica at the Bible on Campus meetings. Even though Veronica was a member of Mt. Olive church, she attended many services at GCC. They had never met directly but Mayson was familiar with her face. He glanced at them as they sat in the back section on the other side. They sat behind a guy Deandra knew from her church name Melvin Sutton. Melvin was also a college student whom Mayson would see from time to time attending church services in the city. Melvin's college was in a different state, but when he came home on school breaks, he'd visit various church services events in Benton. Melvin was so handsome that he modeled part-time, but despite his awareness of his good looks, most people found him to be polite and charming. Melvin was sitting with a few guys from his church. One of the guys with him was Eric, whom they'd sometimes refer to as Mouse because of his beady eyes, long nose, and sharply pointed ears. Despite his comical features, he could talk enough trash with girls to get them in trouble. Eric was loud and immature. Melvin's other friend, Rem, was pretty cool. He just liked hanging out with Melvin and Eric. Rem was of average height and average looks. Nothing like Melvin, but his 6'1" height and broad built frame did catch some girls' eyes.

Mayson would twitch in his seat as though he was trying to get comfortable, but he was really trying to get a look at Melvin on the other side of the church. He turned his head a little as though he was trying to stretch his neck. He got a quick look at Melvin as Melvin sat looking straight ahead at the speaker. Mayson thought how handsome Melvin looked in his suit. He looked like he just stepped out of a fashion magazine, he thought. He saw how neatly cut Melvin's hair was, with stylish sideburns along each ear. His handsome face looked as though he was posing for his next headshot, Mayson thought. He couldn't stop thinking about him.

Then, as if someone poured cold water over him, a sober thought came to his mind. *I have to pretend that I am not attracted to him*. Mayson had justified his need to constantly look for Melvin during church gatherings as simply a need to see what he was wearing. Mayson knew that Melvin always wore stylish suits to church. Mayson was afraid to admit that he had this attraction to Melvin and didn't know what this actually meant for him. He had justified his thoughts about Reanna's boyfriend Branson, as he blamed Reanna. He decided that, if she had not described their sexual encounter in such detail, he would not have thought much about Branson.

Then there were days when he didn't know what to think. He was bothered by the thought that his best friend was female. Mayson thought about his one male friend, Leon. He and Leon had been friends since Mayson was five years old and Leon was six. Leon's left arm and right leg never formed fully. He had an prosthetic leg and arm. Leon was extremely shy and self-conscious about his disability. He never seemed motivated to rise above his physical limitations. His parents died in a house fire when Leon was five and he lived with his grandmother, who was in poor health. Then he had an accident and broke his fully developed arm in a fall. The arm didn't heal well, which limited his ability to take care of himself. Mayson had heard that when Leon's grandmother died, he didn't have anyone to take care of him, so he was placed in a group home. The last time Mayson saw Leon was two years ago.

Melvin represented everything that Mayson didn't see in himself. He saw Melvin as intelligent, smooth, self-confident and, of course, handsome. For Mayson, Melvin's handsomeness was what immediately got his attention when he first saw him with his family at GCC church six years ago. Melvin's father, Evangelist Sutton, was doing a one-week revival at GCC for Pastor Upshaw at the time. Melvin was fifteen, neatly dressed and handsomely built. His skin and soft black hair made him look almost angelic. From that day onward, Mayson would look for Melvin at just about every district, state or national church meeting. When Melvin went to college, Mayson continued to look for him during out of school holidays or summer months when he believed Melvin to be home. His Melvin sightings were not primarily sexual so much as they were full of admiration and hope. Hope that someone like Melvin Sutton could actually like him and make him feel that he mattered. The physical was indeed there, but Mayson made an effort to suppress that side of the attraction, as he'd overrode it by letting his mind go into something completely different. He felt his attraction to Melvin was fine as long as he didn't allow it to become too sexual.

"Glory!" hollered someone in the congregation as they gave praise during the service. Mayson was shaken from his reverie about Melvin and saw that the Praise and Testimony service was almost over. He tried to make it a rule to always say something at this part of the service. He definitely didn't want to miss out during this particular service either. He felt guilty about his thoughts of Melvin, so he repented within himself and stood up to give his testimony in order to get his mind back into praise and worship.

"I'm truly grateful that God has blessed me to be in good health and to know and serve Him."

Mayson continued his testimony as he shared the blessing of his family and friends. He also shared an incident years ago when he was a little boy and was almost hit by a car. He threw up his hands in praise as he told how God blessed that the car was able to swerve past him.

From across the church, as Mayson gave his testimony, Melvin looked at Mayson with a frown.

"Looked at that ol' fag. What a punk," Melvin grunted.

Eric looked at Mayson and laughed out loud. Rem smiled as he too looked in Mayson's direction.

"I could just kick his ass," said Melvin.

Melvin continued his rants about Mayson. Deandra, who was now sitting alone while Veronica went to the restroom, could hear him. Deandra was not a personal friend of Mayson, but from her brief interactions with him, she thought he was a good person. She was surprised to hear Melvin make such comments. Like others, Deandra had questions about Mayson's sexuality, but it was never an issue as to whether or not she liked him. She knew that Mayson could not hear Melvin from his side of the room, but the thought of such hate and disrespect was irritating for her.

"Why don't you leave him alone? He's done nothing to you," said Deandra in a low and angry tone. "You need to grow up."

Unfortunately, Melvin didn't hear her, or if he did he didn't show it. His friends were now laughing even louder. Deandra's formerly admirable thoughts of Melvin changed. She had a short tolerance for mean-spirited people.

Mayson completed his testimony of praise and the congregation expressed inspiration from his words as they clapped along with him.

CHAPTER 5

Young Phyllis and Cliff:
Marital Arrangements

(I)

As the crowd of students mingled through the school halls of Langston High School, Cliff saw Phyllis through a small knot of students near her locker. As the crowd of students lessened, Phyllis saw Cliff making his way to her. As he approached her, she no longer saw a boy she liked, but a man who had recently turned 18, enlisted in the Marines and was about to be a father. As he came close to her, without a word, Phyllis took both of his hands in hers and looked up at him.

"Cliff, I'm scared," said Phyllis.

"Me too, but we have to do something," said Cliff.

"Once my mother gives her word to something, she's usually pretty firm. So, she will help us through this," said Phyllis.

"Yeah, I know, but with the pregnancy, wedding, and enlistment, I can't help but think about how my mother is going to take all this," said Cliff.

"Well maybe my mother will tell her with us," said Phyllis.

"I still don't know," Phyll, he said.

"My mother told me to ask you if February 25th was a good wedding date for you?" asked Phyllis.

Cliff looked at Phyllis as though someone had just hit him in the gut. He didn't want to upset her, so he tried to answer calmly.

"That's 2 weeks from now," he said softly.

"Yes, it is," said Phyllis. "Mama said we could go to the justice of the peace and tell your mother afterwards," said Phyllis.

"After the wedding!" cried Cliff. "I thought my mother would be there with us."

Phyllis felt a tinge of anger swelling when she heard Cliff bring up his mother again.

"Why? So she could talk you out of it?" asked Phyllis.

"No, Phyll. It's just that my mother is going to have to take a lot in, all at once."

"Well, Cliff, you can always marry your mother," said Phyllis sarcastically.

Cliff glared at Phyllis and felt his anger rise as well. He leaned toward Phyllis and rested his arm over her head against the locker next to Phyllis.

"Listen Phyll, I can only take so much. You are at fault for this baby just as much as I am, so you come down off your self-righteous throne and get off my back." He then hit the locker over her head with his fist. It made a vibrating thump.

Phyllis saw the sudden change on Cliff's face and realized that she had gone too far.

"I'm not trying to come down on you, Cliff, but we did go to my mother for help and you seem to squirm at every decision she makes," she said.

"Hell, Phyll! I didn't know that asking your mother for help would be the same as giving my soul to the dev" …he stopped. "…to her."

(II)

Standing in a small room waiting for the justice of the peace at City Hall on February 25th, 12:30PM, were Clifton Harmon and Phyllis Ann Potter. Phyllis didn't go to school at all on the day of the wedding. Cliff went for his morning classes and left during lunch. Justice Walter K. Biel walked into the room. He was a young-looking white man, short, big-bellied, with a full head of dark brown curly hair. Not what Phyllis had expected of a Justice of the Peace. She had anticipated an older man, with white hair. Phyllis, who had been in tears and occasionally throwing up since getting out of bed that morning, attempted to compose herself. She pulled a tissue from her purse and blew her nose. Justice Biel stood in front of the couple and gave a slight grin as he lifted one side of his robe and pulled out a small book from his hip pocket.

"Are we ready for this special day?" asked Justice Biel as he looked kindly at the two teenagers.

Phyllis managed a labored smile and Cliff a tight forward look. They both responded a low "yes." Ida Mae stood near her daughter as the marriage vows began with a look of resolve, but no sentiment. Cliff stared directly at the Justice of the Peace with a stoic look of bravery and tolerance. Justice Biel asked the words of commitment of each of them and they responded "I do" without looking at each other. The vows ended with a nervous kiss from the now-married couple. Justice Biel congratulated them. Cliff and Phyllis then turned to Ida Mae with a look that asked, *What now?*

(III)

After the wedding, Phyllis continued to live with her mother. Cliff returned home to his mother as though nothing had ever happened, certainly not a wedding on his lunch break. Ida Mae had planned their reception for March 2nd at a local pavilion. She had shared the news of her daughter's marriage and pregnancy with her extended family and some of her friends. Ida Mae's younger sister had always been fond of Phyllis, so she had collected money from their family and Ida Mae's friends to help share the expenses of the reception.

The big day of telling Cliff's mother was set a few days after the wedding. Ida Mae planned for her and Phyllis to meet with Ms. Harmon and Cliff at their house. After a few questions on the purpose of the meeting and little response from Cliff, Ms. Harmon agreed to the meeting. Ms. Harmon usually got home from her job at the restaurant in the late evenings but agreed to meet with them at 6:30PM. She was suspicious about the meeting request. She had noticed that Cliff had been nervous for the past few days. She could tell that he was even more nervous telling her that Ms. Potter and Phyllis wanted to meet with her. Ms. Harmon knew she could needle Cliff a little more, but she chose not to because she anticipated that further questioning would spark an argument about Phyllis.

She knew Phyllis was intimidated by her, but the thought of their getting married or wanting to get married had never entered her mind. Pregnancy was not a concern for her because she had had that talk with Cliff. She surmised that the meeting was about her attitude towards Phyllis. She was confident that she knew how she would handle the matter once she met them. She even found herself looking forward to the day. She had a lot to get off her chest to Phyllis and having her mother with her was considered a bonus.

(IV)

As Phyllis and her mother got off the city bus and walked the few blocks to Cliff's home, Phyllis could feel her stomach churning harder with each step. As they walked down his street, they saw old houses, some with weeds for grass and trash around them. In their midst was a beautifully remodeled home that stood out from the others. It stood tall and regal in the midst of its displacement. Ida Mae knocked on the door. After a few seconds, the door opened. It was Cliff. He had on a new white t-shirt, jeans, and house slippers. He smiled but looked as nervous as Phyllis felt.

"Hi Mrs. Potter, Phyll," said Cliff as he stepped aside to let them in.

Ida Mae immediately began to dust her shoes on the rug inside the door, and Phyllis followed suit. Cliff offered them both a seat on the egg-shell-colored sofa. The living room was well lit and full of expensive-looking furniture. From the side of the dining room was a small hall from which came Mrs. Harmon. She walked slowly with her arms loosely folded beneath her chest as she entered the living room with her guest. Mrs. Harmon managed to force a smile.

"Mama, you've met Phyllis," said Cliff with beads of sweat on his forehead. "This is her mother, Ida Mae Potter."

Mrs. Harmon kept her arms folded as she nodded hello to Ida Mae.

"Nice to meet you as well," said Ida Mae, as she looked Mrs. Harmon up and down.

Mrs. Harmon moved the ottoman away from the armchair and sat. Cliff pulled a chair from the dining room table and sat between the wide entrance of the living room and dining area. There was a silence in the room as they all sat and looked at each other. Ida Mae became impatient.

"Mrs. Harmon, I came here to talk to you about our children. They both came to me for help and I provided my help the best way possible," said Ida Mae.

Ida Mae then looked at Cliff.

"Cliff, tell your mother what you and Phyllis came to me about," said Ida Mae.

Cliff was taken aback. He thought Ida Mae would tell the whole story herself. Cliff felt trembling in his hands and a lump in his throat. Ida Mae continued her gaze directly at him.

Silence.

Ida Mae's impatience surfaced once more.

"Just come out and say it, Cliff," prompted Ida Mae.

Mrs. Harmon did not like the way Ida Mae was talking to her son and was about to let her know. But before she could, Cliff finally spoke.

"Mama, Phyllis is going to have a baby," Cliff heard himself say. "It's my baby," he added as his voice trembled.

Mrs. Harmon brows went up as she glared at Cliff. Her mouth tightened. She looked at Phyllis and then back at Cliff. She didn't know what to say. She looked at Phyllis again, as though her mother was no longer in the room.

"Are you for sure this is his baby?" asked Mrs. Harmon.

When Cliff began to open his mouth to answer, Ida Mae interceded.

"Mrs. Harmon, there's no need to insult my daughter. He told you it was his baby."

Mrs. Harmon looked at Ida Mae as she pulled herself up straight.

"Look, you are in my home talking to me about my son. You don't tell me what I can or cannot say in my own home," said Mrs. Harmon.

Before Ida Mae could respond, Cliff spoke up.

"Mama, this is my baby and we didn't come to debate it with you."

Phyllis looked over at Cliff with surprise. She could tell he was getting angry. She never thought that he could show this side to his mother.

Ida Mae opened her mouth to speak again, but Cliff cut her off.

"Not only that, Mama, but Phyllis and I are married, and I have enlisted into the Marines in order to support my family."

Mrs. Harmon's mouth dropped open. Every rehearsed word and

response she had were gone. She had these people in her home and could not recognize any of them, including Cliff. She was quick and knew how to think on her feet. However, at that moment, she felt helpless, and didn't like it.

"I'm sorry we had to tell you like this, Mama, but you were constantly speaking so bad about Phyllis that I couldn't tell you when I first knew about her pregnancy. I have to take care of my family," said Cliff in a stronger manner that eclipsed the tremor in his voice. "I don't want to be like Daddy," he said.

Mrs. Harmon's eyes widened when Cliff added his father's name to his explanation. She looked at Ida Mae and Phyllis and then stood up from the chair.

"Get out of my house," said Mrs. Harmon.

"Mama!" shouted Cliff in surprise.

Ida Mae immediately stood up, grabbed her purse and started walking toward the door. Phyllis remained on the couch in a daze, looking at Mrs. Harmon.

"Come on, Phyllis!" shouted Ida Mae as she anxiously fiddled with the door trying to open it. Cliff hurried to the door to open it for Ida Mae.

"You can go right with them, Clifton. You're Mrs. Loose's husband now, so go," said Mrs. Harmon.

Phyllis dropped her head in shame as she heard the name Mrs. Harmon used for her. Cliff was shocked at his mother's request for him to leave, as he then looked at Ida Mae with another *What now?* look on his face.

"You can come to my house, Cliff," said Ida Mae, as she looked straight at Mrs. Harmon and walked out her door.

(V)

On September 5, 1961, Clifton Harmon, Jr. was born at Oak County Hospital, weighing 6 pounds, 4 ounces. Phyllis rested comfortably in her hospital bed with Ida Mae sitting in a chair on the side. Phyllis had the biggest smile on her face as she looked at her baby.

"I wish Cliff was here to see his son," said Phyllis.

Ida Mae leaned closer to the bed as she stroked the top of the baby's beautiful curly black hair.

"I called the Red Cross to reach him while you were in labor. They're trying to get the message to him," said Ida Mae.

"Why did they have to send him so far away, with a pregnant wife?" asked Phyllis.

"I think they know what they're doing. He'll see his baby soon enough," said Ida Mae, as she placed her finger in the baby's little hand. Baby J.R. held her finger tightly.

"Mama, you think Cliff will hate me now that his baby is here, and his mother is not?" asked Phyllis.

"Phyllis, one thing I learned about Cliff is he has a lot of man that comes out of him when pushed too far. I saw this when he stood up to his mother. He really surprised me," said Ida Mae laughingly.

"So, you think he may be okay without his mother seeing the baby? His very first baby?" asked Phyllis.

"His mama made the decision to cut ties from him, so that's something she'll have to live with. Don't spend time worrying about her. Nobody forced or asked her to do that. If he resents anybody, it'll be his stuck-up mama," said Ida Mae.

"I had thought about calling her," said Phyllis tentatively.

"You will do no such thing," snapped Ida Mae.

Phyllis knew that her mother was thinking more about herself in being thrown out of Ms. Harmon's home rather than what was best for Cliff and the baby.

The hospital phone rang.

"Oh! I hope that's Cliff," said Phyllis.

"Hello?" said Ida Mae.

Phyllis was breastfeeding J.R. while rubbing his soft, beautiful black hair. She could tell it was Cliff on the phone because her mother began to smile. After Cliff moved into their crowded little house a few weeks before going to basic training, he and Ida Mae had grown close. He was helpful around the house and spent a lot of time with Phyllis' siblings.

She could hear her mother's upbeat tone as they exchanged pleasantries. It made her feel good to see and hear her mother speak so well with Cliff. It was good for Phyllis that two people she loved also got along so well. A far cry from the trembling boy who stood in her kitchen asking her mother for help.

She waited patiently to talk to her husband.

"Good, Cliff. I'm glad you are doing fine," said Ida Mae. "Yes, everything is fine here," she said.

She was silent as Cliff said something to her.

"I'll let her tell you that part," said Ida Mae.

She then gave the phone to Phyllis.

"Hi, honey," said Phyllis. "I'm good, baby," she said when he asked her how she was feeling. "When are you coming to see your son?"

She then broke out in a laugh as she pulled the phone away from her ear to talk with Ida Mae.

"He's yelling 'It's a boy!' over and over," said Phyllis.

"Getting a woman pregnant is one thing, but you give a man a son, it changes everything," said Ida Mae as she tickled baby J.R.'s stomach.

Phyllis put her ear back to the phone.

"Honey, I'm glad that we have a baby boy too, but next time we will have our baby girl." She smiled but did not hear a response from Cliff.

"Cliff? Cliff?" called Phyllis.

Continued silence.

"Cliff, are you there?" asked Phyllis.

"Oh, you okay?"

"Why the silence?"

As Ida Mae continued to play with the baby's stomach, she was startled as Phyllis burst into tears and handed the phone back to Ida Mae.

"What's wrong?" asked Ida Mae.

Phyllis continued to cry without answering.

"Cliff, Cliff," yelled Ida Mae into the phone.

"Yes, ma'am," said Cliff in a weak and low voice.

"What's going on?" asked Ida Mae.

"I got to go, Mrs. Potter. Tell Phyllis I'll call back later," he said softly.

"Okay," said Ida Mae in a confused voice.

Ida Mae hung up the phone.

"What happened?" asked Ida Mae.

"He said he wished his mother could be there to see his son and then he started crying," sniffled Phyllis. "Mama, I never heard him cry before."

CHAPTER 6

Deandra and Veronica:
To Tell or Not to Tell?

Wounds from a friend can be trusted, but an enemy multiplies kisses.
Proverbs 27:6

(I)

"Girl, that was a good service," said Veronica as she sat on the edge of her bed, removing her shoes and looking forward to a long, hot shower.

"Yeah, it was nice," said Deandra as she took off her earrings.

"You don't sound too sure," said Veronica, as she looked at her roommate with expectancy.

Deandra knew that Veronica wanted to talk about tonight's church service at Shiloh, but she also knew that Veronica could tell that she was upset about something. When Veronica had arrived back from the bathroom at church, Deandra had a difficult time composing herself after hearing Melvin's hateful comments towards Mayson during the service.

Deandra was poised and most people got along with her, but she knew what it meant to be judged and called names. In middle school and high school, she was often made fun of and called *Goody,* which was short for "Miss Goody Two-Shoes." She felt that because she didn't go through her "terrible teens" like many of her peers, this made her different. She tried to hang out with some of the girls known for their mean-girl reputations for a while, but she felt phony. So, she went back to being Deandra, as she had described it to Veronica.

Rather than thinking of Deandra as conscientious, Veronica would describe her as a prude. Deandra didn't like Veronica's impression of her, but that day she guessed it was that prudish side of her that didn't want to feed Veronica's nosiness. Deandra was highly aware of what she said and to who she said it to. Veronica lived for gossip.

Deandra's church offered more practical teachings about daily living that emphasized, among other things, behavior, outcomes, and applications. Deandra was meshed in the teachings of her church. She sometimes thought that if Veronica's church provided such teachings, Veronica must have been absent for those sermons.

Deandra was not aware that Veronica already knew Mayson. She also didn't know that Veronica had had a huge crush on Mayson from the day she first saw him.

"Do you know Melvin Sutton?" asked Deandra.

"Yeah, I've seen him around. I saw Mr. Fashion Model Melvin at your church when you all had the revival with Evangelist Wakes last year. He's also been to a few BC meetings on the campus. He's handsome," Veronica added.

Deandra anticipated her roommate would be adding something negative to her statement.

"Can't miss that. And he knows he's handsome," Veronica said fervently.

There was silence, as Deandra tried to find the right words. The silence made Veronica that much more anxious. Anxious for Deandra to get to the point, Veronica continued her comments about Melvin.

"With that being said, I didn't like him from the first time I saw him. I heard that he... "

Deandra knew that Veronica had something to say about everyone and didn't want to lose focus on the topic at hand. Deandra had to be careful how she redirected Veronica back to the subject. Veronica had a temper that flared every now and then when she felt someone was upstaging or disrespecting her, as Veronica put it.

"Do you know Mayson Hendricks? "Deandra quickly interjected the question into the conversation.

"Oh, yes!" Veronica exclaimed with enthusiasm.

Deandra was about to proceed with the matter of Melvin's behavior during church service but stopped to give Veronica a second look. Veronica had a dreamy look and wide grin on her face that seemed stuck with anticipation of what Deandra was about to say about Mayson.

Veronica broke out in a laugh. "Mayson Hendricks is going to be my husband," she said with certainty.

Deandra tilted her head to the side as she looked at Veronica in amazement. She doesn't know about Mayson, thought Deandra. Should I continue? Deandra was concerned that if she was mistaken about Mayson's sexuality, she would be just as much of a gossip as Veronica. And if Mayson was indeed gay; would she be exposing a side of him that he was not ready to share with anyone? Deandra felt stuck. She feared that if she decided not to continue with the story, Veronica would not let it go. So, she proceeded to tell Veronica how Melvin called Mayson names at church.

Veronica, with a puzzled look on her face, asked, "What kind of names?"

I knew it, thought Deandra. I knew she was going to ask what names. She thought how guys will sometimes use *punk and fag* to just about any other guy as a joke or in the midst of some sort of conflict. They don't really believe the other guy is actually a *punk or fag*, but just as an insult, thought Deandra.

Slowly Deandra answered, "Punk and fag."

"Punk and fag!" Veronica repeated. "Where does Mr. Model get off calling someone a punk and a fag," said Veronica.

"Anyway, I just told him he needed to shut up. I was so mad. I'm not sure if he heard me, but I wouldn't apologize to him if he did," said Deandra.

"If anything, I'd think Melvin was gay, with all his pretty-boy suits and haircuts. He's just jealous that Mayson carries himself better than him. He's the biggest punk-ass I've ever seen," huffed Veronica. Then she composed herself and regained her smile.

"Thanks for taking up for my husband," said Veronica.

Deandra was not sure where to go with that, so she decided to change the subject.

"Are you going back tomorrow night for the second part of the Appreciation for Pastor Martin?" asked Deandra.

"Oh, yes. Got to see my Mayson again," said Veronica.

Here we go again, thought Deandra.

"Does he know you like him?" asked Deandra.

"Not yet," said Veronica. "But he will."

(II)

Veronica attended the second appreciation service without Deandra, who had to study for a test. At least that's what she told Veronica. Veronica had a feeling her friend's absence had something to do with their conversation about Melvin and Mayson yesterday. But she didn't want to care.

As Veronica was approaching the church, she saw Mayson standing outside in front of the church sipping on a soda. Great! Veronica thought. He's by himself. No entourage with his brother and that other girl. I hope that's not his girlfriend, she thought worriedly.

Veronica's attire was always simple. She never dressed flashy or was overly exposed. She had been a big girl for most of her life. Even as a baby, she was chubby. It was cute back then, but as she got older, she'd look for loose-fitting clothes that she hoped would hide her full-figured shape. Her mother, an elegant dresser herself, would often tell her that she dressed too old for her age. Despite her weight, Veronica's mother knew how to find just the right clothes to complement her own figure. In preparing for tonight's service, Veronica had visited a store her mother recommended and found a black faux wrap dress that hugged her waist a little, but remained appropriate for a church service.

Veronica stepped onto the grass next to the sidewalk of the church building, stepping high as her matching black pumps pressed into the soft ground. She tiptoed through the soft soil of the grass as her eyes darted back and forth from her shoes to her target, Mayson.

He had on his khaki suit, which Veronica found stylish. This service was different from his usual weekly church attendance. Mayson had decided to avoid the mix-and-match clothes he often wore. He knew that everybody who was somebody in their church district would be there tonight. Pastor Martin sat on a lot of boards in the city and just about everyone knew him.

"Hi," Mayson! said Veronica cheerfully.

"Hi," responded Mayson in a similar tone, but slightly puzzled that she knew his name.

"I just wanted to say hello because I see you often at GCC and other churches," said Veronica.

"Oh, yeah," said Mayson.

Mayson knew that he had seen her here and there but wasn't quite sure if he could recall her name.

"I see you at GCC from time to time," he said.

"And, at the BC meetings," she added.

"Oh, right," said Mayson.

Veronica became excited at this response from Mayson. He actually noticed me, she thought to herself.

"I'm Veronica Lambert," she said as she stretched out her hand to Mayson.

"Nice to meet you," said Mayson as he reached for her hand and gave it a firm shake. "I'm Mayson Hendricks. Oh, but you know that."

Veronica felt she could see kindness in Mayson's polite smile as she scanned every area of his face. She looked at his light skin tone, which made him even more handsome in her eyes. Veronica, whose complexion was dark brown, had been attracted to light-skinned black boys for most of her life.

"You're taking a break?" asked Veronica, still grinning at him.

"Yeah, it's a bit warm in there and I needed a soda to get through the service," said Mayson.

A moment of awkward silence lingered between them.

"Your choir will be singing tonight?" asked Veronica.

"Yes, our choir will be singing two selections."

"GCC's choir can move a service," said Veronica.

"Thank you," said Mayson.

"Where is your little entourage that I often see you with during church services?" asked Veronica, hoping to find out who the girl was who was usually with him.

"Oh, my friend Reanna and my brother Lamont," he replied. "They're both in the church saving my seat. It's crowded in there."

Veronica felt a wave of relief when she heard the word "friend" before Reanna's name.

"Crowded again. I hope I'm able to find a seat," said Veronica.

"Don't worry, I'm sure there's enough room for you to sit with us. Reanna saved an extra seat for her purse," said Mayson with a small laugh.

Veronica felt her heart racing. "Okay," she said.

Mayson threw his soda can in the trash can next to the church. He walked toward the church entrance with Veronica, who was still grinning and almost walking on his heels.

Veronica entered the church and could feel the heat immediately. She began to fan herself with her hand as they got closer to the front. Mayson walked toward the left side of the church and stopped at the second row from the front. He stood in front of the row and politely gestured for Veronica to go first. Veronica stepped in front of Mayson and midway down; she saw Reanna's purse on the seat. And there sat Reanna next to her purse, with Lamont sitting next to her. Veronica wanted to make sure that she sat next to Mayson, so she stood in front of the empty space where Reanna's purse was lying, waiting for Reanna and Lamont to move down and give her and Mayson enough space to sit. Lamont moved down. Reanna gave Veronica a look that showed she was not happy about losing her spot next to Mayson. She picked up her purse from the seat and moved down enough for Veronica and Mayson to sit. Veronica straightened her dress and looked over at Reanna.

"Hello," said Veronica.

"Hi," said Reanna in a quick, irritated tone, looking straight ahead.

While sitting next to Mayson, Veronica could feel his arm brush up against her as he clapped or moved around. He had taken off his suit jacket, which allowed her to feel his sharp elbow. Veronica was distracted throughout the entire service sitting next to Mayson. Her imagination began running as she thought about the possibility of her and Mayson marrying. She imagined them having children together, and on their anniversaries, they would tell them about the first time they sat side by side at church.

Veronica saw the side of the church door open and in walked Melvin. This time he was with Rem, but not Eric. She frowned at Melvin as she had when she talked with Deandra about him. She noticed that Mayson seemed to be looking at Melvin and Rem as if in deep thought. She thought that he may be thinking the same as she, how Melvin was so full of himself. She leaned over and whispered in Mayson's ear, "Here comes Mr. Model," she snickered.

Mayson turned and looked at her with a half-smile to his face and gave a faint, forced chuckle.

As Melvin entered the church, Mayson looked ahead, but continued to steal glances at Melvin's movements from his peripheral vision. He didn't want to make it obvious that he was watching him, but at the same time, he wanted an idea of where Melvin would be sitting in order to know where to look after he took his seat. After Melvin and Rem sat down a few rows ahead of Mayson on the other side of the church, Mayson slowly looked in his direction. He stopped and looked to see if anyone was eyeing him as he would be eying Melvin. When he felt it safe to start watching again, he turned his head to resume his longing look at Melvin.

During the course of the service, the main speaker began to minister. His sermon message was *Holiness or Hell: Your Choice.*

In the content of his sermon message, he made reference to "sissies" and their place outside of God's kingdom. He then turned to all the visiting pastors in the pulpit, as he wiped his sweating brow, and yelled:

"Make'em sit down. Don't let them switch their behinds up and down your church, taking up offerings and directing your choir."

He then did an imitation of the way these so-called, "sissies" walked. He acted as if he was taking up the offering as he switched his hips left and right. He then did a mockery of them directing a choir as he stuck his behind out and swayed it back and forth. The church began in an uproar of laughter.

"Make'em sit down!" the preacher yelled again.

Mayson had heard these types of sermons messages before; this time, however, he found himself so engrossed with his attention to Melvin that it took a while before he was aware of what the preacher was saying. Most importantly, when the preacher did his mockery and addressed the pastors in the pulpit to *make' em sit down*, Mayson noticed that Pastor Upshaw didn't laugh with the others. Pastor Upshaw usually stood and supported preachers in the pulpit when they were as lively and rhythmic as this one. But this time Pastor Upshaw was the last of the preachers to stand in support. Mayson's hunch was that he only stood to avoid drawing attention to himself.

Mayson looked over at Melvin again and back at Pastor Upshaw. He thought about how difficult it was at times to keep this side of him suppressed and a secret. He didn't allow himself to fully entertain thoughts about himself and Melvin in any physically intimate moments. Yet, he

46

escalated to fantasies about encounters between them. They involved him stumbling upon Melvin in some sort of mishap, such as car problems, and Mayson offering him a ride to a nearby gas station or phone. Mayson didn't have a car of his own, but in his fantasy, he had a really nice car. He'd let his imagination stop at helping Melvin to the point that Melvin would begin to notice him and from there they'd have an acquaintanceship that would grow. Lately, he found himself having difficulty in letting his imagination stop at that point. *I'm flesh and blood, like anyone else,* was his justification on those days when his imagination wanted to go farther.

Mayson hoped that Pastor Upshaw's lack of response to this preacher was a sign that his pastor was someone he could talk to. Being Human was something Pastor Upshaw had referenced as sinful from time to time, but it had been a while since he had spoken about it. *Maybe he's changed his beliefs about it,* Mayson thought hopefully.

I got to tell someone about this, he thought to himself. His eyes glistened with tears as he looked at Pastor Upshaw with hopes that this was someone who would understand and show some compassion.

CHAPTER 7

Veronica and Mayson:
One Step Further and Behind

It had been weeks since Veronica got to sit by her dream man Mayson at Pastor Martin's appreciation service. It was the third Sunday of the month, and Veronica's church was fellowshipping with another congregation.

GCC! Veronica thought. I'll go to GCC and see Mayson, she thought happily. But I don't want to appear too obvious. I should get Deandra to go with me.

It was 9:43AM and Deandra, who had been up late studying, was sound asleep, but Veronica decided her need to see Mayson was worth Deandra's possible crankiness.

"I'm going to GCC this morning. You want to go?" whispered Veronica in her ear.

Deandra didn't respond. Veronica nudged her shoulder to wake her.

"I'm going to GCC this morning. You want to go?" she asked again.

"What?" asked Deandra, sounding dazed.

"Do you want to go to GCC with me today?" repeated Veronica, louder this time.

"I have to go to my own church. We're also having a second service after that, but thanks," said Deandra. She laid her head back onto her pillow to continue her sleep.

Veronica was pleased that Deandra was not annoyed at being woken up, but disappointed that she would not go to church with her.

What was I thinking? thought Veronica. Of course, she won't go to church with me while her church is having service too. Deandra is such a Girl Scout, Veronica thought.

As Deandra was about to drift back into sleep, the implications of what Veronica just asked her sank in. She lifted her head and looked at Veronica.

"Is this visit to GCC about Mayson?" Deandra asked as she squinted at Veronica.

"Yes, yes, yes," said Veronica in a peppy and excited tone as she put on her slippers to go into the bathroom for her shower.

"Veronica, going to church really should be about Godly fellowship and worship. Not about getting a guy," exclaimed Deandra.

Deandra knew that she was on thin ice with this comment to Veronica. She knew that Veronica could see this as her being a prude, Ms. Goody or as Veronica also put it, a Girl Scout. Deandra despised these descriptions of her, however, she would never let Veronica know this was one of those "don't go there" places that got under her skin.

Despite Deandra's preachy words, Veronica headed toward the bathroom for her shower. A few seconds later, Deandra heard the shower going and Veronica singing Al Green's *Let's Stay Together*. Deandra rolled onto her back as she contemplated whether or not to tell Veronica her thoughts about Mayson. I shouldn't share any of this with Veronica because it's only speculation, she concluded.

Veronica poked her head out the door with her shower cap on her head.

"You're right, girl," said Veronica contritely. "I love church and I know it's a place of fellowship and worship, but this is the only place where I know I can see him."

Deandra looked at her naive roommate.

"Just be careful, Veronica," she said as she pulled her blankets back up and rolled over to look at the wall and think more.

Veronica took out a flowing blue skirt, matching blue jacket, and a pink button-down blouse. Jackets and sweaters were important to Veronica because she felt that they covered what she called her "fat bulges." Her weight was always foremost in her mind. Veronica saw her looks as average, but her mother, in an attempt to boost her daughter's self-worth, complimented her lavishly. Veronica had been slow to approach Mayson in the past as she thought that once she lost about 25 to 30 pounds, she could pursue him with certainty. When her efforts at weight loss were taking too long, she seized the moment when she saw Mayson standing outside the church that day. That day when she sat next to him at church was etched in her mind and had had her walking on air for the past 3 weeks.

Veronica drove to GCC feeling hopeful about the possibility of getting even closer to Mayson. As she stepped through the door, she looked around for Mayson. She spotted him sitting on the right side of the church, close to the front. Nearby were Lamont and Reanna making their way over to sit with him. The church was not as crowded as Pastor Martin's church had been, so there was plenty of room on the pew where Mayson was sitting. Veronica was determined to sit next to Mayson again. She rushed to get to the pew before Reanna and Lamont. Breathlessly, she smiled at Mayson as she sat down next to him.

"Hi," she said, smoothing her dress.

"Hi," said Mayson looking bewildered as he saw that it was Veronica and not Reanna and Lamont.

"How are you today?" he asked

"Fine," said Veronica. She put her purse on her lap and scooted closer to him.

It crossed her mind that she was too obviously interested in Mayson. This was why she wanted Deandra to come with her, so she wouldn't appear desperate or overeager. Her imagination began to wander again. Of course he wants me to sit next to him, she thought. He asked me how I was doing. If he didn't want me sitting here with him, he wouldn't have said anything.

Reanna and Lamont arrived soon thereafter. Reanna was leading the way down the aisle towards Mayson, but she stopped midway when she spotted Veronica sitting next to Mayson. She tightened her lips and had Lamont to squeeze in front of her so Lamont would be sitting next to Veronica rather than her. Reanna sat down with a thump next to Lamont and tossed her purse onto the pew.

Lamont could feel the annoyance radiating from Reanna. "Hi," he said to Veronica. Veronica responded pleasantly to Lamont. Mayson looked down at Reanna and could see she was not happy with the seating arrangement. They all sat awkwardly quiet in the presence of the unannounced addition to their group.

Veronica was distracted during the service. She tried to think of a way to extend her time with him. She remembered that Deandra had told her that her church was having a second service. She thought to invite Mayson to go with her. Mayson did not have his own car, so she would offer him a ride with her.

After 3 and a half hours of service, the pastor was about to do the benediction. Veronica panicked as she tried to decide whether or not to invite Mayson to ride with her to Deandra's church. She decided to take the plunge. She leaned over and whispered to him:

"My roommate Deandra's church, Faith on a Mission, is having a second service. Want to ride with me?" she asked.

Mayson was trying to listen and find out if his pastor would invite everyone to fellowship at My Place Buffet restaurant today. He turned his face in Veronica's direction, put his finger to his lips and softly blew, "Shush." Veronica could feel the blood rush to her head as she felt a combination of embarrassment and anger. I will not ask him again, Veronica decided.

When the pastor dismissed the service, Veronica said nothing to Mayson, who was also standing, as she tried to squeeze past him toward the main aisle. As she tried to cross over him, Mayson touched her shoulder.

"Sorry, what were you saying to me earlier? I was trying to hear the pastor," said Mayson.

Veronica looked into Mayson's good-natured face and her embarrassment and anger lessened.

"My roommate's church, Faith on a Mission, is having a second service this afternoon and I thought you might want to go with me to the service. I can give you a ride," she said.

Mayson put his hand on Veronica's shoulder again.

"Oh, I don't think so, but thanks for the invite," said Mayson,

Veronica felt another rush of blood go to her head. Okay, she said with a small smile. Her humiliation surpassed her disappointment. Why didn't I just leave this alone? she thought. The only thing that she could think of, once again, was getting out of the church as quickly as possible. She vowed within herself to never set foot in GCC again. She managed to compose herself in order to leave without appearing upset.

Mayson watched Veronica curiously as she hurried out of the church. As she was leaving, Reanna stepped over Lamont. She stood on her tiptoes to reach Mayson's ear.

"What did you say to Pushy?" using a nickname she thought of on the fly.

Mayson turned around, startled at the sudden whisper in his ear.

"Who? Veronica?" he asked.

"Yes, Veronica," repeated Reanna impatiently.

"Nothing really. She asked me about riding with her to another service and I said no thank you," said Mayson.

Reanna smiled as she grabbed Mayson's hand and squeezed it. "Pushy got the hots for you, boy," she said gleefully.

CHAPTER 8

"I Have Feelings..."

(I)

"Nice to see you," said Pastor Upshaw as Mayson walked into his office. He motioned for Mayson to take a seat.

Mayson had requested to meet with Pastor Upshaw after he observed his lack of response to the Shiloh preacher's fiery sermon about "sissies." He was yet hopeful that his pastor's lack of enthusiasm was a sign that he did not agree with the other preacher's words. He had thought long and hard about his situation and what to do about it. He knew how much trust and respect his mother had for Pastor Upshaw. He made himself believe that his pastor was the answer to his problem.

Pastor Upshaw seemed like the Norman Rockwell version of a pastor. He was so well-known in the community that he could barely walk a few blocks without someone greeting him or engaging him in conversation. He smiled often, although it didn't come easy to him. During his earlier years of pasturing, some of his congregants complained that he often looked angry and they were not sure how to approach him. Initially, this observation made him reluctant to appease their image of him. His rationale to his wife, whom everyone called First Lady Frances, was that he should not have to change his appearance due to other's insecurities and selfish judgments of him. Frances agreed with him, but also told him that as a pastor, he needed to be more patient with people's shortcomings. She shared a verse with him:

He that is strong should bear the infirmity of the weak. Not pleasing ourselves. Romans 15:1

When Pastor Upshaw heard this, he laughed and gave her a quick kiss on the forehead. From that day forward, she could see her husband's effort to look more pleasant through a smile. This pleasant demeanor eventually became a part of him to the point that Frances could see it was no longer an effort. But with or without a smile on his face, Pastor Upshaw was not a hard man to miss. He often bragged about his years as a football player in high school and a couple of years in college. His broad built yet showed slight evidence of his athletic days. He was balding slightly, but the hair that remained on the sides of his head was always neatly cut.

"Brother Hendricks, what can I do for you?" asked Pastor Upshaw with a wide smile on his face.

Mayson adjusted himself more comfortably in the leather armchair sitting in front of Pastor Upshaw's huge mahogany desk. They looked at one another, each waiting for the other to start.

"Well Mayson, you requested this meeting, so let me know what's on your mind," prompted Pastor Upshaw.

Mayson felt sweat rolling down his underarms. He did not know where to start.

"Uhm, Pastor Upshaw," said Mayson as he cleared his throat." I..." He stopped and stared out the high window over Pastor Upshaw's head.

"I... I have a lot I need to talk to you about, but I'm not sure where I should begin," said Mayson.

Mayson's eyes darted down to his pants and he began to pick bits of lint from his black jeans. Pastor Upshaw saw the seriousness in Mayson's face and heard the trembling in his voice.

"Take your time, son," he said.

Mayson had Pastor Upshaw at a disadvantage. Usually, when members requested time with him, he would have at least an idea of what they needed to talk about. Rumors or other messages would swirl around the church and eventually, the person or persons involved would schedule a meeting, or Pastor Upshaw would call one himself. But he could not fathom what Mayson wanted to talk to him about. Pastor Upshaw thought perhaps Mayson was coming to him with a song that he wanted the choir to sing that he had rejected; he knew there were many . He knew how much Mayson loved being in the choir and his devotion to the other choir members. But Mayson's demeanor indicated something more serious than song selections.

Mayson sat in front of his pastor, drenched in fear. He had heard in the Bible that God was love, but sitting in front of his pastor, the information he was about to share triggered a trembling fear rather than love. His relationship with Pastor Upshaw was not deep or close. Mayson would sometimes deliver messages to their pastor from his mother, or when the choir leader was not available, he'd talk with Pastor Upshaw about the choir selections for service. That was about it.

"I have feelings that I don't know what to do about," Mayson tried again. Am I about to really say these words to Pastor Upshaw? he thought. "I sometimes like people that I should not be liking," said Mayson, still looking out the window.

Pastor Upshaw felt as though a bucket of cold water had been thrown in his face. The words pounded in his head like a hammer. He knew exactly what Mayson was about to divulge. The last time Pastor Upshaw had to address such a matter was when some members of his flock came to him with concerns about the then-choir director, who, they described as a *flaming Human*. One of the members spoke about his soft voice, which was more feminine than hers. These were not the concerns that finally brought them to see Pastor Upshaw, but it was when he began to bring a guy to church with him whom he described as "his friend." Pastor Upshaw listened to their concerns and he informed them that he would talk with the choir director and get back with them. In the course of his meeting with the director, the director did admit that his friend was his partner and he had no interest in women. Pastor Upshaw made the decision to remove him as director of the choir. The ousted choir director could not bring himself to sit in the congregation after that, so he left GCC.

Now here was Mayson sitting in front of him, minus an accusing church member, needing direction about his sexuality.

Pastor Upshaw, not wanting to use confrontation as the first option in his counseling, often preferred the "everybody wins" approach to church disruptions or concerns. However, he knew that "everybody wins" was going to be a difficult, even an impossible, option in this matter. He asked Mayson to tell him more.

Mayson took a deep breath, looked at Pastor Upshaw in the face a few seconds and then began looking back out the high window again.

"I like men, Pastor Upshaw, I like men," said Mayson with a noticeable tremor in his voice.

This is going to change everything, thought Pastor Upshaw. He wished Mayson could take his words back.

"What about Reanna Harrison? I see you with her often," asked Pastor Upshaw, hoping to hear there might be an exception to Mayson's feelings.

"Reanna is my good friend. I just like being with her. She's fun to talk to," said Mayson.

"Have you ever told her about your feelings for men?" asked Pastor Upshaw.

"Heavens, no. I wanted to tell her a few times, but I wasn't sure she could keep her mouth shut," replied Mayson.

Pastor Upshaw wanted to know who else knew about Mayson's confession before they moved further. He was hoping he could help Mayson through this without others knowing about it. Also, he needed more time to plan where to go with the disclosure as well.

"How could she be your friend if you cannot trust her?" asked Pastor Upshaw.

"I know it doesn't make sense, but I just couldn't take the chance of telling her. Being a member here at GCC was not worth me taking the risk to tell her this. To answer your question about my friendship with Reanna, I love her, but I love her for who she is, faults and all. And that's why she remains my friend," said Mayson.

Pastor Upshaw rested his head in his hands.

"Have you talked with your mother about these feelings?" asked Pastor Upshaw.

"No sir, I have not. I just can't bring myself to talk with her about this," said Mayson.

"What about your father?" he asked, knowing the answer, but stalling for more time to think.

"Oh, definitely not my father," said Mayson with wide eyes. "He's barely home enough without this giving him more reason to stay away."

Pastor Upshaw was aware of Mayson's father lack of presence in their home, but he liked Ed anyway. Kind of like Mayson's acceptance of Reanna, he thought.

Pastor Upshaw glared at Mayson, deep in thought. Mayson looked at Pastor Upshaw while repeating in his head:

"Please help me with this, I don't want to leave."

"Please help me with this, I don't want to leave. "

"Please help me with this, I don't want to leave. "

He repeated the words in his head as though they would bring exactly what he wanted to hear from his pastor's mouth.

Pastor Upshaw's glare changed to a firm stare. Mayson's hopes for an open-minded pastor confidant were dashed. The pastor was a man who had much invested in his traditional doctrine.

"This has been an issue in the church for years. I wish I had an answer that could satisfy everyone. As a matter of fact, Mayson, many of the churches in the area have scheduled to meet next month for an interfaith conference on Humans and the Church. I plan to attend, but I don't think much will change. I think the meeting is more about standing our ground than it is about changing our belief," said Pastor Upshaw.

There was a long silence between them.

"Son, I love you and your family dearly. Your mother is one of my best members and all of her children have been nothing but good for our church. With that being said, you, as a Hendricks family member and a member of my church for years, know the church's teachings on being Human. With my understanding and interpretation of the Bible, I can't justify an intimate relationship between people of the same sex. I do not give leadership roles or other positions that represent my church to practicing homosexuals."

Fear gripped Mayson even more tightly as he anticipated the next words from Pastor Upshaw. He knew what happened to others in church leadership or non-leadership activities at GCC and other churches. He had hoped that Pastor Upshaw's high esteem for his mother would make a difference in his case. He didn't want to be put out of the choir or have to leave GCC. Mayson was also concerned about the words "practicing homosexual." He was not happy with the use of the word *homosexual* and the term *practicing*, never made sense to him, but that's what some would include with the use of the word. He decided to address this label.

"Pastor, they use the word "gay" now, for men...men like me," said Mayson. "I have feelings for men, but I've never had sex with anyone, Pastor," he said, hoping his celibacy would make a difference.

Pastor Upshaw could see that he needed to help Mayson better understand the matter from his viewpoint.

"Okay, son," said Pastor Upshaw. He stretched his arms across his desk and laced his fingers together. He closed his eyes as he contemplated his next words.

"I want you to remain at GCC, but would you respect me as a pastor if I disregard my beliefs to accommodate you? My spirituality is who I am. It is not based on what others think; it's based on what I believe as a core foundation of life. I do sympathize with those who feel that they should be treated fairly despite their same-sex partnering. Really, I do sympathize, Mayson. But it is so unfair that those of us who have spiritual foundations in what we believe are considered as bad people because of our God-given and constitutional rights to believe. I don't approve of such relationships, but Mayson, you never have heard me make those terrible *Adam and Steve* jokes in the pulpit. Words such as *fag, dyke, sissy*, I don't use and do not allow my family to use in our home. As outspoken as my wife can be at times, she has never used inappropriate words or jokes when it came to those that are lesbians or..." he paused... "gays."

"I respect others' right to believe and would hope that others would have that same respect for us. It can't be one-sided. I am a pastor; therefore, my beliefs on same-sex attraction, based on my interpretation of the Bible, is not just about me. I have a congregation of people to whom I also minister. I must be consistent."

Mayson could see an almost passion that arose in Pastor Upshaw as he spoke. It was as though he was no longer talking just to Mayson, but many Maysons.

"It's just not right that the church is expected to give up their religious beliefs and Christian teachings in order to appease others. When we stick to what we believe, we then have the Bible thrown back at us and are labeled as bad people," said Pastor Upshaw.

Pastor Upshaw paused, as he felt he was getting too animated in explaining this to Mayson. He had occasionally mentioned homosexuality in sermons while addressing a different subject, but he had never made it his main topic. Like many of his fellow ministers, he talked about the sins of Sodom and Gomorrah and the few words of Paul's references about homosexuality and effeminacy.

Whenever Pastor Upshaw preached on Sundays, he would include a list of scriptures in the Sunday program flyers that were to be included in his sermon message. A few years ago, during one of Pastor Upshaw's sermon messages that included a few biblical references to homosexuality, Mayson decided that when he got home, he would take a closer look at all the biblical references. When he got home from church that afternoon, he reread the scriptures that Pastor Upshaw addressed that day and other related scriptures he recalled from past sermons. After reading the scriptures, a question came to him. He surmised that none of the scriptures ever mentioned Jesus speaking against homosexuality. So how can they say they're following the teachings of Jesus Christ if Jesus himself didn't address it? he wondered. He later believed himself to be trying to make something that was wrong to be right, yet the possibilities of the question remained with him. He never asked Pastor Upshaw or anyone else about the discrepancy, as he was concerned that the question would arouse suspicion.

Mayson sat, wide-eyed. He had never heard Pastor Upshaw speak with such emotions about homosexuality. It all seemed to be coming out like a broken dam.

Pastor Upshaw could see the startled look on Mayson's face and realized he might be taking Mayson's confession in the wrong direction. He feared losing Mayson and maybe his family from his church. But he really wanted Mayson to understand because he knew that he would not say what Mayson wanted to hear.

"I don't mean to become so passionate while talking with you. I'll save it for my meeting with the interfaith conference," said Pastor Upshaw, as he tried to muster up a smile.

He then leaned across his desk and looked into Mayson's eyes.

"Son, other than give up my spiritual and biblical principles, what can I do to help you with this struggle you are dealing with?" he asked.

"I'll try and give this up and hope you can help me," or something like that, was what Pastor Upshaw wanted to hear from Mayson.

"I don't know, Pastor. I'm not sure right now," said Mayson.

"I'm sorry things are this way. Despite my not being able to change things for you, you will definitely have my prayers and my door will always be open to you," said Pastor Upshaw as he sat back in his chair.

Mayson sat in deep thought as Pastor Upshaw looked at him in anticipation of what his next words might be.

What am I going to do now? thought Mayson. I've put it out there and now someone knows and can't help me. He began to regret his decision to confide in his pastor.

"Thank you," said Mayson as he stood up feeling a little light-headed. He turned to leave the office.

"Mayson," called Pastor Upshaw.

"Yes sir," responded Mayson.

"Consider telling your mother? She's a lot more understanding than you may think," he said.

"Yes, Pastor," replied Mayson in an exasperated tone. He knew that he was not going to share this with his mother but said just enough to get out of Pastor Upshaw's office.

Pastor Upshaw felt uneasy with leaving matters the way they were.

"Mayson, one more thing. Sit back down," he said as he motioned Mayson to sit.

"I want you to talk with someone else that may be of help to you. I will give you a referral, not that I believe in homosexuality, but this pastor may be able to relate better to you about this than I can."

Pastor Upshaw took out a small white notepad from his desk drawer. He flipped through a planner on his desk until he stopped on a specific name, address, and phone number. He looked around his desk for something to write with. He checked the middle small drawer on his desk and came out with a thin worn pencil. He quickly scribbled on the small pad and presented it in Mayson's direction.

"This is Pastor Toby McDaniel of United House of Worship. Tell him that I sent you for continued counseling. I really want you to be able to talk to someone about your situation. But remember, this referral does not mean that I condone homosexuality."

Mayson cringed as he heard Pastor Upshaw use the word homosexuality again. But he knew that no matter the changes in its name, his church and many others like it, wanted to stick with its traditional description.

"When you've figured out what you want to do, let me know and we can decide your status at GCC from there," said Pastor Upshaw.

Mayson contemplated whether to tell Pastor Upshaw that he didn't want a referral from him, or to turn his back to him and simply walk out the door. He knew that despite his humiliation and fear, he could not bring himself to address him in that manner.

He took the slip of paper from Pastor Upshaw's hand without looking at what he wrote on it. He stood up and left without a word.

(II)

Mayson lay on his twin bed in his bedroom, waving the referral note from Pastor Upshaw in his hand. He stared at the ceiling trying to decide if he wanted to open up to a second person. Feelings of regret ran through his mind for disclosing to his pastor. He now had added fear that his family would soon find out.

"What was I thinking?" he said to himself.

He placed the note on the nightstand near his bed and turned over in his bed to face the wall. He replayed in his head his meeting with Pastor Upshaw over and over. He went back and forth between anger towards his pastor and wondering how he could take back what he said to him.

"He's right. I did know his teaching about gay people. I'm not sure what I was thinking," he mumbled to himself.

He tried to keep his voice low, as he was not sure who was in the house. His mother was grocery shopping, but he didn't know if Idee and Lamont had gone with her.

He heaved a deep sigh.

I don't want to leave GCC, he repeated in his head. I love my church and I want to be there with my family. Pastor Upshaw may not tell, but when I am no longer going to GCC, they'll figure it out, he thought.

Mayson felt panic take hold.

I'll call Pastor Upshaw and tell him that I was not serious about my feelings, he decided. I'll tell him that I was coming to him for a friend. *A friend,* he repeated. No. That's stupid. Besides, he knows the people that I'm usually with. Reanna is my only close friend, so that won't work. Maybe I can start making moves on Reanna. He giggled at the idea.

Mayson felt his head spinning as he sat up and placed his feet on the floor. He leaned over as he held his head. Suddenly his bedroom door burst open. It was Lamont, who had indeed been grocery shopping with Phyllis. He had an open package of mini donuts in his hand and was chewing on one he just popped into his mouth before entering the room. Lamont would usually accompany Phyllis to the store when he had something specific he wanted her to buy. Mini donuts had been on his mental list that day.

Mayson didn't bother to sit up when Lamont entered the room. He remained holding his head as he sat on the side of the bed.

"Hey," said Lamont.

Mayson didn't respond.

"What's wrong with you?" asked Lamont as he walked over to their television that was sitting on the small television stand. He picked up the remote and turned it on.

"Nothing," said Mayson quickly as he brushed his hand over his bed-pressed hair. He extended his arms behind him onto the bed. He stared at the ceiling while trying to figure out where he could go to be alone or how to get Lamont out of the room.

Lamont slumped into the chair near his bed as he flipped through the television channels.

"Lamont, can you go downstairs and watch the television in the den? I'm in the middle of something," said Mayson.

Lamont, still sitting on the chair with his feet now propped on his bed, looked around the room.

"What? All I see is you sitting on the bed looking like you're about to pull your hair out," laughed Lamont.

"Lamont, please," asked Mayson with a look of annoyance on his face.

"Ok, ok," said Lamont.

Lamont threw the remote on the bed and walked out of the room, leaving the television on. Mayson stood up to get the remote off Lamont's bed to turn it off. As he was about to hit the OFF button, a commercial for BHU came on. The commercial captured his attention because the spokeswoman for the university looked like Pastor Upshaw's daughter, who worked at the university. Mayson looked closer and saw that it was not her. He turned off the television. The commercial about the university triggered thoughts of Veronica. He wondered was she back at the University from their spring break.

(III)

Three weeks after Veronica's humiliating decline from Mayson for a ride to a second church service, she was still trying to put the matter behind her. She dared not tell Deandra what happened. She couldn't bear another one of Deandra's sermons on the purpose of going to church and her last words to be careful.

After her last class for the day, Veronica went back to her dorm. It had been a long day and all she could think of was a shower and bed. After she took her shower and put on her nightgown, she began to put lotion on her legs. The phone on her dorm room wall rang with a loud intrusion into her quiet moment. She thought it might be Deandra, telling her she was going to study in the library.

"Hello," said Veronica.

"Hi Veronica. It's me, Mayson," he said.

Veronica felt her eyes widen when she heard his name. She decided to make the call difficult for him. Despite her agony over the past few weeks of trying to work through his rejection of her, her heart seemed to skip a beat at the sound of his name over the phone. But she didn't want him to hear any enthusiasm in her voice.

"Who?" asked Veronica.

"Mayson Hendricks," he said.

"Oh, hi," she replied in a flat tone.

"I hope I'm not disturbing you and you don't mind that I got your phone number from Deandra. I saw her at the BC meeting yesterday and told her that I needed to talk with you," he said.

Veronica had decided not to attend the BC meeting yesterday to avoid seeing Mayson there. She was surprised to hear that Deandra had actually given their phone number to Mayson, of all people.

"Getting this number from her was like pulling a bad tooth," he laughed. Veronica didn't say anything. "So, I hope you don't mind," he finished lamely.

"What do you need to talk to me about?" asked Veronica in the same flat voice.

"Well, I enjoyed seeing you at GCC the other Sunday. I hadn't seen

63

you in a while and wanted to see how you were doing," said Mayson.

Veronica's mood lightened.

"I'm good," she said, her tone softening. "It's nice of you to call and check on me."

"How was the second service at Mission's church?" asked Mayson.

"Oh, I didn't go. After I got back to the dorm to change clothes, I felt too tired to go back out," she said.

"Sorry I didn't go with you. I guess I was feeling a little tired myself," said Mayson.

Their conversation progressed to mutual acquaintances at church, the national choir competition, their life goals and, as Veronica steered the subject, what qualities they were looking for in a mate. Veronica gave a description that 80% described Mayson with 20% that was added in order not to appear too obvious. Mayson decided to spiritualize the response by simply stating that he wanted whomever God had for him. Veronica accepted this answer from him and decided that it was Mayson's way of telling her that he was open to a relationship with her. Besides, she thought, he does not know me as well as I know him. If he was more specific, he might not describe me correctly and thereby miss his efforts to get with me, she thought.

After three hours, Mayson told Veronica he had to go. He asked if he could call her again.

"Sure," replied Veronica enthusiastically.

Over the course of 10 days, Mayson called Veronica 3 times. Veronica was floating on a cloud. She thought about Mayson from the time she woke to the time she went to bed. She spent every day anticipating his call. She didn't want to humiliate herself again by asking him out, so she waited for Mayson to ask her out. Whether it was to a church service or movie, it didn't matter. As long as they were together.

After their initial phone contact, other than church interest, they also talked about their families, school, or movies and TV. She would flirt with him about his attractiveness or tell him how much she looked forward to his calls. He would change the subject or make his comments more platonic. Veronica allowed herself to believe that he was a little prudish like Deandra, so she decided to take it slow.

One Saturday morning Veronica had plans to visit her family, who lived about two hours away. As she was throwing things into her overnight bag, she was thinking about what she would do while home and how to fit it all in before her return back to campus by Sunday evening.

The phone rang.

With a frustrated sigh, she imagined that it was her mother checking to see if she had left yet. Then a quick thought came. What if it's Mayson? No, it can't be Mayson, he almost never calls more than three times a week. Concluding that it must be her mother, she stuffed another pair of socks in her bag and then reached for the phone on her wall.

"Hellooo," she said in a stretched out "I know it's you, Mommy" tone. Mommy is what she and her siblings called their mother. It was what her mother preferred. Veronica only called her this within the family as she knew it may sound child-like to other people.

"Hi Veronica. How was your week?" asked Mayson.

She felt her heart sank.

"Oh, Mayson," she replied. "Sorry, I thought you were my mother."

Mayson laughed. "Is that the way you answer the phone when your mother calls?" he asked.

"Only when she's rushing me, said Veronica. Its nice hearing from you," she said.

"It's been a busy week and I wanted to find some time to connect with you," said Mayson.

Mayson proceeded to tell her about his job. Veronica didn't like that Mayson was not a college man. She was disappointed when she found out that he worked at a cleaning company. She had hoped that when they married, she could influence him to go to college and advance to a professional career.

While they were talking, Veronica looked at the clock on Deandra's side of the bed. It's getting late, she thought. She had told her mother that she would be at their house at 11:30 am. Veronica's mother had told her earlier that week she was taking Veronica's 11-year-old twin brothers shopping for clothes this weekend and Veronica had asked to tag along. It was now 9:45 am, but Veronica didn't want to end her time with Mayson on the phone.

"What are you doing tomorrow?" asked Mayson.

Veronica knew that she was to stay overnight with her family and return Sunday evening, but she didn't want to miss any possibility to spend time with Mayson.

"Other than church, nothing different," said Veronica, hoping he was about to ask her out.

"Why not come to GCC tomorrow?" It's been a while since I've seen you, he said.

Without hesitation, Veronica agreed to be there. Mayson promised to save her a seat. Once they hung up, Veronica immediately called her mother and apologized as she told her she would not be able to come home this weekend. She told her that something had come up that she needed to attend to. Her mother, annoyed that she was not coming, asked her what it was.

"Mommy, just take my word that I have something that I must do," said Veronica.

She promised her mother that she would be home the next weekend. While Veronica was unpacking her overnight bag, she heard a noise at the door. It was Deandra putting her key in the door. Deandra walked in and expressed surprise that Veronica was still there.

"I thought you were going home this weekend?" said Deandra.

"No, something has come up," she said.

"What can be more important than going shopping with your mother? I know how it is with you and shopping," Deandra said in an amusing voice.

"Well, if you must know, Mayson just called me and asked me to come to GCC tomorrow. He said he hadn't seen me in a while," said Veronica.

"He just called you out of the blue?" asked Deandra.

"No, we've been talking for about 3 weeks and we miss each other," said Veronica with a mile-wide grin.

"Really!" replied Deandra in a surprised voice, as she plopped down on her bed with her purse strap dropping off her shoulder.

"Yes, yes and yes," said Veronica.

"Why'd you try and keep this such a secret with the *something has come up* stuff?" asked Deandra?

"Because I know how preachy you are about my interest in him. I wanted to make sure first that I was certain about Mayson's intentions with me before I told you about us," said Veronica.

"What are those intentions?" asked Deandra.

"Well, it seems that he really likes me. He always initiates the calls

66

to me, and now he's asking me to show up at GCC tomorrow because he misses seeing me. This lets me know that he's getting serious about us," said Veronica.

Deandra was baffled by Mayson's sudden attention to Veronica. She didn't know what it was, but she knew something had happened between Veronica and Mayson that Sunday when Veronica had woken her to go to GCC with her. That same day, when Deandra came back from church to their room, Veronica was in bed with her covers pulled over her head. When Deandra asked her how GCC went, Veronica would not answer. They spent the rest of that evening in silence. After that Sunday, Veronica stopped talking about Mayson. Deandra was relieved. It took care of itself, she thought. Since Veronica never brought up the subject of Mayson after giving him their phone number, Deandra assumed that she decided not to talk with him. Now that Veronica had shared that they had been talking for several weeks, Deandra figured that Mayson must have called during times Veronica knew that Deandra would not be in their room. Deandra felt herself back where she started in this matter. She decided to try and reason with Veronica.

"Veronica, the fact that he initiates calls to you and asked you to come to his church tomorrow does not say much about intentions. Before his calls, you were visiting his church at least once a month, so he and probably other GCC church members who are familiar with your visits there might have missed you. Even I would miss you if you were gone for a few weeks," said Deandra sarcastically.

Still unpacking, Veronica angrily slammed her dresser drawers as she put her clothes back into them.

"See Deandra, this is why I didn't want to tell you about Mayson and me. You always have this preachy, negative spin on things," said Veronica.

"No Veronica, that's not true. It's just that sometimes you see what you want to see, and then when the picture doesn't turn out to be as clear as you thought, you get hurt," said Deandra.

Veronica walked to the door to leave, put her hand on the doorknob and looked back at Deandra.

"Well, it's my hurt, and you need to mind your own self-righteous business," said Veronica.

She slammed the door as she left the room.

CHAPTER 9

Introductions in Action

Veronica arrived at GCC about 15 minutes early. She wanted to make sure that she got the usual seat next to Mayson. She found the spot where he usually sat and anxiously looked around the church for him. She felt a little nervous as she was waiting for Mayson's arrival. There were only a few other people scattered around the church, mostly mingling and talking. A couple of musicians were near the pulpit tuning their instruments. Slowly the seats began to fill, but no Mayson. After 17 minutes of waiting, a well-dressed man came to the podium and knocked on the microphone to see if it was working. He then called the service to order. He asked the congregation to stand as he gave a word of prayer. Veronica prayed along with him, but her mind was constantly wondering where Mayson was. And Reanna and Lamont, for that matter. After prayer, a lady in a choir robe came out from the side of the stage and began to speak inspirational words to the congregation. The congregation gave her greetings back with *Amen, Glory and Halleluiah*. This went on for 20 minutes.

After her inspiring words, she stood close to the edge of the stage and looked to the back of the church as she stated:

"At this time, we will now bring in our choir. Will everyone please stand?"

Veronica stood with the congregation and saw that everyone was looking to the back of the church. She heard the organ with its heavy booming sound, then singing from the back of the church:

♫ Brightness of the world, brightness of the world, ♫

♫Come to His light, shelter for all that are in darkness of night. ♫

♫Come to His mercy and love that is so bright. Jesus the brightness of the world...♫

As Veronica looked back, she saw two more ladies in choir robes singing and slowly marching down the aisle. Behind them were the rest of the choir, singing and marching in step. Once in the choir stand, they began to sway and clap as they sang. As more of the choir marched out from the back lobby of the church, Veronica saw Reanna in her choir robe, looking quite different from the last time she had seen her. She had on very little make-up and had removed the large hoop earrings that seemed to be her trademark look. As the choir continued to march, she saw that the last portion of the line consisted of the male choir members. Lamont was first. After four other men passed by, she saw Mayson singing loudly, carefully enunciating every word of the song. Veronica thought how handsome he looked in his robe. His large afro bounced with each step. As he marched past Veronica, he gave her a quick smile. Veronica broke out in an exuberant smile as she gave a wave to Mayson. He's not going to sit with me, thought Veronica. Oh well, we'll see each other after service.

After an inspiring sermon message from Pastor Upshaw of "Life's Lemon and God's Lemonade," and the choirs' additional selections, despite not being able to sit with Mayson, Veronica was glad she came. She thought it to be a double blessing. With all that was going on in her mind during the service, she found it a challenge to take her eyes off of Mayson, but with such a wonderful service, it became less and less of a challenge.

After the service, Veronica walked toward the choir stand where Mayson was engaged in conversation with an older lady. Veronica had seen the lady at GCC many times but did not know who she was. As she walked toward Mayson, she saw the back of his head nodding intensely as he talked with the lady, as though everything she said was right. Veronica stood quietly behind him. She was relieved that he was talking to anyone from the church other than Reanna, because she knew that Reanna didn't like her. She had decided that Reanna's like or dislike of her was irrelevant to her pursuit of Mayson. His conversations about her usually included something funny she said or did, which was different from the funny things he'd tell her about Idee. Veronica found Idee's behavior funny, but only because she was much younger and didn't seem to know better. However, with Reanna, she saw someone who knew what she was doing and saying, but didn't care. As for Reanna's "guy friends," as Mayson would call them, he'd share this as a means to show Veronica how popular and attractive she was to guys. He never went into detail as to whether or not she was intimate with her guy-friends. Despite Mayson's description of some of Reanna guy-friends as decent, Veronica wanted to believe that Reanna liked bad-boy types. Mayson was definitely not a bad boy by any means, she thought. Therefore, she was no threat to her bid for Mayson.

While she stood behind Mayson, she could hear him talking to the woman about an incident at his home.

"When I tried to wake her up for church this morning, she told me to leave her alone," Mayson was saying.

Veronica knew that he was talking about Idee, because he had told her how difficult she could be to wake up at times.

She could see the lady he was talking to would periodically look past Mayson's shoulder and at her with curiosity.

"She knew I had to get to church early this morning, so she took advantage of the opportunity," said the lady to Mayson.

Mayson could see the eyes of the lady he was talking to were darting back and forth between his face and behind him. He turned around and saw Veronica standing behind him with a patient, but forceful smile.

"Oh, Mama, I'd like you to meet Veronica Lambert," said Mayson.

When Veronica heard the word "Mama," she felt a little panicked. She had seen this lady when she visited the church but didn't know it was Mayson's mother. She straightened her shoulders, which had slumped while waiting for Mayson's conversation to end. Before she could say "Hi" to Phyllis, Mayson continued the introduction.

"Veronica and I have been talking for several weeks and she's become a special person in my life," continued Mayson.

When Veronica heard these words coming out of Mayson's mouth, she felt her heart leap. A warmth came over her as her eyes gazed on Mayson and the words "special person" repeated itself in her head.

Phyllis couldn't help but raise an eyebrow in surprise of this introduction and hoped that the surprise of this news didn't show on her face. Other than his friendship with Reanna, Mayson had never expressed any special interest in a girl, thought Phyllis. She noticed that he had been on the phone a little more than usual, but she thought it was Reanna with more drama from her life.

"Hi, sweetheart. Welcome to GCC, "said Phyllis.

"She's a regular visitor here," Mayson corrected his mother gently.

"Oh yes, I thought you looked familiar," said Phyllis.

"You think you might join GCC? We'd love to have you," Phyllis said as she reached out to shake her hand.

"I don't know," said Veronica as she looked at Mayson as though he could answer the question for her.

"Either way, you are more than welcome here," said Phyllis.

Phyllis, pondering this news of Mayson and Veronica, walked away as someone else in the congregation caught her eye that she needed to talk to.

"Nice to meet you," said Phyllis as she ventured away to talk with another church member.

"You too Mrs. Hendricks," replied Veronica.

Wow, what a nice mother-in-law-to-be, thought Veronica.

Veronica looked back at Mayson with a *what now* look. Mayson began to remove his choir robe.

"Glad you could make it," said Mayson.

"The service was beautiful. I was looking for you when I first arrive. It took a while for me to realize that you would be sitting in the choir," said Veronica.

"I guess I should have mentioned that to you," said Mayson.

"No problem, it was a great service," she said.

"You mind if I introduce you to my pastor and a few more people around the church?" asked Mayson.

"Sure," said Veronica eagerly.

Veronica squealed with delight internally. He wants to introduce me to other people, she thought to herself. This is a good sign. This definitely will lead to the answer of "intentions" that Deandra was asking about, she thought.

"Just a minute," said Mayson.

Mayson walked a little to the left of the choir stand, reached into a nearby closet for a hanger and hung his robe in the closet. He walked back over to Veronica. He grabbed her hand.

"Come on and let me officially introduce you to some of the members here at GCC," he said.

"Okay," she said with a smile that stretched so wide that it hurt her cheeks.

71

Mayson started with Pastor Upshaw who was at the door shaking hands with people as they left the church. As Mayson and Veronica approached the door where Pastor Upshaw continued to greet people, there was a couple talking with him. They appeared to be the last in line for the greeting. As Mayson and Veronica came closer, they could hear the woman telling the pastor about their child who was home sick with the woman's mother. Pastor Upshaw said a few words of prayer with them and they left.

As Veronica walked forward with Mayson to greet Pastor Upshaw, she felt something on her shoulder. She looked to her right and there was Mayson's arm draped across her shoulders. She felt her heart leap again.

"Pastor, I'd like for you to meet a very special lady in my life, Veronica Lambert," said Mayson.

Veronica was astonished once again to hear those added words to their relationship.

Not only did Pastor Upshaw's brows move upward, the words "special" and "lady" rang loud in his head. A quick moment of relief came over him, as though he had been holding his breath for a long time. A wide and joyful smile soon spread across Pastor Upshaw's face. He reached out with his two large hands and engulfed Veronica's right hand and shook it until she could feel her entire arm shaking.

"It is so nice to meet you. I've been seeing you a few times here at GCC. Have you decided to join us?" asked Pastor Upshaw in a hopeful and inviting voice.

"It's something I've been thinking about," said Veronica, although that reflected her feelings for Mayson rather than membership at GCC.

"Here with Mayson, you couldn't be in better hands," said Pastor Upshaw as he looked at Mayson and then back at her.

As they talked, First Lady Frances approached them.

"Hello all," said First Lady Frances as she approached them.

"Hello, First Lady," said Mayson.

Pastor Upshaw placed his arm around his wife's waist. He felt good about the moment as he anticipated what his wife was about to hear.

"First Lady Frances, I'd like for you to meet a special lady in my life, Veronica Lambert," said Mayson with his arm yet around Veronica's shoulder.

As with Phyllis and Pastor Upshaw, First Lady Frances was stunned. She was silent for a few seconds. She steadily nodded her head as she looked at Mayson and Veronica standing before her. She was nodding her head and looking at them as though she was taking in an entire mental picture of them. Veronica reached out her hand to First Lady. First Lady Frances, who was prone to hugging, threw both of her arms around Veronica and gave her a kiss on her cheek.

"We are a hugging church here," said First Lady in Veronica's ear.

Veronica smiled as she was swung side to side from First Lady's rhythmic embrace.

"I was telling Sister Veronica that she has a good man in Mayson," said Pastor Upshaw.

"Oh, okay," said First Lady Frances without agreeing or disagreeing with her husband.

Pastor Upshaw gave a second look at First Lady Frances as he could see that she was not responding with the excitement he anticipated.

"I've seen you come here from time to time," said First Lady.

"Yes ma'am," said Veronica.

Mayson held his breath in hope that First Lady Frances, like his mother and Pastor Upshaw, wouldn't ask her if she would be joining their church. Before he could finish his thought, she blurted out the words.

"So, are you a member of GCC now?" asked First Lady Frances. She didn't ask it with the curiosity and hopefulness of Phyllis and Pastor Upshaw, but Veronica heard in her voice a tone of expectancy.

"I don't know yet," said Veronica.

The question of Veronica's joining GCC scared Mayson a little. It made their being a couple more of a reality. This was somewhat his intent, but each endorsement of her possible membership showed that the matter could become problematic. Despite the implications, Mayson continued his introductions of Veronica to other church members. Veronica became tired of the question of her membership and started answering, "You never know." After Mayson completed all his introductions of Veronica, they stood facing each other.

"I'm hungry," said Mayson.

"So am I," said Veronica, hoping that his next statement will lead to their going out to eat.

"Let's go get something to eat," said Mayson.

This day is getting better and better, thought Veronica. "Sure," she said. "Where do you want to go?" she asked. "I'll drive," she said before he could answer the question.

"Let's go to a seafood place," responded Mayson.

"We can go to the one on Bradley Boulevard," said Veronica.

"Okay, sounds good," he said.

Mayson reached under the pew where he was sitting in the choir stand and got out a cassette tape in a plain white envelope.

"I saw Pastor Upshaw go to his office. I need to talk to him before I leave. The choir director had to leave early, so I have to go over some songs on this cassette tape that the choir wants to sing next week. You can go to the car and I'll be out soon," said Mayson.

"Okay," said Veronica.

After she had waited for 20 minutes, Mayson finally arrived at the car. He was feeling good about himself and the way the day had been going. When he presented the songs to Pastor Upshaw, they didn't talk about Veronica or even his past meeting with Mayson. But Mayson could tell that Pastor Upshaw was happy about meeting Veronica. He could sense this in the big pat on the back Pastor Upshaw gave him after they went over the songs.

When Mayson settled down in the car, Veronica started the engine and set out for Bradley Boulevard. Mayson turned on the radio to a gospel station. He sat quietly as he looked out the window. He seemed occupied in thought.

"Are you okay?" asked Veronica.

"Yes, I'm fine. Just a little tired," said Mayson.

Veronica tried to talk with Mayson about some of the songs and artist on the radio, but Mayson gave little response. He did perk up a little in the restaurant. Most of their conversation centered around Mayson identifying different members of the church who were at service that day. The food eventually arrived, and Mayson was relieved as he found himself running out of things to say about GCC. Veronica had a Cobb salad, as she didn't want Mayson to know what she would eat if he was not there with her. Mayson had fried shrimp, mashed potatoes, green beans, and hush puppies.

As they ate in silence, Veronica tried to think of a way to steer their conversation to be about them as a couple. His introductions at the church to his mother, pastor and church members had her feeling hopeful about their future.

"So many people asked about me joining GCC. What do you think?" Veronica asked hoping this would lead to the "intentions" that Deandra asked about.

Mayson's eyes diverted away from Veronica.

"That's up to you, Veronica. I can't tell you which church to attend. You need to be led by God for direction," said Mayson, as he stuffed shrimp into his mouth.

Veronica felt let down. She decided to make the conversation more spiritual, as Mayson was doing.

"Your right, I need to be led about this," she said.

Mayson pushed his plate away.

"I've had enough. I know I'm thin, but I have a large man's appetite," said Mayson.

Veronica laughed.

As Veronica drove Mayson to his house, she noticed that he was lost in thought again. He looked out the window as though Veronica was not there. He then turned around and looked at her.

"Want to stop by Faith on a Mission Church?" he asked. "They're having an afternoon service today."

After her conversation with Deandra about Mayson, Veronica was reluctant to accept Mayson's invitation to attend Deandra's church. Despite his declaration that he was tired, she wondered what really changed his mind. She allowed herself to believe that he was trying to make up for turning her down the last time.

"Okay. Do you know how to get there from here?" she asked.

"Sure," said Mayson as he sat up in his seat.

As they pulled up to Mission church, they could hear the organ and drums vibrating out from the walls of the church. Mayson bolted out of the car as though he was afraid he would miss something. Veronica hurried behind. Mayson opened the church door as he waited for Veronica to catch up. Veronica stepped in front of Mayson and entered the church foyer. Mayson looked through the inside glass door of the sanctuary as though he was looking for someone. They entered the church and took a seat in the back row. Veronica noticed that Mayson was still looking around the church. Veronica hunched low in her seat as she saw Deandra sitting on the same side of the church, hoping that Deandra had not seen her and Mayson when they came in.

As Veronica sat closer to Mayson, she could feel his every movement as he looked around the church. Then she felt the moving stop, and Mayson seemed to have found what he was looking for.

Veronica whispered, Mayson.

He didn't seem to hear her. She whispered his name again. Again, no answer.

She tried to figure out who he was looking at. She noticed that he was looking on the other side of the church in the middle section. On the other side, she saw the ushers sitting together, a bunch of children passing notes back and forth, and a local popular gospel singer, Lillian Mackey, who was visiting Mission. She looked behind Ms. Mackey and saw Melvin with Rem and Eric sitting directly behind them.

I can't stand that guy, she thought as she looked at Melvin. She thought that Mayson must be looking at Lillian Mackey. She knew how much Mayson liked to sing. Veronica decided that Mayson must have heard Lillian would be visiting Mission Church, and that was why he wanted to come.

After the sermon message, the choir sang as the offering was taken up. Then some last-minute announcements were given, and church was dismissed. Mayson doesn't want to leave, thought Veronica. He sat and continued to look in the same direction as he had since he sat down.

"Ready to go?" asked Veronica, who wanted to get out before Deandra saw her.

"Wait a minute, I'm looking for a friend of mine," said Mayson in an annoyed voice.

I thought he found who he was looking for, mused Veronica. Who can he be looking for now? she wondered. Without a word, Mayson stood up and walked to the other side of the church in the direction where he had been staring. Veronica stayed in her seat and watched Mayson as he wandered around the pews on the other side of the church as though he was not certain what to do.

After a few minutes, Veronica felt someone standing over her head. She looked up and saw it was Eric. He had strayed away from his posse and spotted Veronica.

"Hey," said Eric.

"Hi," said Veronica dismissively.

She continued to try and follow Mayson's whereabouts, but Eric moved in front of her and was now in her view of Mayson.

"I saw you at Pastor Martin's celebration services a few weeks ago," he said.

"Oh. Yeah," said Veronica as she continued to look past him for Mayson. He then sat down next to Veronica.

Oh God, no, she thought. Will you please go away? She screamed in her head.

"My name is Eric Brady," he said.

"Hi, Eric," said Veronica again in an annoyed tone.

"Looking for someone?" asked Eric.

"Yes, if you don't mind," replied Veronica. Mayson was simply standing where Ms. Mackey and the small children were sitting. She also saw Melvin and Rem nearby sitting in their same seats talking. She hoped that Eric would go back and join them.

"Excuse me," said Eric in frustration as he stood up to leave. "Just wanted to say hi and welcome you to Mission."

Eric was disappointed that Veronica appeared immune to his charm. As he turned to leave, he heard Melvin call his name from across the church. Veronica saw Melvin and Rem rushing across the church to catch up with Eric. They gathered near the exit of the church and walked out together. No sooner had they left than Mayson came back over to Veronica.

"Okay, let's go," he said.

As Veronica drove Mayson home, she noticed that he appeared to be in an even more distant mood than before. She decided to break the silence by talking about how annoying Eric was to her. She was hopeful that she might see a spark of jealousy if she made it known that Eric was trying to come on to her.

Mayson didn't respond. He closed his eyes and pushed his seat back and rested his head. She noticed that he had put her car pillow from her back seat on his lap. Veronica allowed the silence for a while but decided that she wanted it to end. She wanted to hurry and get him home and was sure that he would call her later and tell her what was going on.

In order to salvage the uncomfortable moment she was having with Mayson, she thought about Eric. As annoying as he was at that time, she then found it kind of cute that Eric was interested in her. Thinking of Eric made her think of Melvin. She reminded herself again how much she despised him. When Deandra asked her if she knew who Melvin was, she had pretended to barely know him. But she and Melvin had a bit of a past that she had never shared with anyone, which was where a lot of her pent-up disdain of him came from.

She assumed that with Mayson being so different from Melvin, he too would find Melvin's arrogance offensive. She was not aware that Mayson knew Melvin, but she decided to start another attempt at a conversation with Mayson on the topic of Melvin Sutton.

"You know Melvin Sutton, the guy in the gray suit sitting behind Ms. Mackey? That guy is so conceited and pompous, with his cheap knock-off suits. He tries to be more than he is," she said.

She continued with her gossip about how stuck Melvin was on himself and other unflattering remarks about his arrogance. She was too focused on her rants and the road to see Mayson growing restless in his seat, or his sighs with each remark about Melvin. Finally, he couldn't take it anymore.

"Just shut up!" screamed Mayson.

Veronica was shocked. She looked at Mayson, who was now sitting straight up in his seat, eyes swollen and skin pale.

"What do you know about Melvin? You have so much to say about things you know nothing about!" he yelled.

Despite being stunned and confused at Mayson's outburst, Veronica automatically found herself yelling back at him.

"What is it to you, Mayson? I have just as much right to my opinion as you do! she yelled. What is wrong with you? What makes you think you get to talk to me like this?" she yelled.

"Oh, just forget it," said Mayson, as he turned his back toward her and rested his shoulder on the car door.

The remaining of the drive was conducted in silence. Veronica was more hurt than angry at Mayson's outburst. How could such a wonderful day turn out to be so wrong? What did I do? she wondered.

She pulled up to Mayson's house.

"Thank you," said Mayson as he got out of her car without acknowledging what happened between them. Veronica looked straight ahead and didn't respond. He wanted to apologize to her, but he didn't have the words to explain to her what just happened between them.

Veronica made her tires spin with a loud screeching sound as she took off. As she drove, she replayed the day over and over in her mind to try and figure out what happened.

As she drove her thoughts drifted from one thing to another: Ok, so I gossip a little bit. But I think Melvin Sutton deserves to be gossiped about. She then thought about Deandra and her very odd interest in her relationship with Mayson. It's unusual for Deandra to get so involved in other people's business. Maybe she's jealous, she wondered. I don't know what's going on, she thought in frustration. As she was driving down a bumpy patch of road, the pillow that Mayson had been fidgeting with wobbled in the passenger seat. She pushed the pillow back into the seat, wondering why Mayson had suddenly become so attached to it. She retraced their day again and like a flash of light, it came to her mind.

"Melvin!" yelled Veronica as she slammed on the brakes. The car behind her screeched in an effort to avoid hitting her. Veronica looked in her rear-view mirror as the driver punched his horn in anger. She pulled over to the side of the road. She was suddenly out of breath. Her mind began to race as she thought about Deandra's sudden interest in her and Mayson. She must have known, she thought. And he was looking at Melvin during the service, not Lillian Mackey, she realized as she held her head in her hands. She looked at her pillow again, remembering how he kept it on his lap soon after leaving Mission Church. Oh, goodness, she thought. I will not be using that pillow anymore.

As she drove home, flashbacks of all the activities she was engaged in with Mayson flooded her mind. All those people he introduced me to at his church—it was all a lie, she thought.

CHAPTER 10

Rude Awakenings and Deandra's Shoulder

Better is open rebuke than hidden love. Proverbs 27: 5

(I)

Veronica entered her dorm room and saw that Deandra had not made it back yet. She was feeling so burdened that she wouldn't have minded loading it all on Deandra and getting her the "I told you so" she knew she deserved. On the other hand, Deandra's absence gave her time to mull over the shock of what she had just figured out. And anyway, if Deandra had been in the room, Veronica knew that she would have just burst out crying as soon as she saw her.

As she sat on her bed, she heard keys jingle in the door. Deandra opened the door. Once the door was open, the two girls immediately looked at each other.

Veronica opened her mouth to say "Hi," but began to cry uncontrollably instead. Deandra pulled her key out of the door, dropped her tote bag onto her bed, and plopped down on her bed facing Veronica.

"You know," said Deandra as she reached out and squeezed Veronica's hand.

"Yes," said Veronica as she tried to catch her breath. "Why didn't you tell me, instead of letting me make a fool out of myself?"

At first, Deandra was irritated that Veronica seemed to be blaming her for something that was her choice. But she saw how pathetic and naive her roommate looked, with tears pouring out of her eyes. She pulled a tissue from her desk and handed it to Veronica.

"Veronica, I battled with what I should do about you and Mayson, but I decided to let you find out on your own. I know you girl. You're quick to think that someone is jealous of you or just doesn't want to see you happy. And I had no actual proof about his sexuality, so I didn't want to pass on something that I didn't know to be absolutely true. I really battled with this," said Deandra.

"He really hurt me, Deandra," said Veronica as she stood, reached past Veronica and pulled more tissues from Deandra's desk.

"I thought this was the man I would spend my life with," she added.

"Don't you think you were moving too fast?" Deandra asked.

"I don't know," Veronica sighed.

"Out of all the people Mayson would want, with my luck, it would of course be Melvin Sutton," responded Veronica.

"Melvin Sutton!" shrieked Deandra.

"Oh, you didn't know that? yes, Mr. Full-of-Himself Melvin. I don't think the idiot knows about Mayson's stupid crush on him," she said.

Deandra was in disbelief. "No, I didn't know," she said.

"Did I ever tell you that Melvin and I had something going on for a little while?" asked Veronica. She realized that if she was going to confide in Deandra, she wanted her to know everything.

"Melvin Sutton?" repeated Deandra again in a more alarmed tone.

"Yes, Melvin Sutton. Remember that time my car was down and in for repairs?"

Deandra nodded.

"He drove me home that day from a BC meeting. He was home from school visiting with his girlfriend," said Veronica.

"Oh, he must have been home seeing Shante from our church," said Deandra. "Was she with him at the BC meeting?"

"No, it was Melvin and his two shadows, Eric, and I think the other goon's name is Rem," she answered.

"That makes sense, because I think he and Shante broke up some time back," said Deandra.

"Anyway, when the meeting was out, I announced loudly to everyone I needed a ride across campus to my dorm. It was dark and I didn't want to walk alone. Melvin finally said he would take me. At that time, like everyone else, I thought this man was fine as they come. My heart flamed when he volunteered to take me. That night he was a real talker. He started telling me how difficult it was when you're a preacher's kid and all the expectations that come along with this role."

"His father is Evangelist Sutton. We support him on his mission work. He's a really Godly man," interjected Deandra.

"Well, he seemed sincere as he told me that he has girls throwing themselves at him and he can't take any of them seriously because he doesn't know if they like him for his looks, himself or because of who his father is, continued Veronica. He told me that he was weak when it came to girls which is why he kept condoms in his wallet. I told him about my insecurities as a fat girl, and how I don't know if someone wants me for one night or because they see something special about me. He laughed and told me to watch out for Eric. Then he said something so sweet. He said some men like girls with a shape like mine. And, with my being so smart, a lucky man would get much more than he expected. After we got to my dorm, we sat in the car and talked for a while. He was telling me about his studies and his goal to be a news anchorman when he graduates."

"Well, it started getting late as we talked, and things got out of hand and..."

Veronica stopped and looked cautiously into Deandra's eyes. She felt the need to brace herself as she shared the next part of the story.

"We had sex in his car. Don't ask me how I managed that with my weight, but we got it done. I felt so special that night. The last thing I told him that night before I went into the dorm was that I would call him tomorrow and we could talk some more. Well, I called him several times the next day and left three messages, but never got a call back. I was furious and ashamed," said Veronica.

"Veronica, I don't expect you to tell me everything, but why did you keep this from me?" asked Deandra.

"Come on Deandra, you know how much of a goody-girl you can be at times," replied Veronica.

Hearing Veronica with the name calling again, caused a stir in Deandra. Even though the moment was about Veronica, she decided to set things straight with her in the process.

"I've constantly heard you call me a goody two-shoes or a Girl Scout. If that's the way I am then I will not apologize to you for it. Just as you want to be accepted as you are, then if I am this goody-girl, then you can either accept me as is, or move on," said Deandra firmly.

"Deandra, we have been roommates for two years and despite my view of you as Miss Goody, I really like us as roommates. You're the fourth roommate I have had since I've been going to school here and you're the only one I get along with. Despite my little wisecracks about you, I respect your opinion of me. You know me, I often jump the gun when it comes to people in general and even more so when it comes to relationships. I couldn't let you know that I went even further and did something as stupid as had sex with someone who was just supposed to drop me off at the dorm."

With this response from Veronica, Deandra was able to calm herself and resume the conversation about Veronica.

"How long ago was the car incident?" asked Deandra.

"Almost two months ago," she said.

"And you haven't talked to him since?" asked Deandra.

"I only got a wave out of him when we were at Pastor Martin's appreciation service that night. He looked around at me with a silly grin on his face and waved like I was some little kid he knew."

"Oh, I didn't see that," said Deandra.

"Is that why you said you had to go to the bathroom?" asked Deandra.

"I was so furious that I had to go outside and get some air," said Veronica, whose hurt over Mayson was changing to anger at Melvin.

"I thought you were gone too long to be in the bathroom!" said Deandra.

"Yeah, I told you that so I could get away from Melvin for a while. I had to think for a minute," Veronica said.

"So, you missed his antics with Mayson that night," said Deandra.

"I did. But girl, that night I was so glad to hear you say you didn't like Melvin too. I wanted everyone to see him as he was: arrogant!"

Veronica paused for a few seconds.

"Even that fool could see Mayson was gay. Everyone could see it but me," said Veronica with a humiliated look on her face.

"Mayson seemed nice from what I could see. I guess you were stuck on that side of him. I must say, I'm really surprised at him leading you on that way. He doesn't seem to be that type," said Deandra.

"He may be gay, but he has some man in him yet," said Veronica.

"Are you sure you didn't misread his intentions?" Deandra asked.

"Even if he didn't give me anything concrete to show that he had feelings for me, he could see that I had feelings for him. Why would he let me go that far with him?" asked Veronica.

"Good question. I wish I knew," said Deandra.

Veronica continued to share all the details of the story with Deandra that included Mayson's church introductions, his suggestion to go to Faith on a Mission, and the car ride to his house.

Two weeks after her humiliating scene with Mayson in her car, Veronica was still reeling from the shame she now felt when he introduced her to the people at his church and his deception about his feelings for her. They all knew, she figured. She thought about the initial look on Pastor Upshaw's face when Mayson introduced them as a couple. She realized that his wife's reaction was one of skepticism.

He made a big fool out of me, she told herself constantly.

To avoid any contact with Mayson, Veronica asked Deandra to answer all their calls for a while. Mayson left messages with Deandra for Veronica to call him back. Each time she saw a message from him, Veronica found herself getting angrier. She knew that she was too angry to talk with Mayson. She was afraid of what she would say to him.

As for him and Melvin, she and Deandra surmised that Mayson didn't have a clue as to how much Melvin despised him. Veronica wanted to throw that in Mayson's face, but she couldn't allow herself to do it. Veronica knew where her temper could take her. At that time, not returning Mayson's call was the best she could do. She really wanted to hurt him.

On a day when Veronica was walking to her class across the BHU campus, she thought about how Mayson used her and how much she wanted to put him in his place. On that day, not returning his calls didn't seem to be enough. She had thought about telling people about Mayson's attraction to men, particularly to Melvin Sutton, which would be the best payback for both of them, but she decided it might make her look petty and antagonistic. In order to mitigate her usual reaction to things by going too fast, she decided that she needed to take the matter slow.

Mayson Hendricks and Melvin Sutton don't have an inkling who they are messing with, she thought to herself.

(II)

Veronica called Melvin at his home, not really expecting to reach him. It would be her first effort to try and talk with him again. She thought that even if he was home, he wouldn't answer. She knew this due to her efforts in trying to reach him after their special night in his car. Back then, in addition to phoning him at his dorm, she had made calls to his home. She left messages for him at both places, but he failed to return the calls. When she called this time, to her surprise, he answered.

"Hello," said Melvin in his deep, professional-sounding tone.

"Oh, you answered," she said.

"Yes. Who is this?" asked, Melvin.

"It's me, Veronica. Or do you not remember me?" she asked sharply.

"Hey Veronica," said Melvin as his voice softened. "How are you?"

"That's yet to be seen," she said.

She paused.

"I got news for you Melvin. If you'd returned my calls, I could have told you sooner," she said.

"I've been busy Veronica. I did intend to call you back," he said.

"Well, it doesn't matter now. You can avoid my calls, but you cannot avoid the outcome of our night together," she said.

Melvin took a deep sigh, mentally kicking himself for picking up the phone. He had picked up the phone because he was waiting for a call from an internship employer. And now she's bringing up my mistake from the past, he thought.

"Veronica, I don't have time for this. Like I told you, I've been busy, and I'm waiting for a phone call now. What do you want?" he asked sharply.

"Oh ok, it's going to be like this," said Veronica. "Pregnant! I'm pregnant, Melvin, and it's your baby! Is that fast enough for you to get back to your business?" she yelled.

Your baby, reverberated in Melvin's ear.

"What!" yelled Melvin. That's not possible, he exclaimed. "I had on a condom."

"Well, apparently it broke," Veronica shot back.

"No. There's no way this could be my baby," said Melvin.

"Did you check the condom after you used it? Condoms do break, you know. I could feel a lot of you that night. You didn't have enough room to cover yourself fully. It was pretty crowded in that car," she said, hoping to plant doubt in his mind about his protection.

They both were quiet for a while.

"Are you sure you're pregnant?" asked Melvin in a defeated tone.

"Yes, Melvin. When my period didn't come, I added up the weeks and days that you and I were in the car. And my doctor confirmed the pregnancy. And, I know the baby's yours because you were the only one I've been with."

"Damn!" Melvin blurted out. Melvin was not prone to use of profanity but in his shock, the word came easily from his mouth without much effort. His mind raced from the baby to his evangelist father.

"So, you've been to see a doctor. You know sometimes those doctor's pregnancy tests can be wrong?" he said.

"If the test was wrong, what happened to my period?" she said.

Melvin's mind continued to race. He thought to ask Veronica again about the possibility of her being with someone else, but he knew this would cause more nonsense from her mouth. He then thought that he must ask anyway. He considered that this was something that would be with him for the rest of his life.

"Don't get mad," he said as he cleared his throat. "Were you with anyone else soon after that night?"

"Oh, you're going there again," responded Veronica indignantly. "Listen, boy, I haven't been with anyone but you. Even if I had, the dates would still add up to the night you and I were in your car," she said.

"What are you going to do?" asked Melvin.

"What do you mean, what am I going to do?" she responded. "You know our churches' doctrine against abortion, so you will be a daddy. No other options," she said harshly.

"My father is going to peel the skin off of me," moaned Melvin.

"You act as if this has never happened before. I'm sure your other women have had pregnancy scares," said Veronica.

"Veronica, this is not the time to be a smartass. I'm...we're in deep water here. I've never gotten anyone pregnant. I had sex with a girl in high school, and well... there was one time that she and I thought she was pregnant. My father knew about it because I told him. I didn't know what to do. This was the angriest I ever saw him. Fortunately, she was mistaken. After it was confirmed that she wasn't pregnant, he took me out of town with him for two weeks on his evangelist trip that summer. He told me that if this ever happened again, I was going to take full responsibility for everyone involved."

"Wow," said Veronica with a feeling of excitement to hear Melvin squirm at the fear of his father's reaction.

"I've been careful ever since," said Melvin as his voice softened.

Veronica heard in his voice that same moment of confiding connection they shared in the car that night.

"Trying not to have sex didn't work for me, so I started always keeping a condom on me or at least being certain the girl was on some kind of birth control. I didn't expect us to have sex that night, but you were so easy to talk to. I got caught up in the moment," he said.

She thought about how sensitive and vulnerable he sounded. She recalled even more how he sounded the same in the car that night. In some ways they both were lonely. He was such a handsome guy that women had expectations of him. His father was looking for him to live his life based on his reputation as an evangelist. She had shared how she had so much to give and being told in a roundabout way that she was a big girl with a pretty face. Veronica thought about how they did indeed open their hearts to each other.

"This is my last year of college. Why was I so stupid?" said Melvin.

Veronica felt herself softening to let him out of this lie, but as she sat in her room on the phone at her desk talking with Melvin, her eyes fell on a note from Deandra with the message that Mayson had called. She refocused her mind to think back on how he treated her that day in her car. Veronica decided to snap out of her soft moment for Melvin and stick to her plan. Not now. I will not let him off the hook so soon, she decided. I will teach Melvin not to throw me away like an old shoe, she thought.

"My last year in school is approaching too, so this affects my future as well," she said in a softer tone. She didn't want Melvin to feel that this was all about his needs.

"Unfortunately, I will have to talk to my father about this. He's paying my tuition and living expenses. I will have to see where this news will take him. I'll call you back sometime this week," said Melvin.

Recalling how Melvin ignored her after their one night, Veronica decided to return to her tough stance.

"Make sure you do call back. I'd hate to have to go through your father to find you. Do you have my number?" she asked.

"Veronica, don't threaten me. I said I'll call you."

(III)

Veronica sat in the booth at the Brick Pit restaurant waiting for Melvin. Melvin had kept his word and called her back two days later after her news. He asked her to meet him at the restaurant to talk.

Veronica ordered a soft drink as she waited for Melvin. She had managed to keep her false pregnancy and entrapment of Melvin from Deandra. She made sure that she didn't get into any long conversations with her, because Deandra sometimes had an uncanny way of telling when something was wrong with Veronica or when she was hiding something.

Veronica saw Melvin's black sports car in the parking lot. He parked a few cars down from the entrance. She saw his car door open and out came his sturdy athletic legs and movie-star looks. He was wearing a polo shirt that showed off his broad shoulders and well-built pecs. He was also wearing heavy black flip-flops with freshly pressed jeans. As far as Veronica was concerned, flip-flops were only to be worn with shorts, yet the clashing in style made him that more attractive. As he walked toward the restaurant, she could see the stress on his face. It seemed he was anticipating the meeting, which made him look even more vulnerable. Veronica felt a twinge of second thoughts about the lie again.

"Hello," said Melvin to Veronica.

"Hi, Melvin," she said.

She scooted over for him to sit on the same side of the booth with her. He sat on the other side instead. Melvin looked around the restaurant as though he was concerned about someone seeing them. He leaned forward close to Veronica.

"Good news and bad news, said Melvin with a frown on his brow. I talked to my father. To say he's angry with me is an understatement. He also told my mother, who cried for half the day. That's the bad news. The good news is he is going to continue to fund my last year at school," he said.

Veronica felt relieved about this part. A part of her was concerned that he might lose his father's financial support and not be able to graduate. She definitely didn't want it to go that far.

Melvin continued," My father told me that I'm an adult now and the situation is different from the pregnancy scare in high school. He's going to continue to help me until I graduate from college and then he said I'll be on my own. He's leaving it up to us to decide about how to take care of our baby."

Our baby, thought Veronica. He said "our" baby. For a moment, the baby seemed real. Even when she saw him getting out of his car to enter the restaurant with that serious look on his face, she knew that things were going too far. But her interaction with Melvin was contingent on the baby news getting back to Mayson. She imagined how wonderful it would be if she were actually pregnant and the baby's father was a man who looked like Melvin. The trance was broken as she became aware that he must have asked her a question. She started to ask him to repeat it, but she then saw him reach for her glass. He must have asked for a drink, she thought.

"Go ahead. The waitress will be back soon, and I can get another," said Veronica as she could see he was sweating.

"Thanks," said Melvin as he lifted her glass and took a drink. He continued to talk, picking up where he left off.

"But the one thing my father added was for me to remember that he raised a man to take care of his responsibility. Veronica, I've been thinking about this situation day and night. I'm from a large family and the second-oldest of six. I love children and I've always seen myself as a father. I didn't expect to have children in these circumstances, but we have to live with what happens in life. I want this baby and I want him or her to have a good start in life. Maybe what we did can turn out to be something good. I want us to marry and raise this baby together. I don't want my child to come into this world labeled a bastard. We may or may not make it as a couple, but ..." Melvin paused, trying to anticipate Veronica's reaction. He could only see her staring at him with no indication on her face of what she was thinking.

"I want to focus on what is right for the baby more than us. I know that's what a man would do," said Melvin.

He pulled away from the table and leaned back in the booth. He took a deep breath as though he could feel himself having said a lot in such a short time. Veronica felt her jaw drop. She never expected Melvin to propose marriage. She also could read between the lines that he was telling her that he only wanted to marry her because of the baby, and he didn't care about their lack of love for each other. Or did he mean his lack of love for me? wondered Veronica. She could sense that she was beginning to feel something for Melvin, but not the way she ached for Mayson. She was attracted to Melvin's looks and was proud that, of all the girls, she was the one to land him.

Melvin leaned forward over the table again, reached across the table and took Veronica's hand.

"We can do this, Veronica. Remember how long we talked that night in the car? You understood me so well when I told you that people don't understand that there's so much more to me than my looks. I know I'm a good-looking guy, but I can't always live up to other's expectations. There are so many things that I want to do in life, but I can't seem to get people to see my intellectual side. I thought a lot about you in that regard and you seem to get that side. We may not love each other, but that night was a good sign that maybe we have something to share along with the baby."

Veronica could not think what to say but was relieved to hear him say that *they* didn't love each other. For Veronica, *"they"* meant that this pretty boy was not arrogant enough to assume that she loved him. Again, she saw a side of Melvin that contradicted her assumption of him. When she'd try and put him back into her despised thinking pattern, he'd say or do something to contradict her old way of seeing him. When she tried to speak, she could not hear anything come out. She thought to tell Melvin to let her think about it, but that's not what came out.

"I'd love to marry you," said Veronica with a grin that came to her face that she thought was only for Mayson. As she felt Melvin's hands hold hers, she could also feel his hand trembling.

When Veronica drove away from the restaurant, she couldn't believe what had happened. I said yes, she thought. Messing with his head was one thing, but marrying him was a bonus, Veronica thought with a bit of a glee. She justified accepting his marriage proposal by concluding that he was the one who suggested marriage and not her, and telling herself that if he'd called her back the first time she called him, things would not have gone this far.

But later, fear overtook her elation. I can't do this, she thought. What am I going to do when it becomes clear there's no baby? But what if this is the only opportunity I get in life to marry someone this good-looking, with education and a future? She then thought of all the other girls she knew at the university that were engaged and close to graduation. I want to be one of those girls, she thought, but I'm going to show them a wedding ring, not an engagement ring. And why shouldn't I do this? After all, he told me that we had connection. Also, who's to say that I won't get pregnant on our wedding night? As she went back and forth from a little guilt to wanting to pinch herself at the thought that she was about to get married, she looked out of her car to see that she was back at the university parking lot.

Her mood then hit another reality bump. How am I going to explain this to my mother and Deandra?

CHAPTER 11

Meet the Parents...Have a Wedding

What am I going to say to his father? wondered Veronica as she was driving to Melvin's house for their wedding. Melvin decided he wanted to get married before his child was born, so he wanted to marry Veronica as soon as possible. In doing his math from their car encounter, Melvin figured that the baby would come in about six or seven months. He wanted everything settled before the baby was born. He wanted to believe that this was what his father was expecting of him.

With everything going so fast, Veronica decided not to tell her mother about the engagement or the wedding. She was concerned that her mother would try and talk her out of it or become suspicious about this sudden marriage to a man she never met. With hesitation, she told Deandra about the upcoming wedding, but not the false pregnancy. She knew that Deandra would soon find out about the wedding either from campus or through Mission church. Deandra was shocked and suspicious about the news, but she didn't take the matter any further. However, when Veronica invited Deandra to the wedding, Deandra told her that she would not have any part in whatever was going on. That was the end of their conversation about Veronica's marriage to Melvin. Veronica decided to chalk it up to jealousy on Deandra's part.

As Veronica got closer to the Sutton's home, she felt excited but nervous. She held her stomach as she drove. She had never been in a "meet the parents" situation with any boyfriend. Veronica had decided long ago that if she gave away her virginity, it would be to the man she'd marry. In a turned-around way, Melvin was the closest she got to that promise. As she drove, she thought about the day of their sexual encounter and the lonely tormenting days thereafter. They had shared a lot with each other. Veronica thought about how she was a good listener for him. And he had listened to her when she shared her fears, insecurities and life dreams. She believed they had forged a bond that night. When she woke up the next day after their encounter, she continued to feel that closeness. With that feeling of closeness from that night, later came the fear of being pregnant. She had heard of condoms breaking and wondered if it had happened to them. She questioned whether Melvin placed the condom on securely as he was rushing to put it on. She had seen so many girls from her dorm drop out of school due to pregnancy. It was like a monthly parade as the crying girl walked down the dorm hall, suitcase in hand, with her parents lugging bags and boxes behind her.

When she got out of his car that night, she told him she would call him and he said he would call her. She naively believed that he would. That night, she had no one to talk to about what happened. Definitely not Deandra, nor her mother. After waiting three days for his call, she couldn't take it anymore. She had to talk to someone. He didn't return her calls. Veronica was even more humiliated. There was a day in which she was about to share her pregnancy scare with Deandra, but the phone rang in their room, and she was sure it was Melvin. Instead, it was Deandra's mother. They talked for over an hour. Veronica lost her nerve. After getting her period a couple of weeks later, she heaved a sigh of relief, but her relief quickly soured into fury at Melvin Sutton.

Despite the small town of Benton, Veronica had never met the Evangelist Joseph Sutton or Melvin's mother, Rhonda. Melvin had asked his parents a week earlier if they wanted to meet Veronica before the wedding. His father told him that he didn't need to meet someone who was Melvin's responsibility.

"You're a man now. If there is something your mother and I can do to help, we will help if we can," his father said.

Melvin took this opportunity to ask his father to let him have the wedding at their house and for him to perform the ceremony. His father didn't jump at the request but gave a solemn, *okay.*

"You think Mama can be our witness?" asked Melvin.

"You'll need to ask her," he said.

Melvin didn't like how cold and formal his father was being.

"What are you all going to do about a place to live? And will you be able to finish school?" asked his father.

"I checked into this. I would rather Veronica have the baby here in Benton. I don't want to prevent her from completing school by uprooting her. My school advisor told me that I could transfer my credit hours and complete my degree at BHU. So, I'm going to see if I can get into a married student dorm here. It's the middle of the school year, but I'm fairly sure I can do it," said Melvin, trying so hard to show his father how responsible he was.

"I know the president of the university at BHU. I'll ask him if he can help with the process," replied Evangelist Sutton.

"Thanks, Daddy," said Melvin with a sense of relief that his father had offered to help with something other than his college tuition.

Melvin wanted to believe that his father's offer to help was a sign that he approved of his decision, and this was the right thing for him to do. After his father's initial explosion of anger about the pregnancy, he did not offer any hint of approval or disapproval of how Melvin was handling the matter.

Veronica's drive to her wedding that day left her with much time to reflect more on what was about to take place between her, Melvin, and Evangelist and Mrs. Sutton. The more she reflected, the more uncertain she was about this next move. She pulled up to a lovely colonial-style house with its perfectly manicured lawn and felt intimidated. I hope I'm not out of my league, she thought again.

Veronica had been raised in an aluminum-sided house for most of her childhood. The siding would often have to be sprayed down and cleaned on a regular basis. Between the cleanings, their house looked dirty and of poor quality. This would sometimes spark arguments between her parents as her mother would needle her father to hurry and get the siding clean. He eventually died of lung cancer, having been a smoker for most of his life. He was a good man, but a man of very few words.

When Veronica approached the Suttons' door, she used the beautiful brass knocker rather than the doorbell because she was impressed with its shape and heavy appearance. Before she could knock a second time, the door opened and there stood Mrs. Sutton. She was a petite, attractive woman who looked a lot like Melvin. She could see that her soft brown eyes looked so much like Melvin's eyes. He had her warm brown skin color and nice curvy lips. Her soft black hair was in an updo that accentuated her slender neck.

"Hi." Come in, she said in a mild voice.

Veronica put on a nervous smile as she walked in the doorway. Ms. Sutton extended her hand.

"I'm Rhonda Sutton, Melvin's mother," she said as her face quickened in a short smile.

Veronica shook her hand. She thought to give her a quick hug, since she was about to be her daughter-in-law, but decided to follow Ms. Sutton's more formal lead.

"So nice to meet you," said Veronica.

While standing near the door, Veronica looked around the elegant living room with its pale carpet and light pink couches.

"What a beautiful home," said Veronica.

"Thank you. It's a task to keep it up with growing children still around," replied Mrs. Sutton modestly.

"Melvin told me he had a big family. I look forward to meeting everyone," said Veronica. She looked down the hallway as though expecting them to come out at any time.

"They are at Faith on a Mission Church right now. There's a weekend youth program going on," said Mrs. Sutton.

"Okay. I guess I can meet them some other time," said Veronica. Mrs. Sutton gave another quick smile without assuring her that she would. As Veronica stood near the door, she began to second-guess her choice of the dress she chose to wear for her wedding. She usually liked to shop with her mother because her mother has better taste in clothing than she does. But of course, her mother could not go shopping with her for this dress because she didn't know that her oldest daughter was getting married this weekend. She had on a silky, colorful cascade paisley dress with long sleeves. She wore brown pumps that matched a portion of the dress design. Like Mrs. Sutton, she wore her hair in an updo style, but she didn't feel that it made her look as elegant as Mrs. Sutton.

Mrs. Sutton wore white trousers, whose high waistband fit her small waist perfectly, and a patterned sky-blue and white silk blouse that looked as though she paid hundreds of dollars for it. Veronica recalled that not only was Melvin's father a highly sought-after Evangelist, but his mother was a college administrator. Melvin had shared that night in the car that she always kept her job no matter how well his father did as an evangelist. He referred to her career as "the family back-up plan." When Evangelist

Sutton had decided to leave his job as a bank manager to become a full-time evangelist, Mrs. Sutton only agreed to it if he would allowed her to go back to school to get a master's degree in education. Once his mother completed her degree, she found a job at a local university. She later obtained her PhD and eventually worked her way up to VP of Academic Affairs. Evangelist Sutton became so proud of her accomplishments that he would often include her career success in some of his sermon messages.

As Veronica stood near the door, she could see a large figure coming down the hall. It was Evangelist Sutton. He was built like Melvin, broad and athletic. He was not as attractive as Melvin, but his height and built seem to make up for his small-set eyes, rough skin, and thinning hair. He was wearing a dark blue suit that seemed to have been tailor-made to his attractive build.

"Hello," said Evangelist Sutton in a deep voice as he walked to stand next to his wife and put his arms around her shoulder. Mrs. Sutton was about the same height as Veronica, but when Evangelist Sutton stood next to Mrs. Sutton, she seemed a lot smaller. Or was it that Evangelist Sutton had such a formal authoritative presence that it made almost anyone seem smaller than they actually were?

"Have a seat," he said as he motioned Veronica to the full-sized pale pink couch.

"Melvin took his sisters and brothers to the church for an event. He should be back shortly," said Evangelist Sutton.

Veronica felt her heart sink when he told her that Melvin was not home.

Oh, God. They're going to browbeat me into a confession, she thought. They must be suspicious about whether or not there is a baby. Why did I do this?

Mrs. Sutton sat at the other end of the pink couch near the front door and Evangelist Sutton sat in the small armchair near their fireplace. There was a silence as Veronica could hear the faint noise of music from another room. It sounded like gospel music. In the awkwardness, Veronica continued to hear the faint sound of music coming from down the hall.

"Oh, goodness. Daniel left his tape player running again. That boy, that boy, she said as she shook her head. Let me go turn it off. Excuse me," she said, as she got up from the couch and stepped past Veronica.

Their silence continued and became even more awkward when Mrs. Sutton left the room. Evangelist Sutton began to straighten his tie. Veronica was looking around the room at all the family pictures, particularly those resting on the fireplace mantel. With the exception of Mr. Sutton, the family was smiling cheerfully. Mr. Sutton had only a hint of a smile. There was also a photo of Evangelist and Mrs. Sutton in their twenties. In this photo, Mr. Sutton was smiling broadly. I guess time can slowly erase a smile, thought Veronica.

Melvin had told Veronica about all of his siblings when he and Veronica were at the restaurant. He didn't want it to appear to his parents that he and Veronica knew very little about each other. Melvin filled Veronica in on his mother giving birth to Ariel and Melvin, and then years later having his younger siblings: Daniel, fourteen, Luke, twelve, Ben, eleven, and Ruthie, nine. He shared that his parents always wanted a big family, so with the birth of Ariel and Melvin, who were two years apart, they hoped that a larger family was on the way. After Melvin was born, she had a difficult time conceiving. Their doctor suggested that they relax their efforts in order to eliminate stress or consult a therapist. Evangelist Sutton decided that he would not have a secular counselor giving him reasons as to why he was not having more children with his wife. When they finally had more children, Evangelist Sutton often shared this blessing with congregants as a means of telling them to trust God.

"So, your mother will not be able to make it to the wedding?" asked Evangelist Sutton.

Oh my goodness, thought Veronica. The third degree is about to start.

What am I going to say? She thought, as she tried to come up with a response that would not lead to more questions about her mother's nonattendance.

"No sir. She has to take my twin brothers out of town," said Veronica, trying to sound natural. Suddenly, Veronica could no longer hear the music from down the hall. She then heard Mrs. Sutton soft steps walking back toward the living room.

Evangelist Sutton sat up straight in his seat and began to open his mouth as though he was about to say something else to Veronica. Before he could do so, the front door opened and in walked Melvin at the same time his mother had reentered the room.

"Good morning," said Melvin to Veronica as he closed the door.

"Good morning," said Veronica with an internal sigh of relief.

"You all get to know each other?" asked Melvin in a speech that was to address everyone, but his eyes were pointed directly at his father.

"We didn't have much time. She hasn't been here five minutes," responded Mrs. Sutton.

"You got back so fast," added Evangelist Sutton.

Melvin walked over to the couch. As he awkwardly bent down to kiss Veronica on the cheek, his father jumped up from his seat.

"Well, let's get this done," said Evangelist Sutton.

Melvin was startled and aborted the kiss, extending his hand instead to Veronica to help her up from her seat.

As they all stood in front of the fireplace, the wedding was quick and to the point. Mrs. Sutton broke down during the ceremony and Melvin started to leave Veronica's side to console her, but his father lifted his eyes quickly from the wedding script to tell Melvin to leave her alone. Upon completion of the ceremony, Melvin went to his room, got his overnight bag and left with Veronica to finish putting the final touches on their campus apartment. Melvin and Veronica had already moved most of their belongings into the apartment. After two hours of putting things together at their campus apartment, Veronica stopped to go back to the dorm and pick up her remaining items from her dorm room.

When she entered the room, she saw Deandra lying on her bed watching television. Deandra didn't take her eyes off the television as Veronica entered the room. Deandra had decided that she was finished with Veronica. She had concluded that Veronica was someone who could not be trusted. For Deandra, trust meant everything.

"Hi," said Veronica.

"Hi," Deandra responded.

After their greetings, neither said a word.

While gathering her clothes from her closet, Veronica stopped to look at the game show Deandra was watching. She wasn't really interested in the show, but hoped it would spark a conversation about something, anything.

"That was a dumb answer," said Veronica, watching a man from the game show.

Deandra did not respond.

Veronica knew that Deandra was trying to avoid engaging in conversation, so she stopped watching the show and resumed getting clothes
from her closet. Veronica spent a few more minutes rummaging through
her closet, picking up some of her knick-knacks lying around the room.
Deandra knew that Veronica wanted to talk and felt herself weaken at
Veronica's attempt. She also knew what Veronica was usually like when
she was at war with others, but her efforts to mend their disagreements
now was out of character for her. She's trying to make amends, Deandra
thought. Besides, this is her wedding day. Deandra decided to talk with
Veronica for the sake of the fun and heartfelt days they had as roommates.
And she didn't want their ending to be left with them not speaking to each
other. She didn't agree with Veronica's decision, but this marriage was
her choice and life to deal with.

"At least I'll have the room to myself," said Deandra, trying for a
light, bantering tone.

"Unless someone else needs a room," said Veronica as she grabbed
at Deandra's words like a life jacket. She was so happy that Deandra was
talking to her again.

"I hope not," said Deandra.

Veronica made a joke that in case her marriage didn't work with
Melvin, it was good to know that Deandra would still have space available.
Deandra felt her anger stir again, she had hoped they could leave on good
terms, but she felt that same self-absorbed Veronica was resurfacing.

"You need to take this seriously, Veronica," said Deandra. At that
response, silence entered the room once again. Veronica took her remaining items and left.

CHAPTER 12

Marriage-News Pipeline to Mayson

"It's getting late, I need to get home," said Mayson.

"It's only 11:30PM, and it's Saturday," said Reanna.

"Look around, protested Mayson. Just about everyone from the church has left the restaurant. It's just you, me, Lamont, and the Hudson family down at the end of the table. And they look like they're about to leave."

"Why such a hurry to get home?" asked Reanna.

"I was up late last night and the night before. All these late nights are starting to get to me. Besides my mother doesn't like it when I keep Lamont out too late," said Mayson.

"Well, if you've been having problems sleeping anyway, why go home and be wide awake?" said Reanna with a laugh.

"You're being silly. I have Lamont with me. Look at him," said Mayson as he put his hand on the shoulder of Lamont, who was seated at the table with his face down into his folded arms and fast asleep.

"He's snoring. If that's not a need to go home then I don't know what is," said Mayson.

"What's keeping you woke?" asked Reanna, with her head tilted as though she wanted Mayson to tell her some deep secret. "Is it because your stalker is getting married?"

"What stalker?" Mayson laughed.

"You know, Ms. Pushy", said Reanna.

"Veronica?" asked Mayson assuming Reanna was simply making fun of her. He knew that she didn't like Veronica, and she was still miffed at her for taking her seat next to him at church.

Mayson stood up from the table in preparation to leave, hoping Reanna would do the same. Reanna did not follow Mayson's lead, but looked up at Mayson, recognizing that his grin did not show any hint of knowledge about Veronica's engagement to Melvin.

"Yep, Veronica. She's engaged to be married. I thought you knew," said Reanna.

Mayson slowly sat back down. It hadn't been 2 months since they had that scene in her car, he thought. He had tried calling Veronica a few times to make up with her, but she would not return his calls. He felt a little relieved at hearing this news. Veronica finding someone else took the pressure off him to try and make up with her.

"No, I didn't know. When did this happen?" asked Mayson.

"I don't know, but I just found out about it from a friend of mine whose sister lived in her dorm. I thought you knew but just didn't want to talk about her. We both know you weren't interested in her anyway," said Reanna wryly.

"How do you know I was not interested?" asked Mayson, not really wanting to hear a reply.

"Because I know you, a lot more than you think," said Reanna.

Mayson gave a muffled laugh as he looked down.

"Who would have figured?" he asked.

"And who would have figured she was marrying a hunk like Melvin Sutton," said Reanna, as she drank her Cola.

"Who?" asked Mayson, hoping he didn't hear her correctly.

"You know, Melvin Sutton, Evangelist Sutton's son from Faith on a Mission," said Reanna biting into a hush puppy that was left on her plate.

Mayson felt a knot in his stomach. He looked at Reanna to see if she was kidding him, but she was shaking her glass, trying to move around the ice.

"I heard that he dropped out of college in Illinois and transferred to BHU. They're going to live on campus there. He was dating this gorgeous girl from Mission church for a while, so it was a shock when it came out that he was marrying fat, pushy Veronica. Everyone wanted that fine piece of man, she added with a sigh. They may be married already for all I know. I never found out what day the wedding would be," she added as she sipped the residue of water from the ice.

Reanna put down her glass, as she had sipped out as much of it as she could. When she looked across the table at Mayson, she saw that he looked dazed and a little flushed.

"Are you okay?" asked Reanna with a concerned look on her face. "You look sick."

Mayson had never talked with Reanna about Melvin and did not want to give her a hint that among other things, wanting Melvin was a factor in his sleepless nights. He began to feel light-headed and short of breath. I have to get out of here, he thought. He began to rub the sides of his head, which made Reanna more worried.

"My lack of sleep is coming down on me. I really need to wake Lamont and go home," said Mayson.

"Okay sweetie," said Reanna as she looked at him with concern. "If you're that sleepy, do you think you will be okay driving your mother's car home?"

"Yeah, I'll be okay," said Mayson, who was not able to get out of the restaurant soon enough.

"You don't look good, sweetie, so I don't want you to have to make an extra trip to take me home. I see the Hudson family out in the parking lot now. I'll ask them if they can drop me off," Reanna said.

"Thanks," said Mayson, as he shook Lamont from his sleep.

CHAPTER 13
Pastor McDaniel

Understanding and an Open Door

Pastor McDaniel's office was not as well-decorated as Pastor Upshaw's. His office was spacious but old, with scuffed walls and very little furniture. Books and papers were stacked on his desk. There were boxes everywhere, which made it seem as though he was in the midst of unpacking things, yet it was obvious upon closer inspection that the boxes were just another form of office storage. The building was once a Catholic church with thousands of members. But according to a small article written last year in their local newspaper on Pastor McDaniel's "unique" ministry, his congregation was around 200 to 300.

Mayson began leafing through one of the Bibles from Pastor McDaniel's bookshelf. It seemed to be a more modern version of the traditional King James Bible. Mayson was intrigued with this translation, as it gave him a better understanding of the scriptures. He immediately looked for keywords in the concordance for "Sodom and Gomorrah." This was the area of the Bible that his church and many other churches used to condemn gays. He thought perhaps this more modern translation would provide him better insight about the history of the church's stand against gays. He thought that his church might have misinterpreted this area of the Bible. Because his search was in the Old Testament, he had a difficult time finding his area of interest. He was more familiar with the New Testament and the scriptures that used words as "effeminate" from Paul's writings, so he turned to the New Testament. There must be some misinterpretation of God's relationship with those who are gay, he thought as he riffled the pages. This was a thought that Mayson had had in the back of his mind for years; however, because he didn't know the Bible as well as he thought, he had confined himself to follow the lead of his church's interpretation and beliefs. As Mayson stood near the bookshelf searching through the Bible, he could hear footsteps coming closer down the hallway.

He quickly put the Bible back on the shelf and sat on the couch a few feet from the desk. The door opened and in walked a stylish man with a neatly cut afro and a trimmed beard. He was short in stature, casually dressed in jeans and a button-down striped shirt. To Mayson, he appeared to be in his late 40s or early 50s.

"Hello, hello, hello," said Pastor McDaniel as he walked quickly into his office and immediately sat in a wooden chair that was in front of the couch where Mayson was sitting.

"Mayson, it was nice talking to you on the phone. It's good that Pastor Upshaw referred you, and I hope I can be of assistance to you." He reached out to shake Mayson's hand.

"Thank you," said Mayson as he took the pastor's hand.

As his brow raised, Pastor McDaniel's pleasant smile turned into a serious look.

"Mayson before you speak, would you like for me to tell you a little about me and my church? I know you came here at the word of Pastor Upshaw, but if it would make you feel better to know me and my church before you talk, I will be more than glad to do so."

It was Pastor McDaniel's hope that Mayson would say "yes." He knew this was not the way most counseling sessions were traditionally conducted, but he considered himself and his ministry unorthodox in its approach. Pastor McDaniel knew the experiences of people who were Humans and were in churches that preached against being Human. He knew what it felt like to come into someone's office and share this controversial side with another person. Most were filled with fear, confusion and anger. They were usually nervous and not quite sure if they wanted to be there in his office. He wanted Mayson to feel comfortable by setting a background for their conversation.

"Yes, that would be great," said Mayson. He settled back on the couch like a child about to hear a bedtime story.

"First of all, I was born and raised in a Christian church that espoused doctrines and beliefs based on what they interpret the Bible to mean for all people. I specifically say, "a Christian Church" because often when people hear the word "Christian," they assume they know what is meant by Christianity. Christianity does have a main source of belief in the God of the Bible who promotes what is good. We have a written source of who

He is and who we are. How we express our belief and devotion to God varies in our biblical interpretation, ministry, and our style of worship.

Now, of course some things from the Bible do apply to all, but other areas do not fit into a one-fits-all approach. And this is where problems arise.

I believed in much of what was told to me as it pertains to God's goodwill for Humankind. And, I don't have a problem with most Christian churches' basic written biblical doctrine. It's their application of it in the real world that is the problem. Many of the churches would interpret Bible scriptures without a foundation of the time and place in which it was written, or when—or if—to apply it to others. When you read the Bible, you need to ask questions, such as *who, what, when* and sometimes *where* for better clarity of the scriptures. *Who,* because you need to know the foundation of the main characters and their backgrounds. *What,* is needed as a means of determining the actual subject matter. *When,* helps place the time into context. Sometimes you need *where,* for location-specific issues."

Mayson found that key for biblical interpretation interesting. It had been a goal of his to one day take time and try and understand the Bible in more depth.

"That's good to know. Do you have any paper I could write that down on?" asked Mayson.

"I can do better than that. I taught these *Interpreting Questions* to our Sunday School class. I had a curriculum made up that included these areas on better bible understanding," he said.

Pastor McDaniel's got up and went to one of his file cabinets across the room. He began leafing through the middle drawer of the cabinet. It took a minute, but he found the curriculum sheet and gave it to Mayson.

He went back to his chair and sat.

"Sorry to stop you," said Mayson.

"It's okay. I see you want to know the Word for yourself, and that's a good thing," said Pastor McDaniel. "Let's see, where was I?"

"You were saying that some of the churches were not asking the right questions when it came to Bible interpretation," said Mayson.

"Oh, that's right, he said. Many of the churches interpret Bible scriptures without a foundation of understanding. Some are just doing and saying what everyone else was doing or saying in their churches. Or, they got the interpretation or rules from some leader before them. Getting it from prior leadership is not bad in itself, but if you are going to judge people's lives on it, you better know the foundation of whatever you may be preaching. We are all God's people, and you can't just throw anything on them because of what you were told. And it can't be about our need to say or do what is expected in order to fit in. It's not about us as pastors. It's about who we serve as God's servants. And that's really who we are, Mayson. Servants of God's people. This is a highly responsible position that a lot of people in leadership don't really understand. It's about so much more than fancy suits, expensive cars, big hats, large crowds, or seats up front in the church."

"I digress."

"At one time, as a member in a denominational Christian church, I tried to put aside my concerns about the church's questionable Bible interpretations and just let myself fit in with everyone else. I knew I dared not say anything. They'd often tell the members of their church that when people question their preaching, it's because they don't want to adhere to God's word. Therefore, in not addressing my concerns, I thought it showed my love for and commitment to God. What I later understood is that what I thought was a love for God in my commitment was more a fear of what those in the church would think of me. What they would think if I had questions or doubts about some the applications of our teachings and doctrines. I was scared of standing out and being different from the others with my doubts and questions. There were some days when I could not live up to the teachings that were instilled in me from childhood. As a result of living in an unfulfilled life of doubt and uncertainty, I found myself repenting a lot to God because I felt that just about everything I did or didn't do was wrong. As I got older, some things that were taught to me by my church continued to leave me with more questions than answers.

Keep in mind that the church has a right to their teachings and beliefs. The church, like any other institution of faith, does not have to put up with anyone coming to their house of worship trying to change or disrespect them. That's important to know, son. However, I couldn't shake it off when someone was found to be gay or lesbian in the church, and within days or weeks they were gone. My heart went out to what I call the church's outcasts.

My day came when I was 35 years old and was called to the ministry. I was scheduled to meet with the elders for ministry ordination. The ordination board, which included Pastor Upshaw, had concerns about ordaining me as a minister because I was a single man. I recall when the church's ordination board met with me, one of the elders asked me why I was not married. Before I could respond, he added, *You know the church's belief on homosexuals.* I then told him that I had never met the right person to marry and I wanted to use my single years developing my spiritual life. I concluded that I wanted to keep myself free as Paul did in the Bible. To a certain extent, this was true, because I had not found the right person to marry. And I did indeed want to develop my spiritual life. What I didn't tell him was that I wasn't attracted to women, so I was trying to live my life the way a Catholic priest would and not marry at all. What I also didn't tell him was that even at 35, I didn't know exactly what type of ministry God would have me to do. But I knew that it was not what I was seeing them do. I didn't just want to preach, I wanted something that would center around what God had specifically called me to do, but I was lost as to exactly what that looked like.

The elders concluded my ordination meeting by informing me they would contact my pastor with their decision. About a month later, I got a call from my pastor that they had approved me for a provisional ministry license, and he had the certificate. He said he would bring it with him to service that evening. That evening when I went to church, I saw my pastor's car in his parking spot. I went to his study to get the certificate before the service started. I saw him sitting at his desk going through some mail. He then turned to a drawer at the lower part of his desk and pulled out a brown envelope. I reached for it, but he held it close to his chest and asked me to sit for a minute. I sat and saw his face change. He told me that this provisional minister license came with responsibility. He said that the reputation of the church was now placed on my shoulders, and it was my responsibility to uphold the standards and the teachings of their doctrine of the church. I agreed to do so. I held that provisional license for two years. I ministered the word of God and never brought any shame or disgrace to this denomination of churches. My ministry was well received. I had appointments to preach at other churches and was faithful to all my responsibilities of this church. I went back to the board for their final decision on my minister's license. They agreed unanimously to officially finalize my ordination. One of the elders informed me that it was Pastor Upshaw who had spoken up for me. He and my pastor were good friends. Pastor Upshaw felt he knew me because my pastor often referred to me as his right hand. Even with the occasional speculation of some in the congregation of my being gay because I was single, my pastor still thought well of me."

Mayson looked at Pastor McDaniel with amazement as he mumbled with his hand over his mouth: "That part sounds like me."

"Did you say something?" asked Pastor McDaniel.

"Not really. I just can relate to the part of being liked even when there is suspicion of being gay," said Mayson.

"Yes," said Pastor McDaniel with a smile. He was happy to see that Mayson was able to connect with some of his story so far.

"As I look back on his admiration of me, I now think it may be more about my ability to keep myself disciplined as a gay man rather than my spiritual depth. My pastor really needed me in the church because I was indispensable to lots of his programs and ministries. He didn't want to lose that.

After the official ordination meeting, Pastor Upshaw patted me on the back and told me that he was proud of my commitment. I was told that the secretary would send my ordination papers in the mail. When I left the meeting, I was not as happy about the approval of my ordination as I thought I would be. I went home and sat in my living room trying to figure out why I didn't feel happy with the decision. The one thing that stayed on my mind was the people who were turned away or left the church because of who they loved. Many of these people were good Christians whose differences was simply about who they loved.

I need to explain again, Mayson, that the church has its right to its beliefs and biblical interpretations, so my story to you is not to make the church seem full of horrible people. Because, in the midst of those that chose to leave these churches or were told to give up their positions, some were antagonistic and caused trouble before they left.

I concluded that it was not fair to the church for me to accept this license with thoughts and beliefs that contradicted their teachings. I decided that I knew that I was not much different from those that left or was asked to leave the church because they were gay. I knew that this was a side of me that I could not pretend didn't exist.

The next day, I called Pastor Upshaw and told him that I wanted to decline the license. He was surprised by my decision, because I was such a well-received minister. I explained to him all my thoughts and feelings as they related to my spiritual depth. I also disclosed my sexuality. Not because I was coming out of a closet, but because Pastor Upshaw was someone that I thought deserved to know the full story. I'm not much into the coming out of closet approach that is often touted. I don't like being bullied into such an option. As long as it does not harm anyone, I think it should be a matter of choice. I chose to tell Pastor Upshaw because he supported me in getting my license, and I knew I owed him an explanation of my decision. He sounded disappointed and began to inform me of the sins of homosexuality. I listened but didn't make any attempt to share my revelation of the Bible when it came to relationships. I respected the Bible too much to bring it down to a debate level. Pastor Upshaw then asked me whether I had consummated my homosexuality. I told him I had not. I said that I had been in a relationship with someone who I thought would be my life mate, but he couldn't deal with the finality of all that such a union would entail. That breakup crushed me, Mayson; it also cautioned me. It left me with the ability to wait for the right person and thereby see that I had the ability to abstain. Abstinence is not always easy, but it is doable. I would like to be in a relationship with the right man one day, but that day has not come. Our denomination allows for ministers to marry, but for right now, I've made the decision to live a life of abstinence.

Pastor Upshaw told me that because I was not a "practicing" homosexual I might be able to keep my license. I told him that I didn't think I could do that in good conscience. He said he understood. He asked if I wanted to meet with the board to share my reason for declining the license, or did I want him to tell the board? I told him either way would be fine with me. He decided that since he had spoken for me before, he would inform the board of my decision. He stated to me that he would not tell them about my homosexual disclosure because he felt it would cause more problems. I told him okay. I couldn't help but wonder if he didn't want to share the gay part of my explanation to the board because he didn't want to lose his own credibility. Or, maybe he was just a good man who respected my need to disclose to him. Whichever it was, he did me a favor and for that I was grateful.

As soon as I hung up from Pastor Upshaw, I called my pastor to tell him what I told Pastor Upshaw. I never returned to my own church. A few years later, I started this church, and I've been here ever since. We are a church that believes in and teaches the Bible as a whole book, not selected scriptures. My main emphasis to my congregation is not to allow other's beliefs, interpretations, opinions, arrogance or pride, to separate them from God. He does not love us *anyway,* he loves us, period! God has just as much love, direction and purpose for those who are gay as he does for those who are not. Our church is open to those who are married, not married, gay, lesbian, or straight. We also have some of the same teachings as the mainline churches including monogamy in committed relationships. For those who are not in committed relationships, I provide practical teaching and caution them on the dangers of non-monogamous sex and promiscuity. We believe in the covenant of marriage. However, because marriage between those of the same sex is not recognized as legal, we have commitment ceremonies for those wanting monogamous unions. They're just as binding as any legal documents of marriage. Sometimes, the relationships are even more lasting. They have a spiritual binding more than just a legal connection."

Mayson sat up on the couch as he rubbed his face. He was silent for a few seconds.

"Wow, Pastor McDaniel. You have shared a lot," he said.

"That is my story. You share only what is comfortable for you," said Pastor McDaniel.

Mayson looked up at the ceiling for a few seconds as though he was searching for words.

"As you may know, I am attracted to the same sex. I'm not going to say that I wish I was not because I don't. Well, let's say that I don't anymore. I've never acted upon my sexual urges, but if I did, like your church teaching, I would be monogamous. You talked about the possibility of a celibate life. If there is a possibility I could live that way, then I would like to try that. I tried being deceitful by pretending to be straight, but that caused a messy scene for the girl I was seeing...who was actually my cover at that time."

Pastor McDaniel interjected, "Yes, Mayson, we definitely counsel our members about hurting others in an effort to live a lie. And, I know that celibacy is easier said than done, but the choice is a matter about one person rather than two. Is there any specific reason you want to try celibacy?" he asked.

"I have so much to lose by living my life as a gay man. My mother would be devastated, and I don't want to hurt her. It would also give my father more of a reason to stay away from home. And when it comes to my church, the thought of having to leave because of my sexuality is so unreal. I have friends and family there. Pastor Upshaw left an open door for me, but only if I chose not to act on my sexuality," said Mayson.

"Mayson, this will be a lot of pressure for someone as young as you. It's pressure for me, and I'm a lot older," he said.

"I know, I know," said Mayson. Mayson leaned forward in his seat, with his elbows on his lap and hands clasped together under his chin. He looked down at the floor as he began to think.

"Pastor, I currently find myself attracted to a man who will not give me the time of day. I pine for him from a distance, and it hurts. Unless he makes a move or any possible sign of being gay himself, I can't approach him. I fear that this will be my life. Having feelings for guys who don't want me," said Mayson with a sheen of tears in his eyes.

"It gets even worse; I still think about this guy even though I found out that he was engaged to the girl that I was pretending to be straight with. A few days ago, I found out they got married."

The tears ran down Mayson's cheeks. "This is what finally brought me to get help. I think about him every day," he said.

"I'm sorry you are going through this. I've heard many stories like this as a pastor, so forgive me if I don't appear surprised with what you've shared with me. As I said, you are still so young. There are people and places that are still on your horizon, so don't make a quick decision about celibacy based on how you're feeling at this moment. And especially if it's with a broken heart. I know this may not be what you want to hear, but if you and this man were meant to be together, I believe it would have happened for you."

Pastor McDaniel continued in an effort to sound more cheerful. "We would love to have you here at our church, whether you are in a monogamous same-sex commitment or celibate. This is why I think Pastor Upshaw sent you to me. He's a sincere man and I believe he cares too much about you to just let you walk away from God. He wanted to make sure you would be in good hands if you left his church," said Pastor McDaniel.

"Did he call you with specifics about me?" asked Mayson.

"No, but I know your Pastor's heart," replied Pastor McDaniel.

CHAPTER 14

The Early Morning Call

(I)

At 6:30AM on Saturday, Phyllis was up and drinking coffee in the kitchen. After becoming a mother, Phyllis slowly turned into a morning person. She had come to love the stillness and anticipation of a new day. Ed had come in late last night from his usual "overtime." Idee was staying overnight at her best friend Cierra's house. Idee had always wanted a sister to do girl things with. Cierra was the best sister she could have asked for. Cierra was a follower and somewhat shy, so they somehow were a good fit.

Mayson and Lamont were still in bed. Lamont was asleep. Mayson was awake, hands behind his head on the pillow. He would sometimes get up early if he heard his mother in the kitchen. He liked spending time with her in the early mornings, but this morning was different. He had things on his mind that he was not able to talk with Phyllis about.

Mayson looked out of his window while thinking. It was another long night for him, as he had had difficulty falling asleep. It had been a week since his talk with Pastor McDaniel. He was glad to have met him and felt less alone knowing that Pastor McDaniel sympathized with his plight. However, despite the caring counsel, Mayson decided not to join his church. The thought of living his life as a Human man and a member of another church was not something he was ready to do. He had convinced himself that his situation with same-sex attraction was different from most. Mayson had thought about his family-like relationship with GCC, his love for his biological family, and the fact that he was a virgin. He was sure he could continue this normalcy. When he made this decision, he felt a burden lift from him and a freedom of sameness that put everything back in its place. He knew that he still had feelings for Melvin but

113

convinced himself that Melvin marrying Veronica was a sign that Melvin was not meant for him. And that he didn't really have to be in an intimate relationship with anyone.

As he smiled at his solution, he heard the telephone ring from downstairs.

Phyllis gave one more quick sip of her coffee as she answered the phone, hoping the loud ring would not wake anyone.

"Hello," said Phyllis, in her cheery phone voice.

"Good morning," said a man's voice on the phone.

"Good Morning, Pastor," said Phyllis, happy to hear her pastor's voice. "What has you up so early?"

"I'm at the airport, on my way to Shreveport to preach for Pastor Chauncey's anniversary service," said Pastor Upshaw.

"Oh, that's right, you did tell us you would be there this weekend. Have a wonderful trip. I'll be praying for you," said Phyllis.

"Thank you," he said.

"Did Mayson tell you that he came to see me last week?" he asked.

"No, Pastor, he didn't tell me. Is everything okay?" asked Phyllis anxiously.

"Let's just say that your son has begun to face some realities in life. I asked him to talk with you, but I guess he hasn't gotten around to it," said Pastor Upshaw.

"Can you tell me what he came to you for?" she asked, knowing the general answer to that question but hoping it would be different, since it was coming from her.

"I would like for him to tell you," said Pastor Upshaw. "He's an adult now and some things he needs to tell himself. Bear with him, Sister Phyllis. In the meantime, may I speak with him?"

"Okay," said Phyllis uncertainly. She went to the foot of the stairs and tried to call Mayson softly to avoid waking Lamont and her husband.

"Mayson."

Silence.

"Mayson."

Silence.

She then disregarded her initial effort to avoid waking the household and yelled out Mayson's name.

"Mayson!"

Silence.

She went halfway up the stairs and yelled Mayson's name again.

"Mayson!"

Ed opened their bedroom door looking half-asleep and annoyed. He scratched his head while watching Mayson's door.

"Do you have to yell this early in the morning?" griped Ed.

"Mayson has a call from Pastor Upshaw," said Phyllis.

"Mayson! Mayson! Pick up the phone," yelled Ed.

Mayson was startled at the sound of his father's loud, harsh voice. He sat straight up in his bed as he tried to figure out what was going on. He focused on his father's voice and the word "phone."

"Okay," he said as he reached for the phone on his nightstand.

Phyllis put the phone to her ear to make sure that Mayson picked up. For a moment, she thought to stay on the line, reasoning that it was her son and she needed to know what was going on. But she decided to trust that Mayson would eventually tell her about the call.

"Hello," said Mayson.

"Good Morning, Brother Mayson. Did I wake you?" asked Pastor Upshaw.

"No Sir," said Mayson as he trembled with anxiety.

Usually, when Pastor Upshaw called Mayson's house it was to speak with Phyllis about church matters. He had never called to talk to Mayson himself. Mayson was surprised to hear from him this early in the morning.

"How have you been?" asked Pastor Upshaw, in an upbeat voice.

"I'm okay," said Mayson.

Pastor Upshaw cleared his throat.

"I don't have much time because I'm at the airport, so let me get to the point," said Pastor Upshaw. "Have you given more thought to our office meeting?"

Why is he bringing this up again? wondered Mayson. Mayson felt a wave of heat come over him. He threw back his covers off his legs as he swiveled around and placed his feet on the floor. It had been a while since his office confession and his introduction of Veronica to his church family. As Pastor Upshaw had not brought the matter up again, Mayson believed himself to be clear with him. Not talking about it again was his message that things were back to the way they were for him at GCC. He thought his disclosure about his sexuality to Pastor Upshaw was no longer a concern since introducing Veronica to him, so he didn't know how to respond to Pastor Upshaw's question.

Mayson checked to see if Lamont was still asleep. Lamont was lying on his back with his mouth slightly open and his Walkman headphones over his ears. Lamont liked to listen to his self-made tapes, combinations of contemporary gospel and R&B music, as he fell asleep. Sometimes he'd take the headphones off and put the Walkman on his nightstand when he felt sleep coming on. But most nights, Lamont fell asleep with them on. Mayson usually took them from his ears whenever he left them on. However, with the added news of Melvin's marriage and his talk with Pastor McDaniel, Mayson had had a difficult time falling asleep. Therefore, Lamont's headphones were the least of his priorities.

He was fairly sure that Lamont was asleep, so he felt comfortable enough to talk with Pastor Upshaw in his bedroom. But just in case, he made sure not to go into detail.

"Yes sir, I've thought about it," he said to Pastor Upshaw.

"Have you talked to your mother about our discussion?" asked Pastor Upshaw.

"No, sir, I have not," Mayson said.

"Do you plan to talk with her about it?" asked Pastor Upshaw.

"I don't know yet, Pastor. But I did meet with Pastor McDaniel," said Mayson, as though his meeting with Pastor McDaniel would make him seem more cooperative with Pastor Upshaw's earlier counsel. "Did he tell you?"

"No, he didn't," said Pastor Upshaw. "I know you introduced me to the young lady at church some time back, and I thought that was enough for me. But I can't simply overlook what you said to me in my office. You need to deal with this, son."

With a feeling of despair, Mayson felt his shoulders slump. The thought that Pastor Upshaw saw through his charade made him sick to his stomach. Since Pastor Upshaw was not accepting his introduction of Veronica, he now wanted to shift the focus back onto his meeting with Pastor McDaniel. Mayson wanted his pastor to know that celibacy was a discussion that would allow him to remain at GCC. Even with his assumption of Lamont being asleep, he thought that having this conversation now would be too risky.

Mayson abruptly heard a loud, garbled voice through the phone. It was the airport's announcement of Pastor Upshaw's flight. Pastor Upshaw began to sound more rushed.

"I have to go to the gate soon. Since I'll be out of town, I don't want you to sing in the choir this Sunday while I am gone. If you testify in the service, I need for you to be honest about who you are as it stands with God. I need to trust you that you will honor my request while I am gone," he said.

There was a silence for a while. Mayson felt a heaviness settle in his eyes and a feeling of worthlessness when he heard the words, "I don't want you to sing in the choir." He knew what Pastor Upshaw meant by being honest about who he was as it stood with God. He knew that Pastor Upshaw was asking him to state his sins of homosexuality or at least admit that he was not who God wanted him to be.

Pastor Upshaw knew that the silence was a sign that Mayson was uneasy with his words and mandate. Pastor Upshaw had rehearsed the call in his mind before dialing. He decided to be up-front and stand his ground, but Mayson's silence began to tug at his mood. If Mayson was defiant, combative or, vindictive, then he could have held his stance firmly, without wavering. However, Mayson had always been respectful to Pastor Upshaw. Even now, he was meek, which made it a challenge for Pastor Upshaw to remain firm. Pastor Upshaw was consistent in standing for what he believed to be the right thing to do. He wanted to somehow end his call with some positive hope for Mayson. He made his voice gentler.

"Mayson, if you need my support and guidance to be free from any unwanted life choices, then you'll always have me here for you. You are an adult now and I must talk to you as an adult. Telling your mother is not something I can make you do. I just want to make sure that if I'm not the person who can help you through this, that you have someone else who is just as responsible to support you. Other than Pastor McDaniel, I can't think of any other trusted person than your mother for you to confide in."

Mayson appreciated Pastor Upshaw's confidence in his mother, but he knew that he didn't understand their boundaries when it came to his sexuality.

"I can't sweeten this for you. I love you, son, but I need you to decide for yourself what you're going to do," said Pastor Upshaw.

Mayson remained silent.

"Okay?" asked Pastor Upshaw.

"Yes, sir," said Mayson

"God bless you. Goodbye," said Pastor Upshaw.

Mayson didn't return the goodbye.

He hung up the phone and looked over at Lamont's bed again to make sure he was still asleep. He was in the same position. Mayson stood up from the bed and walked over to the chair near the television. He sat and thought about the phone call. He heard a faint knock on his bedroom door. Dread came over him as he realized it was his mother. Terror gripped him at the thought that she might have been on the other phone, listening in. He immediately reflected on the conversation he and Pastor Upshaw had. He consoled himself that they didn't say anything that would allow his mother to know the specifics of the call. Mayson stood up and slowly opened the door.

"Everything okay, hon?" asked Phyllis.

Mayson held the door partially open as though he didn't want Phyllis to enter the room. Phyllis knew that his partial head sticking out the door was not about his trying to hide the dirty clothes that he hadn't thrown into the hamper. She sensed that this sudden secrecy was about his call with Pastor Upshaw.

"Yes, everything is fine," Mayson said in an effort to try and sound upbeat.

"What did Pastor Upshaw want?" Phyllis asked.

Mayson quickly tried to come up with something that would sound reasonable. He knew his mother would know what would sound credible from Pastor Upshaw. Since he sometimes had to provide his pastor with information about the choir selections for Sundays, he decided this would be a good reason for the phone call. He knew that whatever he came up with would have to have some half-truth in it.

"He wanted to know about the choir selections," he said.

Phyllis knew that this was not the purpose of the call. She had been in Pastor Upshaw's office earlier in the week when the choir director came in with the song selections.

"Okay. I was just curious. Are you going back to bed?" she asked.

"Yeah, I think so," said Mayson.

She had hoped he would say no and come down and have coffee with her. Lately, she noticed that Mayson had been avoiding such moments with her. Phyllis decided to let the matter drop for now. In order to avoid worrying about Mayson for the rest of the day, she shortened her morning coffee time and spent the remaining portion in prayer for Mayson.

(II)

"Hello, Sister Phyllis, said Pastor Upshaw as he opened his study door to let her in. I thought I might be getting a meeting request from you soon."

Phyllis was anxious to get into the conversation about the early morning hushed phone call between him and Mayson. She took a seat on the fabric couch, which she found much more comfortable than the more expensive leather furniture.

"How was your trip?" asked Phyllis with very little interest in the answer but feeling the need to start in small conversation.

"The service was truly blessed. We had a good time and they've invited me to come back next year," said Pastor Upshaw.

In an abrupt manner, Phyllis cut off the small talk.

"Pastor, I need to know what's going on with my child," she said. Pastor Upshaw took a deep breath in an effort to get his mind on answering Phyllis' question.

"I don't blame you for being concerned, but Mayson is an adult now. I must let him choose what he wants to share with anyone outside my office," said Pastor Upshaw.

"Pastor, he may be an adult, but he is still my baby. That will never change," Phyllis said.

At that, Pastor Upshaw begin tapping his desk with his fingers as he looked down at them slowly drumming his desk.

"I hope that will change at some point," he said.

"What?" asked Phyllis.

"I hope that at some point you will allow Mayson to be more than your baby."

"Oh Pastor, that was just a figure of speech," she laughed, waving the comment away with her hand.

"No, hear me out. Words can be powerful," he said as he sat more upright, preparing himself to expound on his thoughts.

"Let me explain something to you from a male perspective. No, even better, from one parent to another," he said.

"In my men's group, I often warn the men who have sons not to allow their boys' mothers to treat their teen and adult sons like babies. I've been counseling for several years and I see the difference between parents who see their teen or grown sons as babies compared to those who don't. This is sometimes true for their girls as well, but in my experience the word "baby" is more often used with their sons than daughters. With daughters, it's sometimes the opposite. They are sometimes treated as if they were much older, with more expectations at very young ages. But as for the boys, some may be able to rise above their mother's need to keep them in a toddler state and become responsible, independent adults regardless. However, for those that don't, they lack responsibility and have difficulty in being successfully independent. And for those women who marry these "babies," they are often in my office crying because these men do not or will not put their families first. So, I'm only asking you to be mindful of how you see Mayson. He is a man, not a baby. Allow him his manhood by addressing him for what he is or should be and not what you want him to be," he said firmly.

Phyllis' face dropped as she was stunned at his remarks. Pastor Upshaw could see the offense in her face.

"What I mean Sister Phyllis, is that Mayson is growing up and he is in a position in his life where learning to make adult decisions are vital. He may be your baby, but life is going to require him to make some grown-up decisions and take on adult responsibilities. I don't mean to sound gruff with you, but I asked him to talk with you about the matter because he really needed another ear for what was going on with him. I am aware of his strained relationship with your husband, so I asked him to talk to you about the matter," said Pastor Upshaw.

Phyllis cringed at the thought of Mayson trying to talk with Ed about anything.

"Other than another pastor I know, you were the only other person

I could think of for him to talk to. I couldn't make him talk to you, but I assumed he would. I can see that my assumption that morning on the phone has made you suspicious and worried."

"I know you didn't come here for a lesson in parenting, but you work with the youth group, therefore, this can be valuable perspective to consider when you counsel our youth," he said.

Pastor's more gentle tone made Phyllis feel less defensive. She decided not to focus on Pastor Upshaw's debate of whether Mayson was a baby or man.

"I know he is hurting about something, and it's not like Mayson to avoid sharing it with me," said Phyllis.

Pastor Upshaw opened his mouth as though he was about to say something else. He then brushed his face with his hand as though he was trying to clear his thoughts. He sat back in his chair and put his hand on his desk phone.

"Where is Mayson right now?" asked Pastor Upshaw.

"When I left the house, he was eating his lunch," Phyllis replied.

"I need to get him over here," said Pastor Upshaw.

He picked up the phone and called Phyllis' home number.

Idee answered the phone.

"Hello Sister Idelle," said Pastor.

"Hello Pastor Upshaw. My mother's not here," she informed him immediately.

"I know. I'm actually calling for Mayson," he said.

"I don't think he's here either, but let me check," said Idee.

Pastor Upshaw could hear Idee's footsteps as she raced up the stairs.

"She's checking to see if Mayson is there," said Pastor Upshaw to Phyllis.

Phyllis felt herself getting a little more anxious about the matter. She wanted Pastor Upshaw to just tell her what was going on and stop all the secrecy. She fidgeted with the crease in her linen-blend pants. She kept her eyes downward. She was afraid that if she looked at Pastor Upshaw, holding the phone waiting for Idee to come back, she would lose her patience with his policy on sharing information. Pastor Upshaw has known Phyllis for a long time and could sense that she was uneasy at the long wait for an answer.

A light knock came to the door. Pastor Upshaw was annoyed as he thought it was his receptionist, who was now 15 minutes late, letting him know she had arrived.

"Come in," said Pastor Upshaw in a firm tone.

The door slowly opened. It was Mayson. There he stood, looking lean and pale. He had on faded jeans, white dress shirt, and untied white sneakers. His afro was packed tight and misshapen on one side, as though he hadn't had time to fully pick it out. In his untied sneakers and untidy hair, it looked as though he had come to the church in a hurry.

"Mayson, what are you doing here?" asked Phyllis, startled.

In a daze, Pastor Upshaw stared at Mayson while holding the phone to his ear. He then heard a rustling noise from the phone. Idee had picked the phone back up.

"It's like I said, he's not here," said Idee.

"That's okay," said Pastor Upshaw to Idee.

"You want to leave a message?" she asked.

"No thanks," said Pastor Upshaw. "Take care now, Sister Idelle." He hung up.

"Come in, Mayson. I was just trying to call you," he said.

Mayson walked in, trying not to look as worried and scared as he actually was. He took a seat next to Phyllis on the couch.

Phyllis placed her hand on top of Mayson's shoulder and in a calm voice asked him again, "What are you doing here?"

"I just had a hunch you'd be here. I knew when I didn't go to church this past Sunday, you'd be suspicious about me and my phone call from Pastor Upshaw," he said.

"You're right. And, I knew that your explanation of being sick was not the reason you didn't go to church with us," she said.

"I know my children," said Phyllis as she looked at Pastor Upshaw.

Pastor Upshaw gave a quick smile at Phyllis' statement.

"Mayson, your mother is concerned about you. I think you need to decide what you want to do about this matter," he said.

With these words, Mayson immediately looked away from Pastor Upshaw. He gave a heavy sigh.

"I was going to talk to her, but I couldn't find the right time," said Mayson.

"Your mother came to me concerned about you and I don't feel that it's my place to address her concerns," he said.

Mayson took a deep breath, looked down at his pant leg and began to pick at it as though there was lint on it. He leaned forward in his chair and turned his head to face Phyllis. Phyllis felt her heart beating fast. From the look on Mayson's face and Pastor Upshaw's urging of Mayson to come forward, she knew whatever it was, it would be life-changing. After five seconds of silence, Mayson rested his back onto the couch, as he looked at Pastor Upshaw.

"Pastor, I just don't have it in me. Please help me with this," he said.

"Okay son, in order to take this pressure off your mother, I will do this for you this time, but in the future, such matters are yours to own up to," he said.

Alright Pastor, get over the *be-a-man-Mayson* sermon and tell me what is going on, Phyllis said in her mind.

"Mayson is struggling with decisions he need to make in his life..."

He paused.

"All right, let me get to the point," he said.

"Please do," said Phyllis in a harsh tone.

"He has feelings for those of the same sex. Basically, Phyllis, Mayson believes that he is homosexual," he said.

Phyllis' slumped deeper into her seat. She felt a combination of physical exhaustion and mental relief. Exhaustion from the days of not knowing and relief now that she knew.

With a weak voice and watery eyes, she responded, "I had a feeling about this since you were eight years old, she said as she looked at Mayson. I never wanted to believe this about you, so I tucked it away. I'm not going to be specific as to what it was about you that was different, but after raising J.R., I could see that your path was different. When it seemed that you and Pastor Upshaw had some sort of secret, I didn't want to believe that it was this. We all managed not to make an issue of it for all these years and I had hoped that would continue. But it didn't, so here we are."

To Mayson, his mother's words sounded as though she was describing some sort of medical condition. He knew her words made it official that he was gay. He began to cry.

"I'm sorry," said Mayson. Phyllis put her arm around him. Pastor Upshaw decided to explain things to Phyllis.

"He came to me for help in determining how to deal with his feelings. I explained to him my responsibility as a pastor and my preaching about homosexuality. I couldn't allow him in the choir or any other leadership position in the church. Sister Phyllis, I love your family, but I have a church that I am responsible for. I cannot turn a blind eye to anyone who goes against God's word and have them representing our church. I would love for Mayson to stay at GCC as long as he wants, but until he can come to terms with himself sexually, I need for him to sit out for a while," said Pastor Upshaw.

While hearing the words come out of Pastor Upshaw's mouth, Phyllis felt conflicted. She understood her pastor's position as a church leader, but this was something that involved her own son.

"I understand, Pastor. I know our church's teaching and I would not expect you to make an exception for Mayson," she said.

Phyllis directed Mayson to sit up and look at her.

"Pastor Upshaw is correct: we cannot change the teaching of the church. So you will have to sit out for a while. This is not to punish you, but we need to take this time to figure out what all this means for you. You did the right thing in talking to someone about this, but remember, you can always come to me and talk about anything," said Phyllis.

Mayson sniffled, trying to compose himself. Pastor Upshaw handed him a tissue.

"I never asked anyone to change the church's teaching for me. I just needed someone to help me handle all this," said Mayson.

"I gave Mayson the name of Pastor McDaniel to talk with too," said Pastor Upshaw to Phyllis.

"Pastor McDaniel!" repeated Phyllis, alarmed. She knew Pastor McDaniel and was fully aware of the foundation of his Human acceptance in his church. The reality of Mayson's sexuality hit her even harder when Pastor Upshaw mentioned a referral to Pastor McDaniel. She wanted to take Pastor Upshaw's advice to heart and not baby Mayson. He had to make his own decision, she thought.

"What are you going to do, Mayson?" asked Phyllis.

Mayson sat continuing to look down at his feet and feeling as though Pastor Upshaw and his mother were looking straight through him.

"I don't know," he said.

CHAPTER 15

Late-Night Acknowledgment

(I)

"Hi Mayson. It's 1:30 in the morning. Is everything okay? I've never gotten a call this late from you." said Reanna.

"I don't know, Reanna. I don't know if anything will ever be all right again," he said.

Reanna sat up in her bed when she heard the sadness in Mayson's voice.

"What's going on?" she asked.

"Reanna, I don't have a church to go to anymore."

"What are you talking about?" asked Reanna.

"In a roundabout way, Pastor Upshaw wants me to leave his church."

"What!" said Reanna incredulously. "Why? What happened?"

"He didn't really ask me to leave, but he put it such a way that I didn't have much of a choice. He actually called and told me not to sing in the choir or testify in worship service unless I told the truth about myself or make a change."

Reanna had an idea where this was going. There was a long silence.

"Hello?" she said finally.

"Yes, I'm here," he said.

"What truth, Mayson?"

Mayson felt that it was one thing for his mother and Pastor Upshaw to know about his secret, but once he told Reanna it would be like telling the entire church. He loved her dearly, but love was not enough for news this big, he thought. But why should I care, it's going to get out anyway.

"Reanna for years you've made comments about my sexuality," he said.

"Yes," said Reanna, as she swung her legs out of bed and rested them on the floor in anticipation of the news. She had been waiting for years to hear from Mayson himself about his attraction to men. They were the best of friends, but this part of him that he held to so tightly, formed a wall that made their connection not quite complete. She had been suspicious about Mayson's sexuality since early in their friendship. His eagerness to hear about her sexual exploits and his quiet interest when she described her boyfriends' physiques were signs. He never talked about girls in a romantic sense. Nor had she ever seen him looking at them in that special way that some guys do.

Mayson proceeded to pour out his heart to Reanna: his attraction to men rather than women; the love he felt for Melvin Sutton; using Veronica to evade suspicion; and his meeting a few days ago with Pastor Upshaw and his mother.

"Wow," exclaimed Reanna." Of course, you knew that I knew. I guess I shouldn't have been so playful about it," she said.

Reanna was relieved that Mayson had finally shared this news with her. It made her feel even closer to him.

"From what you said, it seems that Pastor Upshaw gave you a choice. I mean, a choice that would allow you to stay actively at GCC," said Reanna.

"Oh yeah, he gave me a choice. Getting up and telling everyone that I'm gay and can't sing in the choir until I am no longer gay," said Mayson sarcastically. "That's not going to happen."

"Does your father know?" she asked.

"No. My mother said she wants to leave him out of the loop as long as possible. She's concerned about his reaction," he said.

"What about Lamont and Idee?"she asked.

"She doesn't want them to know either. At least, not now," he said.

"Mayson, they're bound to find out. The fact that you won't be singing in the choir, maybe not even going to GCC at all...they'll know something's up," she said.

"My mother and I are more concerned about Idee than Lamont. Idee has a big mouth and we know that this family secret will be out no sooner than it hits Idee's ears, he said with a quick pause...". He then forced a chuckle. "Kinda like you, Reanna."

"I would like to be offended at that remark, but I won't be," she said and paused. "So, you thought I would tell? I do tend to share my mind, so

UNNECESSARY ENEMIES

I get it how you would have thought that. But you have to understand that you're different. I've never had a friend, especially not a male friend, that I've been this close to. You're special. You know I'm here for you," she said.

"I know you care about me, but you know in addition to your unfiltered words, the snide remarks about my sexuality didn't help much with whether or not I could tell you," he said.

"I'm so sorry. I've always wanted you to share this side of you with me, but I never dreamed it would turn out like this," she said.

"Thank you. If I should have told anybody, it should have been you," he said.

There was a long silence.

"I do have something I want you to do for me," said Mayson.

"Sure. What?" she asked.

"I want to start going out with you. I want to go to the clubs and other places that you go to and meet people," he said.

"Well, I don't know about taking you to clubs. The ones that I go to, you have to be at least twenty-one years old. My ID is fake and that means I'd have to get a fake ID for you too. That takes a lot of work and risk," said Reanna.

"I'll be 21 soon, so just get me one," pleaded Mayson. "Pastor Upshaw said I should make a decision and I decided to go for it. I've spent too much of my life scared and brainwashed at that church," he said.

"Come on, do you really think we're being brainwashed?" asked Reanna, alarmed.

"Well, maybe not brainwashed, but this either-or choice he gave me just doesn't make me feel like an individual. More like a, *be like everyone else or else,*" Mayson said.

"I'd never thought Pastor Upshaw would be like this with you," she said.

"This all began snowballing with me and this thing with Melvin. Love or a crush, I don't know, but it changed me. His presence seemed to clear the room whenever I saw him. I had never felt that for anyone. Like everyone else, I want to be loved. I know now I can't get this from Melvin, I was living in a fantasy world, but I want it somewhere out there," he said.

"I figured you found Melvin interesting, but not to this extent. A few times when he was around, I saw how you'd stared at him, but that's all

127

that I thought it was. Who doesn't stare at Melvin Sutton! But, when you and Veronica started hanging out, I knew you were up to something. I didn't connect it with Melvin, but I knew something was going on with you," said Reanna.

"Well, I needed Veronica to help divert attention away from me. Who'd have thought she'd end up marrying Melvin? I didn't think she liked him. Our big fight was over her negative words about Melvin. And then she goes and marries him. If I thought it was that easy, I would have started criticizing him and putting him down a long time ago. Maybe then we would've started dating, if that was what it took," said Mayson as he and Reanna laughed.

"You're crazy," said Reanna.

Mayson was quiet for a few seconds. Then he continued, "Yeah, that marriage struck me in the heart. I was so down. That's what led me to go and see Pastor McDaniel."

"Oh, oh, oh!" said Reanna with excitement. "I knew there was something I meant to tell you last week. I have news for you. A few weeks back, I saw Melvin's goon friend Eric at a friend's party. He was trying to hit on me, of course. Anyway, when I heard Melvin had married Veronica, I was suspicious from day one. Eric got so drunk at the party; he answered any question I asked him. Long story short, Melvin married Veronica because she's pregnant," said Reanna.

"Pregnant!" repeated Mayson in dismay. "This is too much," he said as his mind began to retrace his dates and times with Veronica.

"Let me figure this out. The only argument I had with Veronica was due to negative remarks she made to me about Melvin. Then, a few weeks later they get married and she's pregnant. This means she was pregnant when I was seeing her. Wow!" said Mayson.

"Ms. Pushy gets around more than I do," said Reanna with a laugh.

There was another silence.

"I still have feelings for him, Reanna," said Mayson as the reality of the marriage and his fantasies of being with Melvin became even more of a hopeless dream.

(II)

"You look good, boy!" said Reanna.

"I have to admit, I'm a little scared about tonight," said Mayson.

"Well, you told me you wanted to hang out with me, and you know parties and clubs are what I do. Besides, you'll be twenty-one soon, so you're just getting a head start. So, here we are. Good times at the Jasmine Club!" exclaimed Reanna.

Reanna sat at the bar with Mayson wearing her pink A-line, strapless, to-the-knee dress. It was a bit much for such a small club, but on days when she was not feeling the best about herself, she tended to overdress. She sipped her strawberry daiquiri as she looked around the room. Mayson was nursing a glass of Cola. He had never liked the taste of alcohol. He tried it a few times when his father would leave alcohol in their refrigerator. Reanna had reassured Mayson he didn't have to drink to hang out with her. She was concerned about Mayson's sudden departure from church and emergence into the nightlife with her. She didn't want him to move too fast.

Mayson watched his church friend, who seemed so grown up at that moment. He wondered whether they would be friends if they had not met as children. Reanna liked him whether he was in or out of the church. She liked him when he didn't confirm being Human, and she continued to like him when he confessed it.

Earlier that day, he and Reanna had been out shopping as she helped him prepare for this night out. It seemed to take forever to find just the right outfit for Mayson. He was particular about what he wanted, as though he was picking out something that would define his entire future. He finally chose a collared lavender shirt with a loose-fitting necktie, black jeans and dark brown slip-on loafers. He had braided his hair in large braids the night before so that it would be loose and fluffed the next day. He was excited about this change in his life. He made the decision to live his life on the other side without a lot of rules. He was nervous about this change, as the moral rules of the church periodically battled within him. He knew that he could no longer go back to GCC and simply sit. He was inspired by his meeting with Pastor McDaniel and considered him a good man. But Pastor McDaniel's church was not GCC. GCC was his family and he could not see himself at any other church.

While continuing to look at his grown-up, sophisticated friend, his mind wondered as to how Reanna, who has set under the same church teaching, could balance her two lifestyles. How does she void herself of guilt? He felt the battle of fear and guilt of his new life with every changing step.

"How do you get to do all this and remain in the choir at church?" he asked her.

Reanna laughed out loud as she held her drink, sitting on the high stool, left leg crossed over her right leg as she bounced it up and down.

"Mayson, the reason I'm still in the choir is that everyone knows I'm attracted to the opposite sex. That works to my advantage. For many people in the church, my messing around is a lesser sin than being gay. Besides, I think Pastor Upshaw wanted people to think that we were a couple. This made it so much easier for him to not confront your sexuality or mine," she said.

Reanna had come to terms at a young age that she was excessively attracted to boys and later men. She had started taking birth control pills at the age of 15 after a pregnancy that ended in a miscarriage. Her mother was devastated by her lifestyle, but the pregnancy mishap brought her to a point to see her child as she was.

"Are you sure this is a gay bar?" asked Mayson.

"Yes, Mayson. It's not a place I frequent often, but the bartender at the club I go to regularly recommend this place when I asked him about the best gay bars."

"It seems like a mix of men and women to me," said Mayson.

"Mayson," said Reanna as she looked at him with amusement. "Those aren't women. They're men in drag."

"Oh, God," said Mayson with his hand over his mouth in an effort to compose himself. "Maybe I need to take it a little slower than this."

That first night, Mayson was not approached by anyone, nor did he have the boldness to initiate contact with anyone. Reanna took Mayson to more and more parties and clubs, in and outside of Benton. Eventually, he began to go to these places on his own.

CHAPTER 16

Activism

(I)

"Hey, you look pretty young to be here," said Craig, who had been eyeing Mayson from across the room.

Mayson, sitting at a table with a soft drink, was startled. He had thought this young white man worked at this club. He was worried that someone would be able to tell his ID was fake. But he was only a few months away from twenty-one. I shouldn't look too much younger than twenty-one, he thought.

"I have ID," said Mayson nervously as he reached in his back pocket.

"Keep your ID," said Craig with a hearty laugh. "I don't work here. I was just complimenting you on your youthful appearance. My name is Craig Jameson," he said.

"Hi, Craig. I'm Mayson Hendricks." They shook hands.

"I saw you about 3 weeks ago at Skylark Supermarket. I was several people behind you in the checkout line. I remember your sandy-colored hair and height," he said.

"I don't shop at Skylark," said Mayson.

"Well, if that wasn't you, you have a twin somewhere out there," he said.

Craig was 5'5" and thirty-three years old but looked much younger. He had long, reddish hair that extended to his shoulder blades. He looked like a throwback from the 60s in his black hard-rim glasses, plaid button-down shirt, and jeans.

"I'm a regular here at this club. I know I saw you here about two weeks ago sitting at that same table," said Craig.

"Now, that was most likely me," said Mayson.

131

"You have this new look about you," said Craig.

Mayson wanted to appear grown-up and as sophisticated as Reanna was that first night they went out.

"I'm not too new. It's been a while and I've been to a lot of clubs in and outside of town," said Mayson.

"It's been a while," repeated Craig with a low chuckle. "You must have been in the closet before doing the clubs?"

"Closet?" repeated Mayson.

"That's our way of expressing how some of us resort to living our lives in a shell as Humans in order to keep who we are a secret," said Craig.

"I guess I still have a lot to learn," said Mayson.

"I'm with a Human activist group called "New Times." We meet every month to address issues affecting the Human community. We also offer support and understanding to those living a Human life. I've been involved with them for 8 years. We've rallied and challenged discrimination and other unfair practices against those that are Humans. The group is local and was started by Aaron Locke. He's great. He started the group eleven years ago after losing his life partner, Ben, to suicide," said Craig. He was about to share the details of Ben's life, but he didn't want to overwhelm Mayson.

"Sorry. I don't want to talk your head off with so much information, so fast. I just really believe in what we do and get too eager at times to share it with others," said Craig.

"It's okay," said Mayson. "Go ahead, tell me what happened with Ben," said Mayson, who wanted to learn more about life outside the church and become as street-smart as Reanna. And anyway, he wasn't doing well in meeting anyone special in his new club life, so Craig would help fill his time.

"Okay," said Craig with a smile. He eagerly pulled out a chair from Mayson's table and sat down.

"When Aaron and Ben met, Ben was working as an accountant and Aaron was a freelance writer. Aaron did most of his work from home, so he didn't have to deal with the daily interactions of co-workers. Ben, on the other hand, worked in an office. He told Aaron that gossip was rampant at his job. His first week consisted of his co-workers digging for personal information. "Do you have children?" was the most asked question. "Are you married?" was second. These clowns seem to believe that they could really tell a lot about a person from these questions. So, from that first week of "ask and judge" question-fest, they concluded that Ben was a nice guy, but Human. From that day forward, they made jokes and innuendoes about his possible sexuality.

One day Ben came home from work early, showered and went straight to bed. He later confided in Aaron that on that day, after coming back from lunch, he had a question for his manager, but the guy wasn't there. He asked one of his male co-workers, who was in the copy room, if he knew where their manager was. Rather than answer his question, the co-worker put his ring finger in Ben's face to show him that he was married, like he thought Ben was coming on to him. It was that job and some family issues that drove him into a deep depression. Ben left a suicide note on their dresser that addressed his difficulty in living as a Human in a straight world.

After 8 months of grieving, Aaron started New Times.

Among other things, Aaron is also trying to bring about workplace policies that prohibited employees from asking co-workers about personal matters such as family or marital status. Particularly if the person who is being asked the question has not initiated or agreed to such questions. Sometimes it's their way of trying to glean someone's sexual present or past. These questions not only give people info about someone's possible sexuality, but the kids question can be painful for people who can't have children, or who had a miscarriage, or a child who died. There's a lot more to it, but that's the gist."

Mayson's head was spinning. Suicide was not something he had factored in as a possibility of being Human. He wanted to ask Craig if it was common for people to kill themselves because they were Human, but chose not to, as he wanted to keep that moment to be about Aaron and Ben.

"Wow, that must have been rough for both of them," said Mayson.

"Yeah, it was. This is why I asked you the closet question. I could tell you were new to a lot of this, and I wanted you to know that you can be who you are without closing yourself off. No one should deny themselves because of other people's bigotry. I wouldn't want you or anyone who is Human to end up like Ben," said Craig.

Mayson thought about what Craig said earlier to him about providing too much information too fast. He had barely had enough time to really figure out who he was as a Human, so joining a group and exposing himself even more to the outside world was not something he was ready for.

"Thank you, Craig. That was nice of you, but I don't think I would fit into a group right now. I'm really not ready. I feel a connection to some of what you said, but there are some differences that I don't think can be understood by your group. Especially some racial and religious differences," said Mayson.

"Being different and the right to have our differences is what we are about..." He stopped. "Maybe I'm not presenting this to you in the best way," said Craig as he looked at his watch. "This club provides us a room for our meetings, and we're about to have one tonight. Aaron should be here shortly. I think he can explain to you better about New Times than I can," said Craig apologetically.

"It's okay. I think you did a great job telling me about New Times. I just know that my differences go even beyond New Times's understanding of my being gay reality," said Mayson.

"Like what?" asked Craig.

"Well..." Mayson began to think.

"Wait, here comes Aaron now," said Craig.

Craig walked toward a middle-aged white man, who was just entering the front door of the club. Aaron had a trimmed beard and was wearing cycling shorts and a jersey with the Benton-Hawk University logo. He had a reddish tan, as though he had been out in the sun for a while. His salt-and-pepper hair was curly. As Craig was talking with Aaron from a distance at the door, Mayson could see Aaron glance over at him. After a few seconds they both walked toward Mayson. Mayson felt uneasy. He wanted to leave, but Craig seemed so nice that he didn't want him to feel bad.

"Hi Mayson, I'm Aaron Locke."

"Nice to meet you," said Mayson.

"I understand that Craig has told you a little about New Times," said Aaron.

"Yes, he did," said Mayson.

"We'd love to have you at New Times. Any time you feel you want to talk, call me."

He handed Mayson his card and gave him a warm smile. Mayson took the card and thanked Aaron.

"Okay Craig, let's get to our meeting," said Aaron.

"Okay," said Craig looking at Aaron, wondering why he didn't talk more with Mayson.

"Take care, Mayson," said Craig as he and Aaron walked toward the meeting room down the hall.

"You didn't have much to say to him," said Craig to Aaron.

"I didn't think I could have told him any more than what you already said. He told you he wasn't ready, and we can't make people ready. We've got to respect that. Let him have his time. He has my card. If he needs our support, he'll call," said Aaron.

Aaron had Mayson on his mind throughout their meeting. He battled with the religious and racial concerns that Mayson had with joining the group. He understood that some who voiced cultural concerns had their own means of connecting with each other and the world. Yet, Aaron specifically wondered if he had done enough to address the religious side for the people of faith who joined New Times. Everyone seemed to be okay with their spirituality and it had not cause problems for anyone who was different in that regard. Aaron decided to end the meeting early and see if Mayson was still at his table. He decided he needed to talk with him a little more.

(II)

As Aaron was about to leave the meeting, he saw Louis Johnson. Louis was the leader of Aaron's New Times/African American Approach (AAA) group. New Times/AAA group believed in much of what Aaron's New Times group believed, but they were more discreet and more sympathetic to the parents of Human individuals. They did not feel that their parents were obligated to accept their sexuality, as they felt, within reason, their parents should maintain their religious beliefs. They believe that if their family needed to change what they believed about being gay, God would direct them in that manner, and it was up to them to choose. Most African American attendees who chose to participate in New Times/AAA were able to address areas of being Human on their cultural understanding and addressing it in a more "live and let live" manner. Acceptance and unconditional love were something the initial New Times organization saw as a key to family stability. AAA agreed, but not to the extent that people, particularly parents, would be condemned or seen as not loving their gay children.

It was Louis who had brought it to Aaron's attention the differences that some African American members experience from being Human. Aaron didn't want to hear this at first, as he wanted to believe that the need for gaining acceptance did not need individualized race-based approaches. As time went on, Aaron opened up New Times/African American Approach and positioned Louis as the group leader. It was for the African Americans, and anyone else, who connected with such religious perspective. Louis did not expect all African Americans in New Times to be in the group, but a large percentage did join. New Times/AAA met on a different night, but they would all come together for the monthly meetings at the club.

When Aaron saw Louis talking with Craig across the room, he decided he wanted Louis' help in talking with Mayson.

Louis was a PhD candidate working on his degree in African American studies. He had a recognizable laugh, which sounded like he was trying to catch his breath. He was of medium build, with a noticeable skin problem from shaving that caused bumps within his beard. He was not much into clothes; it seemed as though he was wearing the same shirts each time you'd see him. He was one of Aaron's most faithful attendees and had been with the group for 5 years.

"Excuse me," said Aaron to Craig as he placed his hand on Craig's shoulder, anticipating his interruption of their conversation. "Let me give a quick word to Louis," said Aaron.

"Sure," said Craig.

"Hey Aaron, how's it going?" asked Louis.

"Good," said Aaron, as he shook his hand. "When you leave here, will you look for me out in the club area? I need to introduce you to someone that could use your help."

"Sure thing, Aaron. I just need to finish up here with Craig and I'll be right out," said Louis.

"Thanks!" said Aaron.

Aaron went to the area where he had met Mayson but saw that his chair was now empty. He looked around the club in hopes that Mayson may have moved to another seat, but didn't see him. He turned to go back to the meeting area to tell Louis he did not need his assistance and to say goodbye to the stragglers that still may be in the meeting room. As he turned, he felt a blunt jolt to the side of his body. It was Mayson. He had just come out of the restroom.

"Oh, there you are," said Aaron with enthusiasm.

"You're looking for me?" asked Mayson inquisitively.

"Do you have time for us to talk a few minutes?" asked Aaron.

Mayson thought about saying no, as he was sure that Aaron was going to try and talk him into joining New Times. But he found himself saying, "Sure, I have some time."

"Let's find another table," said Aaron.

Despite all the music and people mingling around in the club, Aaron managed to find a quiet table near the back.

"Let's go over there," he said. He cleared some leftover glasses onto an empty table nearby. He crossed his arms and looked at Mayson, who was sitting rather cramped against the wall.

"Craig told me that you have some cultural differences when it comes to the Human lifestyle. As a Human activist, I'd like to hear more about that. It would help me a lot to hear your side. It could help me with others that may feel the same way," said Aaron.

Mayson thought for a while, looking up toward the ceiling in an effort to find the right words. Discussing his Human side was new for him. He felt a tinge of condemnation as he heard those words describing him. He yet battled with the urge to recant his confession to Pastor Upshaw, and chalk all this up to a confused, lost period of his life. But as he looked at Aaron, just for a moment, he saw a glimpse of life on the other side. He had felt this a little with Pastor McDaniel, but with Pastor McDaniel, his connection was also mixed with his feelings about leaving GCC.

As Mayson began to think more about this other way of living, he became aware that he was developing a sense of his new or deeper self. He no longer felt isolated. He realized that his world could include not just his family and GCC, but people such as Aaron and Craig. He felt himself developing a sense of boundaries or selective merging from a buffet of mandates:

137

Come out of the closet
You must marry a woman
You will need to be celibate
Live your life on both sides

There was no one answer for him. He never had such thoughts and opinions about social matters when it came to his own self. Mayson began to realize that his being Human was not as personal as he thought it was. People would not allow him to just be Mayson – whoever that was. Rather, everyone wanted him to pick a side. His side was to be himself and love people.

"I think you all are a worthwhile cause, but I have areas of my life that you all can't relate to," said Mayson, hoping Aaron would leave the matter at that. He was not in the mood to share or explore this area of his life for what he felt was Aaron's need to make him a political and societal matter.

Aaron looked around for his friend Louis. He didn't see him. He realized that he needed to stall for time.

"Try me. I believe that I know what you're trying to say, but I need you to say it to be sure, said Aaron. What is it that New Times cannot relate to?" asked Aaron.

"I don't really know how to explain it to you," said Mayson. He thought for a moment.

"Okay, it's a fact that I am a black man with deep connections to my family and the church. I am aware of the bad blood between Human groups and Christians. So, what you may advise to your group on how to deal with Human situations may not work for me because of my race and religious background. I know my family and church will not accept my attraction to men. I've already lost my church, but I don't want to lose my family. Having a group of supporters who are Humans will not be enough for me," said Mayson.

Aaron never had any one to put the matter precisely the way Mayson had, but he heard similar concerns before. He was sure that if Mayson would be more open-minded, New Times could be the help he needed. Aaron was surprised at himself for taking so much time with Mayson. His usual approach to helping others was to let them know about New Times and provide contact information if they needed help. He would leave it up to the individual to contact them if they wanted their support. But here he was, encouraging Mayson to take advantage of their acceptance and help. For some reason, Mayson was different. He felt that he already knew Mayson. Or at least, he knew what Mayson did not know when it came to living life as a gay man among those who defy such an existence.

"Mayson, we have people from diverse cultures in our group. And we do get it: everybody is not the same. But what we all have in common is that none of us want to close off who we are sexually, because our sexuality is a part of who we are. No one wants to go through life as a partial person, only showing sides of themselves that others accept. As an African American, Caucasian, Latino, Asian, whoever, you have the right to walk down the street with the one you love holding hands, kissing goodbye, or just putting your arms around them to say "I love you." These are the things that any adult couple should be able to do."

As Aaron took a deep breath, he saw Louis coming out of the meeting room and looking around the club.

"Mayson, I have someone I want you to meet. Will you excuse me for a minute?" he asked.

"Um, okay," said Mayson reluctantly.

Aaron walked a few feet away from their table and waved Louis over to him. Louis saw his wave and hurried over to him.

"Mayson, I like for you to meet Louis Johnson. Louis this is Mayson... sorry, Mayson, I didn't get your last name," said Aaron.

"Hendricks," said Mayson.

"Hey Mayson," said Louis as they shook hands.

"Louis is one of the leaders of New Times. He runs our African American Approach group that addresses some cultural differences in approaching matters of being Human," said Aaron.

"Oh, okay," said Mayson as he nodded his head.

"You mind if I share with Louis what we've been discussing?" asked Aaron.

Mayson preferred that he didn't, but he didn't want to come right out and say *no*. "Go ahead," he said.

"I just met Mayson through Craig. Mayson is new to this side of his life. He is trying to find himself as a Human man. Particularly as a Human black man. Remember, Louis, when you and I first met, how you shared with me the different experience that some African Americans have with being Human? Well, Mayson has shared the same observation. He has a particular concern about family and church when it comes to being Human. Think you can share with him your experience and thoughts about you as a Human black man?"

"It will be my pleasure," said Louis.

Louis took a seat at their table and faced Mayson.

"First of all, Mayson, because you are a black man, I am not going to assume that your life is like mine. I just want to share my experiences and thoughts and hope you can see yourself somewhere in the middle," said Louis.

Louis took a deep breath as though he was about to run a marathon.

"Let me start with the, *to tell others or not to tell*, decision. I decided to let people know about my sexuality 6 years ago. For me, it was not that difficult, because some people knew already. So I only shared it with people who I felt needed to know. As time went on, I was not overly concerned with whether I told people or if they found out on their own. Since I started actually dating guys, I haven't found it necessary to get the approval others for my relationships. As long as I approve of them, then I'm good. Also my sexuality does not define who I am. It's just one part of who I am. But I do applaud those who see the need to take a stand and make changes that are right for them and many others.

My African American upbringing teaches us to respect my elders. This is not to say that other cultures don't teach this, but I think we go about it in a different way. Therefore, I don't expect my parents to throw away their faith in order to make an exception for me. A large part of who you are is what you believe. To ask or mandate that a person reject what they believe for you is asking them to deny a part of themselves. And to say that a parent does not love their child because they won't embrace who they chose for a partner is unfair. As long as a person does not directly violate me or my rights, I have no desire for them to change their religion, morals, or values to validate my life.

As with New Times, I am honest when it comes to who we are and what we share with people. We don't manipulate data or statistics for the sake of promoting our cause. This is not necessary because the true facts speak for themselves. We are balanced in our approach. We like to put things in proper perspective. For example, for children who are Human, particularly teens, sometimes assumptions are made that if they are living on the streets it must be due to their parents' refusal to accept them as a Human. But it can't always be concluded that it was due to their being Human. Some Human children, as with straight teens, may choose to leave their homes due to general defiant teen behavior or unsafe living conditions. Of course, I don't believe in putting any child out on the street. But understanding that there may be more reasons for conflict than the child's sexuality is important. Has New Times ever had children to come to them because they were put out of their home for being gay or lesbian? You bet we have. And the parents had no shame in confirming it, so we know it is a reality. And New Times is here to help. But we must not generalize or assume.

With all that, let me share a little more about my personal background.

I grew up under Pentecostal parents who embraced the teachings that homosexuality was a sin. When I was 12, I recognized that I was Human when I fell hard for a boy in my class. I never told my parents about my feelings, but I never had a girlfriend. My father asked me when I was 15 if I was a *punk*. I knew what he meant, and I said *no*. This may sound strange, but I respected my parents too much to tell them the truth. Three months later, my mother asked me if I was Human. Between when my father and my mother asked me the same question, my thoughts had changed due to a boy I was seeing. My mother was deeply religious and submissive to my father, but she was easier to talk to. I told her that I was Human. She cried and left the room. She told my father and he made me go to church three times a week for four months.

At 16, I still loved and respected my parents, so I would never yell at them or argue with them. But I didn't follow all the house rules. I would stay out past my curfew and bring friends into the home while they were at work. This included the guy I was seeing at that time and another friend who liked smoking weed. My sister told my father and he laid the law down that if I could not respect his house then I needed to get my own house. Despite that talk, the next week he found me, my friends and boyfriend, back in our home. My weed-head friend was smoking on our patio when my father caught us. He told me to pack my clothes and leave. Now, did he ask me to leave because I was Human or because I disrespected our home by doing what he told me not to do? Listen to this, Mayson, he said as he scooted his chair up closer to the table. I didn't want to take responsibility for my actions, so I decided that he put me out because I was Human."

Before he could continue, Mayson interrupted.

"I get that. But you were still a minor at 16 which meant that you were his responsibility, so Human or not, he didn't live up to his responsibility as a parent in keeping you in a safe home," said Mayson.

"You're right. He did have that responsibility. The way I see it, he may have been wrong to ask his minor son to leave, but I might as well be honest about my side of it. I got to own up to what actually led to his poor judgment. The house rules were: a curfew, no friends in the house while my parents were at work, and no drugs in the home. I disregarded all three rules. I would be lying to say that he put me out only because I am Human. But he could have sent me to stay with relatives; he could have monitored my restrictions better; and above all, he could have taken time to talk to me and find out why I was being so defiant. I left and went to stay with a friend until I was 18. For some reason, I was not defiant with his parents. I guess I was grateful they let me into their home and scared at the thought of being on the street.

Now that I am a man, who I love now is no longer my parents' responsibility. They did what they thought was right. I don't need anyone to approve of who I love. If I truly love another of my sex and my parents accept the relationship, then that's good. If they don't accept the relationship, it doesn't make my relationship less valid, nor does it mean they're bad people or they don't love me. I love my parents too much to put them through such guilt and condemnation because of my choices. They have a right to live within their religious dedication. My partner and I are men of faith and no one can take that away from us because of their own beliefs."

Human men of faith, thought Mayson. He was not for sure what faith Louis was referring to, but this reminded him of Pastor McDaniel's counsel on living as Human Christians. He thought how much better it could be if some day they could just be Christians without any other labels attached.

Louis looked at Mayson and sat back in his chair, as if to say he was finished.

"I should have told you that Louis is a talker. He's a good talker though, which is why he's the leader for our New Times/AAA group," said Aaron.

Louis' words inspired Mayson. He could indeed connect with some of what Louis said. Yet, the thought of joining a Human group made everything so final for Mayson. And living life with labels attached to his Christian identity was not who he was. He only wanted to be a Christian—period!

"That was inspiring, but I still need some time to think all this over," said Mayson.

Louis and Aaron looked at each other, a bit bewildered.

"I take a long trip in what I say, but know that I understand, my friend," said Louis.

"Sure Mayson. You take your time. We only want what's best for you. As I said earlier, if you need us, give me a call," said Aaron.

CHAPTER 17

In Walks a Byron

Be sober, be vigilant; because your adversary the devil, as a roaring lion, walketh about, seeking whom he may devour... Peter 5:8

"Nice car," said a voice from behind Mayson as he was putting gas into Tony's BMW. Mayson continued putting the gas in but stopped to looked around in the direction of the voice. There stood an average built, well-dressed man of light brown complexion somewhere in his 40s, in a maroon suit and a close-cropped afro.

"Thanks!" said Mayson with a quick smile.

Mayson often got attention when he drove Tony's Bimmer. He had had a toothache for the past few days and gotten an emergency dental appointment scheduled for first thing that morning. Mayson had no medical insurance, but Tony gave him his credit card to pay for it. He had dropped Tony off at work and decided to get gas before going to his appointment.

Mayson continued to put the gas into the car as he thought how good it was that he had met Tony. He knew how different his life would have been if he had left his family's house with no place to go. He admitted to himself that it was disrespectful of him to do what he did with Tony while in his mother's home. He could not figure out how he let it get that far. While still lost in thought, he could see someone standing near the car out of the corner of his eye. He turned his head and saw the same maroon-suited man, standing alongside him. The man stood there with his hands in his slacks' pockets and his suit jacket tucked behind his arms as though he was posing for a magazine.

"What year is this?" asked the man.

"It's an '81," said Mayson.

"I thought so," said the man as he began to walk around the car and peer into its windows.

"I used to own a similar car but decided to try something different this year. I have my Lexus," he said as he pointed to his well-shined bronze colored car.

"Oh," said Mayson, not knowing much to add to the conversation.

"I had a black BMW like yours, but keeping black cars polished was a bit much," said the man. "How long have you had your BMW?" the man asked.

"It's not mine. It belongs to a friend of mine," responded Mayson.

"I guess that explains why you went to the wrong side of the car to put the gas in when you got out," said the man, with a look of amusement.

Mayson laughed with embarrassment.

"I'm sure you could afford one of these babies yourself. You seem like an intelligent man who could get what he wants," said the man.

Mayson smiled as he continued pumping gas into the car.

"I'm currently between jobs, so I can't afford much of anything right now," said Mayson knowing that he and Tony never discussed Mayson's need for a job.

Mayson had thought about getting a job because he recalled his mother telling Idee that whenever she got married, she needed to make sure that she always had her own money in case the marriage didn't work out. So Mayson had decided he would get a job eventually, but in the meantime, it felt great enjoying each day, relaxing in Tony's condo, watching television, going to the park or the movies, listening to his favorite gospel tapes, reading, and other activities that came with being a man of leisure. But he never wanted to take advantage of Tony's kindness and he was not one to spend the rest of his life sitting around doing nothing. Mayson had decided that when Tony's work schedule changed to an average 40 hours per week, he would then get a job. In the meantime, he saw so little of Tony that if he started a job now, they would see even less of each other. As Mayson replaced the gas nozzle, he hurried back to his car, hoping to end the conversation with the man. As he adjusted his rearview mirror before driving off, he saw the man walking around the car towards his driver's side.

Oh, no. What now, Mayson thought.

The man approached the driver's side and leaned into Mayson's open car window.

"You say you're between jobs?" asked the man.

"Yes," said Mayson.

"You don't say," said the man in an observational manner. He attempted to size up Mayson as he preceded with questions.

"What kind of job are you looking for?" asked the man.

"I'm not sure," said Mayson, who was now running late for his appointment.

"Do you have a college degree?" asked the man.

"Only a high-school diploma," said Mayson.

"I see, he said. I currently have a job opening. I have a distribution company and I'm looking for someone to manage one of my offices," he said.

Mayson became excited at the words *company, manage* and *office.* He thought how prestigious these words sounded and imagined himself in an actual office and managing other people. He only had a high school diploma, which would make the job even more impressive to his family and Tony. Because of Mayson's limited experience in the world of work, he never thought to ask the man about the type of distribution company. The man leaned a little further into Mayson's window with his arm resting on the car door, as he looked Mayson eye to eye.

"You interested?" he asked.

Mayson then saw this man differently. He was no longer a strange guy creeping around his car. Mayson saw an employer who would be his answer to making his own money and proving to his family and GCC that he can do well without any of them.

"Sure, I'm interested," said Mayson with eagerness in his voice.

"What's your name?" he asked.

"Mayson Hendricks," he said.

"Byron Crawford," he said as he put his hand through the car window for Mayson to shake.

"Okay. Can you come to my office at 3548 Palm Avenue at 8:30 tomorrow evening?"

He handed Mayson his business card.

Mayson thought it odd to hold a job interview in the late evening, but he feared he'd turn Byron off if he asked him why the appointment was in the late evening.

"Sure, not a problem," said Mayson.

"It's fortunate that we happened to be getting gas at the same time. This is a lucky day for both of us," said Byron as he stepped away from the car. "I'll see you tomorrow."

"Okay," said Mayson.

Mayson wondered how he would get to this appointment. Tony was out of town for his job and he was not sure what his work schedule would look like whenever he got back. He didn't know if he'd have access to the BMW for his interview. Mayson pushed the car dilemma aside and assured himself that he would get to the interview somehow. He was excited about the upcoming job interview. He visualized all the changes in his life as a result of getting such a prestigious job. As soon as he returned home from his dental appointment that day, he called Tony to tell him about the interview. When he told Tony about the interview offer, he left off where he met Byron, because he thought it would seem undignified telling Tony that Byron had offered him an interview at a gas station. He simply told him that while looking for a job, he was able to get a job interview for a distribution company as a manager.

"Is it a distribution center with specialized products or do they distribute general products?" asked Tony, using the word *center* where Mayson had said *company*.

Mayson was left speechless. He didn't know there were *types* of distribution centers. Not wanting to seem naive, Mayson responded in an assertive tone to Tony's question.

"That's what the interview is for, to get more information," said Mayson.

"Did he give you a job description?" asked Tony.

"No," said Mayson abruptly. "When are you coming home?" asked Mayson swiftly as he wanted to evade more questions from Tony about the job.

"My flight will get me in around 2PM tomorrow," he said.

"Oh Good, I will be able to use your car for my 8:30 interview tomorrow evening," said Mayson.

"Sorry, Mayson, but when I get in, I will only have enough time to come home, change clothes and drive out to Ridgewell for two meetings. I probably won't get home until 9:30 that night," said Tony.

"It's okay, I'll take the bus," said Mayson.

Tony had concerns about this new job. It was strange that Mayson didn't know what type of distribution company it was, and that the interview appointment was being held so late. He didn't feel that Mayson would be in any physical danger but wondered could this be some guy trying to hit on him. He decided he would not share his concerns, as he was not for sure if Mayson would get the job. He congratulated Mayson and told him to be careful.

CHAPTER 18

About Tony: Another Late-Night Call

"Hey Mayson, I haven't heard from you in a while. I left word with Lamont at church for you to call me and never heard from you," said Reanna over the phone.

Mayson was trying to wake up. When he heard the phone ring, he thought it was Tony calling back about his job interview for tomorrow or update on his flight back to Benton. Since moving in with Tony, he no longer had problems sleeping at night. But instead of Tony's voice, he heard a woman, and at first he was not sure who it was.

"When I saw your family at church, I asked about you, but no one would tell me anything. Lamont slipped me a note last Sunday with this phone number on it," Reanna said in a nervous laugh.

Mayson remained silent. Reanna wondered if she had done the right thing in calling him.

"You okay?" asked Reanna.

Mayson was still struggling to wake up enough to respond to Reanna's voice. As it finally sank in that it was Reanna, he slowly put a response together.

"Yeah, I'm fine," he said groggily. He didn't want to talk about himself, so he decided to deflect the conversation to GCC.

"How's GCC?" he asked.

"They're still going strong," said Reanna in an attempt to sound bubbly. "We're having our picnic next weekend. Why don't you come? Pastor would love to see you. You know he never asked you to leave, he only asked you to sit out a while until you decided what you want to do," she said.

She paused.

"I really miss you Mayson," she said in a sad voice.

"No, Reanna. I can't go back. Too much has changed for me over these past few months," he said.

As soon as the words left his mouth, he knew that it was like opening a door for her to ask, "what changes?" He was not ready to share with Reanna things about himself that he was not quite sure he was ready to say. Despite Reanna's open and relaxed lifestyle, their friendship was based on him appearing to have the high ground when it came to morals and commitment to GCC's teaching.

The first couple of weeks when he and Reanna were going out to clubs together was one thing, but when Reanna started going back to her own straight nightclubs, she left Mayson alone to find his own connections. As much as he loved Reanna, actually being in a serious relationship with Tony was sacred ground for him. He wanted to protect his life with Tony, to keep it from being destroyed with gossip and, in Reanna's case, jokes and sexual innuendos. Yet, he knew that this joking side of her was just her being herself, and she would not hurt him intentionally.

Reanna's sudden call didn't prepare him for this moment. In hearing her voice again, there was that side of him that wanted things to go back to the way they were. Him and Reanna, with Lamont tagging alongside at GCC and restaurants after services. He knew those days were gone. Tony had changed everything. There was no going back to the way things were without him. Despite his new relationship, he felt lonely at times. Other than Tony, he had no friends. Reanna could fill in the gap between him and Tony, he thought. She could be the one that he'd spend time with while Tony was at work or out of town. The more he heard Reanna's voice over the phone the more he felt himself wanting to tell her about his new relationship. He wanted to talk to someone about his changes, and even Reanna was a tempting prospect. With that thought, he felt a calmness come over him. He reminded himself how caring and apologetic she was about herself when he admitted to her that he was Human. He loved Tony and he felt that would not change, so what was the harm in telling her, he decided.

"I've been busy, and I actually started seeing someone regularly," he heard himself say to Reanna.

"Really," said Reanna in an intrigued tone. She was also relieved that the silence was gone, and he was opening up to her.

"Yes. His name is Tony."

"Tony," repeated Reanna. "Is he fine?" she asked.

"Of course he's fine. He'd make Melvin Sutton look like a frog,'

150

laughed Mayson.

"I didn't think it was possible to be as fine as Melvin," laughed Reanna.

"To some, Melvin may look better, but through less superficial eyes, Tony carries himself with such confidence and maturity that you can't help but to see him as more attractive. He's a package," said Mayson.

"Is he there with you now?" asked Reanna in a whisper as though Tony could hear her through the phone.

"No, he's out of town on business."

"How'd you meet him?" she asked.

Mayson rested his back on his pillow, as he prepared to share the love story of Mayson and Tony.

"I went back to the Jasmine Club and that's where he and I met. When he came in the door of the club, he immediately got my attention. He's older than me and..."

Reanna cut him off. "How much older?" she asked.

"Eleven years older," said Mayson quickly. "But he looks younger. He's not very tall. He stands about 5'8, but built. You know, like he works out built. He converted one of his bedrooms into a small gym. He has muscles," Mayson said with pride.

"When I saw him for the first time, his hair was cut in a perfect fade that accented his adorable ears. His beard made him look like a college professor. He had one gold earring in his ear, and a custom-fitted silk shirt, and jeans that made him look like he stepped off a Jet magazine cover. I never thought this kind of man would even look at me."

As he shared this part of himself with her, Mayson felt a possible rejuvenation of their friendship. But it was different now. It was him sharing his romantic side of life with Reanna, rather than her with him. He liked her eagerness to hear about Tony. But the knowledge that she was not good at keeping things to herself was still present in his mind. But people were going to know anyway, he thought.

"I was at the Jasmine, which, as you know, is not the best club around town, so I thought he was out of place there. You know, like he was slumming," Mayson said. "I sat there at the club just wanting to look at him. The way I used to look at Melvin," he giggled.

"He went to the bar to get a drink but didn't seem to be looking my way. I assumed he wasn't interested, so I finished my soda and got ready to leave. I saw him leaving the bar and going towards the bathroom. But he must have gone to the back of the room and made his way around back to me. Before I knew it, he was standing over me at my table with a big smile on his face. He asked me could he sit. How he knew I was eyeing him is a mystery to me. I was nervous, and he could tell. But he was so patient with me. We sat and talked at that table for a couple of hours. We've been together ever since. He's a college man, Reanna. He has an MBA. He works for a marketing company over in Westport. Westport," Mayson repeated with emphasis and pride.

"Mayson, this is wonderful. I am so happy for you," she said.

"A few months ago, we started living together," continued Mayson. "I tried seeing him while I was staying with my mother, but it didn't work. When she found out about us, I had to leave," he said.

"What! Sweet Sister Phyllis put you out? Your mother is too kind for that. Remember that time when I was pregnant? Other than you, she was one of the first people I told. Mayson, I'll never forget how she kept my secret until I was able to tell my own mother... I wish I could do that," said Reanna somberly.

"Do what?" asked Mayson.

"Keep my mouth shut and not say so much," she said.

"I know Reanna, but I love you anyway," said Mayson with compassion in his voice. "I know it seems strange to have a best friend who can't keep secrets, but I learned to work around you with that."

"You know my mouth spouts out things mostly when I've been drinking too much," she said.

"Yeah, I know," said Mayson.

"Well," said Reanna with a sigh, "I'm surprised your mom could be that heartless with you. Is there more to this?" asked Reanna with suspicion.

"You misunderstood me. I said I had to leave. I didn't say she put me out. My father actually put me out for being gay, so I have no correction for him," said Mayson.

"Okay, that makes more sense. What was going on that you had to leave?" she asked.

"For one thing, I had become distant with my family. You know I had started making my rounds at the clubs and when I met Tony, I couldn't let Lamont hang out with me like he did with you and me. My days were wrapped up in seeing Tony. I was between jobs, so in addition to seeing Tony at night, I was looking for work during the day."

"What happened to your weekend job with the cleaning company and the temp jobs?" asked Reanna.

"I went through some days of depression and just didn't have it in me to go back to those jobs. They just made me feel worst about myself. Such dead-end jobs," he said softly.

"Oh, I was just wondering. I thought you were doing well in juggling the jobs.... Sorry, go back to your mother and leaving her house part," she said.

"Ok. Well, my mother had been getting on me hard for a few months about my not going to church. But I'm over 18. I didn't feel I owed her an explanation, so I just let her talk. Also, I just couldn't tell her about Tony. It was all so new for me and I didn't want to spoil it by telling her and getting a response that would put a damper on my relationship with him. One week my mother, Idee, and Lamont left to attend the national church convention for 3 days in Michigan. I was left home alone. Of course, my father was at work and working overtime. So, I invited Tony to come over and stay with me during the day."

"Why didn't you go and stay with him?" asked Reanna.

"I thought my home would be a safer place. I was scared that things would get out of hand if I went to his condo for such a long period of time. Tony and I hadn't really been intimate at that point. I guess I thought that if I went to his condo, it would make it real that I was Human. I knew what could possibly happen. I didn't want that to happen yet. Which was odd, because a few weeks earlier, there were some guys from a Human advocacy group, called New Times, trying to help me by telling me about their group. It sounded like something that I should have joined, but, at the time, I thought it would make everything too real. But here I am, living with the guy I lost my virginity to. It doesn't get more real or ready than that, he said.

Anyway, back to Tony. I had been to his home once for him to change his shirt one day, but after that, we mostly were at restaurants, movies and other stuff like that. The most we ever did was kiss a lot in his car.

It was difficult, Reanna. A part of me really wanted him, but the other side was terrified of it actually happening. I felt as long as we didn't go any further than kissing, I could still be a *little saved,* "Mayson said realizing how ridiculous that must sound.

"A little saved," Reanna said laughing out loud.

"Yeah, that's what I was thinking," he said.

"I was completely wrong. When Tony came over to my house, within 30 minutes we were in my room. After we finished, we were lying in the bed cuddling and talking. I heard a noise in the hallway. It was my father. Well, who would have thought that my father would have picked that day to come home right after his shift? I thought he was going to kill Tony. He made me and Tony get out of the house that same day.

He was furious. I'd never seen him that way. I could see that while he was yelling and throwing our clothes out of the room, his hands were shaking.

When my mother came back from the convention, I was at Tony's condo. I wanted to talk with her before my father filled her head, but he must have stayed at the house until she came home from the convention. So of course she knew.

When I talked to her, I immediately explained that I didn't plan for things to get out of hand. But she asked me in this calm, eerie voice, was this what I thought of her and her home? She told me she would pack the rest of my clothes and I could come get them. It was like she was finishing what my father started. If I'd asked her to let me come back, I have no doubt she would have. It wasn't just about having sex with another man. It was also about the planning and scheming to wait until she went out of town to have him come over. I knew that I had betrayed her trust. She'd have been upset if it was a woman that I was having sex with in our house, but it was worse because it was a man."

Reanna let out a sigh. "Wow! A lot has happened since I last saw you." She giggled.

"What are you laughing at?" Mayson asked.

"While listening to you and all your drama, I thought about how things have changed between us. I used to be the one on the phone telling you all my stuff, and now your life sounds more exciting than mine."

Mayson thought of the irony and laughed with her.

"I'm really glad we're talking again. Now that you know my secret, I would hope that I could tell you anything," said Mayson.

Reanna smiled as she heard these words. She had missed Mayson.

Yes, you can, responded Reanna with assurance in her voice. "Our friendship is where it should be."

"I hope so," said Mayson.

"What do you mean, you hope so?" asked Reanna startled at Mayson's questionable agreement.

"I don't know. I feel great talking with you again, but something has changed in me. I want our friendship to continue, but I don't know if it will always be the same. In some ways, I feel I've grown but in other ways, I feel my growth or change is dirty when it comes to people from GCC."

"I am not GCC. I am Reanna."

She paused as to catch her breath. "Okay. First, we are talking as if everything is fine between us. You say to me that you can tell me anything. But now you say you have doubts," she said in frustration.

"I said *hope* I could tell you anything," inserted Mayson.

"How does someone's mind change that quickly?" huffed Reanna.

Mayson could sense her frustration. "Okay. Let me try and explain," said Mayson. "It's all still confusing for me too. You know how GCC teaches that good happens to those that follows GCC's teaching?" he asked.

"Uh-uh," she said.

"Okay, you know yourself that despite the teaching and people who live by them, yet bad things have happened to some people from GCC. Also, prosperous things happen to people who do not follow our..." he paused "...their teaching."

"For the moment," interrupted Reanna. "They prosper for the moment."

It was this comment from her that concerned Mayson about her ability to be open-minded to other thoughts of life outside of GCC. He knew that she, as he had at one time, filtered everything through GCC teachings, whether he or she lived it or not.

He believed that Reanna sincerely loved and cared about him, but they were raised in the same doctrinal teachings. He didn't want her to see him as a Human who was loved by God *anyway*. His meetings with Pastor McDaniel and Aaron opened up new possibilities to who he was in the eyes of God. He often mulled over his conversations from Pastor McDaniel and Aaron. He wanted to make sense of it with someone but was not quite sure if Reanna was that someone.

"Life is not as black and white as we would like it to be. I find the Bible to be based on individuals and circumstances about each individual. I don't see God judging us as a group. I see Him loving us as individuals," said Mayson.

"That's so beautiful," said Reanna.

"Remember our first day at the club? I was terrified. GCC had told us about club people and how degrading it is to frequent clubs with such people. And that's partly true. There are some predators and sleazy people in those places. On the other hand, I met people who were searching for themselves and in need of love, like everyone else. When you took me to the club on my first day, I found myself condemning the people I saw with thoughts from teachings from GCC. How arrogant and hypocritical, huh? You may not be as radical in GCC's teachings, but I still see you as my past GCC. Their teachings are in your head. Which means that you may see me through their eyes. You may see me as "less than," the way I used to when you shared all of your encounters. I loved you and found you adventures interesting, but through GCC, I saw you as less than, when it came to God.

At this moment, I feel close to you and hope I can tell you anything, but after we hang up, I may begin to wonder if rekindling with you is best for me. Will it jeopardize my efforts to grow or is it a bridge to getting back to the way I use to be? I still want to visit GCC, because my family, some of the members that I like so well and you are there. But in my heart, I could never go back," said Mayson.

With each word from Mayson's explanation as to his concerns of continuing their friendship, Reanna felt daggers pierce her heart. She felt her eyelids get heavy, as though rocks were hanging from them. She tried to think of something profound to say that could shake her friend from his concerns, but she was lost from such rich words from Mayson. She wished at that very moment she had the right words to say to her friend.

"Mayson, I've kidded around with you in the past, but you know that with my lifestyle, I've never really judged you or tried to make you feel bad about yourself. Even now, knowing about your relationship with Tony, I have not once condemned you or made you feel it was wrong. From what you tell me, Tony is a good guy. I would love to meet him and be a part of both of your lives," she said.

Mayson felt bad for Reanna. He knew she was close to begging him for his friendship, which was not his intent.

"Reanna, everything I said was not about you being judgmental or critical of me. I'm trying to tell you that I'm going through some changes that battle with my past and future. I don't think you will ever judge or criticize me about my life. But I'm not sure I can completely move forward if we get close like we used to be. I love you and I love GCC, but sometimes I feel I need to get over my past."

"I regret the day I took you to that club," Reanna said in a low, trembling voice.

"I'm sorry, Reanna. I'm in a place where I go back and forth in what I want to do or even know. So, who knows?" said Mayson.

Reanna sighed deeply. She felt drained from their conversation. She wanted to shift to something more uplifting. After a long pause, she cleared her throat.

"Tell me more about you and Tony," she asked.

Mayson had mixed emotions about the change of subject. He wasn't sure if he should try and smooth out what he said to her about their friendship. But it was getting late, and talking about Tony was a good way to change the mood of their somber conversation.

"Tony has been taking care of me for now. But I really need to get a job, whether I have Tony or not. Besides, Tony works so much that he's not home as much as I'd like. He doesn't do that "overtime" stuff like my father, but his job really does require 10 hour work days. I get lonely and bored when he's not home. I'm used to being around people. So, I figured I might as well make money on my own while he's at work."

"Interesting," said Reanna.

"I met a guy, a few days ago. He and I will be meeting about a job opening he has at his company," said Mayson.

"What kind of job is it?" asked Reanna.

"A managerial job in a distribution company."

"Oh, I worked in a distribution center for a few months as a material handler. So, what will you be doing? Floor management or regional management?" she asked.

Mayson didn't have an answer. "He didn't give me much information about the job. He told me to just meet with him at his office," he said.

Reanna, who had had a few jobs in her life, thought it odd that the employer would be secretive about what a job entailed. At least he should have the basics, she thought. But she didn't want to come off as questioning his judgment.

"Well, if you need to save money of your own, then I don't see the problem with getting a job," said Reanna, in an attempt to sound supportive. "As long as the job is something you like, I think everybody wins," she added.

"I don't know how Tony will take it. He has told me that he can take care of me and I don't have to worry about income. When he first told me this, I was floored with gratitude and adoration of him. In my wildest dreams, I didn't think I would be with someone so wonderful. My concern is that if I take this job, or any job, Tony and I will see even less of each other," he said.

"How can you see him any less if he's working most of the day?" asked Reanna.

"He comes home late at night, but he'll occasionally take off early from work once or twice a week and we'll spend the rest of the afternoon together. He works just as hard on Saturdays but does take Sunday off no matter what. I look forward to that. I'm overjoyed when he's able to steal time during the week for us, but if I get a job, we'll lose that."

"Have you talked this over with him?" asked Reanna.

"Not yet," said Mayson.

"I guess some things you never know until the time comes," she said.

"I guess not," said Mayson.

CHAPTER 19

About That Job...

(I)

Fortunately, the bus stop was on the corner from the address Byron gave Mayson. Mayson got off the bus at Palmer Avenue and Glen Street. A rough side of town. Mayson decided not to let the neighborhood discourage him. He recalled that when he had spoken to Byron on the phone for more directions, Byron alluded to having more than one office location, which was separate from the actual distribution center. Mayson allowed himself to believe that this was only one of Byron's many locations and it didn't mean he would actually work at this site. Mayson looked at the address numbers on the building: 3536...3538...3540....3542...As he got closer to 3548, he saw what looked like a restaurant. Mayson pulled Byron's card from his back pocket to make sure it was the correct address. He stood in front of the building, confused. He could see a few people inside sitting at tables. The building was old, and the interior seemed old as well, with gaudy murals on the wall of palm trees and an ocean. Mayson stood frozen. What makes him think I want to work at a restaurant? he muttered.

"Maybe I misunderstood him," he said.

Not knowing whether to go in or leave, he took a deep breath and entered the building. He stood at the door looking for someone to ask about Byron. He stood for almost five minutes, while a woman with papers in her hand walked past him several times as she entered a back door, then came back out. He figured she worked there, and hoped each time she walked past she would acknowledge his presence. But each time, she walked past him as though she did not know he was there. Mayson noticed a man with a white apron on behind the counter sorting through receipts. He walked over to the man.

"Excuse me, I'm looking for Byron Crawford," said Mayson.

The man continued to look down at the receipts he was counting. He was short enough that Mayson found himself looking down on the top of his bald head as he counted. As he was waiting for a reply, Mayson held his breath, hoping that the man would tell him that there was no Byron Crawford who worked there. Finally, the man glanced at Mayson with a bored look on his face and pointed to a dark red door on his far left, then resumed counting the receipts.

"Thank you," said Mayson as he walked toward the door and knocked lightly. He waited about 10 seconds and knocked again. He heard a calm voice behind the door:

"Come in."

Mayson opened the door, and there he saw Byron lying across a large, dark-gray sofa with a phone to his ear. Byron was dressed in tan linen pants, a beige button-down shirt, and a paisley print tie. His suit jacket was draped across his desk chair. His office looked nothing like the shabby restaurant. The wooden desk looked expensive; its chair resembled a Steelcase fabric chair, like one Mayson had seen in his school principal's office. The couch he was lying on was similar to one his mother had admired when she was shopping for furniture but decided was much too pricey. As Byron set upward on the couch, he motioned for Mayson to sit in the desk chair where his jacket hung. Mayson walked past Byron and around the desk to sit. Byron continued his call, but it was obvious that he was trying to end it.

As Mayson sat and waited for Byron to get off the phone, he was tempted to take his shoes off behind the desk and run his feet through the plush carpet. There were exotic and scenic paintings on the walls. Mayson saw beautiful plants and flowers that looked so perfect he thought they were artificial. He touched the plant on the windowsill behind the desk and felt the moisture from the leaf. Hmm, it's real, he thought.

Byron finally ended the call. "Hello, Mayson," he said as he stood up and walked over to the desk to shake Mayson's hand.

"Nice of you to make it," said Byron.

"I'm looking forward to finding out more about your business," said Mayson.

Mayson wanted to appear knowledgeable, so he had written several

160

questions down. Tony's inquiry about the type of distribution center and Reanna's question about the area of management had made Mayson aware that he needed to prepare himself for the interview.

Byron went to a small refrigerator alongside his desk and asked Mayson if he wanted a beer.

"No, thank you," said Mayson.

Despite all the changes Mayson had made in his life, he still avoided alcohol. Tony had different types of alcohol around their condo, but Mayson was never tempted by the thought of drinking, whether Tony was home or not.

Byron got out a beer and closed the small refrigerator door with his foot. He sat back on the couch and rested his feet on top of the glass coffee table in front of him. He started the meeting by describing the type of person he was looking for in his company. When Mayson tried to ask about what type of distribution company it was, Byron talked over him about the different locations of his four distribution centers. He did not provide specific street addresses of the locations, only the sides of town they were on.

"I know you may be a bit confused by the location of my office in this area of town, but I knew the guy who owned this building before I bought it. He sold it to me at a more than reasonable price because he knew I would do well for the people in this community. And, of course, the restaurant is doing well," said Byron.

Mayson's mind was still on getting his questions answered about the company, but he let Byron continue to talk without interruption. When he thought Byron was finished, he took a small breath and opened his mouth to ask his questions, but Byron immediately started up again.

"I asked you to meet with me because of a particular location I have in mind for you. When I met you at the gas station, I figured you must live in the area. I couldn't understand why someone with such a nice car would live on this side of town. When you told me that the car belonged to a friend of yours, I realized that you must live in this area, but the owner of the car must live in a different side of town," he said.

As Mayson was trying to explain to him that he didn't live on that side of town but favored that gas station for its low prices, Byron continued to talk without letting him speak. He informed Mayson that he would be working at one of his other locations nearby, closer to downtown.

"So Mayson, what are some things you like to do?" asked Byron.

Mayson thought for a while, because the question was so broad and came out of nowhere. He also contemplated if he should take the conversation back to where he lived and his prepared questions about the job. Instead, he decided that he would answer Byron's question and get back to his own questions and where he lived later.

"I like a variety of things," said Mayson.

"Any specific hobbies or things that you like to do when not working?" asked Byron.

"I like to sing," said Mayson.

Sing, repeated Byron as he placed his beer on the coaster sitting on the glass table.

"Yes, I love singing. I used to sing in the choir at my church," said Mayson.

"I'd love to hear you some time," said Byron.

"I'm more of a group singer," said Mayson.

"I believe you can sing beyond a group," said Byron with a smile. "As a matter of fact..." he stopped. "How old are you?" He asked Mayson.

"I'm twenty-one."

"Okay, good," said Byron. "In addition to my distribution company, I own a nightclub. It's over on Washington Avenue, and it includes a live band with singers. I can really use another good singer at this club. It would be perfect for you. You can work three to four days a week, depending on the needs of my manager there."

Singing at the club sounded interesting, thought Mayson, but this was not what he was promised.

"Now, the position at my distribution center will not be available for a few months, so in the meantime, you can earn a little income at the club," added Byron.

Mayson was dismayed by Byron's quick statement that the distribution job would not be ready for a few months. Ever since he met Byron at the gas station, his imagination had been spinning with thoughts of his own office, wearing suits every day to work, meetings with staff, and lunch with Byron. He thought about how he would show his mother she was wrong in trying to get him to go to college. From his meeting with

Byron at the gas station, he concluded that it's all about meeting the right people and not so much education. Now, hearing Byron casually say that the position would not be available for a few months, had Mayson wondering about Byron's sincerity. Byron had not given him much time to ask about the delay or any other questions about the distribution job. While he was still lost in thought, Byron made another comment that caught Mayson's attention.

"I have someone else who is interested in the distribution position. I don't have anything to offer him in the meantime like I do for you, but he's willing to wait. I told him that I have you in mind for the job, and this only made him more determined to wait and try to get the job himself," said Byron, as he rested his hands behind his head, while looking at Mayson for a response.

Mayson knew that this could be a scare tactic from Byron, but he feared that even if there was no other person waiting for the job, he didn't want to run the risk of offending Byron. If Byron took the offer off the table and Mayson walked away, he would spend the rest of his life wondering if he had made the right decision.

"I'm really not that good of a singer," said Mayson weakly, still reeling at the prospect of losing the management job.

"Come on, Mayson, I can tell you are the kind of man who can do whatever he sets his mind to do."

What a cliché, thought Mayson. For a moment, he wanted to cry. Cry over a job he never had.

"If you're that uncertain about your voice, I can get my lead singer, Lanelle, to coach you a little before you go on stage. With her help, I'm sure you'll be ready to sing on the first night," said Byron.

"Why do you want to do this for me?" asked Mayson.

Byron picked up his beer, took another sip and sat it back down. He then told Mayson a long, sad story about his childhood and how no one had believed in him. He said that as an adult he became a successful businessman, despite all the negativity. He vowed that after he had become successful, he would help as many people as he could. He reminded Mayson of the day they met at the gas station.

"When you told me that the BMW was not yours, it was then that I saw a big dreamer I could help," said Byron.

He told Mayson that rather than drive a car that belongs to someone else, Mayson could have enough money to own such a car himself.

"This restaurant may not look like much, but I'm helping the community. I bought this place so people could have jobs and others could have a nice place to spend an evening."

Mayson found himself feeling sympathetic and impressed with Byron. Byron has a testimony, Mayson thought.

GCC had an outreach ministry that Mayson had assisted with once upon a time. This giving side remained in him. Mayson didn't want to live the rest of his life with Tony taking care of him. He felt a kindred spirit with Byron, as he felt that they were both reaching for success while helping others.

(II)

"Where'd you get that hair?" asked Lanelle as she lightly pulled at Mayson's afro with the tips of her fingers.

"It gets fluffed like that when I braid it at night," said Mayson, as he sat at one of the nightclub tables with Lanelle, who stood over him with her 5'0" height and voluptuous frame. She looked to be in her forties, but the lighting in the club was poor so it was hard to be sure. He focused on her long, curly, dark-brown wig that framed her plump face, because it reminded him of someone from GCC. Her make-up was light, with lip gloss that shone under the bulb above the small stage. Her aqua dress swirled around the curves of her body.

"My name is Lanelle. Let me officially welcome you to The Encounter Club," she said as she sat in the chair next to him at the table.

"Thank you," said Mayson.

"Byron called me about you," she said as she looked at Mayson inquisitively.

Byron's call had been brief. He did not provide any specific details of Mayson's background, nor the reason he chose him as an alternate lead singer and why he needed help with his voice. Byron was aware Lanelle already had a backup singer who was more than qualified to be an alternate lead singer. So, she was curious about the relationship between

Mayson and Byron.

"Byron is quite impressed with you," said Lanelle, hoping Mayson would share more.

"I'm impressed with him too," said Mayson as he sat across from Lanelle at one of the empty tables.

The room looked rugged and overly done, with cheap posters and Christmas lights strung around the wall. There were 15 tables covered with burgundy vinyl tablecloths. The tablecloths gave the club a uniform look, but some were dingy, which diminished the effect. The small stage took up about a quarter of the room, with the tables arranged around it in a circle.

"I hear you like to sing," said Lanelle.

"Yes, I do," said Mayson as he nodded nervously.

"Ever sing lead before?" asked Lanelle.

"Occasionally at my church," said Mayson, hoping she would not ask him the name of the church. "How long have you been singing here at this club?" He asked, trying to change the subject.

"Six years," said Lanelle. "Six whole years," she added proudly.

"How did you meet Byron?" asked Mayson.

Mayson could see the discomfort in Lanelle's face from this question. From Lanelle's brief observation of Mayson, he didn't seem like one who would ask many questions. Known for her clever one-liners, Lanelle managed to come up with a response that would set the tone as to how she wanted Mayson to interact with her from now on.

"The important thing is we met," said Lanelle.

"Okay. Sorry," said Mayson, sensing he had crossed a line.

Lanelle stood and straightened her dress. "I'll be right back," she said.

She turned and went down a small hall to the restroom. Mayson sat feeling a little uneasy about everything. He felt uneasy about the job offer, working at a nightclub and Lanelle's odd behavior at his question.

How did I get here? he thought. From a managerial job offer to singing at a small ragged nightclub. Mayson wanted so much to make his life mean something. His church's opinion of his love life made him want to prove to them all that he would do well despite what they thought of him. He prayed to God for guidance, and surprisingly, with more intensity since he left GCC.

I must make this work, thought Mayson.

He recalled a lady at Pastor Martin's church. While working part-time as the church secretary, she was also working on her master's degree. In addition, she was a clerk at the city courthouse. It was rumored that she was a lesbian. Despite a lack of evidence, the church replaced her once the whispers grew too loud to ignore. Several years later after completing her master's degree, she moved up the ranks in government positions and eventually became a state senator with an eye on Washington, DC. After that, the pastor and church members sang her praises. And, of course, they called upon her for favors. No one ever asked her whether she was a lesbian anymore. It didn't seem to be important. Once you are successful and people can get something from you, who you are doesn't seem to matter anymore, thought Mayson.

I have to be one of those people who make something of themselves, Mayson thought.

Lanelle came back in the room looking stern. Mayson could tell she was no longer in the mood for small talk.

"Come with me to the stage and let me hear those vocal cords," she said.

Lanelle sat behind the small keyboard piano and began to play, seemingly without much effort. The stage was small, but it managed to hold a nice drum set and speakers.

"You got a song that I can hear?" asked Lanelle.

"Um, let's see," said Mayson as he thought quickly. Most of the songs he knew were church songs. He thought about some of the secular songs that Tony had on his car stereo that he played often. He remembered an old song by Bryson Mack, "My Enchanted Heart." He thought how pretty that song was and how easy it might be for him to sing it.

"My Enchanted Heart," said Mayson.

"Oh, you're going old school," said Lanelle.

No sooner than Mayson said the name of the song, he could hear the introduction being played on the keyboard.

"Okay come in when you're ready," said Lanelle as she played the song with ease.

Mayson closed his eyes and began to sing, mindful of every word. Mayson sang the entire song and then opened his eyes. She didn't say anything after Mayson finished the song. She started to noodle around on the keyboard again, looking down the whole time. Mayson felt embarrassed, just standing there waiting for a response. Her random playing then went back into *My Enchanted Heart*. She then began to sing the song herself. Her voice was smooth and full. She sang each word with feeling. Roberta Flack, thought Mayson. I hear a little Roberta Flack in her voice. He had heard this song several times, yet he was engrossed by her words and expression. She didn't sing the full song, but just enough for Mayson to understand that it was her response to his efforts.

"Well, it's evident that you have some experience, but I wouldn't describe you as a lead singer," said Lanelle.

"I know. I tried to explain this to Byron," Mayson said.

"It's okay. Your voice is good for backup. You can carry a tune and you'll blend well with our group. I'll work with you on your voice and we can go from there. I'll introduce you to the others tonight," said Lanelle.

"Okay," said Mayson.

"You did plan to be back tonight?" asked Lanelle.

"Yes, sure," said Mayson eagerly.

"Okay, we start at 11 tonight, but I need you to come back around 9:30 so you can rehearse with the others. Wear all black, that's our staff color," she said.

"Okay, I'll see you then," said Mayson.

As Mayson walked out the door to his car, he was a little disappointed in Lanelle's critique of his singing, yet he felt a twinge of excitement about singing tonight with the group. He knew that with practice, he could better his singing skills. Lanelle's beautiful, soulful voice played on in his head. He thought that if anyone could bring out his voice, it would be her. As with the thought of becoming a corporate businessman, he allowed his imagination to go wild at the thought of being a renowned singer. He went back and forth between imagining himself as a successful businessman and becoming a performer. They both were exciting prospects, but he decided he would prefer a singing career. He decided not to invite Tony out to any of his shows until he felt he had perfected his voice.

CHAPTER 20

First Night Jitters

Mayson got to the club at 9:15. He sat in the car and waited in the parking lot. Fortunately for him, Tony was on business out of town, so Mayson had the car for the next few days. He looked at himself in the rear-view mirror, making sure that his hair was just right. He saw a late-model car coming into the lot from off the street. Mayson could not see the driver's face. The car door opened and a man got out. He was of medium height, a stout man with dreads wearing a black t-shirt and black dress pants. He looked to be in his thirties. He went to the trunk of the car and pulled out a guitar case and a gym bag. Mayson assumed it must be one of Lanelle's band members for tonight. He seemed preoccupied in thought and he didn't look Mayson's way. He walked toward the back entrance of the Encounter Club and fiddled with his keys, looking for the right one. He found it, turned the lock and went inside. Mayson got out of his car and walked across the graveled lot toward the back-door entrance. As Mayson turned the doorknob, he could see that it was now locked. He knocked on the door a few times and eventually the stout man opened the door. The man looked curiously at Mayson.

"May I help you?" asked the man.

"Hi, I'm Mayson Hendricks. Lanelle..."It occurred to Mayson that he didn't know Lanelle's last name.

"Campbell. Her last name is Campbell," said the stout man.

"Oh, Okay. She told me to meet here at 9:30," said Mayson.

"You must be the new guy. Come on in," said the man as he opened the door wider for Mayson to enter.

Once in, Mayson saw a small, cluttered kitchen. It was packed with drinking glasses, cups, and plates stacked near the kitchen sink. They were clean, but it looked as though they were never put away into the cabinets. The floors squeaked as Mayson walked down the hall toward the clubroom. The stout man led him to the inside of the club near the stage

"My name is Timothy Ralph, but you can call me Tim," said the man, as he unpacked his guitar and other accessories from the gym bag on the stage. "You must be the new singer."

"Yes, but I'll be singing backup for Lanelle," said Mayson.

"Oh, I thought Byron was looking for someone to alternate with Lanelle on some of the songs. She gets pretty busy sometimes, managing the club, and needs someone to fill in for her," said Tim.

"Hmm, I didn't know that," said Mayson, disappointed that he couldn't live up to Lanelle's need for occasional breaks.

"I did audition for Lanelle, though. For now, she found me to be more of a backup singer than a lead singer," said Mayson in a tone that he tried to sound as though he was okay with the choice. "Hopefully I'll be able to lead some songs soon," said Mayson.

"Wait in line. Her current backup singers, Tamara and Monica have been waiting for over a year to lead songs. They were not too happy with Byron when they heard he was hiring another person to come in and lead," said Tim, shaking his head while positioning his guitar strap across his shoulder.

Mayson became uneasy at this news. He didn't like the idea of competing for the position. He wondered if he should just bow out now. Or, he thought hopefully, maybe they can't sing well either. If they can't sing any better and Lanelle is training my voice, then they could see that it would make sense for me to eventually lead.

"Can they sing lead?" asked Mayson.

"Oh yes!" said Tim as he tuned and strummed his guitar. "Tamara can sing just as well as Lanelle. Monica's not as good as Tamara or Lanelle, but the girl can sing. They both had a hissy fit when they were not considered for the lead. Monica's hopeful that Tamara will get the lead, but if it's given to anyone else, she said she'd have a problem with Byron."

More questions came to Mayson's mind. Why would Byron try to hire another lead singer when he had Tamara? Why is he giving me time to develop my skills as a singer?

"I don't get it," said Mayson.

"I don't know either, man, but that's on them. I just come and play my guitar and leave who sings to Byron and Lanelle," said Tim.

As Mayson was about to ask Tim if Tamara sang alto or soprano, he heard the back kitchen door open and footsteps coming toward them in the club room. A 40ish man with a slow, but stylish stride walked in. His build was slimmer than Tim's and he wore a black embroidered guayabera shirt and semi tight-fitting black slacks. What a cool-looking guy, Mayson thought.

"Hey, whose Bimmer is that out back?" he asked in a loud voice, as he was addressing the question to Tim, but eyeing Mayson up and down. The sound of his laid-back, humorous tone voice added to his cool appearance, thought Mayson.

"A Bimmer," repeated Tim looking at Mayson, surprised. "Must be my new friend Mayson here. He'll be one of the backup singers," said Tim as he strummed his guitar. "Mayson, this is Robert Banks, we call him *Urban.*"

Mayson found the nickname cool too. He had a wondering look about the origin of such a name for this guy.

"Three backups now," said Urban as he shook Mayson's hand.

"Good to meet you Mr. Urban," said Mayson.

Urban laughed out loud.

"Mr. Urban!" he repeated with an even louder laugh.

"Okay, take that puzzled look off your face," said Urban. He could tell that Mayson was confused by his name. "I got that nickname from a coach years ago when I was playing college football. The college I went to was in a small rural area and I'm from Detroit. The coach knew where I was from and assumed that I was slick, so he started calling me Urban. I didn't finish college, but I liked the name and kept it. Does that satisfy your curiosity?" said Urban as he laughed a little more and punched Mayson's arm lightly.

"Thanks for clearing that up," said Mayson. As much as he wanted to know more about Urban, he decided to allow everyone to tell him what they wanted him to know about themselves, rather than him asking them. Urban went over to the keyboard, turned it on, made some adjustments on it, and began to play softly. Mayson went to sit at one of the tables. He sat and listened to Tim and Urban adjust their musical instruments. It was now 9:40. Mayson wondered where Lanelle and the other two backup singers were.

At 9:46, he heard the kitchen door open again and voices coming in their direction in the club. It was Lanelle, Tamara, and Monica. A young man was with them. Tamara and Monica went to the stage and began checking on the microphones. They both made an effort not to look Mayson's way. The young man with them looked at Mayson as he raced upon the stage to sit at the drums.

"Hey Mr. 'Fro," said Lanelle referring to Mayson. She waved in his direction while continuing to walk toward the back of the room. She was carrying two large bags. Mayson could see a few bottles in them. She placed them on the small bar near the back of the room. As she began to sort out the bottles, she yelled across the room to introduce Mayson.

"I'd like for everyone to meet Mayson...Baby, what's your last name?"

"Hendricks," Mayson said loudly.

"I'd like everyone to meet Mayson Hendricks," Lanelle said.

"I've met Bimmer already," said Urban as he looked at Mayson in an amused expression.

Two nicknames already, Mr. 'Fro and Bimmer, thought Mayson. Will this ever stop? he wondered.

"Mayson, I'd like for you to meet Tamara Lane, the lady in the long black dress, and Monica Hicks in the black pants," said Lanelle as she put the bottles on the shelf.

As Lanelle was giving the introductions, Mayson was looking at the ladies on the stage, but neither one made eye contact with him. Monica had pulled up a seat next to Urban while he continued playing his keyboard. Tamara was still working with the mikes, one of which kept slipping as she was trying to tighten it.

"Nice to meet you both," said Mayson.

Tamara didn't respond.

Monica mumbled "Hi."

Thirty-three-year-old Tamara was slim and tall, light-complexioned, with long braids that reached to the middle of her back. Monica, twenty-eight years old, had pecan-colored skin and was of average height with wide hips and relaxed blonde hair that she wore in a straight cut. Tamara had on heavy make-up that made her look glamorous. Monica had light blotches on her face but limited her make-up to lipstick.

Mayson felt his heart race. He sensed they were not pleased with his being there. He had hoped that Tim was exaggerating about the competitiveness for being the lead singer, but the ladies had a coldness that made Mayson shiver.

As Lanelle continued to put the bottles away, she also continued her introductions.

"Trenton Strong is our drummer. He'll be finishing college next month, so we may be losing him soon," said Lanelle.

"I never said I was leaving," said Trenton nonchalantly, while tapping his drums. "Nice to meet you, Mayson."

Twenty-two-year-old Trenton was average height, with a high forehead, but his curly soft hair made up for the receding hairline. He was dark-skinned, with a smooth even tone. He was wearing a dark blue vintage oxford shirt, black jeans, and leather black shined shoes.

"By the way, Mayson will be one of our backup singers," said Lanelle.

Urban and Tim immediately looked over at Tamara. Monica had gone to the club's office to make a phone call. Mayson was relieved that Lanelle didn't add more about his efforts to sing lead in front of Tamara and Monica. Tamara gave a quick glance at Mayson but continued to work on the microphones as though she hadn't heard Lanelle.

Mayson sat at the table out on the floor alone, as everyone seemed busy with something.

Would you like a soda? called Lanelle across the room to Mayson, as she rummaged with items at the back of the room.

"Yes, thank you," said Mayson.

"Cola okay?" she asked.

"Yes, that's fine," said Mayson.

She threw the soda can across the room and Mayson caught it. The can was very cold. Mayson was eager to open it. He felt himself sweat and his mouth was dry from the anxiety over Tamara and Monica's edgy reactions toward him. He was concerned that the Cola would splash when he opened it due to Lanelle throwing it. Oh, wouldn't Tamara and Monica like to see soda all over my face? thought Mayson, as he slowly peeled back the tab on the can. A little of the soda shot out of the can, but Mayson immediately covered it with his mouth. While Mayson drank the soda, he saw Tamara walking towards him. Her facial expression seemed a little softer from when she first entered the room.

"What do you sing?" she asked.

"I'm a tenor," said Mayson.

"Any falsettos?" asked Tamara.

"No," said Mayson in an amused and relieved voice. The last thing he wanted was to be at odds with anyone on this job. He realized that Tamara no longer considered him a threat now that he had been introduced as a backup singer.

"How long have you been singing backup?" she asked.

"Other than singing in my church choir, this is the first time," said Mayson.

"What church do you go to?" she asked.

Mayson didn't want to say much more about GCC because he didn't want Tamara to become curious as to why he was no longer there.

"I'm between churches right now," said Mayson.

"How much is Byron paying you?" asked Tamara without blinking an eye.

Mayson was floored. Not just because it was rude to ask, but also because he had never discussed pay with Byron. Since Tamara asked such an intrusive question, it worked to Mayson's advantage that he didn't know how much Byron was going to pay him.

"I don't know," said Mayson.

"You don't know," echoed Tamara.

"No, it just came to me when you asked this question that I never asked Byron about the pay," he said.

Tamara looked at Mayson, trying to determine if she could believe that he didn't know.

"Well, whatever he pays you, make sure it's what you're worth," she said.

"Why do you say that?" asked Mayson.

"I'm just saying, don't get stuck with pay that you later find out was less than what your talents are worth," she said.

Tamara then walked away and joined Monica, who had finished her phone call and was now in the back with Lanelle setting up the glasses in the back of the room.

Mayson continued sipping his Cola. After everyone had finished with their preliminaries, Lanelle came to the front and motioned for Mayson to come up on the stage with her.

"Come on Tamara, Monica, we only have 45 minutes before we open."

Tamara and Monica did some last-minute adjustment in the bar area and joined Lanelle on the stage.

"Do you drink?" asked Lanelle to Mayson.

"No, ma'am," said Mayson.

"Ma'am," repeated Lanelle. "Don't start that with me. I told you my name is Lanelle," she said in an annoyed tone.

"That's what my mama taught me to say out of respect for... Mayson stopped in an effort to think of another word for *elders*. "Respect for other people," he finished.

"So, can I call you sir?" asked Lanelle.

"Well, my mama...." "Lanelle cut him off ...

"You are no longer a child, so rather than say words of respect, show me respect by calling me by my name. I never asked you to call me Ma'am. Ma'am is not my name."

Mayson felt a little angered. He felt that Lanelle was disrespecting his manners and his mother.

"I have to go by what my mother taught me," said Mayson.

"Mayson, apparently you don't know what manners are if you keep calling someone a name that they are telling you is not their name. That does not show respect for me. You need to grow up, boy, and get out of this my mama stuff."

Mayson felt himself about to blow. He was tired of walking on eggshells for Lanelle. When he looked around the room at the others, no one was paying attention to them. I guess she talks to everyone like this, thought Mayson. I don't want to appear too sensitive, he thought. He decided to let the matter go.

As everyone gathered to the stage with Lanelle, she announced that their bartender, Calvin, would not be in to serve drinks tonight, so they would have to take turns at the bar.

"However, we will need to temporarily close down the bar when all of us are on stage. Mayson, since you don't drink and you can't serve, you won't have to be in rotation," she said.

Mayson didn't say anything. He was simmering over Lanelle's "ma'am" words, but tried not to appear angry.

Lanelle went over the evening's songs with the group. Mayson didn't know any of the songs. Tamara and Lanelle gave him a quick run-through

174

of all the songs. Lanelle reassured Mayson that most of the background lyrics were easy and repetitive and he would catch on.

"Church boy, your time in the church came in handy for tonight," said Lanelle.

Mayson thought to push back on Lanelle by telling her not to call him "Church Boy" as she didn't want him calling her "Ma'am." Instead, he repeated in his mind, *let it go.*

At 11:15, people began to gather into the club. For such a small, unsophisticated space, the room soon began to fill. The band was now playing softly. Tamara was in the back office on the phone with her thirteen-year-old daughter, Shyann, who was taking care of her two younger siblings, nine-year-old Marquis and six-year-old Casey. Monica left to get limes for the bar and Lanelle was socializing with some of the customers who had arrived. Lanelle knew just about everyone who came in the door. Mayson left the stage and planted himself back at the same table where he had left his empty soda can.

As people entered the club, Mayson felt himself getting more nervous. At 12:10 the band was playing, and Mayson remained at the same table. As he heard the mumbled voices from the club patrons and the band playing its steady tune, he felt something on his shoulder. He looked at his shoulder and saw a hand. Mayson turned his head back and saw that it was Byron. Byron was standing over Mayson and looking as though he was ten feet tall. He was dressed casually, in a long-sleeved yellow cotton shirt and golden dress pants. He was sporting a brimmed hat that was just the right touch to his look. It was obvious that Byron was a man with power and money, thought Mayson. Despite his recent skepticism about Byron, he was glad to see him. With all the new people he met today, the cold shoulders from Tamara and Monica, and the scolding from Lanelle about his home-grown manners, Byron was a welcome sight.

"Waiting for your turn?" asked Byron, as he eyed Mayson and looked toward the stage.

"Yes," said Mayson with a pleasant smile.

For some reason, at that moment, Mayson felt that he would be safe with Byron being there. Also, with Byron's presence, he could have some of his questions and concerns answered.

"Did you get a chance to meet everyone?" asked Byron.

"Yes, everyone except Calvin. He's not coming in tonight," said Mayson.

"You'll be around to meet everyone you need to meet, so don't worry about who you haven't met," said Byron.

Byron pulled back one of the chairs at Mayson's table and sat. "So, what are you going to sing tonight?" he asked.

Mayson recited the song list.

"And which ones will you be leading?" asked Byron.

"I won't be the lead on any of them. Lanelle wants me as a backup for now," he said.

Mayson decided to leave the explanation at that. He didn't want any more problems with Lanelle and definitely didn't want to appear whiny or ungrateful.

"What?" said Byron with his eyebrows raised in surprise.

Mayson could see that Byron was alarmed. He found it unreasonable that Byron would think Lanelle could train his voice in one night, so he tried to make the matter sound simple.

"It's okay. Lanelle auditioned me and I'm sure I'll be able to develop my singing skills with her training over time," said Mayson.

"That's not acceptable," said Byron as he got up from the table and went to the back of the room where Lanelle was talking with one of the club patrons.

Mayson turned around to see what was going on. He saw the club patron with his shoulder against the wall and a drink in his hand as he talked with Lanelle. Mayson could not hear their conversation, but saw Byron give the patron a friendly slap on the back as he said a few words to him. The man shook his head as though he agreed with whatever Byron just said. He shook Byron's hand and walked to the other side of the room with his drink. Byron then touched Lanelle on her lower back as he guided her to a corner of the room near the door entrance. At one point, he gestured over at Mayson with his hands. Lanelle looked at Mayson and their eyes met. Mayson quickly turned back around. He felt tense, as he didn't know how Lanelle was taking Byron's reaction to her decision.

After 5 long minutes of avoiding eye contact with Byron and Lanelle, with the band now on break and the continued noise from the patrons, Mayson could faintly hear the taps on Byron's shoes. He could tell that he was making his way back over to him. Byron came back to Mayson's table. He made an effort to compose himself as he eased back into the chair and crossed his legs.

"Mayson, I'm sorry you had to go through this change in plans with the singing arrangements, but Lanelle explained that she will eventually get you up for lead songs. She needs to give you more time," said Byron softly.

"I know. I'm fine with that," said Mayson relieved that the matter between Byron and Lanelle hadn't escalated.

"Still, I think you would have been great tonight as the lead," said Byron.

"Thank you, but you may change your mind once you hear me sing," laughed Mayson.

Byron didn't respond.

"I'm still working on getting that job prepared for you. It's taking me a little time," said Byron.

"Don't rush it, Byron. Singing in the meantime is worth the wait," said Mayson.

Worth, thought Mayson. That keyword reminded him of Tamara and her warning him to get paid what he is worth.

"By the way, what will be my hourly pay?" asked Mayson.

"Oh, we never did discuss that," said Byron.

Byron tried to look as though this was something that he simply overlooked, however, because of Mayson's recent talk with Tamara, Mayson wondered if that really was the case.

Byron pulled a pen out from his pants pocket and wrote down a number on the napkin next to Mayson's drink. Mayson saw the number but didn't know if he should approve or negotiate it. He had nothing to measure this pay by in order to determine if it was reasonable, so he simply said, "Okay."

Byron proceeded to tell Mayson about the history of the club and how well-received it was in the community. Mayson was impressed with Byron's words, but the conversation brought on more questions. While Byron was talking, Mayson glanced around the room. He was aware of the cost for the drinks and light food, but it didn't seem to be enough to pay his staff and other expenses in running a club. Mayson decided to believe Byron's other businesses made up for the shortfall.

"How's everybody doing?" came over the microphone.

It was Lanelle at the mike, with the band playing softly behind her. Mayson had been so engrossed in conversation with Byron, he didn't notice when the band came back from their break.

"It's now time for us to sing some love into your evening," said Lanelle softly.

Byron hit Mayson on the shoulder.

"It's your time, Mayson," said Byron in an amusing tone.

Mayson smiled as he wiped the moistness from his hands onto his pants.

"I guess I'm a little nervous. This will be much different from singing in the choir," said Mayson.

Mayson didn't have concerns about singing backup itself, but because he was the only man, with his lone tenor voice, he thought it would be more obvious when he made a mistake.

"You have no reason to be nervous. This is a small club with friendly people," said Byron.

"Yeah, but I am," said Mayson.

"You'll do fine," said Byron.

Byron and Mayson sat silently for a while as Lanelle continued to warm the audience up in preparation for their upcoming selection. Mayson noticed that Tamara and Monica were not yet on the stage, so he decided to stay at the table until he saw them coming.

Byron broke the silence between them as he reached into his pants pocket and opened a small bottle.

"Mayson, I got these from my doctor a few months ago for my back and they really helped to relax me. They are effective, but harmless. They will help you get through this first performance," said Byron.

Mayson looked at the pills in Byron's hand for a few seconds and then at Byron. The offer of the "harmless" pills reminded Mayson of one of those Public Service Announcements that warns the danger of taking others prescription pills or avoiding illicit drug use.

"I think I'll be okay," said Mayson as he wiped his sweaty hands on his pants again.

"You sure?" asked Byron.

Mayson felt his legs getting weak and feared he may not get to the stage.

"They're prescription?" asked Mayson.

"Yeah, but you don't have to take them if you don't want. I just thought they might help," said Byron as he put the pills back in his pocket.

"Let me see them," asked Mayson.

Byron took the pills back out of his pocket and gave them to Mayson.

"They are only relaxers. You can find something similar to these in a local drug store," said Byron as Mayson was reading the label. The label had Byron's name on it and the doses was relatively low.

"Okay, just for tonight," said Mayson.

Mayson shook one of the pills from the bottle and handed the bottle back to Byron.

"I'll get you some water," said Byron.

Byron looked around the room and saw Monica and Tamara coming out from the direction of the club's office. He gave a wave to Monica and made a water-drinking motion to her.

Monica soon brought over the water to the table. As she sat the water down, she looked at Byron out of the side of her eye.

"Don't make this a habit," she said as she put the water down in front of Byron.

Mayson's eyebrows raised at the words of Monica.

"You will bring me water and anything else I want. Even if you have to crawl," said Byron.

Monica broke out in a hearty laugh. Byron smiled as he reached behind her and hugged her from the waist. Mayson felt relieved that their words appeared to be friendly banter.

Mayson took the pill with the water. As Tamara and Monica entered the stage, Mayson came on behind them. He felt light-headed as he walked onto the stage. Around the second song, a calmness came over him. He breezed through the whole set without a problem. He was elated with how well everything was going and particularly how well his voice carried through all the numbers. He decided that this night was the beginning of a whole new life for him.

CHAPTER 21

Mayson's Reappearance at GCC

There he sat in Tony's BMW. Mayson had decided to drive Tony's car for his great reappearance at GCC. As he waited to get enough nerves to get out of the car, he thought about Tony. Tony had Sundays off and was home sleeping in. During the few times that Mayson and Tony had time together, Mayson would tell Tony about the club and his new friends. Tony was glad to see that Mayson had found something to do to fill his time, but he was curious about what had happened with the distribution job offer. When he asked Mayson about it, Mayson told him that it would come in due time. Tony had concerns about Byron and his odd way of doing business, but since Mayson said very little about Byron anymore, he decided to let the matter go. He was just glad to see Mayson happy. Tony had told Mayson several times that he wanted to go to the club to hear the group. Mayson would ask him to wait and give more time for them to "grow their group." In reality, Mayson was not ready to share who Tony was with those at the club. Tony sensed this and after several such conversations, he asked Mayson if he was ashamed of their relationship. Mayson denied it. He reasoned that it was not about being ashamed but more about not being ready for others to be a part of their lives.

Mayson knew that when Tony woke up this day from his late Sunday morning sleep, he would ask more questions about Mayson's whereabouts. Particularly during recent times when Mayson's "I'll be right back," would turn into hours or sometimes the next day. On the days when Mayson's explanation was his job, Tony didn't have many reasons not to believe him. Tony limited himself to address those times when Mayson would not discuss his whereabouts concerning hours that didn't include his job. There were days when he wondered how much he could take when it came to Mayson's well-being and, perhaps, his possible infidelity.

Mayson mused that if he was ever going to visit GCC, Tony's day off would be the best time to do so and avoid conflict with Tony. Despite their occasional disagreements, Mayson's heart still belonged to Tony. But Mayson's desire to spend more time with Tony was now replaced by the world that Byron introduced him to. He had been working at the club almost a year and Byron had him involved in other matters too, although none that had to do with his original promise of managing his distribution center or a career as a singer. His admiration for Byron had changed. Byron had him in a web that he struggled to get out of. Mayson wanted to believe that one day he would get himself together, and away from the world of Byron Crawford. He saw himself and Tony resuming their life as it was when they first met. During those days, he and Tony were not just companions, but also the best of friends.

When he and Tony had words over Mayson's hours away from home and the missing details of his job, Mayson would have Tony believe that it was his fault. Mayson knew this was not the case, but to shut Tony up and avoid further arguments, guilt-ridden words were what he would spew out at Tony. However, when Tony began to make changes on his job for time with Mayson, Mayson no longer could use the "blame Tony" game to justify his behavior and treatment of Tony with avoidance and limited communication. He knew that Tony worked hard to keep his beautiful condo, car and other nice things that Mayson treated as his own. He felt bad about his treatment towards him, but until he finished with Byron, he had to keep Tony at a distance.

Initially, he resented Tony not being around as much and wondered whether he was punishing Tony for spending too much time on his job—and, possibly comparing Tony to his father's supposed "overtime." His mother was not aware that he knew what his father's so called work over times were about. Benton was too small for him not to know otherwise. Yet, deep down he knew that Tony was not seeing anyone else. He knew that in Tony's case, his job was his mistress. With the things Byron had him doing and the time that it now took him away from Tony, Mayson was more frightened at the thought that now, he too was behaving like his father.

With all the changes that had occurred in Mayson's life, there was barely a day he didn't think about GCC. He would call his mother periodically and experience GCC through her. However, the more additional duties Byron assigned him away from the club, the less time he found for his mother and Tony.

As he sat in the car in front of GCC church, he looked at his hair in the sun visor mirror of the car. He hadn't braided it because he had gotten home in the early morning from the club, so it wasn't as fluffy. He had wanted to look nice and well-off for his reappearance at GCC, but his decision to go was spur-of-the-moment.

As he sat, he allowed himself to think about the many wonderful days he had had at GCC. He thought about the first time he and his family came to GCC. He was five years old. He recalled the first time he met Reanna. They were in the same Sunday School class and would somehow always end up sitting together in the class. Sister Emerson was their Sunday School teacher. Sister Emerson died about three years ago from complications of diabetes. She had one of the largest funerals at the church because she was well-loved by all who knew her. It was one of the only funerals where Pastor Upshaw broke down as he tried to preach. She was full figured and always had a glow about her. She was what Pastor Upshaw described as the perfect example of a church member and Sunday-school teacher. Whenever she was pleased with something any of the children did in her class, she would give them a big hug that would smother their faces. Mayson liked getting hugs from Sister Emerson. Not only were her hugs comforting, but she always smelled like whatever she had cooked before coming to church.

He and Reanna didn't begin their friendship at this age. Instead, Mayson spent much of his time at church with his young friend, Leon. Because of Leon's physical deformity, none of the other children would play with him. They made jokes about him and called him Quasi, like Quasimodo from *The Hunchback of Notre Dame*. Mayson was thirteen when he and Reanna joined the young adult choir and officially became friends. Prior to Leon's placement in a medical care group home, Leon, Mayson, and Reanna were the teen tight threesome at the church.

Mayson thought about all the wonderful services that they had at GCC. He thought about the inspiring sermon messages from Pastor Upshaw and visiting ministers that frequented their church. He smiled as he remembered how the church members would organize to stay at church until the next service. They would bring in potluck for dinner or everyone would go out to eat together. He thought about the late-night church musicals that the young people would have and how he and Reanna would make sure they attended almost every one of them. One night, rather than cancel her date, Reanna broke her rule of keeping her social and church life separate and brought her date along with her. The guy was an auto mechanic from the neighborhood, but definitely not a church person. He looked so uncomfortable in the service. About an hour into the service, he told Reanna he was going to the restroom and that was the last that she saw of him. Mayson thought about the fact that she brought her date to church and laughed so hard that he looked around to make sure that no one saw him. With his hands rested on his lap and his eyes glued to the church building, he felt a tear run down his cheek.

"Could I give up my love for Tony, just to be a member of GCC?" he asked himself.

Before he allowed himself to come up with an answer, he felt his left hand opening the car door and stepped out onto the parking lot. As Mayson walked to the church door, he felt surreal. His approach to the church felt familiar and yet strange. He opened the church door and the blast of the music and singing of the congregation overwhelmed his senses. He felt drawn to the familiar smells and sounds of the church. The ushers were standing at the glass doors that led directly into the main sanctuary. Mayson could see the surprised look on their faces. They both opened the doors for Mayson to come in. One of the ushers was Sister Hopkins. She had been with GCC almost as long as Pastor Upshaw. The other usher was Sister Reynolds. She had come to the church around the same time that Mayson and his family joined. As Mayson walked to enter the double doors the ushers had opened for him, he felt like royalty. He could feel his heart leap towards both of them. Sister Hopkins took Mayson's hand, gave it a tight squeeze, and then handed him the order of service brochure. Before Mayson could turn around to walk further, Sister Reynolds put her hands on his shoulder. When he turned around to face her, she gave him a tight hug. Sister Reynold's hug reminded him of Sister Emerson's enveloping hugs. Sister Reynold's whispered in his ear:

"You need to eat boy. You too thin."

Sister Hopkins, with her white usher gloves on and one hand behind her back, extended her hand to the right side of the church to escort Mayson to a seat. She walked in front of Mayson as they walked down the side wall of the church, looking for a seat in the crowded sanctuary. As they walk, Mayson looked on the left side of the church where he, Reanna and Lamont used to sit whenever they didn't have to sing in the choir. He didn't expect to see Reanna or Lamont sitting in their favorite spot among the congregation, because it was the young people's turn to sing in the choir today.

As Mayson looked around the church, he saw both familiar and new faces in the congregation. He could feel Pastor Upshaw looking at him from the pulpit, so he made an effort not to look directly at him. Instead, Mayson looked in the choir, to the right behind Pastor Upshaw, where he saw Reanna who gave him a small wave. He smiled softly at her. He could see Lamont in the choir also. Lamont had spotted Mayson when he first came in the church. When he saw Mayson looking in his direction, he immediately looked away from him. Mayson didn't think much of it, as Lamont was a bit hard to read at times.

Seeing the familiar faces reminded Mayson of how much he missed his family and friends. He realized how much his life had changed from the time he left his home, moved in with Tony, and met Byron. It was not simply a matter of his being too busy for them but more of a matter of his efforts to avoid them. Despite his occasional busy schedule, he felt a loneliness that sometimes disoriented him from who he was. There were times in the night when he would wake not knowing who he was. This scared him tremendously. When it happened a third time, he went to see a doctor who examined him and concluded that it could be attributed to anxiety.

As Mayson sat, he looked around the church for more identifiable faces. His eyes landed on a girl who looked familiar from across the church. She was waving in his direction. In order to avoid embarrassment, he didn't wave back as he thought she may be waving at someone else behind him. Yet, he couldn't take his eyes off this girl because she looked like someone he should know. When a wide grin came across her face, Mayson smiled and laughed. Despite the distance, Mayson recognized that it was Idee. He hadn't recognized her because her hair was cut short, and she was wearing a little more makeup than their mother usually allowed.

Sitting about two seats in front of Idee was Deandra, whom Mayson imagined was either visiting GCC or had become a member since his departure. When he looked at Deandra he thought about Veronica. Veronica was married now. What was even more frightening was the thought that Veronica could be in the church and Melvin with her. As with many other things, Mayson continued to struggle with his thoughts about Melvin. He might have indulged himself by visualizing about Reanna's male companions, but Melvin was someone that he selected on his own. Mayson searched from one end of the church to the other to see if Veronica or Melvin were anywhere, but he stopped looking for fear of actually finding them.

He and Veronica had never resumed their relationship since that day he snapped at her in her car over Melvin. He knew it was odd for him to snap at her like that over Melvin, but he believed that at some point, she would have put the pieces together and realized that he had feelings for Melvin. When he heard about their marriage, he initially thought of the irony, but he also wondered was this union simply payback from Veronica. He shrugged the thought off and refocused his thought away from Melvin and Veronica as he searched across the church for his mother. He looked for her in her usual seat near the church podium, but she was not there. As he sat, he could feel the eyes of those that knew him slowly moving back to the church service itself. He heard the church announcements and the Old and New Testament scriptures read by their head deacon. Nothing much had changed, he thought. They had a visiting evangelist, Evangelist Townsend, who was sitting up front next to Pastor Upshaw. Mayson remembered Evangelist Townsend from a revival they had a few years ago. His controversial teachings of the Bible, which included translations from the original Greek or Hebrew, made some people uncomfortable. For some, it contradicted or denounced some of their traditional understanding of certain scriptures. With much of his translations and interpretations, he showed God in a more compassionate and supportive relationship with Humankind; rather than a constantly wrathful and angry God. For this reason, some pastors didn't invite Evangelist Townsend to their church to teach. They called his teaching a "watered-down" gospel. However, a few pastors in the city welcomed this refreshing understanding of God's word. Mayson thought it odd that Pastor Upshaw would favor this evangelist to come and minister in his services. Mayson always saw a more graceful side to Pastor Upshaw and believed that much of his harsher messages originated from a need to align with other leaders of his denomination. Most importantly, Pastor Upshaw's sermon messages were based on what his senior members expected. It was what they were raised on. And these senior members were also his most faithful tithes and offering payers.

He was excited to see this evangelist as he anticipated that he may bring a *message in due season* that was just for him. He gleefully anticipated what selections the choir would be singing. He looked at the service program and saw that the order of service had not changed much. As usual, after a choir selection, the pastor or visiting minister would thereafter bring the word of God, observed Mayson from the program.

After the deacon read another scripture, Evangelist Townsend stood up and walked to the podium. He spoke how glad he was to be in the service. He explained that he was not there to minister the main sermon message but wanted to come and be a part of the service as he listened to Pastor Upshaw share the word of God. Mayson felt disappointment as he heard those words. He so wanted to hear Evangelist Townsend.

However, Evangelist Townsend said he wanted to share a scripture with everyone. He read from the Old Testament:

"Behold, how good and how pleasant it is for brethren to dwell together in unity!

It is like the precious ointment upon the head, that ran down upon the beard, even Aaron's beard: that went down to the skirts of his garments.

As the dew of Hermon, and as the dew that descended upon the mountains of Zion: for there the Lord commanded the blessing, even life forevermore." Psalms 133: 1-3

He stopped and explained the passage in a way that Mayson had never thought of before. He ended his time with the following to the congregation.

"Your blessing can be in what and how you see it. I describe Behold as a time to stop and look. Not just look, but to hold that look for all its blessings. Don't worry about tomorrow or anything else than the beauty you see and hold in that moment. When you find yourself in good, beautiful, or awesome moments, just "be" and "hold" it."

Evangelist Townsend then took his seat amidst thunderous

applause and verbal praises to God from the congregation.

"Just *be* and *hold* it," muttered Mayson.

Mayson then realized that he was in a *behold moment* as he looked over the church and saw people that he knew and loved despite any past hurts. Despite Pastor Upshaw's choice to seat him during services, that *behold moment* pushed away the ill-will and allowed him to see their relationship from better days. The dominance of love in fellowship had overtaken his need for revenge or spite. Instead, he still felt the hug from the usher at the door, the smiles and waves from his loved ones as he entered the church, and the excitement he felt from seeing familiar faces. As he embraced himself in the *behold moment,* he felt a love from God that he'd never allow to be possible. He was not Mayson, the "homosexual" who left GCC. Neither was he Mayson, the son of a man who had very little to do with him. Nor was he involved with a man named Byron who was shady in his dealings. In this moment, he saw himself as *Mayson, loved by those who see him through the eyes of God.*

After the inspiring words from the evangelist, the church went into their Praise and Testimony service. One of Mayson's favorite songs to sing during Praise and Testimony service was, *My Life is in His Hand.* The inspiring words of the evangelist gave a sparked that caused Mayson to feel, in a small *behold moment,* as though he was back home at GCC. In the midst of the moment, arose his favorite congregational song within him. He could hear the song in his head:

Verse
♫ *Here stand reaching for God's hand*
Never trying to be more than I am
For at the end of the day, all I can say
My Life is in His hands ♫
Chorus
♫ *In His hands*
In His hands,
My life is in his hands ♫

Verse
♫ *When the sun rises beginning its new day*
I look to my Father for every step of the way

No longer bound by what I fear, for God word speaks ever so clear ♫
Chorus

♫ *In His hands*

In His hands,
My life is in his hands ♫

Dare I lead a song now? he thought. He recalled Pastor Upshaw's words:

"I need to ask you not to sing in the choir this Sunday while I am gone. If you testify in the service, I need for you to be honest about who you are as it stands with God. "

He reasoned that Pastor Upshaw would not let him have a position in the church, nor sing in the choir, but he never said he could not sing among the congregation. During a brief lull between congregant's praise songs, Mayson heard a loud voice rang out in his ear. Someone was singing his song:

♫ *When the sun rises beginning its new day*
I look to my Father for every step of the way
No longer bound by what I fear, for God word speaks ever so clear
In His hands, In His hands ♫...

Mayson realized that it was him. He felt himself rise from his seat, with his eyes tightly closed and head raised high as he sang from everything he could pull forth within him. He heard himself singing alone for a while. Later a familiar voice joined in. He knew it was Reanna's. He soon heard scattered voices from the congregation join in. As Mayson sang, he then could hear more and more voices join in. Soon a full complement of voices began singing along with him. Many of the congregants looked to see Pastor Upshaw's response. Pastor Upshaw sat in his chair in the pulpit and looked at Mayson as he nodded his head in beat with the music. His response appeared neutral and unconcerned. As Mayson sang, one by one, the church members began to stand as they could hear the emotion in his voice. Deandra stood to see who was singing with such power. She knew that *My Life Is in His Hand* was one of Mayson's favorite congregational songs, but could it really be him? she wondered. She remembered his voice as a bit overdone and strained with effort. This time, his voice was so strong and powerful that she had to stand in order to see over the heads of others. Others who were also standing in curiosity and admiration. She was aware of what had transpired between him and Veronica. She knew about Mayson's *scandal* and his departure from the church. But at that moment, *Behold!* It didn't matter. Instead, she was overwhelmed with emotion as she heard him sing.

From the side of the church, a door from the church's administration room opened. Phyllis was in her church's finance committee meeting, but when she heard the song and the voice, she and a few of the others from the meeting went out to see who it was singing. Phyllis looked toward the area where the voice was coming from. She saw Mayson standing and singing with his eyes closed. Phyllis clapped her hands over her mouth in amazement. Mayson didn't tell her that he was coming to service. To see him there singing as though he had never left, and with such meaning in his voice, left her in shock. Overcome with emotion, she sat in a vacant seat near the administrative office door. After a few seconds, the others slowly went back to their meeting. Phyllis remained stunned in her seat. She began to thank God that her son had come to church. *Behold!*

CHAPTER 22

Mayson's Work Family

(I)

Mayson had been singing at the club for several months now. He became familiar with all the workings of the club. He knew some of the regular customers by name. No longer was he sitting at an empty table alone, waiting for Tamara and Monica to come to the stage. Rather, he found himself busy doing things around the club that became routine for him. Once it was certain Calvin was no longer coming back to serve the drinks, Mayson attended bartending school. Soon he was able to open up the club, get it ready for the night, and pick up some of the food and drinks for Lanelle. Byron purchased a late-model van for Mayson to use. This team-player spirit caused Lanelle to let down some of her defensiveness with Mayson. She found herself liking Mayson more and more. As for Tamara, as long as Mayson was not leading songs, she felt safe with him and found him to be one of her most endearing friends. She was fascinated with Mayson's biblical knowledge and his obvious church background. She'd also share with Mayson amusing and challenging matters about her children. Mayson didn't mind her talking about her children to him. He missed his family and her stories allowed him to share stories about his siblings as well. Mayson admired Tamara's resilience. He saw her as the queen of Plan B's. Tamara had a routine with her daughter that involved calling her at least every two hours to see how things were going. Everyone at the club worked around her two-hour intervals. They were all supportive except for Byron. He demanded that she take breaks along with everyone else or go home and stay with her children. When Byron was not around, Lanelle disregarded Byron's demand and told Tamara, "Just don't let that fool catch you."

Mayson shared with Tamara many of his family stories, but nothing about Tony. He also shared bits and pieces of information about his church family, GCC. He avoided the specifics of why he was not currently attending GCC. When Tamara asked Mayson a second time why he no longer attended GCC, Mayson changed from his first response of "I'm between churches" to "I've been too busy to go, but plan to start going back soon." He knew this was not necessarily true, but he didn't want Tamara to become suspicious. As for Monica, she was nice to Mayson, but unlike Tamara, she never talked about her personal life with him.

Mayson soon began to feel in sync with the club and all its workings. He learned all the "do's and don'ts" and didn't have a problem with staying in his own lane. As for the club patrons, he was schooled that it was best not to get into personal relationships with them, but if you did, don't let any of the drama get back to the club. He also learned that when it came to lead singers, Tamara was second for the job and never try to change that. As for Monica, let her be nice to you, but don't try and enter her world. Urban being Mr. Romeo of the group, he either came to the club with a woman or found one there; he would later leave with her around closing. Urban was a ladies' man and not someone to take seriously in terms of an intimate relationship. From what Tamara had told Mayson, she learned this lesson about Urban the hard way. She and Urban had been in a relationship for a brief period of time. When it went sour, Lanelle stepped in and told them to pick between either their relationship or their jobs.

As for Lanelle, she seemed to be in her own world. She managed the club and always stayed busy. Once Mayson learned his boundaries with Lanelle, they got along well. Mayson knew that Lanelle didn't like to be asked personal questions, especially about her beginnings with Byron. With Lanelle, he also learned to drop all the traditional formalities of what he considered "showing manners to elders."

Tim and Trenton didn't have any obvious rules. They came, did their work, and were gone at the end of the work shift. They were faithful in their attendance to the club. Tim was married, so he made sure to leave immediately at closing in order to not entertain his wife's imagination. Trenton graduated from college and came in every day with news about his efforts at finding a job in his field.

As for Calvin, the missing bartender, Mayson initially thought Calvin was off work only for that one first night, instead, Calvin never returned.

He later heard that Calvin had quit. No one knew what happened between him and Byron that led to him not returning. After two weeks of Calvin not coming in for his shift, Byron had finally told Lanelle that Calvin was terminated. Lanelle told Mayson that there were some things that you do not want to ask Byron. The abrupt ending of an employee was one of those things.

Mayson and Lanelle stayed at the club after closing. They cleaned up and prepared for the next day. Mayson didn't mind the absence of the guys, because he felt close to Lanelle and liked that special time with her. In addition to eating out together, they also managed a few movies, jazz concerts, and walks through the park, as Lanelle was trying to shed a few pounds. On a few occasions, particularly on weekends, Tamara would join them in some of their morning activities. Lanelle, Tamara, and Mayson were the new Mayson, Reanna, and Lamont, thought Mayson. But this was a little different. Rather than being friends with just one woman as with Reanna, now he was friends with two. Mayson had concerns that it was obvious that he was the "gay male friend." The go-to cliché of not caring what others think of him was not an encouragement for him. He didn't want to care what everyone thought of him, but he did have a few who had earned his respect to care.

Mayson continued to take the muscle relaxer pills for each perfor- mance. He eventually credited the pills for eliminating his stage fright. Byron would supply the pills whenever Mayson ran out. Mayson felt that he was a part of a family now. Still he was unaware that with families, there can be that one that even mama can't control.

(II)

"I'll be back. I have to leave for about 20 minutes to get another shirt for the second set," said Mayson.

"Hurry," said Lanelle, concerned that he would not make it back in time.

Mayson left the club through the back kitchen door to his car. He continued to drive the BMW on days that Tony didn't need it. On days when Tony needed the car, Lanelle or Tamara would pick him up. They knew Tony's condo didn't belong to Mayson but Lanelle never asked him who owned it. Tamara probed without hesitation as to who the condo belonged to. Mayson only responded to Tamara, "It belongs to a good friend." Lanelle and Tamara believed Mayson to be Human because he was so secretive about his relationships and he never talked about any kind of romantic other.

In an effort to get back to the club in time for their second set, Mayson started running across the parking lot to his car. This was a special night at the Encounter Club: Patton Starks was a local singer who had had a few appearances on the national stage, and he was now appearing at the Encounter Club. Patton was friends with Byron at one time and, as Byron put it, "he owes me a favor." In order to have enough room for the crowd of patrons they were expecting that night, Lanelle had her staff park their cars closer to the back of the club. She moved some of the tables around and added more seats in order to make room for the additional patrons.

As Mayson ran, he was amazed at how full the parking lot was. It was so full that many of the club patrons had to park across the street at the laundromat that was now closed. He was out of breath, so he slowed into a fast walk towards his car. He saw an automobile near the back of the lot that stood out. A blue pickup truck that looked like Cliff's truck. As Mayson walked toward his car, he went a little farther to the right, past a row of other cars to see if this was Cliff's truck. He peered in the front passenger window and saw a well-kept truck with no clutter, other than a napkin draped over a coffee cup in the cupholder. This must be Cliff's truck, thought Mayson. "No one keeps their truck as clean as Cliff," he said as he peered through the glass.

As Mayson was peering into the truck, he heard a voice behind him. "Excuse me," the voice said.

Mayson turned around and saw it was J.R. J.R. stood behind Mayson with an amused look on his face. He had on a jersey, jeans and a blue cap with a ball team logo on it. Mayson could feel his face turn red from embarrassment.

"Hey Mayson! What are you doing here man?" J.R. asked.

Mayson shifted his eyes away from J.R. as he backed away from the truck.

"I work here," mumbled Mayson.

"Oh, I didn't know. Mama never filled me in," said J.R.

Mayson didn't respond, because he didn't have the heart to tell Phyllis where he worked. He didn't share this with J.R. It was hard enough that she knew about him and Tony. However, he knew that because of his mother's social network, it was possible that his mother knew about his work at the club. Benson was such a small town.

"I didn't see you in the club," said J.R.

"I must have left out the back when you came in the front," said Mayson.

"Yeah, I guess so... I'm here with a date and I left my wallet in the car," said J.R.

Mayson gave J.R. a brief glance and then looked up to avoid further eye contact with him. He was hoping it would end the awkward conversation between them. This was the first time he had seen J.R. since he moved out from their mother's home. He sensed that J.R. knew the whole story. Despite their divorce, Mayson knew that Phyllis shared a lot with Cliff.

The more J.R. smiled and came up with pleasantries, the more agitated Mayson became. He felt that J.R. was glad that he was no longer in their mother's home. Mayson believed that his absence from Phyllis' home gave J.R. the freedom to visit with his family without having to be around Mayson. One memory of J.R. from years ago had stayed in Mayson's mind. Mayson overheard his mother on the phone with Cliff, trying to get him to ask J.R. to invite Mayson on their fishing trip. He heard Phyllis saying that he needed to talk to J.R. about his attitude towards his brother. Mayson had never been fishing, but he would have liked to go with them and see what all the fuss was about. He'd have also liked to have that time with Cliff and J.R. At that time, rather than being angry or resentful of J.R., he envied him. J.R. had the best of both parents. If I only had that much love, Mayson had thought.

No longer living in his mother's home allowed Mayson to see some things in a different perspective, and J.R. was one of those differences. He looked at J.R. in the parking lot, expecting him to talk with him as though they were brothers and good friends. He felt another shot of resentment as he looked at J.R.'s cap with the sports logo on it. He knew the cap was from one of the many games that he and Cliff had attended together. He decided to cut the conversation short.

"I gotta go," said Mayson. He turned to leave as J.R. stood with his keys in his hands watching him walk away to his car.

"Take care man," yelled J.R., as he turned to open his car. After getting his wallet out of the glove compartment, he saw Mayson drive off the lot in the BMW.

"Wow," said J.R. as he stared at the car driving off into the distance.

CHAPTER 23

The Honeymoon Web

Deception comes with a cost

It had been two months since Melvin and Veronica's wedding. They both were trying to continue their education, but it was a challenge with the additional expenses. Evangelist Sutton was able to get Melvin and Veronica in one of the more upscale apartment dorms. He bought furniture and paid for a few other things, then produced a promissory note for Melvin to pay him back. Melvin and Veronica had started a list of how much they would owe Melvin's parents and a goal date for Melvin to start working to pay the debt. Veronica was also getting monies from the educational account that her mother had opened for her. She knew that if she actually did get pregnant and the money started dwindling faster, her mother would know that something was up. But since their wedding, Melvin had not touched her. Veronica told her mother about her marriage the day after the wedding. Her mother was beyond shocked and angry. She immediately asked Veronica if she was pregnant. Veronica had expected this. She had rehearsed what she would say when this question came up. For most of her life, she had shared almost everything with her mother. But this was something she had a difficult time sharing with anyone. She already lost her friendship with Deandra over her pregnancy lie. She and Deandra were quite different, but those complementary differences made their union as roommates develop into friendship. Veronica helped Deandra loosen up a little and Deandra was Veronica's voice of reason in challenging situations or temptations. Veronica was still grieving the loss of their friendship.

Veronica knew how important it was for her mother to see her graduate from college, so telling her that she was pregnant would be such a letdown. She didn't want her mother to go through such a disappointment for a lie. On the other hand, if she told her mother the truth, that she was not pregnant, it would make matters that much more complicated, she thought. It would saddle with the task of keeping her mother and Melvin apart, because they would have different answers about her pregnancy. Giving them different answers would be a lot to balance, but she couldn't take the risk of them somehow coming together with different answers about her pregnancy. If I tell my mother I'm pregnant, she'll be disappointed for a while, but she'll be okay after she sees that I have graduated anyway, she thought. So, she too will have to live with a lie for a while, she concluded.

Veronica thought about that phone call when she told her mother she was pregnant:

"Ok, yes, I am pregnant," said Veronica in a rushed voice, when her mother asked.

"Veronica!" her mother screamed. "I've always hoped that you'd get married someday, but not like this. How far along are you?"

This was a difficult question for Veronica to answer. She worried that at some point she might get confused when asked again about her months of pregnancy.

"Somewhere in the middle," said Veronica.

"You don't know?" asked her mother, horrified.

"Mommy, I'm just too tired right now to think," said Veronica.

"What will you do about school?"

"I will finish school," said Veronica in a robotic tone.

"Who will take care of the baby while you are in school?"

More questions, thought Veronica.

"I'll finish," said Veronica in an annoyed tone. "Let's get off this subject!" she shouted.

"Don't yell at me!" her mother shouted back. "You can't drop this news on me and expect me to talk about the weather."

They both were silent for a while.

"May I know who this boy is who's keeping you from your education because he couldn't keep it in his pants?" asked her mother.

"Mommy, did you have to go there?" asked Veronica, with frustration. "His name is Melvin Sutton and he is in his last year of college for a degree in communications."

"Where is his family?" asked her mother.

"They live here in Benton," she said.

"You'll need someone to help you with the baby. Maybe they can help you, but I can't. I'm too far away and it's not my fault you got yourself into this," said her mother firmly.

"Whatever, Mommy," said Veronica.

Melvin worked hard to make sure that Veronica had everything she needed to have a healthy baby. With each passing day, she found it more and more difficult to tell him there was no baby. They didn't have a sex life because Melvin told her he didn't want to harm the baby. Veronica wanted to believe that he was naive about pregnant women, but in reality, she knew he had no further sexual attraction for her. What happened in his car that day was something that was done in the heat of the moment. Their now union was all about his wanting the baby. His sole expression of affection was kissing her on the forehead when he left for class before her.

On a quiet evening when they were at the kitchen table doing school-work, Veronica decided to tell him about the baby. They'd been married for 2 and a half months. It was the one time in her life Veronica was glad to be overweight. No one could really tell if she was putting on more weight but Melvin would tell her he could see her expanding. She knew he was seeing what he wanted to see. She often told herself that he needed to know there was no baby. However, she'd always conclude that telling him there never was a baby, was out of the question. Not only would she have to deal with the consequences of his reaction of her deceit, but she would also have to face his parents who were bankrolling her lie. In telling him, her disclosure had to be somewhere in the middle.

Nothing more than to just do it, she thought.

"Melvin, I have something I need to tell you," she said.

"Wait a minute, I'm missing a page from my notes," he said as he rifled through his papers.

His directive for her to wait was not off-putting for Veronica. It gave her more time to think about how to break this to him.

"There we go," said Melvin as he held up the page he was looking for.

Veronica could feel her heart racing. She had the urge to not tell him and wait another time.

Once I tell him, it will change everything, she thought. Veronica felt a heaviness come over her. She stared at the floor for a period of time. She then felt something wet hit her hand. She looked at her hand and it was tears. Her tears. She sniffed and felt another drop fall to her hand again.

Pity, she thought. I'm feeling sorry for myself.

She wiped her eyes and looked up only to see Melvin looking at her as though he was frozen in time.

"What's wrong?" he asked.

"Melvin, I lost the baby!" she shouted. There, I said it. Its out there, she thought to herself.

Melvin looked at her, stunned.

"What!" he shouted.

"Don't make me say it again," she said.

Melvin pushed away from the table while staring at Veronica.

"You mean there's no baby?" he said.

Veronica could see the shock and uncertainty in Melvin's face. Uncertainty with hope that he had not heard her correctly.

"I said, don't make me repeat it," Veronica sniffled.

She saw the look of shock slowly turn into a heaviness in his eyes. The heaviness that blended into sadness that was so obvious to see. He brushed his hands over his thick black hair as though touching it would ease his pain. She saw a hurt in Melvin that made her tears change from feeling sorry for herself, to feeling sorry for his loss. A loss that she knew never existed.

"When did this happen?" he asked yet in disbelief.

"Last week," said Veronica. She had difficulty looking at him in the face.

"Why didn't you tell me?" he asked.

"It was a difficult time for me, and I could hardly believe it myself. Besides, you never cared about me, so I didn't feel the need to rush and tell you," she said sullenly.

"How did you get to the hospital?" he asked.

Veronica had not prepared for that question and had to think quickly.

"I took a cab," she said.

"No baby? I have no baby?" he repeated to make sure.

"I already told you and I'm not going to repeat myself again," said Veronica haughtily as she looked back at her paper in an effort to ignore him.

Melvin quickly stood up. His chair fell onto the linoleum kitchen floor with a loud clang. He stormed out of the room and into their bedroom and slammed the door.

Veronica picked up her pen to continue work on her research paper. As she wrote, she saw the ink smear as she began crying again. She put the pen down and went to the couch and laid on it as she continued to cry. After forty minutes, she heard the bedroom door open. Melvin came back out. His eyes were red, and his hair appeared as though he had continued running his fingers through it in the bedroom.

"Was there ever a baby?" he asked softly.

"What do you think?" asked Veronica sharply.

"Veronica, was there a baby?" he shouted at her. "My parents spent a lot on us for this baby. And I need to—" he stopped. "Maybe I don't need to know," he said as he stared down at Veronica on the couch. "What was I thinking? I should have gone with you on those doctor appointments. No matter how much you urged me not to. I can't believe I was such a dope," he screamed as he beat his fist on the kitchen counter.

Veronica felt a fear come over her. She saw a vein protrude from his neck and his eyes became bloodshot red. She had never seen Melvin that angry.

"Melvin, will you please calm down? People have miscarriages every day," she said in an effort to calm him.

"I got to get out of here," he said as he grabbed his jacket out of the bedroom, then his car keys off the hook near the door and left the apartment.

That was the last time Melvin engaged in direct conversation with Veronica about the baby. He went back and forth with one possibility or the other. Whether it was miscarried or she never was pregnant, both ended with there not being a baby. He leaned more toward her never having been pregnant, but knew that would make him look that much more foolish in the eyes of his father. After walking out on Veronica, he often spent the night at Eric's apartment. Eric and his older brother had an apartment together and it was a bit crowded at times, especially when his brother brought his girlfriend over to spend the night. On those nights, Melvin would go home and sleep on the couch in his apartment. When Eric's brother moved in with his girlfriend, Melvin sometimes stayed at Eric's apartment for days. He hoped his long absence from the apartment would initiate Veronica ending their marriage. That way, his father would not see the divorce as his fault. His father didn't believe in divorce and often preached against it. For Melvin to initiate the divorce would be more of a disappointment for his father. To add insult to injury, there was all the money his parents had spent on them. Once he told his parents about the miscarriage, he promised his father even more that he would pay him back.

Melvin's parents were suspicious of Veronica's miscarriage, particularly his mother, who had a miscarriage herself. She had wondered why Veronica hadn't called anyone to take her to the hospital. The week she said she had the miscarriage, she and Melvin had been at Melvin's parents' house for dinner, and she had looked well and did not express any discomfort or concern.

The day after Veronica told Melvin she miscarried, she decided to call her mother and tell her the news. Her mother also asked several questions about the loss of the baby, which led to an argument as Veronica tried to avoid answering any of her questions.

Veronica felt lonely in the apartment with Melvin gone all the time. Some days she found herself crying over how things had turned out. There were days when she felt hatred for Melvin, but they had put so much into their living arrangements that neither would initiate the topic of divorce. Veronica held onto the marriage our of shame and fear of her lie, but also because of the gentle side of Melvin she discovered when he thought he was to be a father. This side of him stayed with her and, for a time, made her believe that she loved him. Some days she would feel nothing but love for him. Other days the hatred would take its place again.

No matter what happened in their relationship, they both continued school. The times when they would see each other on the college campus, they would walk past each other without a word. On a few occasions, Veronica would wait to talk to him about an overdue bill that she needed him to pay. Melvin would take the bill from her without a word. Some bills he paid, others he did not.

When Veronica and Melvin married, Veronica stopped going to her church and began going to Faith on a Mission church with Melvin. Deandra stopped going to Faith on a Mission due to Veronica's attendance. Veronica had heard she was visiting other churches on Sundays, including GCC. After Veronica told Melvin she had a miscarriage, they both stopped going to church altogether.

One morning, Veronica sat on the end of her bed and looked around at her lonely apartment. She had an early class that day, but the thought of her slowly nonexistent marriage made it hard for her to move from the edge of her bed. Melvin would periodically come to the apartment at night on some days and sleep on the couch, but it had now been seven consecutive days since he had been home. She was in a dither in what to do about his abandonment. Despite her misery of living the results of her sham marriage, she had never missed her classes. She managed to shower, get dressed and left the apartment. When she got out of her car on the campus parking lot, she saw Mayson sitting on a bench near the student center. She was surprised to see him, as she knew he was not a student.

Since the outburst over Melvin, she had not spoken to Mayson since. The news had gotten out about her losing the baby and she was certain that Mayson had heard. Melvin was still friends with Eric, and she heard him tell Eric over the phone about losing the baby. Veronica also knew that Eric occasionally ran in the same circles as Reanna, so she felt her to be the pipeline back to Mayson.

Mayson's back was turned to her, but she knew it was him because of his large, fluffy afro. She gazed at the back of his head and thought how better it would be if she had married him rather than Melvin. I would

202

have fought to keep us together, despite our differences, she thought. I don't have that fight in me for Melvin.

Her class was in the opposite direction of the student center, but she felt she had to connect with Mayson and see how she felt about him now.

She grasped her bookbag tighter. As she walked closer towards Mayson, she could see his head resting on the back of the bench, with his hands on his lap and his eyes half-open. She stood beside him looking down on his head. His hair seemed dry and sandy, particularly in the hot sun. She stood there for a while waiting for him to notice her, but he didn't. She looked in the direction where he was partially looking and there she saw Melvin, about fifty feet away, sitting on his bike and talking to a girl. It was a little before noon and very hot. Melvin tended to take off his shirt whenever he rode his bike. He had his shirt off and tied around the handlebar of his bike. Despite the marriage, Melvin maintained his model-like physique. The glistening of the sun on his muscles made him look like a television commercial for men's sportswear or cologne.

Veronica was not sure if Melvin saw her, but it didn't matter. Given a choice, she would much rather see Mayson's reaction to her when she addressed him than interrupt Melvin while he was charming a girl.

She was not for certain that Mayson was looking at Melvin and didn't want to jump to conclusions, as she did by not returning his calls. It may be the glare of the sun that has him turning in that direction, she thought.

"Hello, Mayson," said Veronica in a surprise-its-me voice.

It was obvious that he had not been asleep, as his eyes popped open as soon as he heard her voice. When she saw his eyes open and he sat up immediately and repositioned himself, she then reassumed the purpose of Mayson's relaxed position in the direction of Melvin.

"Hi Veronica," said Mayson in a cheerful voice. A voice that if Veronica had not gathered such assumptions about his activities on the bench, would have her believe that he was glad to see her.

"What are you doing here?" asked Veronica in an effort not to appear obvious about what she saw.

It had been quite a few months since Reanna had told Mayson about Veronica and Melvin's marriage and later, her pregnancy. Veronica had been so involved in her marriage and its problems that she was not aware that Mayson was no longer attending GCC. But she had no doubt that

Mayson knew about the miscarriage of the baby through the Eric-Reanna grapevine. Veronica battled within herself whether to taper the conversation down and walk away or continue to talk with him and see where they would go. With all that was going on within her, the thought of settling for friendship with Mayson became a desperate option for her.

"My mother is thinking about taking some classes here and I came with her. She's talking with someone in the administration building. She was taking so long that I decided to come out and get some air. You know how musty those old college buildings can be," said Mayson as he stretched. "How are you?" He asked.

"I'm doing well," she said.

Mayson thought to congratulate her on her marriage. But decided not to, as he was unsure if she could see Melvin and the girl near the other building.

"That's good," said Mayson.

As he responded to her, she could see Mayson give a quick glance back in Melvin's direction. She saw a look of both curiosity and disappointment both come to his face. When she looked, she saw that Melvin was gone and the girl he had been talking to was now sitting on the stairs alone.

It was obvious to Veronica that the conversation between her and Mayson was not going anywhere. As much as she wanted to believe in a possible future for them, the realization of Mayson's true nature surpassed her efforts to fight for him. She felt a sadness come over her at the thought that nothing would come from this brief encounter with Mayson. She wanted someone to love who would love her back. But she knew that it would not be Mayson.

What a sad life I have, she mused, as she thought about seeing a man she loved possibly pleasuring himself at the sight of her husband, who was talking with another woman.

"Yeah, well, I just wanted to say hi," said Veronica.

As she turned to walk away, she heard Mayson yell out, "Congratulations on your marriage."

Without looking back, Veronica yelled "Thank you," threw up a wave and kept walking.

She was not sure whether his last comment congratulating her on her marriage was sarcastic or sincere, but it didn't seem to matter anymore

She felt herself go numb; even her tears didn't come like she thought they would.

Veronica went home that evening and called her mother. She told her mother the whole story. From her false pregnancy to seeing Mayson and Melvin at the college campus earlier that day.

"Lying about your pregnancy, falling for a man who is gay, and spitefully marrying someone based on a pregnancy lie," summarized Veronica's mother. She breathed a deep sigh in frustration. "Veronica, you need to get out of this. This marriage was not meant to be. It's not a marriage if it's based on a lie. You can come home, transfer some of your credits to our state college, and start your life over," she said.

"I know Mommy. It's just that some days I think I love him and other days I could just walk out the door and never come back. Seeing Mayson that day was one of those moments when I could just leave Melvin," said Veronica.

"Veronica, there is nothing stopping you from doing that. You have no children with him, so there's nothing else left that ties you two together."

Two weeks after Veronica's talk with her mother, Melvin came home to an empty apartment. Veronica had gone back home to live with her mother. Other than divorce proceedings, neither made an effort to contact the other again.

CHAPTER 24

The Rising Cost of Drugs

(I)

Mayson began to see a change in his relationship with Byron. Byron didn't seem as supportive and kind to him as he had in the past. Mayson noticed that when he would see Byron at the club or talk with him on the phone about his promised job, Byron appeared preoccupied in thought and often cut their conversations short. He especially noticed Byron's change when he went by his office to get more pills. Byron usually would provide him enough for the week and more when Mayson ran out. From that first night, when Byron gave him the pill to relax on his first time on stage, Mayson felt more relaxed than he had in months, since leaving home and GCC. He attributed this to the pills and was grateful to Byron for suggesting them and providing them. However, on one significant day, after giving Mayson his weekly supply, Byron told Mayson that this would be his last free supply. He told Mayson that he was a businessman and giving things away for free was not smart business. He informed Mayson that after that day he would charge him $15 per pill. Mayson was dumbfounded. He could not believe that Byron would charge him for something that he originally didn't want and that helped his singing at Byron's club. Mayson worried because Byron only paid him a small amount for a few hours of work a week. He knew he couldn't afford the pills and dared not ask Tony for additional money.

Mayson told Byron, "I can't afford that. You know how much you pay me."

"What about your friend? You drive around in his nice car. This tells me that there's money around somewhere," said Byron.

Mayson was speechless. He had not talked with Byron or anyone at the club about Tony but he knew he shouldn't have been too surprised that

206

Byron brought Tony into the conversation. Byron had proved to him that knowing about Tony could become a focal point of discussion that could be a source of manipulation.

"I don't have that type of relationship with my friend. I plan to take care of myself," said Mayson in response to Byron's question.

"And I plan to take care of myself too," replied Byron.

Mayson was frightened by Byron's change in demeanor, and more so at his including Tony into the matter. He could now see how Byron methodically groomed him with his charm, praise for his singing, and supply of pills. Now he wants money from me, thought Mayson. Or could this simply be some form of extortion? he wondered.

Mayson decided that this was not a conversation where Byron would outtalk him.

"What about the initial job offer you had for me at the distribution company?" asked Mayson. "If I had that job maybe I could afford to pay for the pills," he added.

"Well Mayson, that job is no longer available," said Byron with a tilt of his head as to say, "What will you do now?"

Mayson's face didn't change at Byron's cavalier disclosure. He was not surprised. After the fifth month of Byron not bringing up the distribution manager job offer, Mayson realized that Byron had either changed his mind or the job never existed.

"However, Mayson, I am a man of my word, so I do have another job offer for you. As you seem to have a need for the pharmaceuticals, so do other customers that I have," said Byron slowly.

"Customers!" yelled Mayson. He felt his fear pass over to more anger.

"I am not your customer and I don't need your so-called pharmaceuticals. You sound like some damn mobster from a corny old gangster movie," said Mayson.

Mayson had never cursed before. But he didn't care. He had nothing to lose. He knew that Byron had him in a corner. He slammed the pills on Byron's desk and quickly walked out of the office.

THE RISING COST OF DRUGS

(II)

"Hello, Lanelle."

"Hi, Mayson!" said Lanelle. She was excited to hear from Mayson as she had been concerned about him. Mayson seemed different lately and didn't have much time for her or Tamara.

"Are you busy?" asked Mayson.

"No, not really," said Lanelle as she changed the phone to her other ear. She was relieved to hear from him. Maybe he'll finally tell me what's going on, she thought.

"I won't be able to come in tonight," said Mayson.

"Are you ill?" Lanelle asked.

"Kinda," said Mayson.

Lanelle sense that something was wrong with Mayson but didn't want to ask too many questions.

"Ok hon. Hope you feel better," said Lanelle.

"Thanks," said Mayson.

After they hung up, Mayson sat for a few minutes while in thought. He looked around the condo and all its nice furnishings. Tony's at work right now, keeping himself, and let's face it, me too, in this luxurious condo, thought Mayson. Why is this not enough, he wondered. I have Tony and all this but can't enjoy any of it. I see Byron's face in just about everything. How did I get stuck with someone like Byron? What is wrong with me, he thought as he grasped his head with his hands.

"Byron. The cliché of the bad man on the street corner," he mumbled.

Mayson laid back on the couch and looked up at the beautiful stucco ceiling.

Since leaving Byron's office in a rage, he was able to get some muscle relaxers from the dentist who had treated his toothache. He had convinced the dentist that he was grinding his teeth at night and his jaw was sore. The pills were okay, but not like the ones from Byron. He had tried the over-the-counter relaxers, but they had no effect on him at all. He was now out of the pills that the dentist prescribed. It had been two days since he had had a muscle relaxer. He knew he couldn't sing through all the anxiety he was feeling, which is why he called Lanelle for time off. He was having problems sleeping again and had thrown up a few times. He found a medical book in Tony's library and read through the section on various types of pills. He wanted to find information on the side effects of muscle relaxers but did not see the same kind as Byron had been giving him. The pills that Byron gave him were much more potent. He eventually closed the book in despair. I have to get more of those pills. I feel like I'm about to crawl out of my skin, and I need to get some sleep.

Mayson got up from the couch, went through the dining room and stood on the balcony. He clenched the railing while looking at the nearby park. Beneath the condo balcony was a line of bushes that extended along the walking path from the parking lot to the building. Mayson eyed the hard concrete walkway between the bushes. He had uncontrollable thoughts of falling, no, *jumping*, off the balcony and hitting the concrete. The thought became so strong that it scared him. He then turned and went back into the condo. He slid the glass door shut and locked it as if to protect himself from himself. A side of him thought how ridiculous the idea of him doing such a thing was. Yet the thought persisted.

I can't go through another evening of this, thought Mayson. I got to calm myself. The thought of calling Byron came to his mind. The humiliation and insult he felt in Byron's office seem to be a distant memory. All he could think about was getting himself calm with the pills. Mayson picked up the phone and slowly dialed Byron's number.

As Lanelle sat by the phone for a few minutes, after Mayson's call, she felt disturbed by their brief conversation. It was not just a matter of his taking the night off. His call reminded her of Calvin's last call telling her that he would not be in that night to tend the bar. He was like Mayson. Taken in by Byron as he slowly moved away from the club and later to become a mystery. She knew that Byron had promised Calvin that he would invest in his dream of opening his own restaurant. But Lanelle was not aware of any restaurants opening with Calvin's name as an owner. Nor was he ever seen working in a restaurant in or outside of the Benton area. He seemed to have just disappeared. Lanelle found him to be just another someone that Byron lured, used, and discarded. It hadn't happened to her yet, but she had put away enough money in preparation of her own end with Byron. She didn't know what Byron had promised Mayson but hoped that this would not be his fate as well.

(III)

Mayson walked across the empty restaurant. He heard the echo of his steps creak on the wooden floor and the stickiness of the floor. He felt a little weak so he held onto the wall as he walked slowly up the stairs to Byron's office. Byron had moved his office off the main floor and upstairs where he was more isolated from the restaurant staff.

He felt a sense of dread as he approached Byron's office door. He knocked on the closed door but didn't hear an answer. He didn't see Byron's car outside, but knew he had to be nearby because the front door of the restaurant was not locked. Mayson thought that Byron must have gone on an errand, so he turned the doorknob of the office door to see if it was unlocked. It was. He entered the office to wait for Byron. He looked around the office, which always looked the same: well-kept and uncluttered. He never saw Byron doing any kind of paperwork in this office. There were no large filing cabinets or other typical business-like furniture or equipment. Most of the items in his office were home-like furnishing. His office desk was the only furniture that made it look like an official office. He wondered why Byron bothered to have an office at all.

Mayson sat on the edge of Byron's desk. He felt too anxious to sit in a chair or on a couch. The desktop was at just the right height. Besides, the desk didn't allow him to sit completely. Since he had not been taking the pills, Mayson had been constantly on edge. He wanted that free supply of pills that he had slammed on Byron's desk. But he didn't think that would happen. He had $95 in his pocket in hopes of buying the pills back. What Byron didn't understand about his relationship with Tony was that they didn't have the kind of relationship where Tony gave Mayson cash on a regular basis. They shopped together for groceries and Tony paid for them. Whenever Mayson needed anything else, Tony let him use his credit card and Mayson would use it only for the amount that they discussed.

Mayson knew that Byron knew, now that he was charging him for the pills, this would become expensive and cost much more than what he was paying him at the club. Mayson also struggled with the thought o asking Tony for cash and not telling him what he needed it for. He knew that Tony was too smart for this.

When Mayson started getting the pills from Byron in unlabeled bottles, Tony had seen the pills in the medicine cabinet and asked Mayson what they were for. At that time Mayson believed they were harmless as Byron had told him. So he felt he was being truthful when he told Tony they were temporary, harmless, over-the-counter meds that helped him relax onstage. After that conversation with Tony, as Byron was steadily supplying the pills to Mayson, Mayson decided he didn't want to depend on Byron for the pills, so he took the pills to a drug store to show to the pharmacist for help in finding similar ones over the counter. When he handed the pills to the pharmacist, the pharmacist did not confirm they were relaxants. Instead, he looked suspiciously at Mayson while holding the pills and asked him where he got them from. He made Mayson wait as he when into the back of the store. The look on the pharmacist's face scared Mayson, so he left before the man could return. It was that day that he knew the pills were not, or no longer, muscle relaxers. As he researched the pills more at his local library, he found out that they were street drugs. But at that point, he didn't care. He continued to call them muscle relaxers and just knew that he needed them.

When Byron first started providing Mayson a supply of the pills, there was enough for him to take them once a day. This lasted Mayson for two weeks. However, when Mayson started taking the pills more than once each day, he found himself running out after a week. Today, Mayson wanted just enough pills to hold him until he could buy them elsewhere or to wean himself off. He figured a twenty-day supply would be enough. But in the meantime, he could only afford a few pills from Byron.

As Mayson sat and looked around the office, he could hear the restaurant door open. He heard the creaking of the downstairs floor and then rhythmic steps of someone coming up the stairs. Soon, Byron walked in with an old shoebox in his hand. At one time the presence of Byron had brought excitement for Mayson. Now that he knew Byron for who he really was, a combined feeling of contempt and hopeful relief surrounded Mayson. As Byron entered the room, Mayson simply glanced at Byron and turned his head away toward the window above the desk. Mayson removed himself from the edge of the desk as Byron walked around to his desk chair.

"Sit Mayson," said Byron.

"I'd rather not," said Mayson in a flat tone.

Byron placed the shoebox on his desk as he sat down into his desk chair. Mayson was now standing in front of Byron's desk. Byron leaned back in his office chair and a grin came across his face.

"Okay. So, you are going to pay the $30 per pill?" asked Byron.

"You said $15," screamed Mayson as his eyes bulged out at Byron. "Besides that, I thought you were going to give me the one more supply for free that last time I was here," said Mayson.

"I was, Mayson, but you chose to disrespect me and storm out of my office, so now this supply not only comes with a cost, but an increased cost," he said.

Defeat came over Mayson. He felt his eyelids droop in frustration and defeat. All he could think of was the need for the pills and the dreaded thought of leaving without them. Mayson pulled up a chair that was next to the couch and pushed it close to the front of Byron's desk.

"Come on, Byron, you know that I don't have that kind of money. Even if I bought the pills for $30 it would take most of my money and I would soon be back here wanting more. I need a supply so that I can slowly wean myself off," said Mayson.

"Mayson, I have good news and bad news for you. Which do you want to hear first?" asked Byron in an amused tone, as though he had not heard a word that Mayson said.

Mayson glared at Byron for a few seconds because he could sense that Byron was not taking him seriously.

"Byron, this is not a game," said Mayson.

"I know it's not a game. It's business, and you have to respect a man's business. You can't expect to go through life with people giving you things for free," said Byron.

Byron's tone was also slowly getting firmer, but Mayson didn't care. A snake is what Mayson saw him as. Just like the serpent in the Bible, a source of evil. He had very little respect for Byron now, but at that moment respecting Byron was not important.

With a worried and helpless look on his face, Mayson asked, "What's the good news?"

"The good news is that you will not have to pay me," said Byron.

Mayson almost felt himself get excited, but he learned better to not allow himself to be enthused by anything that Byron promised him.

"What's the bad news?"

"I don't have any more of the pills," said Byron.

Mayson stood up to leave as he felt that Byron was playing with him like a cat grabbing for an unreachable ball of string.

"Wait boy! Sit back down! I have another piece of good news," shouted Byron.

Mayson decided to continue standing. He crossed his arms in front of him as though he was trying to protect himself from whatever continued nonsense Byron had to say. As he slowly wrapped his arms around himself, he could feel his hands trembling. This time he didn't know if the trembling was from the withdrawals or his feelings toward Byron at that moment. He knew he was fed up with Byron from all this *good news, bad news* playfulness, yet his feet wouldn't move as he stood in front of Byron. "What's that?" asked Mayson in a hollow tone.

He anticipated more games from Byron, yet he was afraid to leave out of concern it may cause more problems as when he stormed out before.

"I don't have the pills, but I have something better than pills," said Byron.

He then pulled the shoebox closer to him and opened it to expose a box full of white rock-like substance in plastic bags. Mayson's eyes stretched as he knew what the substance in the bags were. It was crack cocaine. Mayson saw similar bags in Tamara's boyfriend's car when he took Mayson home one night from the club. The crack was on the floor in the back seat of the car. Her boyfriend had it sitting there as though it was simply a bag of cookies that he would be eating soon. Mayson was surprised that Tamara would choose a man who did drugs. He had admired Tamara's resilience at getting her life stable for her and her children. Seeing that in her boyfriend's car made him sad. When Mayson got into the backseat of the car, the boyfriend calmly told him to watch his feet. While riding in the back seat, Mayson could not help himself but to picked up one of the bags and examine it. Other than on television, it was the first time he had seen crack. Even with Reanna's wild lifestyle, he never saw her in possession of crack or any other illicit drugs.

He began to see the whole picture of what Byron had planned for him. His mind flashed back to their meeting at the gas station. Byron's initial attraction to the car, the bells that must have sounded when he told

Byron that he was not the owner of the car and that he was unemployed. Everything about his relationship with Byron was leading up to this day, thought Mayson. Drug user and dealer. What an obvious relationship, he thought. If it was possible for Mayson's blood to boil, it would have spilled over. He felt his blood rush to his head as he gave Byron a steady glare.

"You expect me to take that? I'm not some addict. I just want the pills!" yelled Mayson.

Byron slowly raised from his chair, looked face to face with Mayson over his desk. He spoke to Mayson in a calm voice, but threatening look in his eyes.

"First of all, keep your voice down or leave my office. Secondly, I didn't say you were an addict. All I did was open a box and you took it from there," said Byron.

Mayson began to shift the weight of his leg to the other as he felt his body weaken.

"What's in this box can ease your anxiety just as much as the muscle relaxers you were taking. I'm sure in these past few days you found out how difficult it was to get prescription meds. This stuff is not that difficult to get, and it won't cost anything at all," said Byron.

Mayson knew anything coming from Byron had strings attached. But he felt such a need for something to help him get through his time at the club and even through the day. He was on his last leg without the pills.

"Why wouldn't it cost me anything?" asked Mayson.

"You know, Mayson. Do you need me to say it?" said Byron.

"I know now exactly who I'm dealing with, so you don't have to tell me anymore," said Mayson.

Byron sat back down in his chair as he could feel Mayson weakening. He stared at Mayson while waiting for an answer. Mayson stared at the box on the desk trying to figure out what to do.

"Come on Byron, just a few more pills and I'll pay you later for the entire supply," pleaded Mayson.

"How can you pay me for something that I don't have? The pill deal is over. Now, what do you want to do?" asked Byron.

Mayson, feeling like he could no longer stand, reached for the chair next to him and sat down. Not just because his legs were tired, but he felt himself weakening in consideration of Byron's deal.

"I'm not a seller, "said Mayson to Byron in a defeated voice.

"You're not a singer either," said Byron.

"You knew I wasn't a lead singer but you used it to win my confidence and put me under pressure for something I wasn't prepared for," said Mayson.

"See it however you want. I don't have time to sit here and bother with you. Yes or no?" asked Byron impatiently.

CHAPTER 25

Cora's Early Morning Breakfast Café

"Mayson? Is that you?" asked Lanelle.

"Hi, Lanelle!" said Mayson.

Lanelle grabbed Mayson's arm and pulled him into her. They embraced as Lanelle rocked his thin body side to side.

"Where have you been?" asked Lanelle.

"Oh, I've been busy," said Mayson, patting her on the back. They slowly eased from the embrace.

"What are you doing here? I thought you moved off the earth," she said as she smiled.

"I have a hankering for hot chocolate, and good ol' Cora's Early Morning Breakfast Café is the only place to get just the right kind," he said as though he was advertising the restaurant in a commercial.

"How have you been?" asked Lanelle.

"I'm okay," said Mayson in a way that led Lanelle to believe otherwise.

Lanelle smiled but felt her heart ache for Mayson. She knew that anyone who has spent time with Byron often ended up in a bad way. His appearance was in conflict with his description. He looked gaunt. However, his clothes had lost that church-boy look and were more urban. He wore a black V-neck t-shirt with a blue denim jacket and a stylish scarf draped across his neck. His black jeans were narrow and fitted slightly snug to his thin legs. His brown sockless shoes were flat with an open face. His hair was cut in a neat trim around the frame of his face as well as around the side and back. His once-large afro was now short and curly as it glistened in the light of the sun that was coming in from the stores' side windows. The drastic difference from the afro to the current hairstyle made it obvious that he had put some sort of processing chemical in his hair. He had on sunglasses, but out of respect for Lanelle, he took them off as they engaged in conversation. His eyes were watery and slightly red. They were not the primary concern for Lanelle; rather, it was his inability to look her in the eyes as they talked. His eyes constantly shifted to the side. Lanelle sensed that in some way he was glad to see her, but he seemed uncomfortable, as though she had caught him in the middle of something.

As with Calvin, Mayson had stopped coming to the club and she knew not to ask Byron about him, because he would not give her a straight answer. In addition, she had a difficult time reaching Mayson by phone. Like Calvin, Mayson seemed to have just disappeared. Even though she was Mayson's manager, she dared not ask Mayson about the details of his disappearance.

As she stood there looking up at Mayson, at that moment, she regretted that one time in their relationship she set such a "don't-go-there" boundary between them. She realized later that Mayson meant no harm when he asked about her relationship with Byron. When he first started work at the club, he was simply unused to waiting, observing and adapting to his new surroundings. Lanelle really liked Mayson because he had a good nature and was eager to please. She knew that her choice to put him with the group as backup was difficult for him, but he never complained, nor did his disposition towards her change. Lanelle's experiences with Byron and the sudden disappearance of Calvin raised Lanelle's suspicions that something was now up between Byron and Mayson as well. She knew how Byron lured people in and then changed his script once he had them at a disadvantage.

Lanelle bored her eyes into Mayson as he stood there with her. It had been a little less than a year since she saw him. He looked so different, she thought. So much more grown-up than when he was working at the club. In his eyes, she could feel that he knew things. Things that he may not have wanted to know, about life and now life in the streets. She wanted to know what he knew since the last time they talked. She knew that he would have the right to tell her to mind her own business, the same way she insinuated this to him when they first met. Without a word, Lanelle took Mayson by the arm and led him over to one of the unoccupied booths in the cafe.

"Sit," she said to Mayson in a take-charge voice.

Mayson sat with a forced smile on his face. He dared not confide in Lanelle for fear it would get back to Byron. He had developed a dependency on Byron that he could not allow anyone to break. Anything getting back to

217

Byron might cut off his supply of the drugs that he so desperately needed. Lanelle looked around the room to make sure that no one was nearby. She leaned forward and looked Mayson in the eyes. She reached across the table and took his long, thin, sweaty hands. Lanelle knew that drugs were involved in his story. She knew about the muscle relaxers he took at the club but assumed they were over the counter, as Mayson had told her. Lanelle's life had educated her on the various kinds of street drugs. In addition, she attended Narcotics Anonymous on a regular basis. In Mayson's eyes were drugs that superseded muscle relaxers or even weed, she thought. He was not taking just any kind of drugs, but drugs that grabbed at the soul of who he was.

"Hon," she said in the most caring voice that Mayson heard her speak, "I know you're in trouble. I don't usually bother people about their stuff. I'm a *live and let live* sort of woman, but I like you too much to stand by and let you become just another statistic. Honey, you need help and I want to be able to get you that help," she said.

Mayson continued with his tight smile. He nodded his head slightly, as though he agreed with Lanelle's compassionate words.

"I'm fine, Lanelle," he said as he pulled his hands away from her." Just a little tired from working hard."

"Working?" asked Lanelle.

Mayson then realized that he had opened a door that required more answers. He dropped his eyes as he tried to come up with an answer.

"What kind of work are you doing now?" asked Lanelle.

Mayson rested his back on the booth seat. His mind was racing.

"I'm Byron's assistant now," he blurted out. "I take care of his appointments, attend meetings with him, and sometimes I run errands for him."

Lanelle, knowing that Byron's so-called business was more fluff than substance, knew Mayson was lying. She realized that she was not winning his confidence. She didn't want to anger him or run him off, so she went along with his lie.

"I didn't know that Byron needed that much assistance," she said mildly.

"Yeah, he's a busy man," responded Mayson.

Lanelle rested her back to the booth as well. She stared at Mayson for a few seconds. She had a sense that Mayson was at a stage where he was not going to let anyone help him. She realized that no matter what she said, he would lie-up another answer about Byron or himself. Mayson crossed his arms over his chest. Lanelle looked at Mayson's hands, so thin she could see his veins coming through the back portion of his hands. His hands were just as frail-looking as his face. She decided to change the conversation in hopes that she may get some sort of truth from him. She asked how his family was doing in an effort to see if he was in contact with any of them. He did not answer. She looked over at the door and saw a sharply dressed man in a gray suit enter the cafe. He looked around the cafe and stopped when he saw Mayson. He then shifted his eyes over to Lanelle. He immediately turned his back to both of them while looking at the pastries near the cafe counter. Lanelle could see they knew each other as the man nervously paced around the pastry counter. Mayson looked at Lanelle without batting an eye.

"I gotta go," said Mayson as he slid out of the booth. Lanelle could see that his eyes were confirming that he knew, she knew.

"It was nice seeing you again," said Mayson.

"Okay. You take care and call me if you ever want to talk," said Lanelle.

Mayson put the tight, "I'm okay" grin back on his face and turned to walk toward the man in the gray suit. As the ma n in the gray suit saw Mayson coming in his direction, he walked toward the door and left the cafe. Lanelle knew what this meant. She got out of her seat to look at them from the large cafe window. She saw Mayson getting into the man's large dark blue Mercedes and they drove off. Lanelle went back to the booth and sat for a while. Mayson's appearance and the man in the gray suit meant that Mayson was in more trouble than she thought. From the booth, she yet could see the Mercedes as it began to drive off. As she watched the Mercedes go farther down the road, she couldn't help but sigh as to what Mayson might have gotten himself into. As she watched, her mind drifted back to when she first met Byron.

CHAPTER 26

How Did You Meet Byron?

"Where is he?" asked Lanelle as she walked the dark street holding her wig in her hand, mascara smeared, missing a shoe and a shivering in her thin sleeveless dress in 45-degree weather. She felt her nose run as she limped along, but she was too angry to care. She could hear a car coming from behind her as she stopped to see if it was her ride. The car drove past.

"Where is he?" she said again as she limped faster, feeling the night air wrapping itself around her arms and shoulders. She heard another car and saw that it was slowing down as the headlights came closer to her. It was Tyson.

When he got closer, he rolled down his window.

"Get in," said Tyson.

Lanelle got into the long black sedan. She wanted to yell at Tyson for not sticking around after her time with the man in the hotel, but she knew that Tyson had a short fuse.

"What happened to your coat?" asked Tyson.

"That fool wouldn't let me get it. He rushed me out of the hotel because he said his wife was calling from the lobby. She surprised him by coming to be with him on his business trip," she said.

"Glad I got my money first," said Tyson.

They said nothing else the rest of the drive. It was the last time Tyson set up Lanelle with a john.

Lanelle was 38 when she met Byron through her pimp Tyson. Byron was known for his association with drugs. He didn't sell them directly himself but had his runners out on the street selling them for him. Tyson had introduced Lanelle to Byron at a bar. Lanelle thought this was just another meeting for her with some sleezy middleman for a high-profile john. But this meeting was different. Tyson was allowing them to meet directly through him at a public bar. In addition, Lanelle had noticed that

Tyson no longer sent her out as he did the other girls. Rather, he'd had her doing more to dress and prepare the girls and buy things they needed. She never complained to Tyson about the changes, because it felt good to not have to be out on the streets as much. She thought that perhaps Tyson was grooming her to be second-in-command for the house. This thought relieved her but troubled her at the same time, because she didn't know if she had the heart to put those girls out on the street. Some of them looked like they were as young as 13, and Lanelle knew that her heart could not let her offer them up to men. She knew that Tyson was doing such things but tried not to think much about it. The drugs helped her focus less on the girls and more on getting her fix. She never wanted to cross Tyson, so whenever she'd see a girl that looked really young coming to the house, she'd numb the prospect with more and more drugs. She'd sometimes try and make up for her part in these young girls' treatment by pampering them when they had really bad days.

The day they met with Byron, they sat in a booth at a bar. Tyson wanted to be blunt with what his intentions were with Lanelle.

"Byron, like I told you, Lanelle is aging, and I have to pay too much for make-up to try and hide the wrinkles and bags on her face. She's handy to have around to help with the other girls, but not having her on the streets is costing me a lot," said Tyson.

Fear overtook Lanelle as she realized that Tyson was selling her. She had been with Tyson for four years and he was her caretaker. She hated being on the streets, but Tyson had also given her a room of her own, which always made her feel special.

"No, Tyson, you can't do this!" she said, alarmed.

"Shut up! Nobody asked you anything," snapped Tyson.

Lanelle immediately stopped talking but could feel the blood drain from her face as they continue to talk about her as though she was not there. Tyson was nice to Lanelle during non-business-related times, but when matters came up that affected his business, he changed quickly. He treated the girls like objects, which sometimes included Lanelle. A few times, he'd confided in Lanelle about his father and mother. They had left him with a neighbor and moved to California. He never saw them again. Whenever Tyson talked about his childhood and his abandonment by his parents, he would get into a depression. When he would get into these moods, Lanelle would find herself feeling sorry for him. But then thoughts of the girls he sold on the street would enter her mind. She always had to remind herself who Tyson really was: a pimp looking out for himself.

Tyson ordered Lanelle to stand up. "I want you to know what you're getting," he said to Byron.

Lanelle was stunned. She thought she meant more to Tyson than some sort of merchandise. The times she spent with him mending his emotional wounds and taking care of the girls she thought was valuable to him. Tyson scooted out of the booth for Lanelle to get out. She stood near the booth as she looked around trying to see if anyone was observing their transaction.

As Lanelle stood, Tyson looked at her as though he was looking at a used car.

"Man, she's aged, but she can attract some of the old-school dudes," said Tyson.

Tyson then grabbed Lanelle's arm to direct her to turn around.

"Turn around," ordered Tyson.

Lanelle slowly turned around.

"Get this man, for the freaks who want to be sung to, she has a damn good singing voice. She can sing to them like she's singing to a child. You know how some of those fools like being sung to like a baby man. She's dependable too. Cause she's got drug needs, she'll do whatever you tell her," said Tyson.

As Lanelle stood out on the floor, she thought about her family and her thoughts went to better times in her life. She wondered how she could have allowed herself to come to this place in her life.

"I'm a piece of merchandise," she muttered to herself hoping Tyson didn't hear her.

"What!" yelled Tyson.

"Nothing," said Lanelle.

Lanelle sensed Tyson's anxiety, which was always at its peak when he was trying to get money out of someone.

Byron quietly listened as Tyson anxiously continued his pitch.

"If you give me no-cost crack to take care of two of my girls' habits for 30 days, we can strike a deal," he said in an eager tone. "I'm a little short on the stuff. I had some unexpected financial issues last month and don'

222

have what I need to keep all the girls on the streets."

"Let's go back to the singing part. You said she can sing?" asked Byron.

"Yeah man. She sings like a bird. Lanelle, sing that song you sang last week for that freak on Madison Street. What's the name of the song?" asked Tyson.

"Forever Heart," mumbled Lanelle.

"Yeah, yeah, that's it," said Tyson.

Lanelle looked at Tyson with pleading eyes not to do this to her, but Tyson demanded that she sing the song. The bar was noisy, so Lanelle knew she would have to sing above the crowd to be heard. A part of her thought was to dissuade Byron by singing poorly, but she knew that when Tyson was this hyped up, he was prone to violence. A lump came to Lanelle's throat as she fought the desire to cry. She fastened her eyes down to the floor and let the song come out.

♩ *I love the way my honey holds me in his arms, I linger in his charm, he protects me from my own harm. He knows his love for me will forever be in my heart. When I think of him alone, he brings a wanting moan, and I know that he can see that his love for me will forever be in my heart.* ♫

She could hear her voice tremble. As she continued to the next verse of the song, she felt a sharp pain across the right side of her face. She could feel her jawbone move and the sharp pain increase. She felt her balance shift and found herself falling to the floor. When she looked up, she saw Byron and Tyson standing over her. Byron was holding Tyson's wrist as he prevented him from hitting Lanelle again.

"Man, what's wrong with you!" yelled Byron as he threw Tyson's hand away from him.

Lanelle looked around the room and saw that everyone was staring at them. The bartender hurried over to them.

"Is everything okay over here?" he asked in a knowing but warning voice.

"We cool, man," said Tyson. He handed the bartender a twenty-dollar bill.

"Sorry for the disruption," Byron added.

Lanelle, holding her face where Tyson hit her, began to cry. Tyson started cursing at her.

"You costing me some damn money. I need that stuff for my women and here you go singing like some sick dog," said Tyson.

Byron helped Lanelle up off the floor.

"You okay?" asked Byron to Lanelle.

"Yes," said Lanelle.

Lanelle stood and straightened out her dress. Byron motioned with his hand for her to sit back in the booth. Byron stepped aside for Lanelle to scoot back into the booth next to him.

"I like your singing. I can do something with that," said Byron.

"So, does that mean we got a deal?" ask Tyson eagerly.

"Wait, I'm talking to Lanelle," said Byron to Tyson, annoyed.

"Lanelle, I can get you into entertainment. People would love to hear that beautiful voice," said Byron.

This was the first time Lanelle experienced the Byron charm and his words of a better tomorrow.

Despite the disrespect, humiliation and beating she just experienced from Tyson, she still didn't want to leave him. But she knew that under no circumstances did Tyson want her back. She had committed the ultimate sin of aging, and there was not a lot she could do about that.

With Byron's acceptance of the trade, it was a done deal. Tyson allowed Lanelle to say goodbye to the girls.

Byron explained to Lanelle that if she wanted a singing career, she had to protect her voice, so her drug habit had to go. He told Lanelle that he was going to put her in rehab. These words brought fear and hope for Lanelle. On bad days, Lanelle would think how much better her life would be if she was not an addict. Yet, the thought of not having her drugs terrified her.

Despite her fear of treatment, she felt her future was going in the right direction with Byron, so she trusted that rehab would be the right step. The 45 days in treatment were a tremendous help for her. She developed a strong will to succeed in her recovery. In addition, she was able to connect with the staff and other recovering addicts. Most importantly, she readily comprehended her addiction and her need for recovery. She was advised of the necessity for NA meetings after the treatment program, as well as a sponsor after her release date. Byron agreed for her to attend drug meetings, but told her he would pick the sponsor for her.

When Byron picked up Lanelle from rehab, a middle-aged woman was sitting in the front seat of his car. He introduced her as Ruth and told Lanelle this would be her sponsor. Ruth provided a halfhearted greeting to Lanelle without turning around to look at her. Ruth looked frail and appeared nervous as she shifted positions in her seat and looked straight ahead. As Byron drove, Lanelle asked Ruth a few questions about her drug use past, treatment, and recovery. Ruth mumbled her answers. She was indeed a recovering addict but had only been clean for two months. This left Lanelle feeling uneasy about Byron's choice of sponsor.

After a long and silent drive, Byron slowed down as he drove through a seedy area of town. Lanelle looked out her window curiously. She knew the area but was not sure why Byron was taking them there. They soon stopped in front of an apartment building. As he shifted the car into park, he announced to Lanelle that this was where she would be staying. Lanelle looked helplessly out the back window of the car at the building. The apartment was an old brownstone two-story building. Its weather-beaten roof had several shingles missing. But there was a sturdiness about the building, that left a possibility that it had once been a nice place to live. It might have once been a building that housed hardworking families. But its unkempt yard, full of high grass and weeds, made its past of little concern. Byron advised Ruth that if she ever had to come and meet with Lanelle this was where she could find her. He cautioned her to call him first before going to her apartment. He told Lanelle to let him know whenever she needed to talk with Ruth, and he would get the message to her.

After that day in Byron's car, Lanelle never saw Ruth again. Lanelle knew that they were not a good match. In addition, Ruth didn't seem to be a willing participant with Byron's choice of her as her sponsor. Therefore, instead of waiting to hear from Ruth or going through Byron to contact her, Lanelle used a pay phone on the corner and called a sponsor she had met in one of her NA meetings. This sponsor had been clean for four years, knew the message of recovery, and communicated it well. They met at NA meetings and maintained a recovery friendship but did not have any personal ties. Byron never followed up on any later connection between Lanelle and Ruth, which made it easy for Lanelle to keep her relationship with her actual sponsor a secret.

On that first day when Lanelle entered the apartment, it was almost as unsightly as the outside of the building, but Lanelle saw potential. It was the first individual home she had in a long time. Byron paid her rent and utilities at first, but they agreed that once she obtained her own income, she would begin to make the rent payments herself. She imagined that Byron's source of income for her would not be much different from her initial job on the streets for Tyson.

Despite the impoverished neighborhood, Lanelle liked her new apartment. She thought she was special when Tyson gave her a separate bedroom from the others, but having her own apartment made her feel like a queen. In addition to rent and utilities, Byron gave her furniture, including a couch. It was new, but Lanelle could tell that it was cheap. She could see the large staples that held the upholstery together. He also gave her a small used color television. The television had a few cracks in the case, and in the cracks were caked-in food particles and rings where it appeared someone had set down their drinking glasses. The kitchen had a dinette area that included an eating counter with a stool, so Byron didn't bother to give her a dinette set. She planned to purchase her own dinette set once she obtained her own income.

Byron also provided her with a small weekly allowance for food and other household needs. She used the money to buy food and home decor from a thrift shop. She purchased pictures of lakes, flowers, trees, and other natural scenery to adorn in her apartment. For the first time in her life, she bought real plants. Byron didn't give her a phone, telling her she needed to focus on her upcoming career. If he needed to call her, he'd contact the apartment manager on the ground floor. Of course, the manager was a "friend of his."

The third day in her apartment, Byron came over to take advantage of his "kind deed" of taking care of her. Unlike many of the johns and Tyson, Byron used his charm. But it would not be accurate to say that Byron seduced or enticed her. He simply took advantage of what he had paid for. Lanelle's life with Tyson programmed her to believe that whenever a man did something nice for her and didn't expect money, she was to provide sex in exchange. As time passed, Byron came by less and less. For Lanelle this was a hopeful sign that he no longer needed to exert his control over her or claim what was his. Over time, he would come by primarily to give her allowance. Lanelle wanted sexual favors to be the end of that chapter of her life, period. But it was all she knew as a means of survival.

For those first two weeks, Lanelle went to bed every night filled with thoughts of a better way of living. Her life of struggles and suffering were coming to an end. She had her own place and was fifty-nine days into her recovery. Each day without drugs was a struggle, but she fed herself on the possibilities of change. Despite her efforts at optimism, she had days of nagging doubt in the back of her mind. She was alone now. She was left in the apartment for days to reflect and wonder. She had no Tyson or anyone else to tell her what to do during the day. With Tyson, she knew what to expect. But she didn't know Byron very well, and waiting to see what he was really going to do with her was torturous. Unlike some of Tyson's girls, who could come to her for comfort, she had no one to talk to. Without a phone, she could only tell her sponsor so much. She worried the stress would cause her to start using again.

She had not prayed in years. Her life had been filled with so much shame that she stopped praying. She didn't feel she was in a place in her life to talk to God. One evening while flipping through the channels on the old television in her small living room, she saw a minister that she had never seen before. He looked different from most ministers that she had seen in the past, with shoulder-length hair that was long for a preacher, she thought. He was casually dressed in jeans, green untucked shirt, and sneakers. She heard him speak about *God's Love for You—No Qualifications Needed:*

"When we seek jobs, they often require qualifications for acceptance. Unlike the requirements of man, God has a love for us that does not require specific qualifications. There's nothing that you must have or possess for Him to love you," the minister said.

Lanelle had heard ministers and church people talk about God's love. She had people to walk up to her with gospel tracts and tell her that God loved her. None of it meant much to her. She felt like people were just throwing religious words at her and hoping she would figure it out later. Just as she was about to press the button to turn the channel, the minister said something that stopped her:

"If you are waiting for everything about yourself to be perfect before you reach out to God, then it will never happen. None of us will ever reach that place of self-perfection. It does not exist. None of us have that amount of perfect goodness to earn God's attention. You already have it. He wants you in a place to know that every day is the best day to come to Him. It's not about your goodness that brings his love and favor. It's about His goodness. His goodness is every day, which is why every day is the best day for you to reach out to Him."

She had indeed been waiting to make her life better before going back to church and eventually praying to God. This sermon message gave her the freedom to pray about herself and her life. From that day forward, Lanelle watched the minister every week. She started to pray whenever she felt alone or fearful about Byron's intentions for her. The more she listened to the minister, the more she prayed. Soon her prayers became daily, no matter how she felt.

His preaching often made her feel that he was talking directly to her. She needed a friend. Even if that friend was coming from a television. People often condemn TV watching, but television can be a good thing. It just depends on what you're watching, thought Lanelle. While in her apartment-paradise of isolation, insights like this became common.

After not seeing Byron for several weeks, he came by the apartment. He looked around the apartment and saw how nicely Lanelle had adorned it on the meager allowance he had given her.

"I see my perception of you was correct. Not only are you beautiful, but you are a smart woman when it comes to money. Get dressed and come with me. I want to take you to your future," said Byron with his charming smile.

"What does that mean?" asked Lanelle, as she looked firmly into his eyes.

"You'll see, just trust me," said Byron.

In Byron's plush, quiet Town Car, they pulled up in front of a rundown building about half a mile away, in an old business district on a forgotten side of town. They stepped out of the car and stood as they gazed at the building. The building used to be a fabric store. After it closed, a different merchant remodeled it to open a restaurant, but only kept it running for a year. It was Byron's building now. He rented it out to a friend who wanted to open a fish market. When his business did not go well, he abandoned it and left the remaining product in the store. Byron had to pay thousands of dollars to clean out the building and get rid of the smell of rotting fish. He didn't know what to do with the building after that. There were a few nightclubs in the Benton area, but most of the successful ones were located outside of town in surrounding counties or cities. So he thought to convert his old building into a nightclub for those on that side of town.

"I need for you to fix up and manage this place and make it a place people will want to come and hear you sing," said Byron.

"What?" asked Lanelle, astonished.

"I want this to be a nightclub where you will be able to manage and sing in," Byron repeated.

In hearing the word "sing," Lanelle felt a smile surfacing itself to her face but quickly pulled her lips back. The word *manage* surprised her, but she could only deal with one emotion at a time. She wondered why Byron would think she could manage anything, let alone a nightclub. She thought about Tyson's pitch to Byron on all her good qualities and guessed that at some point he must have told Byron how she managed the girls. The thought of singing in front of people excited her, but she still could not trust Byron.

"Is this how I will be making a living?" asked Lanelle.

"Yes. With you being able to sing, I get double my money," said Byron.

Lanelle was so relieved to hear that this was how Byron was going to get her to earn her income. However, if it was contingent upon the old building in front of her, then her income may be nonexistent. She had never managed a business before, and she didn't know if her singing was good enough to bring people out.

"Byron, you'd need a miracle to make that building a place where anyone would want to come to for any reason," said Lanelle.

"Lanelle, you have a future in singing, and I think you're a smart lady. You have to start somewhere, and this is your start. I know a lot of people in entertainment. Once the club is moving, I can get these people out to come and hear you sing. But you must establish a foundation first. We need to get this club up and running," said Byron.

Lanelle looked at the building intently. "Let's go in," she said with a sigh. Maybe the inside will look better than the outside, she hoped.

Byron unlocked the security gate and then the door. He stepped back and let Lanelle in first. Lanelle's heart sank as she saw the cracked walls, scarred floors, a musty smell, and debris everywhere.

"Lanelle, you start here and in two years I'll have big names coming in to see you. Get it cleaned up, hire musicians and get some local advertising. You'll be on your way. You just let me know how much you need, and I'll get it. This will take you somewhere, I guarantee," said Byron.

"Okay, let's get started," said Lanelle with an even bigger sigh.

After eight months of work, Lanelle was preparing for the opening. The club was coming together like her apartment. Byron didn't provide her a lot of money for the club, but she had learned to work a budget, no matter how small. As with her apartment, she found furnishings and other décor in from local thrift stores. There was a few major construction work needed, which included building a stage. Byron was able to get another one of his friend's company to get the work done. The thought of making her own money and no longer relying on Byron's weekly allowances was her best motivation.

The more she worked at getting the club together, the less she relied on Byron for direction. Her lessened dependence on him diminished his need to claim her sexually even more. Lanelle knew this and made sure that she always seemed strong and in charge around Byron. She had not seen that side of herself in years. She would never let Byron know that he brought out a productive side of her. Byron was manipulative, arrogant, and deceptive, but once he saw that you knew what you were doing, he stepped back and let you do your thing. At least that's what she felt he did for her.

After a year, as Lanelle's club became more presentable, she hired musicians and a few backup singers. A lot of them left within a year, but she finally found a team that became almost like the family she never had. Her family, Tamara, Tim, Urban, Monica, and a man named Rance Clyburn. Rance was their drummer. He had been working at the club for three years. He died in a car crashed after leaving the club late one night. Trenton came along six months after Rance's death. Rance was a good drummer, but Trenton was better. Rance didn't seem to let himself loose on the drums as Trenton did. Trenton kept his beat but was able to add a little spice between the beats. Trenton would get out of his academics and give all he had to that moment on the drums. Lanelle liked Rance a great deal, but she was proud of her choice in hiring Trenton. Trenton showed her that she had advanced in her hiring skills. Whenever she would see her club family laughing, talking or blending their talents on the stage, she'd felt a smile come upon her. *I did this*, she would think in amazement. But she was not completely surprised. Her grandparents had owned a laundromat and dry cleaners. She remembered her grandfather's business savvy. She felt her grandmother's hard work ethic come alive in her. Lanelle remembered her grandmother saying, "Give them what they come for and they will come back." A club and a cleaners may not be the same, but the basics of her grandparents' ability to manage and organize stayed with Lanelle.

Lanelle sang every night. She felt her voice was at its best now that she settled into the club and had a stable life. But Byron had not brought in the people from the singing industry to hear her like he promised. When she would ask Byron about the entertainment execs coming to hear her, his response was always, *I'll arrange it when I can…you have to be patient.* After three years of never being "discovered," Lanelle became suspicious. Even though the club was not making a lot of money, she'd see Byron in nice cars and clothes. He had been paying for her apartment in the past, bought the building for the club, and paid a lot to get it off the ground. It didn't take long for Lanelle to realize that Byron was using the club to cover for his drug-dealing income. She faced the reality that Byron only needed her as a cover and she never was going to meet people who would launch her singing career. But by then, she didn't mind. She had come to love working the club. She would sometimes call it *her baby.*

CHAPTER 27

Tony's Call to Reanna

"Hello, is this Reanna?"

"Who's calling?"

"My name is Tony Rayburn, I'm Mayson Hendricks' friend."

"Tony, hi!" said Reanna in an upbeat voice that made it known to Tony that she had heard of him and was happy to hear from him.

"Hi Reanna," said Tony in his melodic bass voice. "I hope it's okay that I have your number. Mayson talked so much about you, so I got your number out of his address book."

"It's okay. Is Mayson alright?" she asked in an alarmed voice.

"Yeah, as far as I know, he's okay," said Tony.

"What does that mean?" asked Reanna.

"Well, that's the reason I'm calling. I'm not for sure what is going on with him anymore. I figured that if anyone knew what was going on with him, it would be you," he said.

"What's happening with him exactly?" asked Reanna, feeling a bit calmer.

"He's seldom home, and when he is, he seems preoccupied with phone calls, which he takes in the other room. When we do find a little time to talk, he becomes my old Mayson again. As long as I don't ask him about those calls and his whereabouts away from home, we're good. If I try to bring them up, he becomes defensive and then we argue. We didn't use to be this way," said Tony.

"I get that. He speaks about you in glowing words. But..." She paused. "He did have concerns about your working too much," said Reanna hesitantly.

"We discussed my long work hours and I told him that in a couple of months, my hours would decrease. He seemed okay with this, but he still occasionally disappeared and was constantly on the phone. I'm not much of an eavesdropper, so I'm not sure who or what he's talking about when he's on the phone," said Tony.

"The only time I talk with Mayson is when I call him after not hearing from him for a couple of weeks. He does the same with me. When we talk, he seems like the same old Mayson, but when I ask him why I haven't heard from him in a while, he just says he's been busy," she said.

"He must be referring to his part-time job. It's part-time," Tony emphasized.

"That shouldn't have him that busy," he said. "I'm not the jealous type, Reanna, so this isn't about whether he's seeing someone else. I'm worried about his safety. When Mayson and I started talking, he told me he was not too experienced when it came to dating. So, if we end our relationship I want to make sure he's safe. I'm really worried about where he is and what he may be doing. I haven't seen him in weeks. It's never been this long," he said.

"I wish I knew where he was, " said Reanna, sounding just as frustrated as Tony.

"Do you know if he's been in contact with his family these past few weeks?" he asked.

"I don't think so. I ask about him whenever I see any of his family and they said it's been a while since they've seen or talked with him," she said.

"I know you don't want to tell on your best friend. That's not what I'm asking you to do. He may be in harm's way and I was hoping that you and I could keep in touch to make sure he's safe," said Tony.

"I know, but I honestly don't have anything to tell you," said Reanna. Silence.

"Okay. Well. Keep me posted if you hear from him," said Tony.

"I sure will," she said.

CHAPTER 28

A Meeting with Caring Others

(I)

It had been months since Phyllis heard from Mayson. At first, she was not concern because he had become inconsistent in calling her. And there had been times when two weeks had passed before he would call. She called him a few times, hoping Tony would not answer, which he often was not home to do so. When she got their answering machine, she would not leave a message. After several more weeks, she knew something was wrong. One evening she decided she would no longer sit around, waiting and hoping for Mayson to call. She got into her car and scoured the areas where she thought he might be. She included the Encounter Club in her search. It was noon, and she hoped someone would be at the club to tell her something about his whereabouts. Mayson had not told her about his working at the club, nor had J.R. told her about his interaction with Mayson in the parking lot. They both knew it would be devastating for Phyllis to know where he worked. However, Phyllis found out when a neighbor's son told her he had seen Mayson working there.

When Phyllis drove up to The Encounter Club building, she gasped when she saw the old, run-down building with its failed efforts at looking like an upscale establishment. Lanelle had purchased a used portable marquee sign. One of the legs was bent, which made the sign lean, and a couple of the letters were missing. Lanelle had put blinking Christmas lights around the marquee in order to attract attention to the sign. It was tacky, but it let people know the name of the club, that it served drinks and had a live band. Lanelle wanted a better sign, but Byron hadn't given her enough in the budget for anything nicer. In addition, the paint on the building was peeling in places. Graffiti was unreadable but still visible under an inadequate cover-up paint job. Phyllis thought about how far

Mayson had come to be employed in such a place. She had never seen the club before, but Mayson often mentioned Lanelle as a new friend of his whom he worked with at his part-time distribution job. Phyllis eventually put it together that the distribution job was a lie and Lanelle was someone he worked with at the club. This would be the first time she and Lanelle would meet—if she was there. Phyllis knew it might be too early, but she was desperate. Phyllis braced herself before getting out of her car.

There were no cars parked in front of the building, therefore, she assumed that no one was there. She then saw an extending back lot behind it. She thought to check and see if there were any cars parked in the back. She saw one car. She thought it was an abandoned car that someone left unrepaired on the lot, but she decided to try her luck and knock on the back door anyway. After her second knock, she turned around to go back to her car. As she reached for her car door handle, she heard the creaking sound of the building door open. She turned around and saw a woman in a tight button-down brown blouse, flower-patterned head scarf, and jeans that looked at least one size too small.

Lanelle was indeed at the restaurant, giving the place a thorough cleaning. Lanelle saw a beautiful, sky blue, like-new four-door sedan, and an attractive, casually but distinctively dressed middle-aged woman standing next to it.

"Hello, may I help you?" asked Lanelle.

Phyllis took every part of Lanelle in as she saw a haggard woman with street-like appearance and poor-quality clothing. She hoped her stunned observation of her did not show.

"Hi, my name is Phyllis Hendricks," she said.

The name didn't mean much to Lanelle at first.

"I'm looking for my son," said Phyllis.

Immediately Mayson came to Lanelle's mind. She could see a slight resemblance to Mayson in her eyes.

"Oh, you're Mayson's mother," said Lanelle delightedly.

Phyllis felt such a relief from hearing a positive tone in Lanelle's voice. Despite Mayson's fond words about Lanelle, Phyllis had preconditioned herself to talk with a crude and unfiltered woman based on what she saw from the neighborhood.

"Come in," said Lanelle warmly.

"I don't mean to take up your time," said Phyllis apologetically, partly because she had hoped she wouldn't have to go inside the club to talk. She had thought herself to be open-minded when it came to meeting people or places for the first time, but she felt a side of prejudice rise within her. She was sad and hurt to see that Mayson worked with someone who looked like Lanelle and in such a deplorable neighborhood.

"No, you're fine," said Lanelle as she opened the door wider for Phyllis to enter.

Phyllis stepped in and saw a small, cramped, dimly lit kitchen, with worn-out appliances sitting on two counters that surrounded a small stove. But all the appliances seemed clean and well cared for. The dish rack on the side of the sink was full of dishes. The dishes were clean and neatly stacked in the rack. The neatness and cleanness of the dishes and appliances were a wakeup call for Phyllis not to make prejudgment of Lanelle or the club. She was even more pleased to see a dishwasher that appeared to be new. To Phyllis, a well-organized and clean kitchen said a lot about a person.

Lanelle pulled a chair back from the small kitchen table to sit. Phyllis couldn't help but glance at the rust that dotted the metal legs of the table. Lanelle had covered the table with a flowered-patterned vinyl tablecloth. It looked clean, but Phyllis felt the need to test the cleanliness of the table before she sat her purse on it. When Lanelle looked down to position her chair up closer to the table, Phyllis quickly ran her hand across the table.

"So, Mrs. Hendricks..." began Lanelle.

"It's okay to call me Phyllis."

"Okay. Thank you," said Lanelle.

"I am looking for Mayson. It's been a while and I am worried," Phyllis said.

"Okay, Phyllis. Let me see if I can help you," said Lanelle pleasantly.

Lanelle was happy to see Phyllis. Mayson's warm description of her had Lanelle imagining Phyllis to be the world's greatest mother. He had spoken so well of Phyllis that Lanelle wanted to meet Phyllis one day. Even with Lanelle's family-like group at the club, she had no special relationships and wanted to keep it that way for a while. Lanelle wanted a close friend, but it had to be someone much unlike her, someone who would help her grow as a person. From Mayson's description, Phyllis seemed like she would be the perfect friend for her. She was hoping Phyllis' visit would lead to them keeping in touch.

"I don't know if Mayson told you, but he no longer works here at the club. The last time I saw Mayson was at Cora's Cafe on Wedgewood Boulevard about 3 or 4 months ago," said Lanelle.

Lanelle recalled the concerns she had had for Mayson that day at the cafe. She wondered if she should tell Phyllis about the man that he got into the Mercedes car with. As she took more time to see Phyllis in the light of a worried mother rather than a possible future friend, she decided to wait a while and see where the conversation would go. Mayson had never shared with Lanelle the reason for his leaving his mother's home. The departure sounded abrupt, but Mayson did not offer any details. It was like one day he was happily living with his family and the next day he was not. Therefore, Lanelle knew she had to be careful with what she told Phyllis.

Phyllis pulled a tissue from her purse to dab her brow that was covered with beads of perspiration. The long drive to the club and the anticipated meeting with Lanelle increased her anxiety.

"May I get you something to drink?" asked Lanelle.

"No, I'm fine. I've been out in the sun a little," she said. "So, he no longer works here?" asked Phyllis, as she balled up the sweaty tissue in her hand.

"No. He worked here for almost a year, then one day called to say he wasn't coming in, and he's never been back since," said Lanelle, trying her best not to bring up Byron's name. "I wish I had more to tell you," said Lanelle as she rubbed her ear, which was a sign of discomfort when she was not being completely truthful.

"Well, I'm not going to waste any more of your time," said Phyllis as she reached for her purse.

"If you find out anything, please give me a call. Let me give you my number," said Phyllis, as she stood and reached to go back into her purse.

Lanelle watched Phyllis as she dug through her purse looking for paper and a pen. While Phyllis was rifling through her purse, she found another tissue and used it to wipe her nose, which was running.

"It's been a while since I've talked with him," said Phyllis as she pulled out a piece of folded-up paper and a pen. "When he moved out, he and I used to talk at least once a week. I don't hear from him at all now," said Phyllis as she handed the piece of paper to Lanelle.

"I'm going to keep looking for him. But if no one knows where he is, then I'm going to file a missing person's report. What concerns me is that if they ask me if he's ever done this before, then I will have to say yes. Since he has moved from my home, there have been long periods of time where I haven't heard from him. But this time is different. I haven't heard from him in months. And, now you tell me that he stopped coming to work and it's been months since you've seen him. I'm now more than concerned about him, I'm scared," said Phyllis.

Lanelle heard the fear in Phyllis' words as she tried to keep her composure. Maybe this information about the man at the cafe could help. Or, it may plunge her into deeper despair, thought Lanelle.

While determining whether or not to tell Phyllis about the man in the cafe, Lanelle knew that this was not the primary reason for her dilemma. She knew that lingering in her mind was the biggest lead to the whereabouts of Mayson. Byron Crawford was where much of the information she needed would come from, she thought.

Phyllis stood up to leave.

"Sit down again, please Phyllis, I think I can give you some tips on where to find out where Mayson may be," said Lanelle.

Phyllis sat down slowly as she looked at Lanelle with intensity and anticipation of what she was about to tell her.

"First of all, Phyllis, from the first day I met Mayson I could tell he was a good kid. Brought up in a good home. My boss often hires people without giving out much information about them, so I usually keep my relationships with my coworkers strictly professional. But Mayson was different. I saw the greenness in him the first day I met him," she said.

She shared the time length of Mayson's employment at the club, the sudden ending of his employment and Byron's possible false promises to him. She shared that since leaving the club Mayson later told her that he was working with Byron as his assistant. She informed Phyllis of her concern that Mayson was using drugs. As she saw Phyllis' posture sink into the chair with every word, she chose not to tell Phyllis about seeing Mayson getting into a car with the man at the cafe. She didn't want Phyllis to worry that her son was not only an addict, but also someone to be bought.

When Lanelle finished relaying all she felt Phyllis could take about

Mayson, Phyllis' head was buried in her hands as her elbows rested on the table.

"Lord, Lord, Lord," said Phyllis as she rocked her head from side to side. "I thought about drugs, but I didn't want to believe it. I knew he was staying with some man, and I thought maybe this man had got him into drugs. I never imagined he would have been involved with some low-life, street thug named Byron," said Phyllis.

When Lanelle heard Phyllis use the word *some man* in describing who Mayson was living with, she became more suspicious that Mayson was gay. She recalled seeing Mayson being dropped off to work one day in the BMW by another man. She was almost certain that she saw them kiss in the car before Mayson got out. When she saw this man with Mayson that day, she had thought, "Good for Mayson. He seems to have found someone that will treat him right." After dealing with Byron and Tyson, Lanelle considered herself to be a good judge of character. Her instincts told her that this guy was good for Mayson. The man who drove Mayson to work looked nothing like the creepy, nervous guy she saw him with at the cafe.

"As for Byron, it would do well if he was a street thug, as you put it. If he did his own dirty work on the streets, then I'm sure he would have been locked up by now. Instead, he lets others take the fall. I fear that Mayson is involved in some of his dirt," said Lanelle.

"Have you ever talked with this guy who Mayson is living with?" asked Lanelle.

"No," said Phyllis in an exhausted tone. "His name is Tony. I never could accept that union, but always wanted to keep my son. I wouldn't ask Mayson much about this guy and he would not mention him to me unless I brought him up. When I would call Mayson, I worried about this guy picking up the phone. Most of the time Mayson or their fancy answering machine would pick up. That machine made me nervous. I was never sure what to say and felt silly talking into a machine."

"When Mayson used to come by my house, he would arrive in this guy's car and claimed it was his, but I knew that it must belong to the guy he was living with. I just couldn't make their relationship feel normal. It's just too much for me to take," said Phyllis.

Lanelle began to have second thoughts about the possibility for friendship with Phyllis. If she disapproved of Mayson and Tony's union, her blood pressure would go through the roof if she had something to really worry about. Such as Lanelle's sordid past, she thought.

"I see. Well, you may need to contact his..." Lanelle paused...she started to say his *boyfriend* but was aware of Phyllis' response about the relationship.

"... his live-in friend to see if he could tell you if he knows where Mayson is. I'd advise you to contact this guy before you make any effort to contact Byron. Actually, I caution you not to contact Byron at all. He can be dangerous. And he knows a lot of people who could be harmful to you too," said Lanelle.

"Good Lord. Is he that dangerous?" asked Phyllis.

"Well, if you consider manipulative, controlling, and self-serving to be dangerous, yes, said Lanelle. You really need to talk with the guy Mayson is living with. Let me work on Byron before you make a move to go see him," she added.

"Thank you," said Phyllis as she reached across the table to shake Lanelle's hand.

"Do you know his friend's phone number or address?" asked Lanelle as she was about to get her address book.

"I have the phone number, but not the address. But I'm pretty sure Mayson's friend Reanna knows," said Phyllis.

Lanelle decided to let Phyllis get the address from Reanna. She figured she had already told Phyllis too much.

(II)

It had been over twenty-four hours since Phyllis' meeting with Lanelle. She was in her car now, on her way to see Tony. Phyllis had gotten Tony's full name and address from Reanna. Phyllis preferred to go to his home unannounced. She thought that talking with Tony over the phone would not be the best approach. If Mayson was there, a phone call might tip him off and he'd leave. The element of surprise was not the most respectable approach, but she had to make sure she eliminated any obstacles in connecting with Tony or catching up with Mayson.

240

Mayson had given Reanna his home phone number. On the day Tony called Reanna looking for Mayson, he had called her back and given her his office phone number as well. But neither Mayson nor Tony gave Reanna their home address. Tony's phone number was private, so his address was not listed either. Reanna told Phyllis how she was able to get Tony's address. She told her that she had gone to the Encounter Club with her date one evening. Mayson was thrilled when he saw her. Unbeknownst to him, when the club closed, Reanna had her date wait in the parking lot for Mayson to finish up and come out to his car. When Mayson finally drove off, Reanna and her date had followed him home. Once she followed him to the condo, she jotted down his address and told her date that she needed it in order to keep up with her best friend. He found her explanation amusing.

While driving to Tony's condo, Phyllis began to think about her visit with Lanelle yesterday. She liked Lanelle, but knew that if Lanelle didn't have any connection to Mayson, then she would not be someone that Phyllis would want to know. She knew that Lanelle's outward appearance would have been enough for her to keep her distance. In talking with Lanelle, she had a sense that she was an anchor for her son. Yet she could tell that Lanelle was someone who may have had an interesting past that was not too far behind. Meeting Lanelle, with her less-than-appealing external features, but underlying strength, forced Phyllis to take a look at a side of herself that was not her best. I'm a religious snob, thought Phyllis. She was not proud of this observation, however, at that moment, it was not a priority of concern for her.

Phyllis pulled up to a luxurious two-story building with a sun deck. Beneath the building were large garages. She saw the car that Mayson had driven to her home parked in front of one of them. Phyllis took a deep breath. Why am I so nervous? she thought as she walked to the building. After ringing the doorbell, she looked with admiration at the sturdy well designed door. The door opened and there stood a man with a perfectly cut beard and mustache. Despite his strong facial bone structure, he had a slightly boyish look to him, yet she could tell he was much older than Mayson. She was 5'6" and he only seemed a few inches taller than that. He was wearing a white t-shirt that fit snugly across his muscular chest and arms, sweatpants, and white tube socks. He had on wire-rimmed eyeglasses and looked as though he had been reading, because he removed them when he opened the door.

"Yes, may I help you?" asked Tony.

"Hi, I'm Phyllis Hendricks, Mayson's mother," she said.

Tony's eyes widened. He stared at her without saying a word. She took him by surprise because other than Lanelle and Tamara, he and Mayson made it a rule not to give out his address. It was actually Mayson's idea, because he did not want any of his family or friends doing drive-byes of the condo or popping up at their home unannounced.

Tony was not sure why she had come to the condo, but three thoughts of her abrupt presence flashed to his mind. The first and most dreadful thought was something had happened to Mayson and she was coming to tell him or blame him for it. Or that Reanna had told her that he called looking for Mayson and she was coming by to ask him to leave Mayson alone. Lastly, like him, maybe she didn't know where Mayson was and wanted to know if he was at the condo.

"I'm sorry," said Tony as he was coming out of his trance. "Come in, Mrs. Hendricks," he said.

"Have a seat," said Tony as he pointed her to his couch in the living room.

Phyllis walked over to the couch as she looked at the immaculate living room with its expensive couches, lamps, tables, and décor. The inside looked just as impressive as the outside, she thought. On a small dinette table near the living room, were stacks of papers, two notebooks, and a pen on the floor that must have fallen when he got up to answer the door.

As she was about to sit, she saw the balcony that overlooked the front of the building and a beautiful view of the park.

"May I get you anything?" asked Tony.

"No, thank you," replied Phyllis.

Tony took a seat in his wing back chair facing Phyllis. Phyllis looked around the living room, trying to take everything in.

As she looked at Tony she thought, "Who is this man to me?" If she had a daughter and Tony was seeing her, then he could be a potential son-in-law, but he was not. She had a son he was seeing, so his presence was unsettling for her. She had to admit that seeing Tony in such an upscale manner; the beautiful condo, expensive car, well-kept appearance and seeming intelligence, eased her a little about the relationship. At that moment, Phyllis saw Tony and all his surroundings that identified him as an individual and a person. Not just a Human label. She had hoped that if he were less well-off, she would feel the same in her sense of ease of him. Maybe his intelligence and sense of maturity without the money would have won her over just as well, she thought. She wondered whether she would have felt the same if he were more effeminate. She could only take so much reality of her newly discovered superficiality and hypocrisy within a twenty-four-hour period. She was still trying to resolve herself from her reality with Lanelle. But seeing Tony helped ease her fears. She had not been sure what to expect, but she felt a peace about him the moment he opened the door. She saw a person, who, if she had not known about his being Human, she hoped her sons would have turned out to be like him, educated, responsible, and intelligent.

They sat in silence, hoping the other would speak first. Phyllis knew that since she was the one who came to his home unexpectedly, it was she who should begin the conversation.

"I'm looking for Mayson. I have not seen or heard from him in a while. I was hoping he would be here, or you'd know where he was," said Phyllis.

Tony felt a combination of relief and worry. Relieved that Phyllis was not coming to tell him that something terrible had happened to Mayson, or confront him about his relationship with him, but worried that she didn't know where he was, either.

"I'm sorry Mrs. Hendricks, I don't know where Mayson is. He came by to pick up his clothes months ago and I have not seen him since."

He paused a few seconds wondering whether he should tell her that they argued that day. Tony had gotten fed up with Mayson's come-and-go habits, which included a day in which Mayson stayed out all night without explanation. He decided to leave out the argument. He did not want her to know that it resulted in him telling Mayson to get all of his things out within 24 hours.

"When he came by, he picked up a few clothes and I asked him to come back and get his remaining items as well," said Tony hoping she could read between the lines.

Phyllis gathered that they had an argument but was not highly concerned about it.

"Does he still have things here?" asked Phyllis.

"Yes, he does. He never came back to get the rest," responded Tony.

"So, you have not seen him since that day?" asked Phyllis.

"No ma'am, I haven't."

They both lapsed back into silence.

Phyllis stood up to leave.

"Well, if you hear from him, will you please have him call me?" she asked.

She reached into her purse and pulled out her card that Pastor Upshaw had made for her. It had her name and title as the Youth Coordinator for Greenlawn Community Church (GCC). The card had the address and phone number of the church, but she had written down her home number on the back.

"My home number is on the back," said Phyllis as she handed the card to Tony.

Tony looked at the card then turned it over to look at the phone number. He didn't have the heart to tell her that he already had her home number from the days when Mayson lived with the family. They had set up a day and time when it was okay for Tony to call in order that Mayson would be there to answer the phone.

"Sure thing, Mrs. Hendricks. I'll let you know if I hear from him," he said.

(III)

For the past week, Phyllis felt like an amateur detective. It had been two days since she had talked with Tony. She made an appointment to meet with Pastor McDaniel at his office.

Upon her arrival, Pastor McDaniel sat at his desk as though he had been expecting her for a long time.

"Hello Mrs. Hendricks," said Pastor McDaniel as they shook hands. "Have a seat. Can I get you anything?"

"No, I'm fine," said Phyllis.

"I was glad to hear you wanted to meet with me. I've been thinking a lot about Mayson and wondering how he's been doing," said Pastor McDaniel.

"That's a good question," said Phyllis, pleased that he would start their conversation in that manner.

"I'm not sure how Mayson is doing. He seldom calls me and these past months I haven't heard from him at all, which is why I wanted to meet with you. Pastor Upshaw told me that he referred Mayson to meet with you. Because Mayson keeps some things secret from me, I was hoping there was something you could tell me that could help me find him," said Phyllis.

Pastor McDaniel could see the frustration and hurt in Phyllis' eyes. He wanted to help her, but since Mayson was an adult, there was only so much he would share with her about their meeting.

"Pastor Upshaw did refer Mayson to see me, but out of respect for him, I can't share the specifics of my conversation with him. However, I'd be more than happy to be a listening ear if you need me to," said Pastor McDaniel.

Phyllis had anticipated that there was only so much that Pastor McDaniel would share with her, but she needed to see him and try to get something from him. She had prayed the night before that Pastor McDaniel would make an exception to his rule of confidentiality, considering that Mayson was missing. Despite her initial flabbergast in Pastor Upshaw's referral of Mayson to Pastor McDaniel, she needed someone to talk to; therefore, she decided to take advantage of their time together and talk with him about Mayson. Phyllis was quiet for a moment. She fidgeted with her purse. These past months left her with so much, she was not sure where she should start.

"I knew that Mayson would be different when it came to girls. I could tell he was trying so hard to be what the church told him that he should be. He had one male friend named Leon who had a physical deformity. Leon was terribly shy and self-conscious about his disability. Children were cruel to him, but he and Mayson were friends no matter what. As I look back on that friendship, I now see it as a means of them coming together because they were different. They understood each other and needed that connection.

When it came to girls, Mayson had such an awkwardness about him when we had our talks about his future after he graduated from high school. I came so close one time in asking him if he wanted a wife in his future, but the words would not come from my lips. Instead, I told him to never allow "anybody" to put him in their box of who he should be. I specified "anybody" rather than "anyone." Any 'body' would be any human being. Any "one" would include God. God is a Spirit, not a body, therefore

I wanted to make sure he knew that God would be the exception to that rule. Whether he recognized that difference, I don't know, but I needed that to be clear to myself," said Phyllis.

"Anyone and anybody," repeated Pastor McDaniel. "I never thought about the difference."

Phyllis smiled.

"That's just my way of viewing God. I'm sure some scholarly intellect can find problems with that distinction," said Phyllis.

She continued, "I also told him that who he is to be in life is something he would have to discover on his own. This bit of wisdom just came out. I didn't plan to say this to him, so it surprised me when I heard it. He didn't ask me why I was saying these things to him, but just said, *okay*."

"When he moved out, he would come by the house every week for lunch to see me and his brother and sister. I could tell that he looked forward to it. I think he missed us and his home. He'd always come with some kind of treat for his brother and sister. His younger brother Lamont loves mini donuts and sister Idee has a sweet tooth for candy bars. He'd bring those things with him every time. I told him that he didn't have to bring them anything in order to come to the house. I also told him to stop feeding them so much junk. One day I told him that his sister Idee didn't need so much sugar because she was already bouncing off the walls. He laughed at this but then started sneaking the treats to her anyway. When I confronted him, we both found it funny and I just let it go. I figured that it was his way of trying to feel needed by his siblings. These were the better days after his departure from our home.

On the rare days that my husband was home, rather than Mayson coming to the house, he and I would have lunch at a restaurant. My husband and Mayson don't get along, but that's another story. After a while, our time together changed. These luncheons became occasional. Sometimes he would not show up, or call. I'd have to call him, and he'd apologize but do it again.

When Mayson left my home, he went to stay with a man. I found out his name was Tony. Mayson and I had an unspoken agreement. He would not provide specific information about his relationship with Tony, and I would not express my feelings about his life choices. During these earlier times with Tony, Mayson always looked well. But a few months later, it seemed something had changed. I was afraid that at some point he would lose so much weight that he'd disappear. He explained that he keeps busy with his job, which I later found out was at a nightclub. He also claimed his weight loss was from working out a lot, but I didn't believe that because Mayson has never been much for exercising.

A lot of our conversation was also about our church. Even though he no longer attended services on a regular basis, he continued to be interested in what was going on at GCC. I could tell he still loved GCC, so I would ask him to come back to the services. He'd respond "maybe." He did visit the church last year and I thought he was back for good, but it wasn't so."

She paused to think for a few seconds.

"I understand that my pastor had to do what he thought was right," said Phyllis with the assumption that Pastor McDaniel knew about the ultimatum that led to Mayson's leaving GCC.

Pastor McDaniel leaned forward.

"It seems you are caught in the middle between your son and your church. I can imagine how difficult that is for you," he said.

Phyllis found it refreshing to have a pastor hear her without making a judgment. She had expected most other pastors in her denomination to preach to her as to why Pastor Upshaw was right, and her son was wrong. But Pastor McDaniel didn't preach to her about the rightness or wrongness of either person involved in her dilemma. It was even more comforting to hear the empathy in his voice that was specifically directed at her.

Like so many people from her denomination, she had heard about Pastor McDaniel's break from their denominational church and his openness to those who were Humans. His name was often spoken of as though it was a taboo. She looked at Pastor McDaniel and smiled.

"Indeed, it is difficult, Pastor, she confirmed. During our weekly luncheons, Mayson would often ask about services, people at GCC, and especially the songs sung by the choir. We'd also talk about our family. My husband Ed stays away from home on a regular basis. When the problems involving Mayson in the home were looming, Ed began to stay away for even longer periods of time. He used to do this before Mayson moved out, as he said it was due to overtime on his job. Since Mayson moved out, he stopped bothering with that excuse and comes home days later without an explanation. Anyway, as I said, his father is another story," said Phyllis with a look of disgust.

Phyllis felt a lump in her throat. She coughed to suppress the urge to cry. Hearing her words about her family sounded sad in her ears. Sadder even than living them, she thought. She decided to find something more upbeat in order to avoid shedding tears in Pastor McDaniel's presence.

"Mayson and I enjoyed talking about his sister Idee. She is my fun, happy teenage daughter. I'd tell him how much she missed him or share something amusing that only Idee would do or say. Talking about her always brought the laugh I wanted to hear from Mayson, or that smile on his face that I so wanted to see. Mayson had trouble talking with me about Lamont, his younger brother. Mayson knew that moving out would affect Lamont significantly. In terms of friends, Mayson was all Lamont had. He thought the world of Mayson. Lamont never made much effort to try and make his own friends because he had Mayson. He's a nice boy, but a little shy. Sometimes he can be difficult to read, but Mayson was often able to connect with him."

Phyllis suddenly stopped talking. "I'm sorry. I am rambling on and on," she said.

"It's not a problem. I want to hear whatever is on your mind," he said. Phyllis was not for sure why she was telling all this to Pastor McDaniel. But she sensed that he seemed genuinely interested in what was going on with Mayson. She was so overwhelmed in what was going on with Mayson and her family, that she wanted to see them in her words that were entering into the ears of Pastor McDaniel.

She continued. "Mayson and Reanna are Lamont's best friends. Reanna adores Lamont just as much as Mayson does. I knew Mayson was feeling guilty about not being around for Lamont. So to help ease his guilt and show him Lamont would be okay, I told him about an evening when Reanna called Lamont to go with her to My Place Buffet after service. I think she was feeling sorry for Lamont and missing Mayson herself at the same time. Mayson said it was nice for Reanna to reach out to Lamont like that. He also said that he felt his life with Reanna and Lamont hanging out at the church or the buffet was hundreds of years ago. I didn't bother to ask him what that meant, because the way he said it sounded like an end."

"An end to what?" asked Pastor McDaniel.

"And end to his life as I knew it," she said.

Silence.

"As you can see Pastor McDaniel, Mayson's situation and the eventual move have affected my whole family. We are a close family and what happens to one affects the other."

Phyllis' eyes began to water. She pulled out a tissue from her purse and blew her nose.

Pastor McDaniel leaned back in his chair. He waited for Phyllis to compose herself.

"This would be so much easier and better for you if Mayson was here. He could allow us to have the dialogue that is so necessary to address the hurting that is going on within him and his family. One thing that I can say to you about this matter is that whatever Mayson's sexuality may be, he is going through changes that most people must address at some point in life. That being, who am I, and where is my place in the world. Granted, for those with the added pressure of being gay or lesbian, the journey can come with an even greater task," he said.

There was a silence as Pastor McDaniel waited to see if she had more she wanted to share.

"I'm not sure why I shared that with you, but it did help me to see my family and situation in a nutshell. Well, a large nutshell, she laughed. I guess I just needed to hear all that myself," she said.

Phyllis dropped her tissue into a small trash can next to Pastor McDaniel's desk and put the strap of her purse over her shoulder.

"I'm sure you are a man with a lot to do, so I won't waste any more of your time," she said.

"No, no, you're fine," he said.

"I'll continue my detective work," said Phyllis in an effort to lighten the moment.

"We are going to believe that he is okay and safe. If—when you see Mayson, let him know that my door is always open to him," said Pastor McDaniel.

"I will," said Phyllis.

"Can I pray with you before you go"? asked Pastor McDaniel.

"By all means," said Phyllis eagerly."

They both stood and joined hands. Pastor McDaniel begin to pray:

"Dear Lord, this family is in pain and turmoil. Help them to find peace in their lives as it is in Your divine order and steps. Bring healing to the hearts and minds of all that are suffering in this household of division. Father, give this mother healing from worry and fear.

We pray for the safety and peace needed for our son Mayson. As for his earthly habitation, I asked that You lead him home. Bring him to the home that is best for him. Not our personal direction for him, but Your will, as it will be for his salvation and peace of mind.

I stand in the gap for this family. The Hendricks family. I pray and receive Your will for them for deliverance and peace. I also pray they receive the knowledge and wisdom you have for them for the days to come, as they will hear many voices. But in the midst of all the voices, I ask that You make your voice known to them. I ask that You open their hearts and mind as they are led in your voice of truth.

And God, I ask that You bring Your church together under Your grace and love for all of your children. Help us to be patient and open to Your will and way as we come together as one in You.

God, we acknowledge You as God of all that is good. Thank You, Father God. Amen."

(IV)

The worried look on Phyllis' face and the possibility that Mayson was missing left Lanelle with a few sleepless nights. One evening while driving to the Encounter Club, she found herself turning down a different street, towards Byron's office. In the blink of an eye, she was standing in front of Byron's office door.

"What are you doing here?" asked Byron, surprised to see Lanelle. Showing up at his office unexpectedly was something she never did. He also knew that around that time she was usually at the club setting things up for the night.

Lanelle stood in the doorway for a while as she took in the sight of Byron. He was sitting at his desk with a small television perched on its corner. He had on a crisp white button-down shirt that looked fresh from the cleaners. She could see a portion of his tan pants and black dress shoes beneath his desk. Byron made a great effort not to look like a stereotypical drug dealer. He despised being described as a drug dealer as he thought he was too advanced for such a title. But as far as Lanelle was concerned, he was no different, or better.

Lanelle had come to Byron unannounced to find out what happened to Mayson and hopefully provide some information of his whereabouts to Phyllis. She had developed a boldness with Byron over the years. Lanelle knew she was valuable to Byron. Her boldness had grown along with Byron's developed trust of her.

When the realization hit Lanelle that she was not going to be in the "big time" in terms of her career, she never confronted Byron again about his promise to bring people in the entertainment field to come hear her sing. They both had a silent agreement: she protected him by managing his club without a lot of questions, and he, for the most part, left her alone to do it. In addition, whether the actual profits from the club were large or small, she and her staff would be paid. Lanelle felt good that she was able to earn her own money, even though some of its protective legitimacy was questionable. Her allowances from Byron were a thing of the past. Lanelle loved the club and worked hard to keep the customers who frequented it. These steady customers brought in other people, which contributed to the increased profits. Lanelle's hard work, respect, and caring presence for the clubs' patrons, like her grandparent's business sense, brought in the revenue to cover a portion of the salaries and the needed financial image for Byron. Lanelle was also aware that Byron needed her and could not bear the thought of losing her and starting over with someone else.

"We need to talk," said Lanelle as she sat on the couch.

Byron sat back in his chair and began to swivel it from side to side with his elbows on the arm of the chair and his fingers overlapped.

"Okay," said Byron, in a deceptively casual tone.

"Mayson!" blurted out Lanelle as she looked Byron straight in the eye. "Why is he no longer working the club?"

Byron could pick up a bit of tension in her voice and knew that this was not an isolated question.

"Mr. Mayson found that the club was not for him and had other career goals that he preferred," said Byron.

"Come on Byron, cut the bull!" This is me you're talking to, Lanelle snapped. She was tired of the "Byron charm" that lured so many people to dead ends in order to support his lifestyle.

Byron sat up in his seat.

"Lanelle, what the hell is wrong with you?" he asked with less charm in his voice.

"Byron, I've sat by and watched so many people come to you with hopes and dreams only to find themselves hooked on drugs and God knows whatever else. When Calvin came and went, I decided to keep my mouth shut because I felt he was old enough to take care of himself and old enough to know better. Mayson was my last straw. You knew this boy was from a good family and was about as green as they come. Why couldn't you have just left him alone? No, he didn't have a solo singing voice, but he was a good backup singer. And he helped me open and close the club without ever being asked, or paid extra. He was a friend, Byron. Something you can't seem to be to anybody," she said.

With all his charm now gone, Byron stood up from his desk and straightened out the crease in his pants. "You need to leave," he said to Lanelle as he pointed to the door. "I have things to do and what you are talking about is none of your damn business."

He then leaned over his desk and looked Lanelle in the eye.

"You only need to be concerned with what I give you. You go beyond that and I'll see if someone else would like to have your life, with no questions asked. Mayson made his decision and you need to mind your own damn business," said Byron.

Lanelle stood up. Despite Byron's threat, she felt desperation come over her.

"Byron, I know you have a compassionate side to you. I know what you can do," she said.

"I'm not going to ask you again to get out of my office!" he yelled. She saw a rage in Byron's eye that she had not seen before. She started to press him more, but her instinct told her not to. Instead, she turned toward the door and walked out.

CHAPTER 29

The Other News of Mayson

(I)

A long, loud, and horrifying scream came from the Hendricks' home. No one in the neighborhood opened their doors or went to inquire about the blaring shriek. When two official-looking gentlemen got out of their unmarked car and headed for the Hendricks' house, it was no surprise that such a scream would follow. The day before, the local television news announced that a body had been found in a wooded area near Willard's Pond. Rumors went through Benton that the body was that of Mayson Hendricks, who had been missing.

When the doorbell rang that day, Phyllis knew it was the police. Ed opened the door and saw two suited detectives looking stoically back at him. Detective Lawrence House, clean cut, average height, slim and tidy appearance. Detective Quinn Smith, a little heavier than Detective House, sporting a full mustache, top button of his shirt undone, necktie pulled slightly down, and hands casually placed in his pants pocket. Phyllis sat in the den anticipating words that she did not want uttered from these men. As she anticipated the possible news, still hoping, "it's not so," she thought how good it was that Idee and Lamont were upstairs in their rooms at that time. Ed directed the detectives into the den. Detective House, who had talked with Phyllis and Cliff at the police station when they filed the missing person report, introduced his partner, Detective Smith. Detective House reiterated that a body had been found near Willard's Pond. Without any other preamble, he told them that, at this time, it seemed to be that of their son, Mayson. These were the words that sent Phyllis' voice piercing throughout the room, their home and beyond their walls. The scream immediately brought Idee out of her room. She raced down the stairs to her parents and held onto Ed, who was holding Phyllis. She cried too without ever asking what was wrong. She knew the scream and tears from her mother meant her brother was dead.

"Honey, please give us a few more minutes with the detectives and we'll come to your room and get you," said Ed to Idee. Without a word, Idee ran to her room, crying hysterically.

Once Idee was out of the room, Detective House told Ed and Phyllis that it appeared he had been beaten to death. He informed them that the matter was yet under investigation, but they had two possibilities about the motive of the murder. He stated that no wallet was found directly on the body, nor money, which could mean that it was a robbery. However, with the brutal beating of the body, it could also signify that it was done by someone who knew him and was angry at him.

"A crime of passion?" asked Ed, thinking about the possibility of Mayson's *friend*. He never bothered to know Tony's name as he didn't want to recall the thought of Mayson and Tony in his home that day.

"Pretty much," agreed the detective.

Detective House asked if they knew anyone who could have had problems with Mayson or whom Mayson had problems with. Phyllis did not say anything. She was still crying and rocking back and forth on the couch while Ed kept his arms across her shoulder. He looked at Phyllis for an answer to the detective's question, but then he realized she was too far gone to give an answer.

Ed tried to think of some kind of generalized answer to give the detective. He knew it would look bad if he didn't seem to know anything about his own son.

"Mayson was an even-tempered person. I don't know of anyone who was angry with him or he with them," said Ed, as he continued to wonder about Mayson's *friend*, but assumed they had already made contact with him.

Detective House explained that a backpack with clothes and a picture ID was found near Mayson's body. He added that the picture looked like Mayson. He noted a slight height difference in the body and the ID, but mentioned that people tend not to be too exact about their height on IDs. The detective added that their former neighbor, Harold Watson, who lived near Willard's Pond, stumbled upon the body and unofficially identified it as Mayson.

As Detective House talked with Phyllis, Detective Smith eyed Ed and motioned with his head for him to go with him from the den into the kitchen. Ed gently moved away from Phyllis, who was still in tears, but a little more composed. Ed told her he would be back. Detective House continued to talk with Phyllis as he tried to get more information from her.

Once in the kitchen, Detective Smith told Ed that it would make matters more certain if a family member could ID the body. However, he also told Ed that if his wife was to be that person or one of them to see the body, then he wanted to warn him that the body had been beaten severely and picked over by animals.

Once Ed and the Detective reentered the den, Detective House was at the door waiting for his partner. Before they left, Detective House told Ed and Phyllis they would keep in touch as other matters would need to be attended to regarding the body and further investigation.

After they left, Ed explained to Phyllis that a family member should ID the body and he wanted to be the one to do that. He urged Phyllis that she should not go. He explained the condition of the body to Phyllis in an effort to discourage her from trying to go with him. Phyllis cried even more at Ed's description of the body, but she still couldn't decide whether or not she should go.

Phyllis was so devastated over the news of Mayson's death that she didn't bother to think about how unusual it was for Ed to take charge of the moment. When Ed walked in the house yesterday, Phyllis oddly felt herself glad to see him. Any man should want to be with his family when their child could possibly be dead. But she knew Ed was a parent in name only. For the moment, she ignored any thoughts about his lack of parenting in the past. At that time, she needed someone, and there was Ed.

After the detectives left, Phyllis felt too weak to stand. She asked Ed to check in on Idee and Lamont. While Ed was doing that, Phyllis thought about everything the detectives had told her. She thought about her poor son lying outside like trash. At that moment, she wondered what happened for such a day to come into her life. As much as she needed Ed for that moment, she blamed him for what led up to Mayson's short life. She included Pastor Upshaw and GCC in her blame. She also blamed herself for not doing more when Mayson left GCC. She blamed herself for not addressing Mayson's differences when he was much younger. When she initially reported Mayson missing, she was angry at the detectives for asking her questions about Mayson's personal and social life. A part of her knew that they had to ask those questions, but she still resented them, and anybody who knew Mayson but didn't help him.

Throughout the day, Idee cried and stayed glued to Phyllis. She lost her appetite, until Phyllis had to insist that she eat something. Lamont stayed in his room most of the time and watched television. When Phyllis checked in on him, he'd simply state that he was okay, but would not come out of his room. During the times she came to him, she noticed that the television was on an animal program or home construction show. She knew that Lamont didn't have an interest in either program but had the television on for noise. The last time she checked in on him, he was listening to his Walkman. Phyllis knew that he was grieving in his own way, but he needed to stay detached from the family. The only time he came out of his room was when he heard Phyllis scream. When he came out of his room and saw Phyllis crying, he knew that Mayson was dead. He stood at the top of the stairs and stared at his family. He saw his father embracing his mother on the couch and Idee also sitting on the couch lying against Ed's side and crying. Without a word, as he stood there in silence, he walked slowly back to his room and stayed there for the rest of the day.

Relatives and neighbors came by to console the family with food and companionship. Ed's sister took Lamont some food in his room. Phyllis was able to get Idee to eat a bowl of cereal and drink some orange juice. The church came by every day with meals and moments of prayer for the family.

(II)

Lanelle prepared the club for the evening as usual. While singing onstage, she was annoyed that Tamara had not come to the stage to sing backup with Monica. As usual, Tamara was in the back office on the phone checking on her children. Most often she'd make it back to the stage before their next number, but this time she remained in the back all the way through the end of the song. When they finished, all Lanelle could think of was going to the back office to yell at Tamara for missing the last number.

As she put the mike back on the stand, the band continue to play softly. As Lanelle was about to leave the stage, she saw Tamara walking slowly out from the backroom looking dazed.

"Where have you been?" hissed Lanelle. She failed to see that Tamara's eyes were red and puffy.

"He's dead," said Tamara softly.

"Who's dead?" asked Monica, who was now standing next to Lanelle.

"Mayson is dead," said Tamara.

"What are you talking about?" asked Lanelle, trying to make sure she understood Tamara.

"While I was on the phone, I turned on the television. The news was on and they said a man was found in a wooded area. The body was later identified as Mayson Hendricks. They're still investigating who did it and why," said Tamara.

Lanelle was stunned. Monica began to cry. Urban stopped playing the keyboard as he saw Monica crying. Tim and Trenton followed suit. Urban walked over to Lanelle, Tamara, and Monica to find out what happened. He put his hand on Monica's shoulder to comfort her.

"What's up?" asked Urban.

"Mayson is dead," said Lanelle.

When Lanelle repeated Tamara's words, Tamara began to cry.

"Damn!" said Urban.

"What happened?" asked Trenton.

Tamara, still crying, tried to calm herself in order to answer Trenton's question.

"It was a murder. They said he was beaten to death. They don't know who did it or why he was killed," said Tamara.

The patrons in the club were all now looking at them on stage.

"You talkin' about the dude found dead across town? yelled out one of the club's patrons. I heard about it on the news before I got here," he said.

"First, they didn't know who he was, but must have found someone to identify the body later," said another man.

"I heard it was a drug deal thing," said a woman.

"I didn't hear that on the news," said the man.

"It wasn't. I just heard somebody talking about it when I went to get my hair done," she said. "Mayson Hendricks, I thought his name sounded familiar. So he used to work here, huh?" the lady asked.

Tim slightly nodded his head to confirm.

Lanelle walked to the front of the stage.

"We will be closing the club early tonight. We need this time to deal with this. He was a part of our family, she said, her voice trembling.

"We got you! It's cool," called out a man.

CHAPTER 30

Coming Together: The Cycle of Ending and Beginning

Phyllis and Ed arrived together at Mayson's memorial service minus Idee and Lamont. Idee and Lamont didn't want to go to the service. They had a difficult time at his funeral, and she didn't want to make matters worse by having them come to the memorial service and experience the pain again. It was difficult enough for her to muster up enough energy to go herself. She wanted to remember her son in her own positive memories of his life. With the murder still unsolved, it made the memorial service that much more taxing to attend. As they walked into the large auditorium, Phyllis stopped short and Ed bumped into her from behind. He started to ask her what was wrong, but instead, he followed her eyes to the side of the stage. There he saw a large picture of Mayson with an enormous smile on his face. The smile that he would have whenever he was around people that he loved or inspired him. Phyllis kept a photo album of her family but didn't recognize the picture. Wherever the picture had come from, it lit up the entire room. The picture of Mayson was as though it was welcoming her to the service as she entered. For a moment, it made Phyllis forget that Mayson was dead.

After a few minutes of looking at the picture, they made their way into the auditorium. It had been over a year since Mayson's death. For Phyllis, it was still unreal. When she heard about the memorial service, she was not quite ready to relive the moment of his death with others. She was also battling bouts of depression. She assumed that the service was put together as a kind gesture from those who loved her and her family. On the other hand, she also thought that it was insensitive for them to put on the service without asking her in advance. She received word of the service by mail with only 2 weeks knowledge of it. She figured that many of people's so-called kind gestures are more about their needs than those that they are supposed to be doing it for. She didn't want this memorial service, at least not this soon. But she was concern how it would look if they did not attend.

Ed looked around the room at all the people there for Mayson's memorial service. Despite his pending divorce with Phyllis, Ed never left Phyllis' side, hovering over her, almost stepping on the backs of her shoes. He desperately hoped that Phyllis would have a change of heart about their divorce. After Mayson's death, Phyllis blamed so many people for letting Mayson down, including Ed and herself. She went through weeks of "should-haves" and "could-haves." She included just about everyone in her "should-haves," including Pastor Upshaw. She was only able to stop flinging blame at everyone around her because of something Idee said to her. One day when Phyllis was lying in bed after an argument with Ed, Idee came to her room and got into bed with her. She curled up under the covers and she looked at her mother.

"Mama, it's nobody's fault. Mayson did what he wanted to do, and we have to accept that. I'm still going to miss him, though," she said, as she pulled the covers up to her face. Phyllis never thought she would hear such sober words coming from Idee. It was at that moment she realized that Idee was more than just a happy-go-lucky teenager. It took Mayson's death to see her daughter possessed the capability for insight, which she hadn't acknowledged before.

Seeing Phyllis at the memorial service was the first time in months Phyllis and Ed had been together. After a failed attempt at marriage counseling, Ed moved out and only saw her whenever he picked up the Idee and Lamont for visits.

"It's been over a year and I still cannot believe he's gone," said Phyllis to Ed.

"Who do you think put all this together?" asked Ed as he continued to look around the room.

"I don't know," said Phyllis.

Phyllis looked across the room and saw someone waving at her. Nathan Hightower, one of GCC's deacons, came into her view. She observed him say something to his wife Maureen as he walked away from her and came across the room while continuing to wave at Phyllis.

"Oh, here comes Deacon Hightower. I'd imagine that he and Sister Maureen put this memorial service together," said Phyllis.

"Hello, Sister Phyllis," said Deacon Hightower, embracing her.

Phyllis was glad to see Deacon Hightower. He was Pastor Upshaw's most dependable member and always seemed to be in an upbeat mood. Idee often made fun of Deacon Hightower because of his baldness and the slight dip at the top of his head. His suits often seemed a bit small despite his thin frame.

"Brother Hendricks, how are you?" said Deacon Hightower as he shook Ed's hand.

"I'm good," said Ed, with a curious do-I-know-you look. Ed had only been to GCC on a few holidays and other special occasions, so he didn't know most of the members. Deacon Hightower looked familiar to Ed, but not anyone he would recognize outside a congregational gathering.

"Looks like a large group," said Deacon Hightower as he gazed around the room.

"Yes, it sure is," said Phyllis. "I wondered why it was scheduled here at Prestwood Community Center, but with all these people, I can see why."

"Yeah," said Deacon Hightower as he looked around.

"Did you organize this?" asked Phyllis.

"No, I didn't," said Deacon Hightower in a startled look at Phyllis. "I heard about it when Pastor Upshaw announced it at church a few weeks ago," he said.

"I heard about it through mail and I also heard the pastor announce it," said Phyllis.

"So, you don't know either?" asked Deacon Hightower in a surprised voice.

"There was no name on the letter. Do you think Pastor made these arrangements?" asked Phyllis.

"No," said Deacon Hightower immediately. "He just asked me a few days ago if I knew who was over the memorial service. You'd think whoever arranged this gathering would have given the Pastor their name," said Deacon Hightower, puzzled.

"Is that Pastor Upshaw and..." Ed didn't know if to call her First Lady Frances as he'd hear most members call her, or Frances as sometimes Phyllis would slip and call her ..."his wife coming in the door?" asked Ed.

"Yes, it is," said Phyllis.

Deacon Hightower began another animated "over-here" wave to

Pastor Upshaw. Pastor Upshaw waved back at Deacon Hightower to let him know that he saw him. It took a while for Pastor Upshaw and First Lady Frances to reach them, as various members approach Pastor Upshaw in greetings or to engage in conversation.

"When Pastor gets here, I can ask him again if he knows who organized the service," said Deacon Hightower.

Pastor Upshaw and First Lady Frances made their way over to the group. Pastor Upshaw shook Deacon Hightower's hand and First Lady Frances gave him a quick embrace. Pastor Upshaw and First Lady Frances greeted Phyllis with an embrace and a small kiss to Phyllis' cheek.

"Brother Hendricks, it's so nice to see you," said Pastor Upshaw as he shook Ed's hand.

"Thank you, Pastor Upshaw," said Ed.

First Lady Frances greeted Ed with an embrace.

"It's good to see our church leader enter the room," said Deacon Hightower as he looked at Pastor Upshaw with a large smile. "Pastor, this is a wonderful gathering. We're wondering who organized this memorial service?" asked Deacon Hightower.

Pastor Upshaw and First Lady Frances looked startled as they looked at each other and then at Phyllis.

"We thought this was put together by someone you knew," said First Lady Frances.

"No. If you didn't do it, then I don't have a clue as to who put this together," said Phyllis.

"I received a letter about this gathering in the mail. I thought it strange that it didn't have a specific name on it. It had a PO box address and a business name of "Coming Together." I read this in the announcement a few Sundays back. I assumed you knew something about it," said Pastor Upshaw.

Phyllis then looked over the crowd again. Other than the members from GCC church and surrounding churches, and a few people that Mayson had come to know, she did not recognize the other faces.

"I don't know a lot of these people," said Phyllis.

Their group fell silent as they all looked around the room.

262

CHAPTER 31

Coming Together II: Opening A Door

Phyllis saw Lanelle on the left side of the auditorium, sitting shoulder to shoulder with a group of people in the third row. They sat in a corner far away from the other mingling attendees. Lanelle, Urban, Tim, Tamara, Monica, and Trenton were seated already and not interacting with the others. Their isolation was not only due to them not knowing most of the others, but also because of their clothes, which was obviously different from the others' "churchy" or conservative attire. Trenton, now a post college man, was the only one in the group whose clothes match the formal attire of most other males in attendance. He wore a black suit and tie, unlike Tim and Urban, who were dressed in black jeans and silk shirts. Lanelle had on a shiny, low-cut green dress that snug around her hips. Tamara wore a leopard print, ankle length, free flowing dress. Monica, in her effort to be conservative in her appearance, wore a white blouse with ruffles at the front and wrists, a deep lavender color suit jacket, and a matching skirt that accented her curves.

Phyllis had planned to go over and greet Lanelle, but she was engrossed in trying to figure out who organized the memorial service. She looked near the front of the auditorium and saw another group of people to the right of the stage. There were eight of them, isolated from the others like Lanelle's group. This group consisted of Aaron, Craig, Louis, and five others that were in attendance from New Times. The five others had never met Mayson, but came to support Aaron, Craig, and Louis, who were devastated when they heard about Mayson's death. Phyllis had not met any of them, but she surmised that they were not just friends. They seem to have a purpose that extended beyond friendship. They were not only different from others in the auditorium, but there was a difference in appearance about them within their own group. Phyllis saw that some were dressed more flamboyant than the others. From those dressed in such flamboyancy, she assumed that they were Humans. Her assumption did not include those in this group who wore casual jeans, plaid shirts and pullover tops; it was the couple of men with stylish bouffant hair. With the bouffant hair, one man's shirt had a pattern of hearts and another's sported a large pair of lips. They both wore makeup and Phyllis had to admit they looked good. She then thought about Mayson. He didn't dress like that, but he too was Human. Phyllis then thought that maybe the group was from Pastor McDaniel's Church, but some in the group of eight were white and she was not aware that Pastor McDaniel had white members at his church.

Phyllis saw even more unfamiliar faces. Small groups of about five or six people huddled together talking, couples clinging to each other and individuals walking around as though they were looking for someone. Phyllis agonized that she didn't have the time to personally greet everyone for coming to her son's memorial. She thought about her failure to greet Lanelle's group and the Human group and wondered if she had really come to terms in accepting them in association with her son. The thought stayed with her through much of the service.

As Phyllis, Ed, Pastor Upshaw, First Lady Frances, and Deacon Hightower stood in silence looking around the room, a voice came over the speakers from the stage.

"Hello. Welcome, everyone. Will everyone please take their seats so we can get started," the strong, articulate voice said. The attendees slowly scattered to their seats.

The man behind the strong voice wore a stylish blue suit, with a white handkerchief in his upper jacket pocket. He had frameless glasses that made his tanned skin more noticeable. His hair was tidy and snow-white.

"He looks familiar," said Phyllis, squinting slightly without her glasses.

"It's Art Peters from WWQW News, Channel 2," said Deacon Hightower.

"I thought he had retired," said Pastor Upshaw.

"He did. My boss went to his retirement party a couple of years ago," said Ed.

"Let's get a seat and see what's going on," said Phyllis.

Phyllis, Ed and the Upshaws sat together in the center aisle four rows from the front. Deacon Hightower went to the other side of the room and sat with his wife. The other attendees took their seats as the mingling voices soon came to a silence. The auditorium was almost completely filled. A few seats near the stage were empty with a reserved ribbon draped across them. A few minutes after everyone was seated, an elegantly dressed usher in a black suit, white shirt and white bow tie and gloves, graciously approached Phyllis and Ed with a smile and silently gestured them to follow him as he walked them to the front of the auditorium. He removed the reserved ribbons and Phyllis and Ed took their seats. Phyllis smoothed out the skirt on her light-blue linen suit and placed her purse on the floor. She looked over to the side of her row and saw the group she assumed were Human.

"Who are these people?" she continued to wonder.

As Lanelle sat waiting for the service to begin, she felt an elbow nudge her in her side. It was Tamara who was sitting next to her. She looked at Tamara, a bit annoyed at the distraction.

"What?" she asked in a sharp whisper.

"I meant to ask you how you knew about this memorial service. With the churchy crowd I'm seeing here, I wouldn't think we would be invited," whispered Tamara.

"I got a letter in the mail," whispered Lanelle as she tried to compose herself.

"Was it from Mayson's parents?" asked Tamara.

"I don't know, but I guess it was from them or someone they know," said Lanelle, looking straight ahead.

Tamara sensed Lanelle's annoyance at her talking and thought maybe she was nervous. She knew that she herself was nervous about the memorial service. Not because she was unfamiliar with the environment, but because she had been crying about Mayson frequently and uncontrollably. She was not sure she would be able to contain herself during the service. Tamara refocused her attention to the stage. From her peripheral vision, she could see movement further down from her row. She turned her head and saw a familiar face coming through her row to be seated. Alarmed at the sight of the man coming down their row, she felt an urge to renege on her decision to no longer bother Lanelle. As a result, Lanelle felt another nudge to her side. Lanelle frowned in surprise that Tamara continued to bother her. She looked over at Tamara to show her displeasure. This time Tamara did not say a word but tilted her head sideways three times in a

COMING TOGETHER II: OPENING A DOOR

pointing manner. She was directing Lanelle to look down toward the end of their row. Lanelle looked in the direction and saw Byron coming down their row sliding past the attendees to get to a seat. He finally sat in the seat next to Trenton. He and Trenton gave each other a short handshake. Byron could see from the corner of his eye, the heads of Lanelle and Tamara extended outward down the row looking at him. He turned his face toward the stage in an effort to ignore their stares.

"Hello again, everyone. This is our special day for Mayson Hendricks," said Art, as he pointed to the large picture of Mayson.

As Art continued to speak, an odd, small-statured man sat down on one of the two metal folding chairs about five feet behind Art. As Art spoke, the odd man behind him sometimes gave a hint of a smile as though he knew what was to happen next in the program. It was difficult not to look at him because he appeared to be someone who was a vital part in the program; yet it was not clear why.

"Do you know who that man is sitting behind Art?" whispered Pastor Upshaw to his wife.

"No honey, I've never seen him before," she whispered back.

"Odd-looking man. Don't you think?" asked Pastor Upshaw.

First Lady Frances, thinking how unusual it was for her husband to focus on someone's looks, hesitated to respond. However, she was thinking the same as her husband.

The man's skin color made it difficult to distinguish his race. At one angle his complexion looked pale, then brownish or even silver. His shaved head made it impossible to determine his hair color or texture. There was tranquility about him that radiated, which made his presence even more impactful.

Art informed his audience that when he heard about Mayson's tragic death, the thought came to him that it could have been his son. He said that when he was called to facilitate this memorial service, after consideration, he told the audience that he had said, *Count me in*. He added that he wanted to be a part of the movement to eliminate such horrific deaths in communities.

"Before I continue, I'd like to bring the gentleman forward who put this service together," said Art.

Everyone was eager to see who had spearheaded such a worthwhile and thoughtful service for Mayson's memory. Art turned around to address the mysterious man sitting behind him in the folding metal chair. The chair was empty.

"Hmm, where did he go?" asked Art as he spoke loudly with his back now fully turned away from the audience. He looked to the side of the stage and into the audience searching for him.

"Anyone see where the gentlemen went who was sitting behind me on the stage?" Art asked in an amused tone.

Mingled low talking arose from the audience, but no one answered.

"Well, I guess he must have evaporated," said Art whimsically. "He said his name was Jonathan David and he contacted me a few weeks back to moderate this memorial service. Hopefully, he will be back shortly. Now I'd like to introduce, Spencer Willette, who was my cameraman years ago when I used to do street reporting," said Art.

A huge man with long hair and a full beard was standing in the center aisle behind a large, expensive-looking camera perched on a tripod. He moved his head away from the camera and gave the audience a wave.

"I asked him to come and videotape this event so Mayson's family would have something to remember the service by. Also, it might be worthwhile to the community to show footage on our local news, if they choose to broadcast it," said Art as he looked down at Ed and Phyllis, who were seated off stage but directly in front of him.

"Are you the parents?" he asked.

Phyllis gave a nod and quiet smile and Ed gave a quick wave.

"Do I have your permission to videotape this service for your later viewing and perhaps our community audience?" asked Art.

Phyllis nodded again.

"Thank you both. I hope this will bring warm memories, as you see all who came out to honor your son's life," said Art.

Art began to read from a list which had the names of people who were scheduled to speak during the memorial service.

The reality of Mayson's death clutched at Phyllis' heart again hearing the names of those that were to speak. She turned her head and looked at all the people who were there for her son. As those on the list got up one by one and spoke of their fond memories of Mayson, some touching and other humorous, Phyllis' sorrow slowly turned to anticipated interest.

A lady from their previous church, before GCC, who was over the small children's program, shared a story about how Mayson, at four years old, ad-libbed and changed the last part of his Easter speech. Rather than saying that Jesus rose from the grave, Mayson said he rode from the grave in his new car to heaven. When asked why he change the last part of his speech, she said Mayson responded, "I didn't want Jesus to ride out the grave with no place to go."

Pastor Upshaw shared with the audience Mayson's faithfulness to the choir and willingness to pitch in when needed.

Leon attended the memorial service also, accompanied by a large middle-aged lady who was dressed in a loose black dress, flat shoes, and a short brown wig. She appeared stoic but attentive to Leon as she occasionally whispered in his ear and patted him on the shoulder. She was a staff member of the group home where Leon was living. When it was Leon's turn, she gestured for Art to bring the microphone out into the audience for him. Leon told them about the name-calling and his being treated as though he was subhuman when he was a youth. He said that Mayson always made him feel that he had a friend, and his disability was never an issue in their friendship.

After Leon, Reanna, who had her 8-month-old baby girl in her arms, nervously stood up to go to the stage as she placed the baby into the arms of the child's father. Reanna had her baby shortly after Mayson's body was found. Mayson was difficult to find during his troubled days and she was not able to share with him the news of her pregnancy. It was a heavy burden for her to know that her baby would never know Mayson. As she approached the stage she reached for the mike and tried to speak. She felt her emotions welling up. Her throat closed as she tried to refrain from crying.

"I can't stand it when I cry. I am not a cute crier," she said to the audience as her voice broke.

The audience gave a low laugh.

She paused for a few seconds and tried again. In a weak and wavery voice, she spoke about Mayson's caring and gentle nature. She shared the comfort and security their friendship had brought her. Without going into detail, she stated that Mayson had brought balance to her life. As much as she wanted to keep her comments upbeat as with others, she began to cry again. "I miss my friend every day," she said. She left the stage in tears.

After Reanna, Art came back to the podium. He opened the floor for others who were not on the program to come and share about Mayson. No one else came forward. Before he introduced Phyllis and Ed, he spoke for a moment about the meaning of community, building stronger ties and seeing tragedies as opportunities for change. He then introduced Phyllis and Ed as the last of the speakers. Phyllis who had ceased crying until hearing Reanna's speech, was now wiping her eyes. She and Ed approached the stage. Art handed Ed the mike and took his seat. Ed then handed the mike over to Phyllis. She looked around the room through her teary eyes. There were a few seconds of silence.

Phyllis scanned the faces of the audience. Particularly, Lanelle's group, the group that included the assumed Humans with the bouffant hair and others that she did not know. At that moment, in order to really know Mayson, she felt an urgency to know those in the audience that she couldn't identify.

"I don't think the lineup of speakers is complete," she said.

Silence.

"If we..." she paused.

Her eyes then scanned across the room again.

"If we leave here without hearing from everyone in my son's life, then this whole service would have been more about us than him," she said softly.

The room was deafeningly silent. Every eye and ear was glued to the stage.

"Before I go on, I want everyone to remember Reanna. The young lady who was here before I came up. She may not have prestigious titles and high places in the church, but she is more of an example of what to do than what not to do when it comes to loving a friend. She was a friend to my son no matter what he declared himself to be. If you want to know what truly unconditional love is, then look hard and long at Reanna," said Phyllis.

Phyllis gave a wave to Reanna, who was now back in her seat with her baby in her lap.

Phyllis then refocused her thoughts to address what was going on in the moment of the service.

"My tears are more than just those of a mother grieving for the loss of her son. I grieved also because I and many of us in this room let my Mayson and many other Maysons down. Yes, he was a man whose choices eventually cost him his life. For that, he was responsible. But there are things that I, and many others who have Maysons in our lives, could do better without us abandoning or disrespecting our own beliefs and values. To some extent, I believe that we are our brothers' keepers. My son was a pliable person who was easily influenced by his environment. I think we all knew Mayson had a different side, but we wanted to address him in a manner that suited our own needs and purpose. I want to hear about my son as a whole person not just bits and pieces," said Phyllis.

The more Phyllis talked, the more boldness she heard in her choice of words. She felt the tears dry on her face and the weight on her chest ease. She put her tissue on the podium as if to say, I don't need tears anymore. She opened her mouth again as though she was about to say something that she knew would be difficult to say, but she cleared her throat to go on. Her eyes pierced through the audience as she continued to speak:

"This has to be more than a memorial service. I want us to talk about Mayson, and not just what is comfortable for us to hear. I want what we call "his secret" to be a part of who he was as a whole man. This secret has nearly torn our churches and country apart. Since Mayson's death, I have been so preoccupied with him, his secret and our society. We as a church, community, and country are at each other's throat of who is right and who is wrong when it comes to same-sex attraction. I am a Christian, but I am not one to simply throw out-of-context Bible verses at those who are attracted to the same sex and use the tired phrase of "I didn't say it, it's in the Bible." I love God's word, but there is so much more to God than a small group of religious people's interpretations. Yes, I do believe God loves same-sex couples. Not because they are Human, but because He loves all human beings. Whether same-sex or not, we all have to give an account to God for what we do or don't do. Which also mean that I don't believe that heterosexual Christian couples are more loved by God. Both unions are subject to behaviors and choices that must be taken under consideration in determining right or wrong. Its more about the "what" than the "who." There is a middle ground of respect. A truce for the sake of God and all that He loves. Let's start that middle ground right here today. With that being said, please let me hear others honest thoughts

270

and experiences about my son, who…"

Phyllis paused for a second as she searched for the right words. She continued…

"…my son, whose love does not fall in line with social commonality. Social commonality," Phyllis repeated with a small laugh. "This is a phrase that was never a part of my vocabulary until Mayson's death. I've done a lot of research, which has helped me understand my son more. So, let us allow all these different areas of life come together and talk about my son and his life. Forget that this is a memorial service. I even want to hear thoughts, feelings and beliefs that are associated with my son as a…as a…Human. That's the name I sometimes use. Because, in the long run, that's who we all are. Forget tradition and let's give this gathering meaning," said Phyllis.

CHAPTER 32

The Unmasking: Reflection, Bridging and Diversity

Unmasking: Reflections

(I)

A s Phyllis waited for someone to speak more about Mayson, she felt Ed's hand touch her hand as he took the mike from her. Startled, Phyllis took a step back to give him space at the podium. Ed looked down at the floor as he awkwardly held the mike in his shaking hand.

"This is hard for me," said Ed, his voice was low and strained. "Since my son's death I have thought about him more than when he was alive," he said, as he held the microphone in one hand while his free hand was shoved deep into his pants pocket.

"Since my son's death, I had to face who I am as a man with a family. And with this realization, my wife and I have begun to have serious talks. As parents, we never existed. Instead, my children grew up with one parent, my wife. And for that, I am sorry. I'm sorry that I placed that responsibility on her," he said as he pressed his hand even deeper into his pocket.

"This realization of who I am has brought my wife to the point where she wants out of our marriage," he heard himself say.

"I love my wife and I can't imagine my life without her," he said as he turned around to engage in eye contact with Phyllis.

Phyllis still standing behind him, looked directly at Ed with no expression. How dare he use this time to expose our personal marital problems, she fumed internally. Despite her efforts, Ed could see the displeasure in Phyllis' face slowly emerge. He felt his heart race as he found himself between the displeasure of his wife and an audience full of people glaring at him. As he looked at Phyllis' expression, he saw the end of his marriage once again. In frustration, he decided to proceed with expressing his true feelings about the entire matter of his relationship with his family.

"My wife has asked for our honesty about Mayson. I know it would be touching to hear me say that despite my distance from my son, I really did love him. But love does not allow for outright abandonment. None of my children deserved my disregard for their life. So, if you asked me if I loved my son, my answer would be "I don't know." When he died, and I saw how it affected my wife, it reminded me of the woman I fell in love with. My wife's caring nature is what I love about her. I know it sounds terrible to hear a father say he loves his wife, but questions whether he had love for his own son. This is something I continue to try to understand, but it is my truth."

At those words, Ed knew he was finished with his speech and possibly his marriage.

"Thank you," he said, as he stepped away from the podium and stood next to Phyllis. As they walked back to their seats, neither said a word.

Art returned to the podium, picked up the mike, and walked out into the audience looking for more people to share their stories about Mayson.

(II)

The auditorium was full. There was not much room for spreading out one's arms across empty chairs or stretched-out legs that touched the chairs in front of them. Sitting like that was what J.R. was accustomed to, but he couldn't manage it now as the chairs were so close together. Cliff and J.R. sat four rows from the back of the room. J.R. didn't like attending funerals, or anything relating to death for that matter. But Cliff, uncharacteristically, had stood his ground and demanded that J.R. attend Mayson's memorial service. J.R. was not usually a pushover, but he had respect for his father.

As they sat side by side at the memorial service, Cliff wondered what J.R. was thinking. He could tell when his son had something preying on his mind. J.R. had a way of rubbing his chin when he was preoccupied in thought. It was obvious when he was in such deep thought because when someone would call his name, he would blink his eyes heavily as though he was coming out of a trance. Unlike his sister Idee, whom Phyllis described as one who speaks without a filter, J.R. did not blurt out whatever was on his mind. But when he decided to speak, it would sometimes be as though he had no filter. J.R. was thinking about the last time he saw Mayson in the parking lot at the Encounter Club, and Mayson's brush-off at his attempt to hold a conversation. With such an attempt at trying to be brotherly with Mayson that day, J.R. had long summed up the matter as, "Well, I tried."

As much as they both were enthralled by Phyllis' bravery in changing the tone in the memorial service and Ed's heartfelt honesty, neither Cliff nor J.R. were inspired enough to motion Art for the mike or go on stage.

While out on the floor with the mike, Art continued to look for speakers. "Anybody else…floor mike or stage?" he offered.

(III)

Lanelle beckoned for Art to come to her with the mike.

"Hello, my name is Lanelle Campbell. I was Mayson's boss," she said without adding what kind of work they did.

"I could tell Mayson was in search of his place in life. He never shared the details of himself with me, but I knew. I knew who he really was, and I came to care about him. I tried what I could to help him because there is so much evil out in the world that would take advantage of someone like him."

Lanelle tried to avoid looking in Byron's direction because her words were not intended to call him out. Still, she could not figure out any other way to express her story without a hint of Byron being in it.

"Before I could take a second wind, I got the news that Mayson had left us. I've always asked myself, could I have done more? Ultimately it was Mayson's decision to help himself, but sometimes we need help in helping ourselves. So, in looking back, if I could have done something more, I would have tried to reach out to him sooner rather than later."

(IV)

Pastor Upshaw motioned Art to let him know he was going to speak from the stage.

"I need to add one more thing," said Pastor Upshaw. "Mayson came to our church as a young boy. He was always a polite and well-mannered young man. He sang in our choir and was willing to do almost anything that I asked. Sister Phyllis would often speak about her children to me, especially Mayson. He was her support and someone that Sister Phyllis depended on in helping to manage the household and being there for his younger siblings."

Upon hearing this, Ed began to squirm in his seat. He knew that what Pastor Upshaw was describing as Mayson's family support was actually Mayson stepping in for a missing father.

"When I heard of Mayson's death, my heart was broken." Pastor Upshaw paused as he searched for words to transition into his purpose for wanting to speak again.

"I saw Mayson driving one day. He pulled up beside me at a stoplight. I don't think he was aware of me in my car next to him. He looked different. Not only had his appearance changed, but I became concerned because he looked sickly. He looked as though he was carrying the world on his shoulders. A young man who was deep in water that he couldn't swim his way out of. The last time I talked with Mayson in depth was the day he came to my office with concerns that affected his life and his standing in the church. He shared with me things that I will not go into details about, but I knew from that day forward his life would be different. My choice and decision for Mayson was not the most shining time in my life as a pastor, but I did what I thought was right for him and, in the long run, for my church."

"Don't apologize, Pastor!" called a man from the crowd.

Pastor Upshaw usually responded with amusement or enthusiasm at such vocal support from his congregants during his sermon message, but he was in no mood for that at the moment. He ignored the man and continued.

"As a church, we have doctrines and beliefs that we must abide by and do not ask that everyone agree with them, but in a country that allows religious freedom, we do ask for respect and our right to exercise our beliefs. Instead, other groups expect and get their rights for acceptance or tolerance for who they are and what they believe, but this does not include the church. It's a double standard that has been in place for years.

I didn't leave Mayson without a place to go but asked for the help of another colleague for assistance. As a man, Mayson made his choice. It hurts that his choice may have eventually cost him his life; but looking around this room, regardless of his choice, people are here. It shows that he was loved and cared for. No matter what."

(V)

Sitting in the back of the middle aisle of the auditorium was Veronica Lambert-Shaw. She had gone back to her maiden name after her divorce from Melvin. Melvin hadn't remarried, but she heard that he was involved with a beautiful girl from a different church. Veronica's self-worth had plummeted after her divorce from Melvin. Shortly after divorcing and moving back home, she married a man who was not her ideal choice, but he was not Mayson or Melvin, which became her new standard.

When she moved back home, her heart was still with Mayson and trying to recover from her divorce from Melvin. She knew that neither relationship would ever be, and that neither was hers to have in the first place. She also asked herself what she was thinking to believe that a man as attractive as Melvin would want her. As she ground down her self-worth more, she wondered why Mayson would use her in the manner that he did.

She and Deandra no longer had a friendship, but it was Deandra who called her to tell her about Mayson's death. Deandra had gone to Mayson's funeral but didn't attend the memorial service.

At the memorial service, Veronica saw many people from the churches that she recognized. Yet there were a few faces she didn't know. It had been a while since she had left BHU. A side of her felt nostalgic at seeing some of the familiar faces, and other faces reminded her of a very sad time in her life.

She reflected that her revenge on Mayson didn't go the way she planned. She never really knew if her purpose to hurt Mayson ever played out. Based on that time she saw him at the university, he seemed like someone who was not really heartbroken over his loss but making the best of his time whenever he saw Melvin. Melvin being married didn't seem to have crushed Mayson the way she wanted it to. She continued to see Mayson as her first love, but her resentment of what he did would often overshadow her romantic thoughts of him. She was not able to make Mayson's funeral because of her job, but she felt compelled to be at his memorial service, no matter what.

(VI)

Aaron and Pastor McDaniel found themselves walking toward the stage to speak at the same time. They both stopped and motioned for the other to go ahead. Aaron gave a thank-you wave to Pastor McDaniel as he continued to the stage.

"Hello. I am Aaron Locke. I am the founder of an organization called *New Times*. Thank you, Mrs. Hendricks, for allowing this open and honest space. I will just get to my point," he said.

"It's not right. It's not right that people cannot be who they are without being rejected and made to feel less than," said Aaron as he looked over the audience.

"When are we going to allow people to come out and be loved no matter their sexual orientation? When are we going to stop withdrawing our love from Humans when they don't meet our standards? This is why so many of our Human youth are committing suicide at alarming rates. When will you learn that people are born this way?

If I had to see your God through your behavior, I would not want your God. We as Human activists will continue our fight of acceptance, or at least tolerance.

And you, African Americans, how can you of all people not support the rights of Humans? Think about what you went through and the support needed to change things around in this country for your rights. You of all people are now fighting against Humans and their right for equal treatment. We have African Americans within our group who are supportive of Human rights, but many of them have to choose between their church or what is right for Humans. It should not be that way. Our group, New Times, take people in without any prejudice of their color or religion. Why can't the church grant this kind of acceptance when it comes to being Human?

I know this is a time about Mayson and the celebration of his life, so let me honor him in that manner.

I only knew Mayson for a short time, but when I heard of his death, I was heart-broken, but sadly not surprised. When I met Mayson, I could tell he was struggling to come to terms with who he was. I tried talking to him, but he was not ready to accept who he was and the reality of how others saw him. I didn't want to push him, so I let him know he could come to me anytime. Unfortunately, he was never able to take me up on my offer."

Aaron looked over at Phyllis and Ed.

"He seemed like a fine man and I wish that I could have helped him. I'm so sorry this was Mayson's end," he said.

Unmasking: Bridging

(I)

On the stage, standing behind Aaron was Pastor McDaniel, waiting to speak.

"For those who do not know me, I am Pastor Toby McDaniel of United House of Worship Church. Mayson was not a member of my church, but he did come to me for counsel. My church has its doors open for all people and this includes those who are Human. Our church shows that when it comes to the word Christianity, it expresses itself in many ways, but the common union is our Heavenly Father.

Mayson was introduced to me because he was told of our acceptance of Humans. I had some quality time to sit and talk with him, and what I could see in him was what Sister Lanelle saw. He was indeed on a journey for his place in the world. I also saw a young man confused, full of condemnation and even some anger. As a pastor, I have had many to come to me as Mayson did. Some who come to me on their journey, after hearing about my church of acceptance, find my invitation to join our church a relief; others leave my office with a continued search. Mayson left with a continued search. Unfortunately, it led him to a short life. I grieve over Mayson and other people that have left my church in continued search and tragic outcomes.

I am grateful to Sister Phyllis for being so open and allowing us to recognize the complete side of this life for our beloved Mayson. People, this is a wonderful opportunity to address Mayson's whole life. I tried to share with Mayson the acceptance of our church of Humans, while at the same time trying to respect other churches that have moral issues with Humans' participation in their church. Just as Jesus himself didn't treat everyone the same, it must be understood that not all Christian churches are the same in how they address Humans. Some pastors use the talents of gay members to benefit their ministry, while closing their eyes to the realization that these in-denial or undercover Humans, are the "Adam and Steve" that they make fun of or ridicule in their Sunday sermon messages. While we were busy condemning and laughing at them, there were changes and shakings going on in this country. We, as a church, woke up one day to find that we were no longer the empowered, self-righteous, cross wearing, suit and tie do-gooders of this country. Those Humans that were oppressed, condemned, made fun of and most importantly were not allow space for in our services or pulpit (other than repenting for what we saw as the ultimate sin) had emerged to become a strong community that we are now in submission to. Those rejected souls that were coming to us for fellowship and a place of spiritual belonging, found their own space to fit in and belong. A powerful place that protects them through our laws. The influential platform that the church had in the past has now become a shared space (almost dominated by) Humans who have found their acceptable place. The tides have turned in that now the Church has concerns about being discriminated against and not allowed their religious freedom. Church, where are your Adam and Steve jokes now!

We've all heard about the scandals of those ministers who speak so vigorously against being Human, only to later see these same ministers caught up in some type of Human sexual encounter. Each time I hear about a Human sexual scandal involving one of the church leaders who preach against being Human, it only makes the need for the church to address this in a more Christ-like manner more evident. Condemning, joking, removing, false sympathy, and even despising Humans has not been working for the church in the past, so why is it still being tried?

People, listen to me. In regard to gays and lesbians, who someone loves isn't the enemy. It's how we respond to it that causes the problem! It's a spiritual matter that can't be resolved through earthly means. It can't be resolved through anger, spite, manipulation, deceit, control, pride, self-power, self-willed effort, or the use of the media.

A segment of the Christian church does not believe that one has to change themselves before coming to Christ. They believe that through Christ, the needed change will occur. For these churches, this seemed true for most people, except for Humans. Humans have special sins that need to be dealt with before they can be considered church members. These churches would state:

Oh, we must maintain our reputation. We cannot have them being Humans and telling others they are members of our church.

Or if they are already members of the church, they lose their membership and are not allowed to participate in church ministries.

When the church went from emphasizing God's wrath and began to acknowledge his grace and truth through the gospel of Jesus Christ, and defining it as His unmerited favor, I thought, great! We are now about to come together as a whole. No more judging when it comes to Humans and the church. The wall between *us* and *them* is now coming down. Grace teaches the love of Jesus Christ through his death on the cross. His sacrifice on the cross has taken care of our inadequacies and pointed it toward Christ's adequateness. This sermon message that emphasized grace and what Christ did for us and not just what we can do for Him, put such a peace in the hearts of many.

I thought the time of unity for everyone had come for all. But no. Humans have been judged by some in the church to be excluded from his grace- unless they follow their religious interpreted rules first.

Humans, God does not love you *anyway*. He loves you, period! Don't let others' opinions and biblical interpretation exclude you from receiving God's love and grace for you."

(II)

Without a word from Art, Mark walked over to Art with his hands outstretched for the microphone.

"My name is Mark. I'm a member of a Human activist group called *New Times*. I've been with *New Times* for more than 5 years."

Mark took a deep breath as he looked over at Aaron.

"I know that many people assume that Humans' primary interest in life is sex. It's not all about sex. It's more about relationships for many of us. Like heterosexuals, we have layers in our lives and relationships. In addition, we have a need for God, to be loved by others, cared for, respected, responsibility, good citizenship and other things for a happy fulfilled life. People tend to see us as flamboyant, sex-crazed, immoral, ungodly, perverted, and other things that have been prejudged of us over the years. Just as some of those labels may be associated with heterosexuals, it does not apply to all of them. It's just to say that we are individuals when it comes to Humans. I have to admit that some Humans flaunt these stereotypes in Christian's faces and that doesn't help the cause. I've always had problems with anyone who flaunts affection for the purpose of spite."

Mark scanned the audience. A few of his friends were squirming in their seats, while others nodded their heads in agreement. Aaron looked stoically at Mark with a steady gaze.

"If Pastor McDaniel can share the unpleasant side of his religious groups and their short comings, I can do the same. Sooooo..." he stretched the word as a means of transition.

"Some Humans punish those who don't agree or accept us, by use of extreme sexual behaviors directly in their presence or by use of the media. And some Christians have disrespected who we are, we, in turn, have degraded and disrespected their religion by using Jesus' name with profanity or comical disregard. Two wrongs don't make a right.

Why is it that we as Humans find it necessary to get the personal acceptance of others who oppose us? We often state that we don't care about what anyone thinks of us. However, we become outraged when people have a view of same-sex relationships that does not align itself with the way we think. Apparently, we must care about what others think of us or else we would not be fighting with such vindictiveness. I understand the legal side of what we do, but we have to come up with a more inclusive approach to get it.

We have spent much of our time fighting for our rights to be who we are without discrimination. I'm tired of fighting. Fighting does not allow for time to look around for any possibility of coming together for a more peaceful resolution. Fighting makes us more angry, spiteful and vindictive. When was the last time an olive branch of peace was presented between the Human activists and the church that condemns being Human? I hope it happens in my lifetime.

I say again, as for the fussing and fighting for who's right and who's wrong between the church and the Humans, fighting is not doing any of us good."

(III)

In the audience, Pauline waved her hand for Art to bring the microphone over to her.

"Hello, my name is Pauline. I am a Christian and lesbian. I am not a member of any church, but I am a believer.

I just want to add something that may just be my need to vent. A lot of in-fighting goes on in the Human community. I lost my job at a bookstore as a result of another Human who forced my resignation. At that time, I had not come out as a Human, as the job itself did not require me to be. A co-worker of mine, who is lesbian also, shared with me a relationship that she had with another Human whom she had fond memories of. Her conversation then evolved into her belief of how Humans are born to be the way they are. I shared my belief that I felt that some Humans are the result of nurture as well because of the influences and experiences of those close around them while growing up. However, I emphasized that it really should not matter whether being Human is from nurture or nature, no one has the right to judge, discriminate, condemn, or try and separate them from God. She went and told my belief to our boss, who is also lesbian. As a result, my boss made my time on the job difficult. Whenever I'd enter the room with them, my coworker and my boss would began to display open signs of affection in my presence. This had never happened before, and I knew that they were both involved with other people. For days they only spoke to me if they had too. I started getting fewer and fewer hours. After a few weeks of this, I gave my resignation. My boss never asked me why I was resigning. I really liked my job so, I have to admit; I was hurt and then later angry.

The bottom line, even among Humans we discriminate and disrespect those that do not *fully* think or believe the way we do."

(IV)

As Pauline was talking, Hosea rushed from his seat to stand behind her in order to speak next. As she turned to hand the mike back to Art, Hosea tapped her on the shoulder to take the mike. Pauline, with a slightly nervous laugh, handed him the mike and took her seat.

"Hi, I am Hosea and I am a gay man. I want to add to Pauline's experience." First of all, Pauline, I want to say that I feel bad that happened to you. It shouldn't have."

He turned to address the audience.

"I applaud and thank God for those of us who advocate for the equality and nondiscrimination of gays and lesbians. I love being an advocate for what is right. However, as with Pastor McDaniel's boldness about some of his religious groups' short comings, I too would like to share the flaws within some of our gay advocacy approach too.

"The word *homophobia* is a word that Humans use to describe those who don't accept Humans. I know that it means one who does not accept gays or lesbians, but it also describes one as being fearful of them. Or afraid of becoming gay or a lesbian themselves. Granted, this may be the case for some who denounce same-sex couples, but it can't be that everyone who denounces it is gay or lesbian themselves or fearful of becoming a gay or lesbian. Come on now! We use the broad brush of homophobia for all as deemed enemies in order to hurt, spite and get ahead in our fight. What's even more hypocritical and unfair is that we were able to get the mental health professionals to remove homosexuality as a mental illness from their manual, but no sooner than they did, we reached back and grabbed the word homophobic and began to lash it at those that don't accept us. Once we got that word out of the DSM manual, we turned the tables and labeled anyone who had issues with gays or lesbians as homophobic, which, as with the word homosexual at one time, can signify as a word for being mentally ill. What a double standard!"

Unmasking: Diversity

(I)

Latice motioned for Art to bring the microphone over to her.

"Hi, I'm Latice Thomas. I am a member of Pastor McDaniel's church, United House of Worship. It's the only church in the city that opens its door to everyone, including Christians who are Human. When it comes to life's basic morals, we are like most others. Just as some heterosexuals are chaste and discreet in their sexuality, so are many of us Humans. Our sexuality is not the basis of who we are; it's only a part. We believe in monogamy in our relationships. If we have problems within our relationships, our primary source of help is God and his word. We may also go to our pastor or his staff for counsel. I share this to express that we should get to know people before putting them in a category. God has many people and the Bible is too wide-ranging to be reduced to only one group's interpretation. Those who really want to know God and his word will not use biblical interpretation to harm or exclude others. As I heard it said, God saves individuals, not groups."

(II)

Tony had positioned himself on the stage, waiting for Latice to finish.

While at the podium, Tony rubbed the side of his beard as he prepared to speak. Phyllis waited hopefully to hear what Tony had to say about Mayson. She felt that his presence on the stage represented the crux of her move to open up the service to show the complete spectrum of Mayson's life. However, she could feel Ed's uneasiness as he sat next to her. She glanced at him as he sat lower in his seat, teeth clenched and jawbones moving back and forth at the sight of Tony.

"My name is Tony Rayburn. I have heard some wonderful things here today. What is happening here is new to me. I've never been in such a place where I have shared anything personal about myself with a room full of strangers. Mayson and I were partners in love. I hope that does not offend any of you because I know that we have audiences here with different views about being Human.

Let me tell you what drew me to this wonderful person. I saw something different in Mayson. One of the first things I liked about him was that he seldom used vulgar or harsh words to express his frustration. Also, unlike me, with the exception of holiday dinners, Mayson always prayed over his food before he ate, but he often did it without purposely calling attention to himself. I have to admit, initially I was a little embarrassed when he first did this in public. Once while he was saying grace over his food, a waiter noticed him. When Mayson got up to go to the restroom, the waiter came to me and asked was my friend okay. I responded, *Yeah, he's fine. He often drops his head and takes a quick nap before he eats."*

A quiet laugh rippled across the audience. Phyllis laughed and sat up in her seat, eager to hear more.

"His time of prayer became a special part of who he was and what he brought into my life. I began to join in his before-meal prayer. I now do this every day before my meals. No matter where I am. That was Mayson. Influence without words. He had a way of bringing you into things without being loud, demanding or showboating. I've never been to the church he left, but he'd spoke of it with such fond memories."

"GCC, Mayson missed you," said Tony as he looked over the audience without eyeing Pastor Upshaw specifically.

"Mayson had a mission in life to succeed. He focused on this mission as though he was trying to prove something to others, rather than himself. He, like many of us, didn't always make the right choices. He had his moments and his days when he was not the most pleasant guy to be around, but I loved him.

Despite the distance later in our relationship, he continued to have this focus or mission in life to prove himself relevant to himself, or others. I was not always sure which it was. His focus eventually closed me out on a lot of things that were going on in his life. I loved Mayson and tried to protect him, but in some ways, I was like him in my focus to prove something. I had a job that kept me away from him for hours and hours on end. When I would come home and try to be a couple, he was slowly moving into other things. Mayson was a man who was indeed responsible for his own choices, and I don't believe he would allow anyone to feel responsible for his outcome. I personally think his choice to come to live with me was one of his better life choices. We were happy for a while, but you can't expect the challenges of change to come sometimes without consequences."

Tony looked over at Phyllis before taking his seat. Without any acknowledgment to Ed he said, "Mrs. Hendricks, even with such a sad finish to his life, you raised a wonderful man and thank you for bringing him to all of us."

(III)

Melony made her way to the stage rather than use the floor mike from Art. She was a middle-aged woman in a pink long sleeve custom-fitted blouse and pleated black skirt. She came to the stage soon after Tony. Her hair was in an updo with little stray hairs sticking out from her hairband. She had a few acne spots on her face that she had covered with powdered foundation but they were still visible.

"Hello, I am Melony Fulton." She pressed two of her fingers downward around her mouth as she prepared to speak.

"I have been a Christian for 34 years. My pastor and other church members are here today, but who the pastor is and what church it is, is not important because this message is for all that are of the Christian faith."

She then briefly gazed in the air as she took a breath.

"I'm going to change the direction here. I have concerns for the Christian Church. Our beliefs, morals, and values as a church are slowly dwindling away. With every cycle of resistance and disapproval from those that come against us, we bend and change. We don't want to look bad or have people think poorly of us, so we wave our olive branch to every anti-Christian bully or critic. We must take a stand and allow ourselves to remain true to who we are, and most importantly, to God."

"Say that! Say that!" yelled out a lady in the audience.

"You got that right!" shouted a man.

"I hear those talking about the poor treatment, the jokes and exclusion, that the church has inflicted on homosexuals. That may be true for some churches. But, even if we didn't embrace gays as the world thinks we should, does that give homosexuals the right to now make fun of us, disrespect out religion and try and make us fit into their way of thinking and living? Other than a few words of protection of the Christian church I've heard today, I'm pretty sure that I am not the only other person in this building with these thoughts and words. But I am the only one who had the holy boldness to come up here and speak it.

I'll conclude with this: Christian church! Get off the fence and take a stand—no matter what!"

She hurried off the stage. As she was leaving, sporadic applause was heard around the auditorium.

(IV)

Standing behind Melony was a Faith on A Mission member, Rondale Coleman. He looked straight ahead to the back wall of the auditorium to avoid any eye contact with the audience.

"These past years I've been going through some changes myself. I am a deacon at a church," he said without naming Faith on a Mission Church. "My name is Rondale Coleman," he said swiftly. "Some of what I have to say is a repeat of what Pastor McDaniel said," he declared. "During the years at my church, we have had wonderful preaching from our pastor, evangelists, television ministries, and books. We've witnessed revelations of better insight from traditional beliefs and ways of living. With each decade, inspiring sermon messages were bringing in all sorts of life-changing revelations or expounding on areas of the Bible that held much more insight than what we knew. Yet they were dancing around any positive insight on being Humans. You'd think with all the scandals in the church about ministers who are exposed as Human, something would be done about what is going on in the church as it relates to same-sex relationships. Instead, they'd simply agree with what has always been said and move on to some other breakthrough.

One day it dawned on me, Jesus never said anything specifically about homosexuality. He talked about sexual infidelity and other sexual immorality, but he never went back to the Old Testament and started talking about Sodom and Gomorrah or told Adam and Steve jokes. He never talked about gays or lesbians and then after making derogatory or angry remarks about them, tried to clean it up with false sincerity of how he loves them and will keep praying for them. Jesus never did these things, but today's church does. I knew that in this area of Christian teaching, something was wrong. We have been fighting against Humans for years and years and have only built a wall of disconnect. We have removed Humans from leadership positions in our churches, humiliated them when we knew that they were in our services, and used their talents as long as they kept silent about their sexuality. But when it comes to heterosexual men in the church committing adultery, fornication, sexually harassing church members and physically or emotionally abusing their wives, we give them passes for their sins and put them back in their leadership church roles as soon as possible.

Over the years we have been told how to think, act and feel about people who are Human. Because we want to fit in and not be seen as spiritually weak or as a backslider, we go with the flow. I know that some of us are simply afraid of being excluded from the Christian others, so we keep our mouths shut.

Coming to God should be more about who comes in and not so much pride about who should be put out. Other than my wife, I have never disclosed all this to anyone," he added as though he was stalling for time and making sure if he wanted to continue. "I was concerned about sharing these thoughts with her because I was afraid that it would affect our marriage. When I shared these thoughts with my wife, she didn't take it well at first, but she eventually came into agreement. She later told me that she had the same thoughts as I did but was afraid of what would happen to her if she ever voiced them."

He looked at his wife, who was sitting next to his empty chair in the audience. He began to speak to her directly.

"Honey, I know you were not expecting this, but I need you to help me with this."

He beckoned his wife to come forward. She shook her head no. He asked her again. She refused again.

Art came to her with the microphone. She gave him a look. As he was about to remove the microphone, she quickly grabbed it.

"My husband is not completely wrong, but I am not ready to voice myself in public on this matter," she said.

"You don't have to agree with him. I still say it's a sin!" yelled a woman from the audience. There was mumbling and snickering throughout the room.

Rondale could feel the heat of embarrassment. He was in a moment of trying to figure out how to transition from her refusal.

"Well, I did throw this on her on the spur of the moment. I guess she's not ready," said Rondale with his head down and a half-smile on his face. "I shared this with my pastor. At first, I had thought my timing in sharing this with my pastor was not at its best, but it was. It was around the time that I had heard that Brother Mayson had been put out of his church."

Pastor Upshaw flinched when he heard the words, "put out of his church."

Phyllis winced at the words, while still finding it funny.

Pastor Upshaw leaned over to his wife. "Wouldn't you know it. They have a way of spinning things around. I never put him out and they know it," he whispered.

"Now, I see that the timing could not have been better. It was an excellent time for us to show our support for Brother Mayson and others like him. Thank you for your time," said Rondale as he went back to his seat. He did not look at his wife as they both sat like statues facing forward.

(V)

Kimberly was in the audience standing next to Art waiting for her turn to speak. As Rondale Coleman left the stage, Art handed the mike to Kimberly.

Kimberly had struggled about whether she should get up and speak. She was a member of a church that did not allow Humans in leadership positions or other active roles. She had never told anyone from her church that she was Human herself, but she wanted to share her experiences. Like Rondale, she decided to share her beliefs about God and Humans, but not specify her church. She knew her pastor was at the service and she felt that what she had to say would be something he needed to know. She and her life partner had discussed in the past that they should at least tell their pastor about their relationship, but neither had had the boldness to follow through. But Kimberly felt that no better time would be more suitable than this moment.

"Hello everyone, my name is Kimberly Bolden-McFadden. I am a member of a Christian church. My hope is that I will be able to add something good to what is happening here today. My life partner and I are both in college. We were from different churches, but she has recently joined the church that I am now attending. We decided to cement our relationship just as heterosexual Christian couples do, so we had a commitment ceremony. We love each other dearly and we do not try and convince anyone to do what we did or accept us as a couple. The one thing I should have did a long time ago was tell my pastor about my union with my life partner. He does not endorse same-sex intimate relationships, so I was wrong to stay at his church in my leadership role and not tell him. So today, I am letting him and others know about me and my life partner. This is what I needed to share in this moment," she said as she handed the microphone back to Art.

"Anyone else?" asked Art as he looked around the auditorium.

A hand went up from the back of the building. It was the back area of the room that was roped off because of repairs needed for a row of seats. Yet, there sat someone in one of the chairs at the end of the row. Because of the dimly, flickering fluorescent lighting above this person's head, it was difficult to determine if the person was male or female. The person also wore a cotton cap that covered all of their head. This person was oddly dressed in a light blue pull-over top, a black tie, and a red jogging suit with white stripes down the arms and legs. Because the pants didn't quite touch the work boot shoes on their feet, a pair of pink socks were exposed. While this person's hand was raised, a gold bracelet slid down their wrist. Come on over, waved Art to the person, but the person didn't move. Art found this person's behavior strange. He was curious also as to why this person would sit in an area of the auditorium that was restricted for repairs. He started to take the microphone over to the odd person, but suddenly stopped. He was not quite sure if he wanted to approach this person. So he didn't.

CHAPTER 33

Dawnings

I knew a man in Christ above fourteen years ago, (whether in the body, I cannot tell; or whether out of the body, I cannot tell: God knoweth;) such an one caught up to the third heaven. 2 Corinthians 12:2

(I)

Dawning: The Ventures of Unfamiliar Surroundings

An old armless wooden chair sat in a dimly lit room. The chair was perched against a scuffed white wall. Beneath the chair was a beige carpet matted from years of foot traffic. Mayson's eyes quickly opened to this scene, relieved to be out of his surreal dream. Or was it a vision, he wondered. His dream-vision had left goose bumps on his arms, but the unfamiliarity of his surroundings temporarily distracted him. He felt the softness of the light-blue bedsheet beneath his chin and its lavender scent from the dryer sheet. He pushed the sheet off his chest and saw that he did not have a shirt on. Fear gripped him as he threw the remaining sheet off his body. He saw that his white cotton briefs were still on. He gave a short breath of relief. He sat up and lowered his legs to the floor of the single bed. He touched the long, narrow wooden headboard attached to the bed in an effort to make sure that it was real. He rubbed the mint-green blanket on the bed for further assurance of his existence. It was the same color as a blanket he had seen at one of the GCC church mothers' houses. The elderly woman had had a stroke, so Phyllis and a few other members from the church took turns caring for her. Phyllis would go to her home every week to help her with chores. On one of Phyllis' days, the church mother sat in her armchair in her living room looking out her window. She asked Phyllis to bring her blanket from the foot of her bed. Phyllis went to the bedroom and brought the blanket back to her. The senior mother told Phyllis that the blanket always reminded her of a time when she was unemployed, homeless, and sleeping in a storage shed in the back of a hotel. One cold night she could not get warm enough to sleep. She heard a knock on the shed's door. She looked out the small window and saw a man. He was standing in front of her door with a woolen blanket draped over his arm. He was a middle-aged white man in a white shirt and tie and a name tag with the hotel's logo. She opened the door and rather than telling her to leave, he gave her the blanket, saying only, *it's cold out here.* She said that either the blanket was just what she needed to keep warm enough for sleep; or the fact that someone cared enough about her to give her a blanket, brought with it the warmth that helped her to fall asleep. She said the blanket gave her a peace that God had good people surrounding us during some of our most difficult days.

Mayson had not thought much about that time with the church mother and her story. But when he saw the woolen blanket on the bed, it was the first thing that popped into his head. He reached for the blanket, pulled it back onto the bed and held on to it.

Further examination of the room showed an old dresser, repainted light blue. There were a few scrapes and scratches on it, but it had sort of a regal look as it sat firmly on the old carpeted floor. The tarnished dresser knobs were in place on three of the five drawers. A colorful, new-looking poster of people in a club playing musical instruments hung above the dresser. The small size and worn furnishings of the room might seem depressing, but it was obvious that the owner of the room had included a few things—the mismatched sheets, the print, the dresser—that held special meaning for them. They made the room cozy rather than depressing. Mayson twisted himself around in the bed to look behind him. A window over the bed was framed with, long flower-patterned curtains. Mayson could see a streak of sunlight coming through the curtains. He moved them aside. The outside view was an alley filled with overflowing garbage cans and a large apartment building that would appear to be uninhabited if not for the clothing hung over the back railing to dry. There were a couple of dogs eating from the garbage cans that had spilled or been knocked over.

As Mayson looked down at the dogs, it became obvious to him that he must be in an apartment building, as he could see the ledge of a window beneath him. Based on his viewing of the building across the alley, the building he was in appeared to be at least two stories high. Neither the buildings nor the alley gave Mayson a clue as to where he was. He twisted his body back around in the bed to see a new-like light brown door. The door looked to be just as new as the poster. Because there were two doors in the room, he was not sure if the light brown door was to a bathroom, closet or an exit out of the room. He thought to get up and look, but a part of him was afraid to see what was behind either door. He was worried that the situation might not be what he wanted it to be, so he sat and stared at the doors. He looked around the room again and this time, despite the moment of fear, a peace began to fill the room, draping over his shoulders like a blanket. He looked back at the uncertainty of the doors and relaxed. I'll check it out later, he thought, as he was feeling a little weak. He was not sure why he became so peaceful about the doors, but he went with the overwhelming change to let the fear go.

He looked around the room for his clothes and didn't see them. He sighed heavily. His mind went back to what seemed like a movie playing in his head just before he woke. It was far from a dream, he thought. It was crystal clear with people and conversations. Some of it was like a dream and some of it was like a vision, he mused. It was difficult to determine if he was actually seeing and hearing all this while he was awake or asleep.

"If it was only a dream, then it was the clearest dream I ever had in my life," he muttered to himself. Maybe it was a little bit of both. He patted his stomach for more assurance that he was actually in his physical body. He wondered more about the dream-vision in an effort to see if there was some meaning in it. Unlike any other awakening, it had stayed with him.

(II)

Dawning: The Dream-Vision

He recalled seeing people running, lots of forest, water, drowning children, and a room full of people. What was all that about? he wondered. As he pondered over the dream-visions a frightening thought came to him. I saw a lot of people in a building and they sometimes seemed sad, as though they had lost something or someone.

I was there, yet not there, he thought. I felt like I was invisible, because I didn't interact with anyone and no one interacted directly with me. I must have been out of my body and I could see everyone from different angles of the room. Mayson's eyes widen with this reality. This thought superseded all the other occurrences in the dream-vision as he mesmerized himself in the thought of his death. He felt his heart race from the possibility of his death. What if this was a premonition that I will die soon, he thought. I'm being punished by God, he despaired. I am gay, I do drugs, I do things for drugs and I have used people. From there, Mayson's curiosity of where he was, became secondary to his dream-vision experience that seemed to signify his punishment of death. He slid off the bed. He pulled his legs up to his chest and rested his head on top of his knees. He stared straight ahead as he voided his mind of thought. His eyes were fixed on a dull, chipped segment of the room's wall. His eyes slowly closed as he began to pray.

"God, forgive me for my sins. I did things that I thought were right and some that I knew were wrong, but I did them anyway. Help me to get my life back on track and spare me from an early death...."

Mayson stopped his prayer as another flash of the dream-vision came to his mind. He thought about the people he saw close to the end. He remembered hearing loud noises of different ranges in the dream-vision that seemed to be contention but later changed to a unified hum. Noise of conflict to a unified hum, he repeated in his mind. That means that something changed, and it was for good, he thought. Like the church mother being given that blanket that night. Something changed for her good and she took it with her throughout her life. The loud noise in the dream-vision was almost deafening, but the hum was like an angelic choir.

"The hum showed something good happened," he mumbled.

I don't know exactly what, but it felt good close to the end of the dream-vision, he thought. Maybe it's not about me dying. And, there were too many people doing things in the dream for it to be only about me, he encouraged himself to believe.

He braced one arm onto the bed for leverage and stood up. His eyes were intense in thought as the dream-vision opened itself up to him more. He focused on the beautiful harmonized hum at the end of the dream-vision. It was much better than GCC's choir at their best, he thought. So that blended hum sound coming together may be more of an answer. If there was death in it, it may be that death could have been symbolic for the end of some sort of conflict in me or me and others. Maybe the death part was the end of something and the beginning of something else, thought Mayson. He recalled an evangelist who had come to GCC about four years ago who taught a sermon message on, *Death, My New Beginning*. In that sermon, the evangelist stated that what we often see as an end can sometimes be the prelude to a new and better beginning in our lives. It was a message that Mayson never forgot because he had grown up to believe that death was always what it was, the end. What a feeling of enlightenment and relief of this other interpretation, thought Mayson. *"A symbolic death,"* he muttered.

"Enlightenment!" yelled out Mayson as he felt he was actually interpreting a dream or vision. He smiled. "I sound like some spiritual guru," he said to himself.

What a spiritually deep sounding word coming from someone who does not know where he is, thought Mayson.

He felt a peace come over him again. He looked at the mint-green blanket on the bed and rubbed it against his cheek. There has to be some good in the world, he thought. His effort to interpret this dream-vision in a more spiritual light, led him to recall those times when he would give an inspiring word at GCC. Or when he'd belt out a powerful congregational song. It was often during one of those Sundays that people would come to him after service and tell him that he should be a preacher, or that God was calling him into "the ministry." Most meant well, he thought. Many people at GCC often told Mayson they could see him as a preacher, but Mayson never really saw himself as "deep" enough to preach or insightful enough to lead others. Despite the days when he would feel condemnation about his sexual identity, he considered going to Pastor Upshaw and declaring his calling as a preacher. Maybe God was calling him to preach in an effort to help him eventually move away from his attraction towards men, was one of his rationales. There were days when he talked about his potential preacher calling over with Phyllis. Rather than being happy that her son wanted to be a minister, however, she asked Mayson to wait until he was sure that it was what God wanted him to do, rather than what others wanted from him. Despite not getting the reaction he expected from his mother, Mayson took her counsel well and was actually pleased that his mother was not one of the nudgers. Mayson believed that the nudging from some of the church members for him to preach may have had more to do with his faithful church attendance, his inspiring testimonies, being a choir member and his leading songs in Praise and Testimony service. When he left GCC, he had wondered what all those nudgers had to say now.

Mayson paced the floor in the mysterious little room. He felt excited about all the positive possibilities of the dream-vision. He perceived that death could mean the end of the conflict between him and his struggle with his sexuality. With such a wonderful alternative to the dream-vision, it became difficult for him to imagine God putting him to death for being Human.

Taking a broader view, he wondered if the dream-vision meant that those that were running and struggling in the dream-vision represented him and others who were gay. And the other people represented those who were not gay. It would make sense as he felt he couldn't make the matter only about him. At that moment he didn't want to be a preacher. Instead, the dream-vision gave him the hope of normalcy within the church without a "camouflage" title of minister, reverend or even pastor. No longer did he want the title of Minister Hendricks or someone's heterosexual love interest in order to be who people wanted him to be. He loved GCC but felt himself wanting to acknowledge God more. He raised his hand in reverence to God as he continued to pace the floor.

As he praised and rejoiced, a dark doubt lodged itself into his mind that stopped him in his moment of inspiration.

Who in the world do I think I am? How dare I? I'm a drug addict, who just woke up in a room I don't recognize, half-dressed and probably did who knows what with someone last night. And now I put God in my blasphemous imagination that I've been given a revelation that could change the world?

These words hit Mayson to his core. He plopped into the chair next to the bed as he mused more about the matter. I need to get myself together before I try to act as if I have received a word from God through a dream-vision, he thought as his feelings of inspiration turned to despair. But how do I do that? "Get myself together?" I know that there are things that are outright wrong in my life, but is it mostly being Human that needs to change in my, "getting myself together"? I think it's more about what I did as a result of being Human, he decided. Before people actually knew I was Human, I went to church every week, I was good to my mother and family. I believed in and worshipped God. I got along with most people. I was not the church troublemaker. I was a good person. But in actuality, I was a good person who was Human. That's what people were seeing, but most didn't know it or wanted to admit to it. The problems came when I tried to cover up my Human side while hurting others. I deceived others, estranged myself from church and family, which pushed me out into a part of life that I was not ready for. My sin may not have been about me being Human. Rather, when "a need-to-know moment" (he remembered this phrase from Pastor McDaniel) came in my life, my active deception of being Human became the beginning of where I am now.

He thought about Pastor McDaniel. He seemed like a spiritually devoted man. And he believes you can be Human and a Christian, he thought. He thought longer about Pastor McDaniel's counsel with him. He remembered the pastor's testimony and braveness in leaving his mainstream church. He remembered some of the Bible verses that Pastor McDaniel asked him to read about God and man. He yet admired Pastor McDaniel's openness and honesty. He didn't resort to deception, like I did, he thought. I'll accept that, like Pastor McDaniel, I too am a Christian believer who happens to be Human, thought Mayson. My past sins were not that I was Human, but what I did as a result of it.

Get myself together, he thought again.

"It's the drugs and the…" he paused…"the prostitution," he said quietly. Yeah, I prostituted myself for drugs, he admitted to himself. "Illegal drugs and prostitution, that's a part of the *get myself together* thing," he said softly.

"Getting myself together. Can't hurt myself or others because of who I truly am. Can't do that," he said.

At one time he had come to justify his actions to believe that Veronica may have deserved to have been used. He thought she was pushy, just like Reanna had said. If she had left him alone once he showed her he had no interest in her, then she wouldn't have been there to be used, he had justified. After he yelled at her over Melvin, he knew that he was not in a position to apologize to her, because it would lead to more discussion as to why he would get that upset over Melvin. His confession to Pastor McDaniel's of his use of Veronica was not all that sincere. He knew that while he was confessing what he did to her was not said with conviction, but he didn't think that Pastor McDaniel would go for his "she deserved what she got" conclusion. Besides, that's not why he was there to see him, he had thought.

However, at that moment, while sitting in that unfamiliar room, he knew that he was wrong and didn't want to use the same excuse. With this thought in mind, he mused, Yeah, I need to get myself together.

"The drugs and prostitution got to go," he said softly.

Mayson sat quietly and continued to reflect. He reflected as though his thoughts were being narrated by someone putting his life together like a puzzle. He smiled as he thought about Tony. Tony was always good to me. He was my soft blanket. I wish I'd kept a monogamous, unselfish relationship with him. I don't think our failed relationship was really about his work hours. I just used that as an excuse to pull away from him. He was a reality that represented who I really was. There were days when that reality represented the loss of my family and church.

"Wasn't fair to him though," he muttered.

Rather than trying to make new friends after I left GCC, I hid in Tony's apartment and got too close to Byron and all his shady dealings. I had friends at the club, but they had ties to Byron. If I had ventured out to make other friends, I probably could have filled my time with different types of people while Tony worked.

"Byron Crawford," said Mayson out loud.

"Everything was good and then it wasn't. That's what you get with Byron Crawford. No real job, night clubs, pills, then heavy drugs and selling drugs. Drugs," he repeated. "Drugs and then he later looked the other way as I got into prostitution for the drugs. He had me mingled in all his underhand dealings, thought Mayson with a tinge of anger."

When people from the church talk about "homosexuals," this is what they'd think of. People who are into constant, promiscuous, wild sex. No moral compass. Just doing anything with anybody, as long as they are same sex, thought Mayson in frustration. I know I must look like a Human stereotype. I give Humans a bad name, he thought as he gave a chuckle. He looked down at himself, with only his underwear on and in someone's bedroom he didn't know. I'm not representing anyone in a positive light. Not as a Human, a black person, a man, nor the church. I give everybody a bad name.

Mayson began to feel more frustrated and impatient with himself.

"I'm too good for this!" he said with fire.

He knew he shouldn't have allowed himself to move away from good people. People like Tony, his mother, and even Reanna, he mused as he smiled almost as much at the thought of her as he did when he thought about Tony. Maybe even Lanelle? he wondered.

He felt a resolve about his ponderings of what "getting himself together" would mean. Maybe the answer would be in his dream-vision. He got up from the chair and back into the bed. He leaned his head back onto the headboard as he stretched his legs out from him and placed his hands behind his head.

Something in this vision, dream... whatever it was, I feel driven to find out its purpose. It was just too real to be ignored, he thought.

As he sat on the bed, he saw something across the room that got his attention. Beneath the dresser was a pencil on the floor. Its yellow brightness made it look out of place under the shadow of the dresser. It was sharpened and ready to use as though someone started to use it but dropped it on the floor.

I need to write this dream-vision down before it all becomes a blur, Mayson thought. He got up from the bed and picked up the pencil. He looked around the room for something to write on. He looked at the dresser and opened the top drawer. Electrical tape, thread, scissors, pliers, screwdriver, outlet adapter, and other odds and ends. He closed the drawer and opened another that had a few socks in it. This drawer, however, was lined at the bottom with brown paper-bag covering. He pushed the socks aside in the drawer and pulled the brown bag lining up from the drawer. He wrote about the forest and other experiences in the dream. His mind focused sharply on the part where he found himself in the building with a crowd of people. He stopped for a moment as he was about to write more concerning his mother. He felt a brief moment of emotion that came as he thought about his mother and the time that had passed without him contacting her. He knew she must have been worried about him. His writing about the dream-vision also caused him to think about Pastor Upshaw, who, despite their less-than-ideal parting, still struck him as a man of intelligence and a small amount of spiritual insight. Like Pastor Upshaw, he felt he was developing spiritual maturity in getting insight on matters. In that room, he found himself seeking answers in ways that he had not experienced in his life. He noticed how he had been asking himself questions in order to come up with answers about himself. He wondered about the possibility of this dream-vision taking him into an actual ministry. It might not be preaching, but surely there were ways that didn't involve a pulpit, he hoped.

The size and quiet of the room made the perfect atmosphere for Mayson to write steadily. Mayson liked writing, but never considered himself to have any talent at it. But in putting this dream-vision on paper he felt he recorded it better than he thought. When he ran out of space on both sides of the paper bag, he pulled open the third dresser drawer in search of more paper. When he opened the drawer, he saw an electric heating pad. This drawer also had a brown paper-bag lining at the bottom. He took the brown paper from under the heating pad and closed the drawer.

He had been writing for over an hour. The way all this is pouring out of me, I may need even more paper, he thought. Before he continued his writing, he checked the fourth drawer, which was stuffed with mismatched bedsheets. He saw a brown paper-bag lining sticking out from the side, but he didn't feel like taking out all the bedsheets in order to retrieve it. He checked the last drawer, and could see a small, broken fan and three neatly folded cotton headscarves. This drawer also had a brown paper-bag lining. He took the items out of the drawer and retrieved the bag to continue writing. Finally, he got the dream-vision all out on paper.

Mayson took the three brown papers with him back to the bed to read over. He sat on the edge of the bed reading the notes as though it was the first time he had seen them:

I saw myself running through a dense forest. I was not alone in the forest; there were other people running with me. We were pushing our way through plants, grass, small trees, bushes, and shrubs. We didn't have shoes, so our feet were muddied from the moist dirt. As we were running, we started hitting up against each other in our effort to have enough room to run. I couldn't see the people I was running with, but I sensed they were there. I felt such terror coming from all of us. At some point, I felt myself getting tired, so I pulled away and ran in a different direction to find a place to rest. I continued to run and soon saw a clearing ahead. It was a beautiful clearing with shade trees, a small water stream, and rich soil. I also saw the sun that was shining brighter than I had ever seen it for a while. The forest was initially devoid of sunlight, but it shone brightly in this area. I saw pretty green leaves that were in a pile that looked comfortable enough to rest in. I saw something that looked like a drink next to the pile of leaves. It looked like one of the drinks that Lanelle would make for some of her non-alcohol customers. Kind of a pink tropical drink, minus the umbrella. I started to run towards the clearing, but as I got closer, I became afraid. I had been in the forest for so long that I didn't trust what might be in the clearing. I turned back and continued to run away from the clearing. I saw a large body of water and heard the voices of children as though they were under the water. I could not see the children, yet felt they were struggling in the water and calling out for help. I ran toward the water to help them, but the closer I got to them, the farther away the water became. The sound of the children's voice began to disappear, and the body of water turned into a large white building. As with the children in the water, the closer I tried to get to the building the more distant it became. I was not able to enter the building, but I was able to see inside. Then at some point, I was actually in the building. I could see people inside. At different times I could see them from different viewpoints. Sometimes I could only see the back of their heads.

I saw a large box in front of everyone. It looked like a huge casket. It was the largest casket I had ever seen. I felt pulled towards it. I was so drawn to this box that I felt I should be in it. Every time I tried to open it, the top of it kept closing. I don't know why I wanted to get in it, because the thought of it scared me.

Even though I was trying to get into the box in front of everyone, I felt that no one was looking at me; they were focused on the box.

There were lots of people inside the building, but they were divided into groups. Some groups had on some kind of uniforms that were the same color, and other groups had on the same colors but were dressed differently. I could sense who they were, but not actually see their faces. I guess another way to put it might be, I could feel them. I could feel them without touching any of them. I sensed that my family, people from the church, other people I knew and some I was not sure about, were there. For a brief time, I was able to see my mother clearly. She looked the same as she did when I was a little boy. She was so beautiful but looked so sad. In her eyes I could see the body of water from outside the building in her eyes. The water in her eyes swayed back and forth as they did when I heard the children calling for help. The water flowed from her eyes down her cheeks and then I was no longer able to see her clearly.

I stood in the back of the room and I could hear their conversations. I don't know exactly what they were saying, but their words gave off a feeling. During some of the conversation I felt scared and unsafe. Then there were conversations where even though I didn't know exactly what they were saying, I felt a peace about me like in the calm clearing earlier.

All of a sudden, everybody became angry with each other. I don't

*know what or who they were talking about, but the room was
filled with anger. Then I heard a loud sound. It sounded like
thunder. Then eventually there was calm. A beautiful unified
hum came out from all the groups. It was peaceful and soothing.
After the humming, I saw that the colors, which were once all
the same, change to a variety of colors. The colors together were
so breathtaking that I no longer could tell who had on uniforms
or other types of clothing. It didn't seem to matter. It was all so
colorful, yet, somehow, one solid existence. I could see all this from
the ceiling view.*

*All of a sudden, I was no longer at a ceiling view. I was now
back in the building in the rear of the room. I then saw everyone
resumed their original groups, complete with color and uniforms.
This time, I saw a group of people who I was not familiar with
standing before me. They were in the room before, but not right
before me as they were now. I could not feel them or sense them in
knowing who they were. But this group had some kind of weak-
looking fence or border around them. They seem to be waiting or
looking for something. I felt a connection to all the groups, but
I couldn't commit myself as to which I wanted to go for help in
understanding what I was seeing.*

*I heard the loud thunderous noise again and later that same calm
humming. When I turned to look in the direction of the humming, I
found myself here in this strange room.*

After reading everything he wrote, Mayson took a deep breath. The
reading of it exhausted him. He repositioned himself on the bed to think
again about any meaning or purpose from the notes. How to make sense
of this, he wondered. He recalled the copy of the Sunday School paper that
Pastor McDaniel had given him. The paper addressed "The foundation
of *who, what, when* and *where,*" when applying Bible Scriptures. When
leaving Pastor McDaniel's office that day, he had put the paper in his Bible
believing that he would study it and put it to the test one day. He had
taken his Bible with him, which had the paper in it, when he moved out
of his mother's home. He never did pick that paper back up for use, but he

could remember the questions to ask and roughly how Pastor McDaniel defined each of the questions.

Mayson decided to try this formula in determining meaning for the dream-vision. He turned over the last sheet of the 3 papers and saw that he had about a quarter of the bag left on which to write out his *who, what, when* and *where* about the vision.

Who
  Me, a Christian and a Human who lost his way
  My mother
  Other people I knew and could feel
  People who I didn't know
What:
Death (represented by the casket he saw)
  Differences / Sameness
  Meeting / Gathering
Where: Unknown
When: Unknown

Mayson pondered the content on the pages for several minutes as he tried to use his *who, what, where* and *when*. This does not work for me. Maybe it's more for Scripture understanding, he thought.

He knew that this dream-vision was more than just about him. Through most of the dream-vision, very little was said, but much was seen, heard and felt. The dream-vision gave him a constant sense of what was occurring, but not why it was occurring. Mayson summed up his sense of feeling:

The positive of the dream-vision was unity and harmony and the negative was fear and uncertainty. From the peaceful humming, something seemed to work together in the end, he wrote on the brown paper-bag page.

While in the dream-vision, when he was in the building with the crowd of people, it was then that he became aware that he was in some place that was not actually in existence at the moment. He sensed that something spiritual or Godly inspired was going on in what he was seeing. Among all that he was feeling in the dream-vision, he had a fearful anticipation that something about his being Human was going to come into the dream-vision and reprimand him. He recalled his fear that all the things that he had been told about him, or people like him, would specifically come up at some point in the dream-vision. But it didn't. He didn't see or hear anything outwardly or with clarity personally condemning him in the dream-vision.

He stood again and paced the floor. He thought more and more about the possible power within the dream-vision. He mumbled to himself about some of the *Who's* and *What's* from the dream vision:

"If some of the *Who's* represented the church, then nowhere in the dream-vision did it seem they were directed or told to abandon their faith to please others.

If some of the *Who's* were Humans, none of them were asked to change their love relationship in order to be accepted by God.

If my mother's tears were about the *What's* of death, I only sensed the sadness of loss, not right or wrong.

If the *What's* of differences was about separation, then one of the most beautiful sites of *What* is when the differences blended together in beauty.

All the other *Who's* were mingled around some kind of a border. The border looked temporary as its edges looked fragile. I had a feeling that these *Who's* were waiting for a place to belong and a voice to tell them when and where."

If this dream-vision was for me as a Human to personally or others like me, to "get ourselves together," then why didn't it directly address these areas of my life that have been my burden and condemnation? Without any direct, clear word from God in this dream-vision, one thing I know already is that I must get myself together from the drugs and prostitution, he said within himself.

All this process takes back to my original conclusion. It's not about an end, but a beginning. He thought. Mayson put the papers on the bed and moved to sit in the chair.

"I don't know. Maybe I'm overthinking all this," he sighed.

Drugs and prostitution. *I need to get myself together,* thought Mayson again. But apparently, that's not something I can do on my own. He recalled hearing a preacher on television talking about living in God's grace, and the stress of trying to "clean ourselves up first" for his acceptance. Mayson recalled that his initial thought was that this guy was making it sound too easy to get right with God. He then thought of a *What* question to ask himself. His question would put to test the man's sermon message of living in God's grace versus the struggles of, "clean-up first" salvation.

His *What* question was:

"Have my efforts to do it on my own got me where I want to be in life? No, they haven't!" he said vehemently.

He then asked himself another question.

Where do I want to be in life? Definitely not where I am now, he thought.

As Mayson explored this thought, he was startled by a soft knock on the door. Not for sure where he was or why he was there, he was hesitant to answer the door. After a few seconds, he heard the knock again. It was coming from the new-looking brown door. Mayson had wondered if it was a bathroom or closet, but it couldn't be if someone was knocking on it, he reasoned. After a silence, the door slowly opened, and a head popped in through the door.

(III)

Dawning: An Unlikely Source

"Hey man, you up?"

Mayson looked up intently from the chair to see who this familiar voice was. He was shocked to see it was J.R.

"J.R.!" yelled Mayson. "What are you doing here? Where am I?" He asked. He didn't think this was J.R.'s home because J.R. lived with Cliff.

J.R. opened the door further and walked in. He walked toward the dresser and rested his back against the dresser and perched his elbows onto the top of it.

"Well, it's not pretty man," said J.R. with an amused look on his face.

From J.R.'s look of amusement, Mayson was not sure if he wanted to hear this story coming from his superior brother. If Mayson had not found himself in such a curious and vulnerable state, he may have chosen not to hear J.R.'s story of what happened to him and just leave. But here he was, in a place that he was not familiar with, partially clothed, weak from whatever just happened to him, and not certain where he would go if he walked away from J.R.

J.R. could see the uncertain look in Mayson's eyes, as though he was not too sure if he wanted to hear the story.

"You want to hear it?" asked J.R., still looking amused.

"Go ahead," Mayson mumbled, as he felt he didn't have much of a choice.

"Okay, about 11:45 last night I was driving on my way to drop off my girlfriend Alana home. At 9th and Vermont, I saw a man staggering across the street."

Mayson felt his blood rush to his head from the words," staggering across the street." He knew this man must have been him. The thought that anyone would see him like that was humiliating enough but coming from his own pompous brother was difficult for Mayson to hear. However, the humiliation overrode his curiosity as to why he was there in the strange room.

"Alana pointed to the man and said she hoped no one would hit him. Mayson, even though I had been to your funeral and knew…."

Mayson stopped J.R. in the middle of his sentence.

"What does that mean, you went to my funeral?" asked Mayson as more confusion entered his mind.

"Yes Mayson, we all thought you were dead," replied J.R. with a touch of impatience in his tone. "I'll get back to that."

Mayson still had a startled look on his face and wanted to hear more about their thinking him to be dead and the funeral.

"J.R. you can't just say everyone thought I was dead, had a funeral, and then go on like it's nothing. What about it?" yelled Mayson.

J.R. was surprised to hear Mayson be assertive with him. He's changed, thought J.R.

"Man, I give you my word, I will get back to that part," said J.R.

"All right, all right," said Mayson as he folded his arms across his body like a little kid who had not gotten his way.

"Okay?" asked J.R. sensing Mayson's agitation.

"Go ahead," said Mayson

J.R. continued.

"As dark as it was out on that street, and as different as you looked, I knew it was you. I knew I had been to your funeral, but still I just knew it was you. Man, I was scared as hell. Alana was freaking out trying to convince me that it was not possible. She wanted me to keep going. That's how scary you looked. But I just couldn't keep going. I had to know if it was just my imagination. I pulled over to the side of the road. Once I saw it was you, I guided you out of the street. I knew you were high man. Alana kept screaming that this can't be true. I couldn't tell her she was wrong, but I did remind myself that your funeral was closed-casket. But I couldn't explain to myself how it could be you when your body was IDed. At that point it just didn't seem important. Alana eventually calmed down and kept telling me to take you home to Mama. I couldn't let Mama see you like that, especially with her thinking you were dead. It would be a shock to her system. I couldn't take you home with me to my father because you know that as soon as he saw you, he would tell Mama. I wasn't sure what to do, so I put you in the backseat of my car until I could figure out where to take you. You passed out. Alana and I rode around for a few minutes trying to figure out what to do. Lanelle from the club came to my mind. I drove you over to the club and asked her could she let you sleep this off and I'd come and get you in the morning. After she almost passed out herself from seeing you, she agreed to let me take you to her apartment. I told her I would be back in the morning to get you. So this is where you are, and this is why I'm here."

J.R. tilted his head with the amused look back on his face.

"Any more questions?" he asked.

"I'm at Lanelle's apartment?" asked Mayson.

Mayson had never been to Lanelle's apartment. Whenever he, Lanelle, and Tamara spent time together away from the club, they'd eventually end up at Tamara's house with her children. But neither Mayson nor Lanelle would ever open their homes for such gatherings. For Mayson, being in Lanelle's apartment was like being in a mysterious cave. He knew it existed, but never knew how to get there.

"Yep," said J.R.

Silence.

"Alright, now tell me about the, *everybody thought I was dead*, thing," said Mayson.

"Okay," said J.R. quickly. But as he was about to tell Mayson about his assumed death, the thought came to J.R. that a lot had happened since then: Idee and Lamont's struggle in dealing with his death; their mother's bouts with depression; the separation of his parents and the aftermath of his memorial service that was held only a few months ago. The attendee leaders at the memorial service had agreed to have monthly meetings to include civic groups, activist, church leaders, and others in the community for mending the rift between the church and Humans. They had vowed they would be a model city for how these two communities could coexist in mutual respect and peace. After only two meetings, however, they abruptly stopped, but no one would explain why. Everyone went back to their various corners in the community.

J.R. didn't want to share all this with Mayson until he found out what Mayson had been doing since his disappearance. He thought it was only fair before he shared more. He owes me an explanation before I tell him anything else, J.R. thought.

"Before I get to that, you need to tell me where you've been all these months. It's been over a year since what we thought was your death. We just had a memorial service for you a few months ago. The family is still trying to deal with this, man," said J.R.

Mayson started to tell J.R. that he gave his word that he would tell him about his assumed death. He wanted to be firm with him in sticking with the plan. However, he gathered that it made sense that he give an explanation because he was the one who left, not the family.

"Fair enough," said Mayson. "Here it goes. You sure you are ready for this?"

"I'm an adult. I can take it," said J.R. firmly.

"Okay. From finding me last night you can see I have some issues with drugs," said Mayson.

"You think?" said J.R. sarcastically.

"Ok, J.R., you asked me to tell you, but you're making a judgment before I can answer your question," said Mayson with frustration in his voice.

"Sorry, man. Go ahead," said J.R.

"Okay. From one drug to another, things started going fast. I soon found myself high every day. I couldn't afford to get the drugs based on my pay from the club, so..." Mayson paused. He decided to leave out the transaction of himself as a commodity from Byron to a pimp named Montrell. "Let's say that I had to go into a different line of business in order to get the drugs," Mayson said.

Mayson saw J.R.'s eyes shift to the floor. He could tell his euphemism had registered with J.R., and he appeared uncomfortable with the thought.

"The people I had to deal with in this business required a lot of my time and demanded things from me that had me going from one place to another. One of my...."

Mayson tried to think of a title other than *john* for J.R.'s macho ears.

"One of my *clients* supplied me with a drug that I had never used before. He put me in his car and the next day I found myself in his house and in a different state. I knew I was out of state because he had the television on, and the local news and the weather forecast was for Greenrow, Kentucky."

Mayson was careful not to give the client's name because the man had threatened him that if he ever told anyone about their interaction, he would kill him.

"I was in and out of consciousness for days. When I was finally able to realize what was going on, I had no money and no way to get back home.

Whatever he was giving me was potent. Just to let me know how much I needed him, one day he refused to give me the drug. I thought I was going to die. To make sure he kept control over me, he would not tell me the name of the drug. From that day, I stayed under his control.

Those days living with this guy went from weeks to months. My life there consisted of staying at his house while he was at work. I listened to a lot of music and watched a lot of television. I slept a lot. He kept the house dim and the blinds shut all day and night. Getting fresh air consisted of opening the small bathroom window on those days I was feeling closed in. The bathroom window faced a tool shed in the backyard, so no one could see me. I was not allowed to sit in front or back of the house because he didn't want the neighbors to see me. Sometimes he would let me walk to a grocery store to get him cigarettes or beer. On those days I had to leave out the back door and make sure no one saw me. He was my only source for the mystery drug, so he knew I wouldn't be going anywhere other than to the store and back. I longed for the times he asked me to go to the store for him. It was the few times that I actually had the sun on me.

One day he sent me to the store for cigarettes. When I was leaving the store, a man approached me. He was a dealer. He was selling weed. I needed something stronger than weed. Even if I wanted the weed, I didn't have the money to pay for it. And the guy I was staying with made sure he gave me only the exact amount to pay for the cigarettes, so taking the cigarettes back to get the money for the weed wouldn't work because I still wouldn't have enough to pay him. Besides, the weed wouldn't get me the high I needed. So, I went home and continued my dependence on this man.

One day we got into a loud argument. I can't remember what it was about, but I knew I had to leave. I also knew that I had to find out what the drug was and find another source for it. Even though he kept me shut in, I was able to get information about stronger drugs from that weed dealer I had met at the store. He gave me a location to go to for the dealer I told him that I was looking for a specific type of drug that I didn't have a name for, so I asked him if he thought this guy could find out the name of the drug if I gave him a description of it. He said he didn't know, but I'd have to talk with him to see.

I found a city map in the kitchen drawer. I saw that the area was near downtown. I decided to follow the map, go there, and see if I could get the drugs from the dealer myself. Other than the small amounts of money to go to the store, the guy never gave me money, so I couldn't catch a bus to get downtown. Even if I had bus fare, I had no way to pay for the drugs So, I decided that once I met with the dealer, I would barter with him for the drugs," said Mayson, mumbling the word *barter*.

Again, J.R.'s eye gaze dropped to the floor. He knew what Mayson meant by "barter."

Mayson continued.

"When the guy I was staying with went to work the next day, I left soon after he did. I still didn't have bus fare, so I ended up walking 7 miles Once I reached the right part of town, I hung out there for a while until the dealer approached me. I told him I was looking for a specific kind of drug and described what it looked like and the effects of it. He acted like he knew what I was talking about and could get it for me within twenty-four hours. He said I had to pay him for giving me the name of the drug and the drug itself. Of course, he wanted cash. I had no cash and bartering was a joke to him. So, I had to walk all the way back to that creep's house without anything. When I got back home that day, he was there, and furious that I had left the house. He put his hands around my neck, pushed me up against the wall and threatened to kill me right at that moment. He told me that if I ever left again, to never come back. I was terrified at the thought of being out on the street without the drugs. So I never tried to leave him again. Before I knew it, several more months had passed.

The only reason I'm back in Benton is that the guy and his wife decided to get back together. I'm pretty sure she didn't know about me, so he had to get me out of the house before she moved back in. He gave me a few days' supply of the stuff and put me on a train back home. I used the drug before and after I got off the train. That's all I remember. Getting off the train and using. Then you found me in the street."

"Wow," said J.R. He was speechless as he looked at Mayson. This used to be a church geek, thought J.R. He wished he had not heard all the details. He was grateful that Mayson did not tell him the specifics of what he and his captor actually did in that house. However, he was curious about Mayson's addiction to the drug. He knew that at some point Mayson was going to see their mother again and he wanted Mayson to be as close to normal as possible.

Before Alana, J.R. had had a girlfriend whose brother was an addict. He remembered her brother telling him that his every waking thought was how to get more drugs. He wondered was Mayson feeling this way right now. He didn't want to invest too much time in Mayson if his only thought was to get back out and start using again.

"How do you feel right now?" asked J.R.

"It's something that you should ask me that," said Mayson, surprised that J.R. seemed to care.

"I feel a little groggy, but as for drug-craving or withdrawal, I'm not feeling it right now. Which is bizarre, because every day I had looked to this guy like a dog panting for a bone. Even if I had the craving, it wouldn't matter because I don't know what happened to the rest of the supply. I remember having it in my suitcase," said Mayson.

"We didn't find a suitcase with you," said J.R.

"It figures," shrugged Mayson.

"You said you don't know what the drug is?" asked J.R.

"No, but I was going to take it to this guy I know and ask him to find out what it was," said Mayson.

The guy Mayson was referring to was Byron. He knew that his pimp Montrell was still fuming over his disappearance, so Byron was the lesser of two evils to ask for help.

J.R. decided to avoid any further details of the matter. Rather, he decided to keep up his part of the agreement and tell Mayson why they thought he was dead.

"Alright, let's talk about you being dead," said J.R. "Okay, so, while Daddy and I were watching the game on television one evening, Mama came by the house just out of the blue. She looked lost and kinda sick. She had just come from Tony's condo looking for you."

Mayson felt electricity rush through his body at the thought of his mother being at Tony's condo. He was also taken back as to how casually J.R. spoke Tony's name, as though he were part of the family.

"She was crying. She said she hadn't heard from you in a long time and no one knew where you were," J.R. said.

J.R. looked at Mayson, hoping to see some remorse when he told him that their mother was in tears looking for him. Mayson was devastated about their mother's heartbreaking search, but he didn't want to yield to J.R.'s expectation of guilt, so he looked directly back into J.R.'s eyes without a hint of expression.

"Daddy took her to the police station, and she filed a missing person's report. The next few weeks were a nightmare. We passed out flyers and waited to hear from the police. There were constant calls from people saying they saw you at different places. But these sightings couldn't be verified. Then the police found a body about nine miles away from Mama's house, near Willard's Pond, where we used to live. Remember Mr. Watts, who owned the Fish Shack in that area?"

Yeah, said Mayson.

"He was the one who found the body. He was out walking his dog. When I saw Mr. Watts a few days later, he told me that he found the body and told the police that it looked like Mayson Hendricks to him. With the face bashed in and animals had picked away at the remains, I couldn't figure how he could have come to that conclusion. He said the police thanked him but told him that it most likely had to be identified other ways. Near the body was a backpack. In it was a picture ID with your name on it and some clothes. The detectives came by the house to tell Mama a body was found in a wooded area near Willard's Pond. They told her that it had a picture ID near it with your name. Idee said Mama started screaming and Ed had to hold her up. I have to admit, man, old Ed was there 100%. He told the detective that he would ID the body. He confirmed that it was you even though the body was in even worse shape by then."

Mayson was quiet. He believed he knew who the body was. John Morris, whom he had met at the Encounter Club. People at the club often said he and Mayson looked a lot alike. Urban would call him "Mayson 2." It was when Mayson met John, he realized that it must have been John that Craig saw, when Craig thought he saw him at Skylark Supermarket. John told Mayson that at least three times, strangers had approached him and talked to him as though they knew him. Mayson joked to John that if he had known about him when he was twenty, he wouldn't have needed to use a fake ID to get into the clubs. He could have used John's. John asked him to show him the fake ID. Mayson told him that he no longer used it because he was now twenty-one years old, with a real driver's license to prove it. He still kept the fake ID in his wallet, intending to throw it away but never got around to it. He pulled it out of his wallet and handed it to John to look at. Around that time, Lanelle had called Mayson to come and help her with something. Mayson was busy all evening and never retrieved his fake ID from John. After that night, he never saw John again. He figured John must have been using his fake ID.

Mayson decided he would not tell J.R. any of this because it would be one more thing for J.R. to look down on him for. But he knew at some point he would have to correct this matter with the police, so John's family would know what had happened to him.

"Isn't it like Ed not to know his own son," said J.R.

Mayson was feeling proud of his father's efforts with helping his mother, and agitated that J.R was now making light of him.

"You said the body had been beaten and animals had gotten to it, so it made sense that he could misidentify the body. And, he was under a lot of stress too," said Mayson.

"I get that, but he could have at least followed it up with a dental check for certainty," said J.R.

"I guess," said Mayson.

"Do you know how this guy got your ID?" asked J.R.

Mayson shrugged, hoping J.R. would not inquire further.

"Bizarre, man, bizarre," said J.R. as he shook his head.

"The body was supposed to be autopsied, but we got it back so quickly for burial that Ed questioned if it was actually done," said J.R.

"Because your...the face"...he corrected himself, "was bashed in and some body parts were missing because of animals, Mama said she couldn't bear to see you that way. So, she had a closed-casket funeral. To this day, we never found out who committed the murder, or why. It's still considered an unsolved case. Now I know why, because the body wasn't correctly IDed," said J.R.

Mayson felt overwhelmed and guilty from hearing the story about the guy who was mistakenly identified as him. He also was surprised to hear how supportive his father was with his mother during this time. However, of everything J.R. told Mayson, he was most upset to hear what his mother went through thinking he was dead.

"Mama only had family attend the funeral. The following year we had a memorial service and it was open to everybody. It was packed."

There was silence as Mayson tried to take everything in.

"As I said, despite all this drama of your death, I just knew that was you out on the road that night. I can't explain it, I just knew," said J.R.

Mayson was torn. Pleased that he and J.R. were talking and the fact that J.R. seemed to be looking out for him as his younger brother. But at the same time, he felt ashamed that J.R. had to see him that way. Mayson's mind went back to the dream-vision. He thought about the building and the people in it. The funeral service J.R. described was small, so it didn't seem to jibe with the large body of people in his dream-vision. He thought that maybe the people in the building in his dream-vision were the people at his memorial service. To be certain, he asked J.R. who attended the memorial service.

"Oh, everybody, man," said J.R. without much thought.

"Like who?" asked Mayson.

J.R. looked up at the ceiling to recall.

"Um, Mama, Ed, Daddy, me, our relatives from Chicago, Atlanta, Louisville, people from GCC, other churches, Lanelle, her friends and some other people that I didn't know," said J.R.

"Where was it held?" asked Mayson.

"The funeral was held at GCC and the memorial service was at Prestwood Community Center," said J.R.

In an effort to connect the memorial service to the dream-vision, Mayson wanted to ask more questions about who attended and what they did. But J.R. shifted the discussion away from the funeral and memorial service and back to Mayson's present state.

"Now that you are rested and conscious, what do you want to do?" asked J.R.

"I don't know," said Mayson in frustration as he readjusted himself in the bed.

J.R. moved away from the dresser as though he was about to leave the room.

"Lanelle asked me to come in and check on you because she made breakfast. If you were awake, she said to tell you can come and eat," said J.R.

J.R. quickly left the room. He returned a moment later with Mayson's jeans and shirt that were clean and nicely folded.

"Lanelle washed your clothes," said J.R. as he tossed them onto the bed. "Get dressed, man, and come eat," he said as he walked back toward the door.

"Why did you do this for me?" asked Mayson.

J.R. was about to close the door but opened it back up.

"What?" asked J.R.

"I get that you wanted to make sure it was me in the road when you thought I was dead. And it makes sense to get someone out of harm's way if they're in danger, but finding me a place to sleep and coming back for me the next day...we've never really had much of a relationship, so what was different now that you did all this for me?" asked Mayson.

J.R. shifted uncomfortably.

"I didn't want Mama to see you in that condition," he said.

317

Mayson knew that was not the reason for J.R. to go the extra mile in helping him. He had suspected in the past that J.R. thought his relationship with their mother was too close. So he was baffled as to why J.R. didn't use his drugged-out condition as an opportunity to show their mother that her second son was not so perfect.

Mayson gazed at J.R. A look that made it evident that he didn't believe that it was all about their mother's feelings.

"Okay. I did it because I'm a good guy. Now come on and get something to eat," said J.R. as he started to close the door again.

"Come on, J.R. There was a lot more going on than being a good Samaritan in getting me out that street. I really need to know what you were thinking when you stopped and helped me," said Mayson.

J.R. knew that Mayson was trying to take him to an area of the conversation that he didn't want to answer. But, as he looked at Mayson sitting on the bed, bone-thin, hair dry and flat, with his pale skin and the dark circles around his eyes, he knew that Mayson needed someone to talk to. He never considered himself a source for personal disclosure, but at that moment, in that room, he was all that Mayson had. In addition, he saw a little of his mother in Mayson's face. It was the face that Phyllis wore when she was worried. He had never seen this face in Mayson before and found it strange to see his mother during a time when Mayson was at his worst. Was it a matter of Mayson being in a state that made J.R. feel like "the good one?" Or was it the reality that he was now more vulnerable since everyone knew his secret? J.R. was not completely sure; he just knew that he needed to talk with his brother.

J.R. reentered the room, leaned his back on the dresser and perched his elbows on top of the dresser again.

"I saw more than a man out in the street, I saw family. I saw you, Mama, Idee, and Lamont. That's who I saw in that street and that's what I do for my family," J.R. said.

It was good for Mayson to hear those words coming from J.R. He knew that J.R. would do something like this for anyone else in the family, but he was never quite sure if he was worth J.R.'s time and attention.

"Thank you, J.R. I just needed to hear that," he said.

"Why? Why does that make you feel better? It bothers me that you need that much attention from me, man, said J.R. as he frowned. It makes

318

me uncomfortable," he added.

"Uncomfortable," repeated Mayson. "Uncomfortable because I am Human?"

"Oh, here we go," said J.R. as he threw his hands in the air.

Silence.

J.R. rubbed his hand around his face in frustration. He had avoided conversations about Mayson with his father and mother for most of his life, and now Mayson himself wanted to talk about his being Human.

J.R. knew that the root of his resentment towards his brother involved Mayson's relationship with their mother and his own suspicions of Mayson being Human. Mayson's lack of relationship with girls and the churchy clothes he wore to school made him stand out. Despite his effort to ignore the other kids' comments about Mayson, he eventually fought with a classmate who constantly referred to Mayson as J.R.'s "sissy brother." J.R. knew that there was something different about Mayson sexually, but he would not allow himself to believe that it was because Mayson didn't like girls. Mayson's relationship with Reanna was also a justification for J.R. to believe that Mayson must like girls. He had thoughts of Reanna for himself at one time, but for him to make a move on her meant he really didn't believe there was a relationship between her and Mayson. J.R. never shared his school problems because of Mayson with either of his parents; instead, he distanced himself from Mayson more and more. Once he finished high school, he thought he had put his resentment behind him. After many years of living with his father, he continued to find himself uncomfortable around Mayson. He faced the fact that the resentment was there, but not as much. Once Mayson left GCC and began living with Tony, J.R. tried to justify his continued distance from him based on the church's teaching that being Human is a sin.

As a young boy going to church with his family every week, J.R. often heard the GCC congregational song called *Less Than Will Not Due*. He distinctively remembered a portion of the song that troubled him:

♫ *In pleasing God, I must live his perfect will.* ♫
♫ *Less than 100 will not due, considering all He's done for you.* ♫

The song basically said that if your Christian whose life is less than perfect, then God is not pleased with you. Based on what J.R. learned from GCC, he knew that percentage left him out. J.R. felt that like many people, he had the occasional bad thoughts and made choices that were not always right. One of his church violations would be his being sexually active. He knew that having sex outside of marriage put him on the outs when it came to the church's rule. He agreed with this church's teaching and never had a problem with it because it was biblical, and he had caused pains for girls in his past as a result of it. He had hoped that someday marriage would remedy it for him. After he found out about Mayson's secret, he figured that, in comparison, at some point he himself could give his life to God, follow all the church's rules, eventually fall in love, and marry a woman. This could possibly put him at 100%. However, for Mayson, if Mayson has attraction to males and it never left him, no matter what other biblical good qualities he has, the song, and therefore the church, would still have Mayson at less than 100%. After Mayson's outing, J.R surmised that Mayson would never have a chance for salvation. It was one of the few times he felt a little bad for Mayson.

When J.R was 16, Phyllis had asked him a few times why he would not give his life to God as Mayson had. J.R. was concerned that he may have to do something that meant giving up something that was pleasurable for him. He knew that the church described some activities as worldly, which meant it was ungodly. J.R. assumed that whatever "worldly" meant, sports was probably included in that terminology. The possibility of sports being worldly was one of those areas that concerned him and not something he wanted to readily give up. He knew he could ask his mother or Pastor Upshaw to explain what "worldly" meant, but he felt no urgency in what the answer might be, therefore, he allowed himself to live with the assumption that sports was considered a *worldly* activity.

J.R. found it difficult to express an answer to his mother's question of getting saved or giving his life to God. He believed in God, but he found himself more attuned to his qualification as a church member rather than his having an actual connection to God. On the other hand, he could never be like Mayson because he didn't find himself capable of submitting to the expectations of others in what he did or didn't do. At lease, not at that stage in his life.

In his effort to answer Phyllis' question of his salvation, he'd give her a brief response that he was "not ready." He later stated that he didn't feel he should go to church and sit next to hypocrites. Phyllis was highly offended. She asked J.R. did this hypocrisy description include all of GCC?.

"Not everyone," was J.R.'s response.

"Then that excuse won't work," responded Phyllis.

From that day, Phyllis stopped asking J.R. about being saved or giving his life to God. When J.R. moved in with his father, rather than going to church every Sunday, as he did when living with Phyllis, he applied the "church's hypocrisy" as his reason for not attending. However, he knew, when asked by his father, he didn't really need an excuse for not going to church because his father seldom attended church either.

Now, before him was Mayson sitting there asking another difficult question. Of all things, he was waiting to talk about his being Human. He decided that he would not run, yet he would not back down from being honest in what he had to say.

"This is not going to be a moment where brotherly love is going to flow over us in this room. We both are men. You are a gay man and I am not. We are who we are," said J.R. as he stretched one of his legs out.

"That day I saw you at the club peeking into my car, I was really glad to see you. We're not friends, but we are brothers. The older I get, the more I accept the importance of that connection. I've learned that my problem with you is just that -- my problem. Yes, it may have something to do with your being Human, but it's my problem and not yours. It gets frustrating at times trying to keep the bond of our brotherhood over your being Human.

When it comes to having someone in your family who is Human, I hear people who don't know me or my family personally telling me who I am, what I should believe, what I should think or how I should act when it comes to having someone in my family who is Human. Your life may be hard for you Mayson, but people like me have a little battle too. Hearing all the mouths yapping about what we should do and how we are supposed to act with a Human in our family, makes me wish they would all just shut up and mind their own business. Just let us do what works for our family," said J.R.

J.R. didn't expect to say all this to Mayson, but once he got started, he felt he couldn't stop. Occasionally, his old self would edge at him to stop talking and just leave the room and get away from all this Human stuff. But his feet wouldn't move.

"So, if I'm not on board with you or other Humans, does that make me gay or homophobic?" asked J.R. with a trace of resentment in his voice. He inherited this thought from his time at Mayson's memorial service when he heard from the various attendee speakers.

Mayson knew how loaded that question was and didn't respond. He was mesmerized at the outpouring of words coming from J.R. The fact that he knew what homophobic meant was astonishing. He had only recently found out what that word meant himself. It was obvious that J.R. had put much thought into being Human and the acceptance or nonacceptance debate, thought Mayson. But he kept silent, as he could see that J.R. was not finished.

"When my resentment of you was at its peak, I really didn't want to talk to you because I was concerned about what I would say to you. I knew that if I really told you what I thought of you, it would affect our entire family. When I was resenting you, man, I was resenting the problems you were putting me through because you were so different. I resented your relationship with Mama. I'm close to Mama too, but I don't hang out with her. That's creepy, man," said J.R.

J.R. saw the attentive look on Mayson's face turn to insult.

"I told you that I was not in a place to tell you any of this back then," said J.R.

Mayson composed himself. "Go on," he said.

"Even though Mama would not acknowledge you as Human she seemed to want to protect you in your Humanness. Women seem to always want to protect you guys. You Human guys," he clarified.

J.R. paused.

"No offense man, we know Mama loves Idee, but you seem to be the daughter that she really wanted," said J.R. as he scratched his head hoping the words would not cause a problem.

Mayson could feel his breath shorten and eyebrows raise at this comment. He felt his mouth part to scream at J.R. But he reminded himself that this was an unusual time for him and J.R. He had to hear more. He forced himself to remain silent.

J.R. could see from Mayson's facial expression that he was not happy. He abruptly tightened his lips as though he was trying to keep more words from coming out.

"Okay, I'll not say any more about that," said J.R. "Isn't it obvious that when it comes to your safety or well-being, I'll look out for you? You're family, man. Can we just leave it at that?"

I have to deal with one thing at a time with J.R., Mayson thought. For now, he's talking to me, so this is a start. At that moment he saw more than his self-absorbed estranged brother. Instead, he saw a man who had thoughts, views, and opinions in and outside the Hendrick-Harmon household. He saw someone who had feelings and thoughts that went beyond ball games and sports equipment. Like me, he was more than just a stereotypical label, thought Mayson. As to how he would respond to everything J.R. just said, Mayson found himself speechless. He pondered if he should confront some of the ugly sides of what J.R. said, or deal with them later.

Mayson gave J.R. a halfhearted smile.

"I guess we can leave it at that. For now," Mayson emphasized.

Mayson expected J.R. to leave the room as he often did when he was in an uncomfortable spot. Instead, J.R. stayed perched with his back against the dresser and elbows resting on its top. He seemed as though he was about to say more, but his eyes shifted toward the bed.

"What is that next to you?" asked J.R. pointing to the brown papers with Mayson's notes.

Mayson reached for the papers and looked over them with a fond look on his face.

"Just some notes I was writing about a dream I had," he said.

"Can I see what you wrote?" asked J.R.

Mayson was hesitant to hand the papers over to J.R. The dream-vision was still new and personal for Mayson. But the fact that J.R. picked him up off the street, found him a place to stay, and was making efforts to better understand Humans, showed a maturity about J.R. that allowed Mayson to hand the papers over to him. Who knows, maybe he's grown a brain, thought Mayson.

Mayson handed the papers over to J.R.

J.R. walked over to the chair next to the bed and sat down to read. Mayson watched J.R. curiously as he read, wondering if his brother would throw the pages to the floor as utter nonsense.

Mayson's eye fell on his nicely folded and laundered clothes lying on the bed. He decided to put them on while J.R. was reading. Lanelle had washed and pressed the clothes so carefully that they looked as though they had been professionally done. He was impressed with the crease in his jeans and the smell of the dryer sheet in his cotton sweater, the same smell as the bed linen. Mayson didn't think Lanelle had this homespun touch to her. He picked up the aroma of coffee entering the room. He wanted to follow the aroma to Lanelle while J.R. continued to read. No, he thought. I want to hear J.R.'s response first. Mayson sat quietly waiting for J.R. to finish.

J.R. placed the first page to the back of the other and continued reading.

"Hmm," said J.R. His eyes widened as he read about the people in the building and his mother:

> *I sensed that my family, people from the church, other people I knew and some I was not sure about, were there. For a brief time, I was able to see my mother clearly. She looked the same as she did when I was a little boy. She was so beautiful but looked so sad. In her eyes I could see the body of water from outside the building in her eyes. The water in her eyes swayed back and forth as they did when I heard the children calling for help. The water flowed from her eyes down her cheeks and then I was no longer able to see her clearly.*

J.R. could tell this was possibly referencing Mayson's memorial service. His mother had cried at this service, but he was concerned that the tears from the notes seemed to be more than about her missing Mayson. Other areas of the notes were more of Mayson's feelings and descriptions of him running through a wooded area, feeling people's presence and other things that J.R. could not interpret. Sounds a little spooky, he thought.

For a moment, J.R. stopped reading and looked at Mayson. Not only was he engrossed in the content of the notes, but he was also confounded in Mayson's ability to write in such graphic details and expression. He recalled his mother telling him that Mayson did not have the best writing skills. But from reading these notes, he was impressed with how Mayson had transcribed his memory onto the paper. After a few more minutes of skimming the notes over again, J.R. looked up at Mayson. Mayson could see the hazy look in J.R.'s eyes as though he too had just emerged from a dream or vision.

"Wow, man. You dreamt this?" asked J.R.

"Yeah," said Mayson. "I don't know if it was a dream or a vision. I can't say I woke from it. It was more like I came out of it. It was like watching a movie. Sometimes you're watching it and other times you're in it. Sometimes I think I was dead, but at the other times, I was not. I don't know," said Mayson. "I call it my dream-vision," he added.

J.R. stared at Mayson in disbelief.

"When did this happen?" asked J.R.

"I experienced it while I was here, in this room," Mayson replied.

J.R. riffled through the papers again.

"If I didn't know what I know from the past year, especially the memorial service, I would think that this was all just a dream coming from some druggie. But some of this stuff I can identify with, man," said J.R. looking stunned at Mayson.

J.R. then shifted through the notes around to give them another look.

"Are you kidding me with this?" asked J.R.

"Kidding you? Why would I be kidding you about this?" asked Mayson.

"Some of what you wrote sounded a little like your memorial service," said J.R.

"The memorial service," repeated Mayson.

"Yes, the memorial service that maybe you came to," said J.R. in an accusatory response.

"I had no idea that people thought I was dead. And, that a memorial service was given for me. Why are you accusing me of lying about the dream-vision," J.R.? asked Mayson.

Mayson didn't feel any anger at J.R.'s insinuation that he was lying about the dream-vision, rather he sensed that there must have been something in his notes that had occurred at the memorial service that sparked J.R.'s accusation. The accusation prompt fear in Mayson as the dream-vision began to extend itself beyond the confinements of the room and outside of Mayson's head.

"Some of what you say in these notes were as if you were at the memorial service," said J.R.

Mayson felt a chill come over him.

"Like what?" asked Mayson.

"Well, the part where you said that you were in a large building. Your memorial service was in a large building at the Prestwood Community Center. You said that Mama was crying. She was crying at the memorial service. Other things like the divided groups. There were a variety of people there from different backgrounds at the service. Church people, Humans, people from the club, college students, a couple of media guys and some people I didn't know. And they were divided into their little cliques in the building, but they were not dressed the same or in the same colors. Creepy man," said J.R. as he looked back over the papers.

They both were quiet for a while. Mayson stared out the window as he thought more about J.R.'s words and the dream-vision.

"I think I was dead in the dream-vision. I also think it goes beyond me personally being dead. It's another message in there somewhere. I was trying to figure it out when you knocked on the door," said Mayson, continuing to stare out the window.

(IV)

Dawning: An Unlikely Union

As J.R. was about to respond to Mayson, Lanelle stepped in the room. She was wearing a flower-patterned house dress, sneakers without socks, and a blue bandana on her head. Mayson was glad to see her. The last time he saw her was the day they talked at Cora's cafe. He knew she was fully aware that something was not quite right with him that day. When the nervous guy in the suit came into the cafe, Mayson saw Lanelle look over at him and then back at Mayson. It was then Mayson knew that she had put things together.

Male escort, thought Mayson. That's what Montrell called it. I did sexual favors and Montrell supplied me with drugs. That day in the cafe caused Mayson to think about Lanelle almost every day. He wanted to tell her everything, but he was so deep into the drugs and obligation to Montrell that he knew she could not help.

"I guess you're waiting for breakfast in bed," said Lanelle, as she eyed both of them.

She then looked at Mayson.

"I see you've risen from the dead," said Lanelle in amusement.

Mayson smiled at Lanelle. At the same time, he was also feeling ashamed of what had brought him into her apartment. He finger-combed the top of his hair back in an attempt to look a little better.

J.R. looked at Mayson, combing his hair with his finger as though he was trying not to look dead. He let out loud a hearty laugh. Lanelle looked puzzled at J.R.'s outburst. She tilted her head to the side as she looked at Mayson then back at J.R.

"Am I missing something here?" asked Lanelle.

Before either could give an answer, she saw the torn pieces of brown paper bag in J.R.'s hand.

"Where did you get that paper from?" she asked J.R.

J.R. followed Lanelle's eyes from the papers in his hands and back to the partially open dresser drawer. He figured that the papers must have come from the drawer.

"Oops!" said J.R. in a playful manner as he looked at the papers in his hand and then over at Mayson.

Mayson knew he was busted. Who goes through someone's dresser drawers and steals the paper lining? I know this looks bad, Mayson thought.

Lanelle stood there as she looked at Mayson, waiting for his answer.

"I really needed to write down some thoughts and couldn't find any paper. The only thing that was available was the paper bag linings in your dresser drawers. Hope you don't mind," said Mayson apologetically.

J.R., who had found his way back to leaning his back against the dresser with his elbows perched on top, was flapping the brown paper pages up and down in his hand. He still had the amused look as though he was waiting for some sort of "uh-oh, you're in trouble" moment between Lanelle and Mayson.

Lanelle elbowed J.R. out of the way. She opened and shut each drawer, confirming that the brown paper was indeed taken out of her drawers.

"You could have come out and asked for paper," she said to Mayson.

"Sorry, I didn't know where I was at the time and I had to write some things down before I forgot them," said Mayson.

"What was so important that you had to take my drawer linings out to write on?" asked Lanelle, trying to sound annoyed. She was not really annoyed or angry at Mayson because she was so happy to see her dear friend, but her shield of roughness automatically closed over her.

"You want her to read it?" J.R. asked Mayson.

"Might as well," said Mayson defeatedly, as he could tell J.R. wanted her to read it anyway.

J.R. handed the papers to Lanelle. Lanelle scanned through the pages as it was obvious that she was not in the mood to do a lot of reading.

"Mayson what is this about?" she asked.

Mayson gave her a synopsis of what he and J.R. had discussed about the notes and their attempt to make sense of it. Lanelle began to read the papers more carefully. J.R. was now sitting back on the chair near the bed. After a few minutes of reading, she walked over to the bed where Mayson was still sitting with his back against the bed board. She sat at the foot of the bed as she continued to read.

As Mayson sat on the bed waiting for Lanelle to finish reading, he heard his stomach growl. It occurred to him that he had not eaten much since yesterday.

With each shuffling of the pages, Lanelle found herself fascinated at what she was reading. She was thrilled to see that Mayson mentioned her name in the dream-vision, even if it was only about the similarity between the soothing drink in the clearing of the dream-vision and her own style of making drinks.

"I get a shout-out in the dream-vision!" she yelled, with a couple of playful cheering sounds towards Mayson.

Mayson laughed.

If the notes had come from some theologian or some other professional intellectual writer, she would have dismissed them. But they came from unsophisticated Mayson. Like J.R., she was aware of some of the similarities between Mayson's memorial service and what was written on the pages. At the moment, Lanelle could not explain the relevance of importance of everything she read. But she knew she was reading something special. She felt excitement and inspiration at the reading but kept her face stern. While reading the notes, she was inwardly jumping up and down like a little girl as she connected the notes to some greater good. Hearing all the people talking at the memorial service had her thinking how good it would be for them to start some sort of initiative on community and city-wide peace building. Even though the community leaders from the memorial service had agreed to meet regularly after the memorial, it became evident that it was not enough. She had learned about social and civic matters from one of the club patrons who worked for a social service agency. From their time together, she had thought that someday she would get involved in such social advocacy causes. That day at the memorial service had inspired her. And now that she was reading Mayson's dream-vision, she was even more excited. Whatever the meaning of it, she knew that she wanted to be a part of it. She imagined that the dream-vision could include their community coming together. Maybe something could be done to sever the link between people like Byron and the people he preyed on, like her, Calvin and Mayson, she thought.

As she looked at Mayson sitting on her bed looking misplaced, she thought how out of place she had felt at his memorial ceremony. Not the entire ceremony but a portion of it. There were two brief periods of time when she felt connected with all at the memorial. It was something about the, later missing, small statue man who sat behind Art Peters at the beginning of the service that caused her to have less focus on herself. His appearance soothed her and yet she did not know why. And later, the unidentified gender person with the cotton cap and mismatched clothes, who sat in the back of the building in the roped off chairs, had her mystified. Yet she felt paradoxically safe at this person's presence. People around town talked about these two for a few months with speculation of who they were. Some thought they were some odd couple in disguise with money trying to anonymously do a good deed for the community. Others saw these two as angels bringing a town together. And for those in which who they were didn't matter, they bottom-lined that something good happened which brought a town together, even if it was just for that "behold" moment. For Lanelle, whether they were angels or people doing good deeds for the city of Benson, she believed that either way it was from God.

Unlike Mayson, she hadn't grown up in the church, but she felt an awakening inside of her. She knew that Mayson referred to his phenomena as a "dream-vision" because of his uncertainty if he was asleep or awake, but she chose to believe it was a dream because she had had an interest in dreams for most of her life. As a girl, when Lanelle lived with her grandmother, her grandmother read the Bible to her about Joseph and his gift of interpreting dreams. Lanelle would try to analyze her dreams as Joseph did in the Bible. Sometimes her efforts of interpretation made sense. Other times, she felt herself over-analyzing some areas in her dream that eventually left her exhausted and more confused.

"You mean someone who was found on the street, so high that he had to be put to bed, laid down and dreamt this?" asked Lanelle in astonishment.

"I know," laughed Mayson nervously. "It was so vivid. Unlike those weird dreams where people you don't think much about just pops into your head. Or those odd dreams where you are falling off a mountain or a building. This dream…vision," he corrected himself, …"didn't have all the weird stuff that happens in a lot of my dreams. I knew most people in the building and heard all of their conversations, whether they were speaking in front of the room or among each other in their groups or seats. I didn't know what they all were saying, but I could feel their words. Their voices and conversations were placed into category types in my mind: complaining, repenting, criticizing, and optimizing," he said.

"Optimizing," Mayson repeated with a laugh. "I have never used that word in my life. And I'm not certain what it means. But this was one of the words that came to me in the dream-vision," he said.

"Optimizing," Lanelle repeated as she sorted through the papers looking for this specific word.

"It's not in there. Some things I didn't include in the notes. Some things I didn't see the necessity in noting or it just came to me later," said Mayson.

"We need to find out what that means," said Lanelle as she left the room and came back with a pocket dictionary. "Optimizing, optimizing," she repeated as she turned the small pages.

"Oh, here it is "Optimize. Let's see what that says:"

"Make the best or most effective use of (a situation,

opportunity, or resource)."

"Okay. Good," said Mayson, who was not as fascinated with the definition of the word as Lanelle. He wanted to get back to other areas of the dream-vision.

"I could see the entire audience. I could feel a lot of emotions in the room. Sadness, uncertainty, enthusiasm, fear and some anger. My sense of awareness was at its highest. But I'm not sure if I was actually in the room," he said again.

As Lanelle talked about other areas of the notes, particularly where Mayson was struggling through the forest with others surrounding him, she added her observations and speculations on that matter, but Mayson was not listening. Despite his interest in her observation, Mayson found himself in doubt again. Am I making more of this than necessary? he wondered. I was high last night. People can see and hear all kind of things when they're on drugs, he mused. He looked at Lanelle as she talked about the notes and, for a moment, he anticipated sharing his skepticism with her. He then looked at J.R., who seemed to be hanging on Lanelle's every word. He sensed that J.R. had confidence in Lanelle regarding all that was happening. This is the most spirituality I've ever seen in either one of them, thought Mayson. Even after writing the notes, other activities of the dream-vision entered his mind that he had not written down. I usually can't remember much about my dreams as I awaken from them, he thought. But this dream-vision seems to haunt me with its continued presence. I can't just make this about me, he concluded again.

Mayson recalled a verse from the Bible, about a man whose son was healed by Jesus. The man's words had never made sense to him, however, at that moment, it appeared appropriate for him to pray:

Lord I believe, help thou my unbelief, Mark 9:24

As Mayson turned this over in his mind, he could hear Lanelle talking about the notes.

"As Mayson was running through the forest, he seemed to be struggling to get to someplace and others running with him had the same destination. Or maybe there was no destination. He could be running from something but not certain where he is going," she said.

Lanelle believed that his running was his effort to run away from his sexuality. However, Mayson had not confessed the Human side of himself directly to her. Even though his sexuality was touched on at the memorial service, when she spoke about his running away, she used the words "from something" in her observation to avoid the word "Human." Mayson believed that Lanelle knew about his sexuality but was trying to be discreet. At this point, he didn't care who knew. He found it unbelievable that he shared this side of himself with J.R. before he shared it with Lanelle.

"It's okay Lanelle. I already talked with J.R. about my sexuality. I'm Human. So, we get that the dream-vision of me as a runner could be about me running from being a Human," said Mayson.

"Okay," said Lanelle with a wide smile of relief that Mayson was finally sharing this with her. She could feel her own walls coming down more. Crumble, crumble.

Lanelle continued as she rephrased…

"A *gay man* running from his reality from a non-gay acceptance group. In this case, his church. Above everything, I think the one thing that we all see in this dream-vision, in the large building, were people coming together. Like the memorial service. I hope the humming at the end means they stay together. What a powerful experience to have in your head. I didn't know you had such revelations," said Lanelle.

"I didn't know either. It just came to me all at once. This is different from anything I've ever experienced in my life," said Mayson.

"These interpretations are only my thoughts, so we need to search more," said Lanelle.

Lanelle and Mayson went back and forth talking about the content of the paper. J.R. decided he would slowly move out of the room and go home. Leaving or distancing himself from matters that he simply had no interest in or made him uncomfortable was what J.R. did. But this time J.R. found that his feet were not moving. Lanelle and Mayson's discussion of the dream-vision left him wanting to know more. The discussion of the dream-vision notes engaged him in a mystic and emotional way. Mystic because they didn't know what to make of the dream-vision. Emotional, because it was a mystery that involved not just Mayson, but his mother, whom he loved very much. He wanted to make sure that if any sense came out of the notes, it would exclude his mother from any danger. He was brought up under the teaching of God's anger more than his love, so he was anxious at the thought of God's anger being the outcome of the dream-vision, which included his mother in tears.

J.R. was glad that Lanelle had entered the room and merged into the conversation between him and Mayson. She was a much-needed deflection from the awkwardness of where their conversation was going. On the day J.R. saw Mayson in the parking lot at the Encounter Club, when J.R. went back into the club that day, Lanelle greeted him and his date. J.R. introduced himself to her as Mayson's brother. Unlike when he was in high school, where he hoped that no one knew he was Mayson's brother, for some reason that evening, it was not a bad thing for Lanelle to know. She was surprised to know they were brothers. She told J.R. that Mayson was a "good kid." J.R. saw Mayson as someone who needed to be protected. From meeting Lanelle that day, he knew Lanelle was one of Mayson's protective resources. At that moment, he understood why. He too found a safety with having her around.

Lanelle continued to try and analyze the meaning of the dream-vision.

"You know, this is not something that needs to be put aside as though it has no meaning. The fact that it came from you in the state you were in is a message in itself. The communication among the people and the coming together in the dream-vision is a message that belongs outside these walls," said Lanelle.

As Lanelle was addressing all the reasons to take the dream-vision seriously, J.R. had a thought. Art Peters from WWQW news was at the memorial service with his cameraman. Maybe Mayson saw the memorial service on the news, and it found its way into his dream with other personal matters he was struggling with, thought J.R.

"Mayson, is it possible that you saw the memorial service on the news?" blurted out J.R.

"No. I was in a different state, so I couldn't watch Benson area local news there," said Mayson.

"I know what you're getting at, J.R., but the memorial service clip was cut from the local news that day. I know this because I saw Art Peters at the mall a few days after the memorial service and he told me," said Lanelle.

"Okay, people coming together is one thought," said J.R., "but there may be other thoughts to consider. Do you think the dream-vision is also warning about the sin of being Human and those who contribute to it? You know how sometimes when boys are growing up and get too much attention from their mothers. Like you and Mama," said J.R.

Lanelle winced as she heard J.R.'s question and saw Mayson's facial reaction.

Mayson felt anger rise in him at J.R.'s question. He twisted his body to the other side of the bed toward J.R. His efforts to stay positive with J.R. were no longer a priority. He had hoped to let J.R.'s previous comments go, but J.R. had opened the door again. He looked J.R. in the face.

"What sins?" snapped Mayson. "You don't have a clue about who God is. You barely go to church, if at all. If it's all about sexuality, then think about yourself: out with a different woman every week, and now you're going to talk to me about the sin of being Human?" said Mayson.

J.R. didn't return Mayson's tirade of angry words. It was obvious to him that Mayson had been away for a while and was unaware of his long-term relationship with Alana. He could see he should have left the matter alone. However, he felt compelled to know about his mother's place in that dream-vision before he left that room. He had these thoughts about her and Mayson for years and thought this would be the right time to ask. But apparently, it was not, he thought.

"Calm down, man! It's a real question. It's not about you specifically," said J.R.

Despite J.R.'s effort to calm Mayson, Mayson ignored his efforts of appeasement.

Mayson felt words accumulating in his head and coming out non-stop:

"Maybe it's about you, J.R. Maybe that dream-vision is about you and your arrogance. If my being Human is all about getting too much attention from Mama, then that makes you Human too. Before I was born it was just you and Mama. She gave you just as much attention as she did me, so maybe the dream-vision is about you being Human and you won't admit it," said Mayson, knowing it was not true but wanting to insult his masculinity.

Mayson could feel himself breathing heavily. He was more angry as he thought how J.R. lived such a privileged life with the love of both parents, athletic good looks, and a new girlfriend whenever he wanted.

Mayson took a deeper breath and looked away from J.R. in order to compose himself.

Lanelle was momentarily speechless. She had never seen such anger from Mayson. She thought to intervene but decided to let the matter play out. This conversation may have been long in coming, she thought.

"Listen J.R., just like you're in a relationship with your girlfriend, I was in a relationship with a man I loved, and he loved me. Neither one of us were married to other people or in a relationship with other people. We didn't condemn people who were not in same-sex relationships as us and neither did we try to convince people to be like us. So we were not harming anyone because of our relationship. You, and people like you, opinions about us was never our problem. If who I love is considered harm to you, then you brought that harm on yourself. I can't please the "who you love" police. So, if there is a sin, it's the sin of your judgmental arrogance…And another thing! Leave Mama out of this," said Mayson in a stern controlled voice.

J.R. could tell he struck a nerve again, when he involved their mother back in the matter. That moment may not have been the time to find out if their mother was involved in the dream-vision notes, or if it was about repentance, but at some time J.R. knew he had to find out if the dream-vision involved his mother. Give it more time, thought J.R.

"Ok, we'll leave Mama out of this, but you're taking this the wrong way. I'm just trying to understand some things. I'm not on drugs, I'm not gay and I've never been in prostitution, so you need to keep in mind who you're talking to rather than flying off the handle," said J.R.

At these words, Lanelle winced again and dropped her head in anticipation of what was going to happen next.

From hearing the words "drugs and prostitution," Mayson got to his feet. He was fuming at the humiliation of J.R. throwing back in his face something sensitive that he had just disclosed to him. Something that he had not personally share with Lanelle, but there he threw it out in the room.

"First of all, let me educate you. I just happened to be a Human who got into drugs. I had an addiction that took me into prostitution. So, don't talk to me like I am some sort of low-life street hooker who goes around looking for sex. That's what you do. Maybe you're into prostitution. You go through women like you change socks. There is such thing as a male whore.

You fit that description perfectly, but you're too dumb to get paid for it," said Mayson as he sat back down on the bed. His hands begin to shake, as he tucked them crosswise under his arms in order to calm himself.

"Okay gentlemen. I think that's enough," said Lanelle.

J.R. decided not to address Mayson's comments about being gay or a prostitute. Seeing Mayson in the street that day changed him. Rescuing Mayson that night brought questions to him about being Human. That night, he not only saw someone that appealed to his sense of family, but he also felt a piece of himself out on that road. This day, in Lanelle's small bedroom, J.R. felt he had to be the big brother and control his anger for the sake of his younger brother. He had managed not to run this time, and that was a good step. As Lanelle knew, J.R. also knew that this was a moment between him and Mayson that should have happened a long time ago. But there was the insensitive side of J.R. that wanted to get answers and get them fast. The dream-vision was golden for this moment to understand things, thought J.R. Therefore, he found himself needing to keep going.

"Could it be with this whole dream-vision scenario, with all the people telling their stories, that you are being asked to choose yourself among these voices? Choose whether you are a Human or a Christian?" asked J.R.

At J.R.'s question, Mayson reared his head back in disbelief. The friction that had subsided slightly was now rekindled in Mayson. He and J.R.'s brother relationship advancement possibility was no longer a priority for Mayson.

"What! Is that what you got from all this? *Choose*?" asked Mayson incredulously.

"Hey, it was a real question. I don't know what the dream-vision means and I wanted to put the question out there man," said J.R. earnestly.

"What does that mean, to *choose*? If I say I choose to be a Christian, then that means that I cannot love my mate. If I choose *gay*, then that means I don't love God. You see that same word in each answer—love! L.O.V.E. God is love, so don't tell me that I must choose when it comes to love. He's in every good relationship and my relationship with Tony was good, so I have nothing to choose from. You know, J.R., sometimes you seem intelligent and other times you seem like a dumb, airhead jock. Enough air in your head to fill your basketball," said Mayson.

At those words, J.R. moved up from his lean against the dresser and stood square on his feet. He could deal with Mayson's rant about his being gay himself or a prostitute because he knew that these were areas that he was confident in what he was not. He also knew that Mayson didn't believe these words as well but was angry and wanted to hurt him. But he had issues with Mayson repeatedly labeling him as dumb because he liked sports. He gave Mayson a look that dug into him.

Lanelle could see that the matter was about to escalate even further. She stood in front of J.R., who seemed to be ready to either pounce on Mayson or leave the room. Either way, Lanelle knew that it was time for her to intercede. She placed her hands on J.R.'s chest as to keep him in place, while looking at Mayson with an expression on her face ordering him to not say anything else.

"Gentlemen, gentlemen, let's chill. This is getting out of hand. We are getting away from something that may not be just about us. Let's not allow distracting forces to stop our blessing in understanding these notes from this dream-vision. I need both of you to put aside your past differences and focus on right now," Lanelle said firmly.

In an effort to avoid J.R.'s gaze, Mayson looked out the window as Lanelle talked. J.R. dropped his gaze from Mayson, shoved his hands in his front pockets and looked at Lanelle for more direction.

"Before we proceed, I just need to get something cleared between you two. If I don't, we may have round three coming up between both of you," said Lanelle.

Lanelle looked at J.R.

"J.R., you need lessons in being tactful when you ask questions. Use a filter when you want to know something."

She then looked at Mayson.

"Mayson, bring it down a notch. J.R. was asking questions he genuinely wanted the answers to. Don't be so easily offended. Now, let's get back on task."

J.R. and Mayson both looked directly at Lanelle in an effort to avoid looking at each other. She smiled as she looked at both of them.

"If this passionate conversation can affect laypeople like us, can you imagine how powerfully the answer or answers could affect an entire community? Especially in the Human and church communities? Let's put our heads together and stay focused. Maybe as we address its purpose and meaning, it could also mend the divide between you two," said Lanelle.

J.R. was amazed that he was still in the room dealing with all that was going on between him and Mayson. The more Mayson vented during their encounter; the more J.R. pressed his fist down into his pockets. But he didn't leave.

Mayson took a deep breath and tried to refocus, as Lanelle advised.

"Who do you think can help us with these notes?" asked Mayson.

Before Lanelle could answer his question, he proceeded with another thought to the question.

"At one time I would have immediately answered my question, without a doubt. I would have said to give the notes to Pastor Upshaw. But with all that has happened between me and Pastor Upshaw, his interpretations of the notes may be biased," said Mayson.

Lanelle skimmed over the papers again.

"I don't know right now, but let's see if we can figure out as much as possible before thinking about adding anyone else," said Lanelle.

"I'll do what I can, but I'm not that spiritually deep," said J.R.

"Neither am I, but I want to be," said Lanelle with a glisten in her eyes that reflected a long-held desire. "I love spiritual insight. I always thought that people who denounce being spiritual or religious did it as though it was a proud badge of exclusion. As if not being religious or spiritual made them somehow more intelligent or better than those who were," said Lanelle.

"I've thought that many who said they were atheist or" … Lanelle stopped as she searched for the word.

"Agnostic," Mayson added.

"Yes, agnostic," she said. She continued, "I thought maybe the atheists and agnostics were angry with God or put off with what they see in relation to God. You know, things like innocent children dying of hunger or disease," she said.

"Maybe so, true or not, atheist and agnostics have that right to their disbelief. Anyway, what do atheists or agnostics have to do with this dream-vision?" asked J.R. He saw Mayson roll his eyes.

"Listen, man, I'm just putting out thoughts and questions that others might have. So, you can roll your eyes to the back of your head for all I care. If you can't take uncomfortable questions here then you won't be able to take them anywhere," said J.R.

Lanelle decided to intervene, again, in this brotherly conflict.

"He's right," she said to Mayson. "Let's ask uncomfortable questions and make remarks that may not be what we want to hear, but let's do it with respect," said Lanelle as she looked at J.R.

"I think the reason we are having such difficulty in addressing this dream-vision is due to our efforts to try and address one thing when something else is going on in the room. We're also dealing with issues involving your family past as brothers. One thing that I do see from this moment is dialogue involving the strained relationship between two communities and two brothers. Two brothers who come from the same mother, but different in how they approach life. Two brothers who may represent these two communities," said Lanelle.

Mayson and J.R. looked at each other in disbelief.

"That was deep," said J.R.

"Something to think about," mumbled Mayson, not quite ready to align himself with J.R yet.

"If it's difficult for you two to work together on this, I can understand. I can see that being in the same room and talking has its own issues for both of you. If so, we can hold off on this or show the notes to someone else for help in understanding it. Or maybe discuss the matter at a later date when you two have a better relationship," said Lanelle.

"No, no. This can't be about just me and J.R. I don't want something this good to be hindered by my past with my brother. Let's keep going," said Mayson.

"We'll be good," added J.R. as he laughed at his attempt to sound like a little boy.

"Sorry man, I meant no harm," said J.R.

"It's okay," said Mayson.

"Alright! Let's give it a try. Let the dialogue begin," said Lanelle.

"Okay, let me dive back in," said Mayson as he tucked his legs beneath him while sitting on the bed. He leaned forward toward Lanelle.

"Dialogue, dialogue. I've heard this word come up so many times when some social unrest has come about. Whether it's crime, racial or Human-related, people get in an uproar and little groups are formed to discuss whatever the social injustice may be. As time passes, these groups break up," said Mayson.

"Like they did at the memorial service," put in J.R.

"Okay," said Mayson, not certain what J.R. meant. He continued, "Or they'd stay together and simply continue *dialoguing* the matter with no action. This is something that I don't want to happen. I want more than just dialogue. We have an inkling that it does involve the church and the Human community, but there are other parts of it that seem to have answers in what to do about it. Once we know what that is, I want a plan in getting something done and not just spend more years in dialogue."

"Hold your reins," said Lanelle. "You must talk to acknowledge the problem and resolve it. Just like the conflict between you and J.R. We were not able to move forward in our efforts to talk about the dream-vision until we were able to see that there was a problem between you boys. Once we acknowledged the problem, and came to common ground, we were able to move forward with this discussion," said Lanelle.

"That's true," said J.R.

"Don't get me wrong, boys, there are still things for you to work out. They may require spiritual or other professional help. Also, Mayson, we have to acknowledge that you may need to get treatment for your addiction," added Lanelle.

She had heard of people who had stopped using drugs immediately, without ever going into a treatment program. They often attributed it to divine healing. Mayson had stated earlier that he had no craving for the drug. Unbeknownst to Lanelle, he had already made up his mind that he was open to treatment as he figured either way, God would be with him. Mayson had confidence in Lanelle ever since he met her. When they first met, he saw her as someone who had "worldly wisdom." But at that moment in the room, he saw a spiritual side of her that had more discerning qualities than just street survival skills. He assured himself that she indeed was among those "good people" that he needed to keep in his life.

Lanelle also felt a different side of herself in that room with Mayson and J.R. She was not completely surprised at how adeptly she had handled the conflict between Mayson and J.R. For years this gift in her was suppressed because of life distractions. Now it had been awakened and utilized for two estranged young brothers and notes from a dream-vision.

"Yeah, of course I need treatment," replied Mayson.

Lanelle continued, "So, if your relationship as brothers or Mayson's addiction is not miraculously healed, then time will be needed to deal with these contributing factors. I'll add myself to that fray as well," said Lanelle without being specific about what her need for healing was.

"In the meantime, I think the three of us are a good start for a more meaningful dialogue in understanding some of the dream-vision. Our next step will be in determining who or where we should go for more insight in this dream-vision meaning also. If needed," she added.

Lanelle looked at J.R., who was staring down at the floor, in thought, as he rubbed his chin. She snapped her fingers under his eyes, trying to get his attention.

"Earth to J.R," she said.

J.R. looked at Lanelle, slightly startled.

"I was thinking about what you said about the three of us getting started on this dream-vision. Are we the right people to try and find meaning in something we believe is from God? I don't see myself as a part of a think tank for resolving spiritual or social problems. And, no offense, look at what we have in this room in getting more insight into something that seemed to be so deep in this dream-vision."

He looked at Lanelle. "Someone who works in a nightclub." He looked at Mayson. "A gay druggie-prostitute we had to scrape up off the street last night." He planted his hand on his chest to acknowledge himself. "And me, a fornicator, who questions the Human way of living and who has not fully ventured out in the world. Man, I still live with my father!" said J.R.

Mayson decided not to take offense at J.R.'s description of him. He chose to understand J.R.'s doubts. He knew the fear that J.R. was going through as he sized himself against their church's teachings on who is accepted by God and who is not. He could see that J.R. was questioning his own worthiness in dealing with such a spiritual matter. It was what he had experienced himself before either of them entered the room.

Mayson felt his past biblical understanding coming forth in addressing J.R.'s doubts. He remembered one of his favorite evangelists that came to GCC during a revival preaching on *A Better Way*. Mayson had purchased the tape of this sermon message and would listen to it over and over. He could almost recite the evangelist's words from memory. The memory of that sermon message began to soothe his earlier doubts, and perhaps they could help J.R. in his struggle of worthiness. He decided to take some of that sermon message and address it to J.R.'s doubt. He decided to blurt out what he recalled from that message:

"Sometimes the most unlikely people have the most likely answers. Think about some of the people who Jesus brought in as disciples or who he fellowshipped with throughout his ministry. There was impatient Peter, the repented denier of Christ, murderous Paul, the former Christian murderer and Mary Magdalene, the former prostitute, who devoted her life to Christ as she witnessed his crucifixion, burial and resurrection. Just to name a few. They had flaws that only could be healed as they open themselves up for a better way. A way that didn't cause harm to others. That way opened itself for the good of all, not just those who fit into a certain group. Jesus didn't condone or excuse their sins but showed them a better way as they grew in grace. Those who were determined to do things their own way, he didn't stop them, but they were led to their own demise. We are not disciples, but we do have flaws that can be mended as we follow what may be beyond our own understanding," said Mayson.

"Amen. Preach it, Brother Mayson," said Lanelle as she applauded him. "I couldn't have said it any better," she added.

Mayson felt amused and encouraged by Lanelle's supportive words, but the amusement and encouragement was short lived. He knew he had a lot before him. Like some overly done soap opera script, he had to deal with the mess made from the fact that everyone thought he was dead. Especially with his mother and family. He knew that he also had people that he had to make amends with and others that he was yet not certain if or who they were to be in his life. He could see that once J.R. opened that new-like brown door in that room, the reality of his life was now back in motion. Some new and others old realities. So, he decided that, for that *behold* moment, while yet in that room, Lanelle and J.R. and a dream-vision was what mattered.

For a brief moment, in hearing Mayson's words, J.R. was surprised to discover that he had missed the old Mayson. J.R. accepted Mayson's words, as they were good enough to keep him from walking out of the room. The old church-boy Mayson, once the object of his scorn, was now a welcome presence. He knew that Mayson would never be the same, nor was he expecting him to be. Mayson had life experiences that changed him, and J.R. could see that from the moment he saw him roaming aimlessly in the street.

Lanelle pushed Mayson's long legs away off the bed to give herself more room to sit. She handed the first page of the brown paper bag to Mayson and another to J.R.

"Let's read and talk," said Lanelle.

"What about breakfast?" asked J.R.

"What was once our breakfast has now become our holy communion. Read now and eat later," said Lanelle.

Epilogue

"I never thought my hair would ever be this gray. At least not this soon," said Phyllis.

"I think it flatters you," said Cliff as he and his wife Irene sat at Phyllis' kitchen table drinking coffee. Irene felt a tinge of jealousy as she heard those words coming from her husband's mouth to his ex-wife. Her jealousy was not based on any concern about his having any continued intimate feelings for Phyllis, but more so from the fact that Cliff rarely gave her such compliments. She understood that he was trying to make Phyllis feel better after all that she had been through over the past couple of years, yet her neediness wanted that kind of attention from him too.

"Thanks Cliff, but I look like my grandmother in the last years of her life," she giggled.

"A death, memorial service, a 2nd divorce and now the reemergence of Mayson. I wouldn't have seen this if I had written the script for it myself. After all this, it's a miracle that your hair is not snow white," said Irene.

"I'm just glad to have my baby... she stopped...my Mayson back. In due time, Idee and Lamont will warm back up to him. Idee has grown up a little more over these past few years, so she's not as fun-loving with Mayson as she used to be. Lamont seems a little frightened of Mayson since his return. He's more formal with him now," said Phyllis.

"They'll get over it," said Cliff.

"I hope so," said Phyllis. "Poor little Reanna. When Reanna heard the news of Mayson, she was in shock. Once it all sunk in, you would have thought it was Christmas and she was given a million dollars. When she saw him, she hugged his skinny little body so hard that they toppled over," said Phyllis with a big smile as she lowered her cup back to its saucer.

There was a long silence as they all were in thought.

"Did they ever find out who those 2 odd people were at the memorial service? You know, the one that was on the stage with Art Peters and then nobody could find later. And the oddly dressed person in the back of the room sitting in the off-limit chairs?" asked Cliff.

"No. We never found out who they were. Everybody have their thoughts on who they may be. Good Samaritans, community philanthropist and my hope, that they were angels," said Phyllis.

"I wasn't there, but when Cliff told me about them, it gave me chills," said Irene.

Silence.

"Think Mayson will ever go back to GCC?" asked Irene.

"You know, that is no longer important to me and it does not seem to be for Mayson either. I just want him to know God and believe in Him, no matter what church he goes to," said Phyllis.

"Here, here," said Cliff as he raised his coffee cup in a manner of giving a toast to Phyllis' words.

"I still wake up in the morning wondering did everything that happened, really happened. I can't get over all this. Everyday, I think about the poor man that actually died," said Phyllis. She sipped her coffee down as she gazed out the kitchen window.

"The one they thought was Mayson?" asked Irene.

"Yeah. I can imagine what his mother is going through. Especially since they still don't know who killed him," she said.

"You said you called his mother some time back, didn't you?" asked Cliff.

"Yeah, I had to. I knew what she was going through, and I had to reach out to her," said Phyllis.

Another long silence as they drank their coffee.

"I hope he's happy," said Phyllis.

"Who?" asked Cliff.

"Mayson. I hope he is happy."

"As happy as anyone can be in rehab," said Cliff as he put more cream in his coffee. "I think he'll be okay. He's been in rehab for a few weeks and I think he will be ready to get back into life," said Cliff.

"Since he's been in rehab, Tony calls me every day," said Phyllis.

Cliff became silent at this information from Phyllis. He didn't dislike Tony, but he was never sure how to respond to such a union. Even though J.R and Mayson's relationship had improved since Mayson's return and J.R. spoke about Tony with ease, it was not enough for Cliff to relax when the subject of Tony came up.

"He calls me to check in on me. He's kind," said Phyllis as she took another sip of her coffee.

"You think they'll get back together," asked Irene.

"I don't see why not. But that is Mayson's decision to make," said Phyllis.

"How's that lady from Mayson's job? The one J.R. sent Mayson to stay with when he found him," asked Irene.

"You mean, Lanelle?" asked Phyllis.

"Yeah, I think that's her name," said Irene.

"I think she's doing good. The last I heard, she joined Pastor McDaniel's church. Mayson told me that she and he were working on some kind of forum that had something to do with an experience Mayson had while he was missing," said Phyllis.

"J.R briefly told me something about that. Something about a dream or vision on a document. They supposed to be meeting about it," said Cliff.

"Yeah, and they were including Pastor McDaniel in the forum. Mayson seemed mesmerized by whatever this meeting is about," said Phyllis.

"They didn't give you any specifics?" asked Irene.

"No, but Mayson seems motivated at the thought of it. The fact that it has gotten J.R.'s attention, amazes me," said Phyllis. As Phyllis drank the last sip of her coffee, she leaned back in her chair. "I hope whatever it is, it brings good news. I can't take any more of what has happened over the past few years," said Phyllis.

"I hope it doesn't turn out like those meetings they were supposed to have after the memorial service. They ended no sooner than they started," said Cliff.

Phyllis stood up and began clearing the table.

"Mayson said these meetings will help him find his place. I don't completely know what he means by that, but whatever it's about, let's hope and pray that at the end of their meetings, all of us will know our place," said Phyllis.